Dream Catcher

A Morphean Chronicle

By Tracy M Thomas

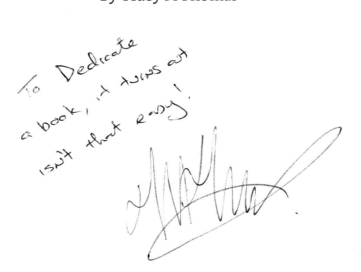

To Dedicate a book, it turns out isn't that easy!

CHAPTER 1

Will Cooper could swear that every clink of every coffee cup in the shop vibrated through his very brain. It was true he hadn't been sleeping well. Too many late nights, too much caffeine and enough stress to fuel a small combustion engine, if such a thing were possible. But then, to Will, a whole lot of the impossible seemed to be coming to fruition at the moment. The woman in front of him was apparently ordering beverages for the entire postal code district, and the barista seemed in no rush. He rubbed the bridge of his nose and tried not to fidget as life-changing decisions between caramel and chocolate muffins were discussed.

In his faux tweed three-piece suit, Will was quite aware that he had been middle-aged forever. It wasn't a look he particularly minded. From virtually his teens, he had realised that being cool was something that happened to other people. With his slightly rounded physique, smart side parting and precise nature, Will had nurtured an excessively grown-up air that others failed to achieve long past his tender thirty years.

'Oh, come along, woman! Just take a bloody muffin and be done with it; it's not as though you need the calories. And yes, you pasty-faced waste of space. I am sure that she will be able to remember who had an extra shot and who had the cinnamon. No, no, you do not need to write it on the cups. Oh, wait you do.' And so, Will's thought process went on.

Seven minutes into his impatient internal rant, it was finally his turn to be served. The girl behind the counter barely glanced at him, preferring instead to chat to her colleague. Will felt his teeth begin to grind. He coughed politely. The girl flicked an escaped piece of hair out of her eyes and looked at him questioningly. 'I would like two coffees to take away, please. One full-fat double mocha with an extra shot, whipped cream and sprinkles, and one latte.'

She turned away without a word and began the process of pressing buttons on machines to make them spit and hiss and whisk and whatever else they did. Will wondered how so much hype could be produced by the simple act of adding milk and water to ground up coffee beans. 'Full fat double mocha, shot, cream, sprinkles and... a latte.' The last two words dripped with disdain. 'Eight pounds seventy-nine.' Will felt his left eye twitch ever so slightly. 'Nearly nine pounds for two cups of coffee?' 'Eight pounds seventy-nine. You do get a free muffin? It's organic.' Will glanced at the bite-sized muffin neatly wrapped in its cellophane jacket. 'How much is it without the muffin?' The girl held out her hand. 'Eight pounds seventy-nine. The muffin is free.' Still holding her stare, Will reached into his pocket and reluctantly handed over a ten-pound note. Awkwardly collecting his change and his coffees Will was just about to go when the girl called out. 'Don't forget your muffin.' Will turned back, and she balanced it carefully on top of the cups. 'You have a nice day now!'

The little pink chicken on the muffin's label wobbled dangerously as Will stomped back to the car park. He was still muttering to himself as he turned the car into the neat drive of the semi-detached house, nearly hitting an unfamiliar bright-red mini. 'Typical.' He growled before reversing and parking on the road.

Juggling the coffee, muffin and car keys, Will shoved the car door shut with his hip causing the muffin to make a final lurch for freedom. As he twisted to catch it, the motion dislodged some of the molten cream sprinkle, which slopped angrily onto his shirt. Will hung his head and sighed. Crushing the now escaped muffin into the pavement with his heel, he stomped towards the house.

Voices were coming from just behind the door: one male, one female, and both, in Will's present mood, incredibly nauseating.

'I have to go. I'll be late for work.' A feminine voice cooed, clearly making no move to leave.

'Yeah, I know... Will will be here any minute... just five minutes.'

Will saw shadows moving behind the glass of the front door.

'Nooo, I really do have to go.' The smaller figure disentangled herself only to be drawn back straight away.

Will rolled his eyes and attempted to press the doorbell with his nose just as the door was flung open. He stood unnoticed as a small dark-haired girl was trying, without too much conviction, to escape, while being smothered by a shock of dirty blonde dreadlocks.

Will coughed. The girl looked around, startled, but the man only grinned. 'Right on time. Will this is Louise, Louise, this is Will.'

The girl smiled sheepishly. 'Hello,' she said, looking at her feet.

'Morning.' Will replied without much warmth. 'And morning Adam, nice to see you up and about so early.'

His friend ignored the comment completely as the newly introduced Louise bolted to the mini. 'I'll call you later, yeah?' Adam called after her. She waved in reply, dived into the car, and, seconds later, was reversing down the drive.

'Will you?' Will asked.

'Possibly.' Adam shrugged as he took the exploding coffee and ushered Will inside. 'I think you embarrassed her.' He added with a laugh.

'Who was that?' Will asked. 'Louise. I just introduced you. Met her at a gig last night. Isn't she hot?'

'I'm sure she's lovely. But what were you thinking?' Will asked in exasperation.

Adam looked confused. 'I was thinking she's hot.' He waved his cup vaguely. 'You know you've got a brown mark on your shirt?'

'Yes, I know.' Will said irritably, scrubbing at the offending stain with his fingernail. 'I don't suppose you have any stain remover?'

Adam got up and lazily reached under the sink before handing him a tube.' 'So that's why you're in a shitty mood?'

'Is a stained shirt why I'm in a shitty mood?' Will snapped. 'Or is it possibly because it's eight-thirty in the morning, we have a meeting at nine o'clock with a man from one of the greatest promoters of computer games, REMCORP no less, who is hopefully going to write us the biggest cheque we have ever seen; and you look like you haven't slept for a week, smell like a brewery and haven't even got your trousers on yet.' He finished with his voice an octave higher.

'I have trousers on.' Will rubbed his forehead as he looked down to the creased combat pants he wore.

'Technically, perhaps they are trousers. If we were about to complete an assault on a Columbian drug baron's jungle lair, then I do not doubt that they would be the perfect attire. To meet a man like Murray Leibowitz, who only thinks in dollars, I am thinking something a little more formal, more... I know where the washing machine is?'

'Ok, ok, you should try and chill out.' Adam held his hands up in mock surrender. 'I will go and get changed.' He moved towards the door got halfway then turned back. 'Oh, man, though. You should have been at this gig last night. It was awesome!'

'Clothes!' Will almost screamed. Adam winced. 'Relax,' He said soothingly, 'I'm going...' Almost out of the door, Adam

6

stopped again. 'You remember that gig at the Uni bar where that girl... oh no, wait. You didn't go, did you, some final or other? Anyway...'

'Will you please for the love of all things holy, go and put some clothes on!' Will pleaded.

Adam pretended to be hurt. 'All right, all right, but you'll give yourself an ulcer at this rate, mark my words.' Almost twenty minutes later, Will was still pacing the floor of Adam's kitchen. His shirt was passably clean. He'd listened to the shower. He'd heard many doors banging, which suggested activity, but the finished product had yet to arrive.

Will tried to breath and resisted the urge to shout up the stairs. Just as he was about to lose the battle, a half-naked Adam arrived with a crumpled shirt in one hand.

'You haven't even ironed a shirt!' Will said through gritted teeth. He could feel a small vein pulsating in his temple.

'It won't take a second,' said Adam moving Will out of the way to pull out the ironing board. 'And, by the way, you are turning into my mother.' He complained, pulling his hair back into a band.

'Your mother lives five thousand miles away, lets you live here rent-free, pays all of your bills and as far as I am aware, probably irons your shirts too when she's home. If she had ever occasionally asked you to put on some clothes, I suggest we would not be having this conversation now. Your mother is a Saint.'

'Last time I checked you couldn't be beatified if you have been living in sin with a sixty-seven-year-old Spanish vintner called Philippe.'

Despite himself, Will felt the corners of his mouth turning up. 'What and *you* disapprove?'

Adam shrugged. 'Am I detecting a note of bitterness in you this morning?' He said, changing the subject.

'Not bitterness. I had to deal with the world's slowest coffee waitress this morning behind the representatives of the English coffee drinking association who were getting their practice beverages in. We have to present to some American, who is going to be looking at his watch the whole time and probably won't believe us anyway, and you are not helping my nerves!'

'Hello! Who put the thing together in the first place? I think I'm helping.'

'All I am saying is you don't have bills to pay...' Will continued.

'I have to pay for things,' Adam countered petulantly. 'Beer tokens do not grow on trees, you know.' The iron hissed.

'I know that.' Will softened. 'But you don't have a mortgage or utilities. I mean the credit card bill alone.'

'AHA!' Adam pointed the iron accusingly. 'How is your lovely wifey?'

'This is not about Cassandra,' said Will wearily. 'This is about our chance to make our names as well as more money than we have ever dreamed of, it could set us both up for life, and you don't seem to be taking it very seriously!'

'I see new wifey is turning the screws and making sure that you are going to keep her in the manner to which she will quickly become accustomed?' Adam said buttoning the still steaming shirt.

'She wants a decent life; what is so wrong with that?'

'Nothing.' Adam replied, slipping on his suit jacket. 'How do I look Mum, is this grown-up enough for you?'

Will looked him up and down and had to admit when he chose to, Adam could look like he just stepped out of one of those magazines Cassandra read avidly. 'I hate you!'

Adam slapped Will on the back. 'That was the look I was going for. So, let's go charm Mr Money.'

~~

If money were a person, in this case, it would be short, bald, round, and incredibly American. 'Mr Leibowitz, it's really good to see you again.' Will said as his hand was pumped up and down.

Murray Leibowitz smiled expansively. 'My father is Mr Leibowitz; you can call me Leibowitz. Otherwise, I am looking over my shoulder for the old man... eh?' Leibowitz slapped Will hard on the back. 'I can't tell you how excited I am fellas. This is an amazing opportunity. I haven't been able to stop thinking about it. I am very excited, very excited indeed!'

'Shall we sit down?' Adam asked. He showed the American through to what they grandly called the conference area.

Technically, of course, this was Adam's garage, or more accurately his mother's garage, which, up until only a few days ago was a space exclusively reserved for sprawling bits of dissected radios, half mobile phones, plastic thingies, brackets, pizza boxes, coke cans and possibly some primitive forms of life. However, that was before Cassandra had been allowed in and taken over the décor. The workshop had been tidied to the point that they now couldn't find anything. With the addition of a few essential pot plants, some outlandishly modern furniture and the small corner was transformed.

Murray settled into a seat designed clearly for a lesser man. Opening a file in front of him, he made great plays of taking the lid off a solid gold pen and stopped with it paused above the page. 'So, fellas,' he said, 'Time is money, and if you want either from me, you'd better sell me your idea.'

~~

'You were at university together, discovered your mutual love of computer games and decided to take it one step further?' Leibowitz said, looking up from his notes.

'It wasn't quite as simple as that.' Will snorted. 'It began as an idea.'

'Most things do fellas, but as my old great-granny used to say, if wishes were horses, beggars would ride, the same goes for ideas.'

Will continued. 'It did seem impossible at the time. We'd come up with some games, ARPG's, they were good, but it wasn't enough.'

Murray raised an eyebrow in question.

'Action role-playing games.' Adam supplied. 'They were pretty sweet, but we wanted something more interactive.'

'We wanted to really be in the heart of the action.' Will added enthusiastically. 'We'd developed this game based on Australia. Adam had been there while he was travelling, and it seemed a great basis for a very exciting scenario…'

'While we were working on it, things were getting pretty intense, ramping up the graphics, sound, even trying to work out a smell.' Adam continued.

'It got so crazy that I found I was dreaming about the game…' Will said, looking at his friend.

'That was when the idea began to take shape…' Adam supplied.

'How completely awesome would it be if you could play a game while you were asleep?'

'And remember the whole experience with no sleep deprivation.' Will said. 'Cognitive sleep; dreams you can control and remember. You can't get any more interactive than that.' The two inventors sat back in their seats.

'You truly can't.' Murray agreed. He tapped his pen on the notepad. 'And you set about working out how it could be done?'

'Remember there was once a time when the idea of making a phone call without being wired up to the grid seemed impossible.' Adam leaned in.

'Wireless technology and computers the size of a matchbox?' added Will. 'It was only a matter of time before we found out how to tap into the dream centre; the part of the brain that we only use when we're asleep.'

'After that, it was simply a case of making the module and creating the stories to go with it.' Adam finished.

'And you have managed to do all of that?' Murray said with some disbelief.

'Well, it wasn't overnight…' Will started.

'Yes, we have managed to do all of that.' Adam cut him off mid-sentence.

Will placed his closed fist upon the table and opened it slowly. He removed his hand to reveal two small electronic devices. 'Introducing the Vio spelt V10,' he said.

The American gawked at the little black earpieces. Each had a thin silver wire ending in a rubber pad. Will and Adam stared back at the American.

'That's it?' Murray breathed.

'That's it.' The pair said together.

'So how does it work?' He asked eventually.

Will opened his mouth to speak, but Adam beat him to it. 'How're your advanced electronics?'

Murray looked confused for a moment. 'Huh? My what?'

'In layman's terms, the black plugs go into the ears. The diodes are then placed next to the temples, like so.' Will held one of the devices to the side of his head. 'A wave is then transmitted between the two diodes corresponding with the current frequency of brain waves. Alpha waves occur when a person is relaxed but awake. These have a frequency of between eight and thirteen Hertz. When we sleep, these waves are replaced by beta waves at a lower frequency of nought point five Hertz. The device modulates and alters these waves to fool the brain into…'

'What we mean,' interrupted Adam, 'is that we could go into a long and complicated explanation about how it works, but ultimately what you need to know is it manipulates the brain's activity to produce cognitive dreams.'

'And you can do that?' Murray said slowly.

'It's not only what we can do; it's what we've done. This here is a working model. We have been testing it, and it is amazing!' Adam said.

'You've tested it? Murray's eyes were shining now. 'You're telling me that I could put those… those things on my head, and I could be part of my very own dream?'

'Well, you could be part of a dream that we have devised for the machine.' Will said. 'You simply download the scenario to the machine via any laptop or home P.C.'

If this were a cartoon, the pound signs would have been kerchinging in Murray's eyes like a fruit machine. 'So you are telling me, you have complete control over what is downloaded, and also the licence for those dreams. All of which have to be purchased?' The American licked his lips.

'Exactly.' Adam said, leaning back in his chair. Murray did the same. He linked his fingers and looked pointedly at both inventors. 'You wouldn't be shittin' me now, would you? You're not trying to take this good 'ole boy for a ride?'

Again, Will tried to speak, but Adam got in first. 'The only way we're going to prove it to you is for you to try it.'

'What!' Will spluttered.

'If Leibowitz wants to know it works. He had better try it then.'

Will began to go red in the face. 'He's not taking it away with him.' He hissed to Adam. 'We developed this, all that work, how do you know he's not going to take it apart and steal our idea?' Adam turned to Murray.

'It's not that my colleague here does not trust you; it's just he has a more naturally suspicious nature. Obviously, you wouldn't be expecting to take the device out of this building?'

Murray's attention was entirely on this potential goldmine. He shook his head. 'I wouldn't expect my boys to trust anyone, not yet anyway. Do you know what you've got here boys if this works? You have a licence to print money. You will not be able to spend it as fast as you are earning it. You will be retiring before your time, and you will be millionaires!' Murray reached out to touch the probe and then changed his mind. 'And there are no side effects? It's safe?'

'Safe as a big fluffy pillow.' Adam stood up. 'What about now; fancy a little nap, Leibowitz? We have programmed a medieval scenario into this one; it should give you a good idea of how it feels for the consumer.

'Merry old England, huh? Well, that would be something to see and no mistake,' said Murray, his voice a little high.

'That's settled then,' replied Adam. He gestured towards the door adjoining the house. 'Shall we?'

CHAPTER 2

With his free hand, Ceun Hawke pushed open the glass door marked Morphean Police and negotiated his way through the busy reception. He was currently dragging a tentacle behind him at the other end. A creature was changing shape in a desperate attempt to find one that would be the means for its escape. Ceun dinged the bell. A round face appeared from behind a mountain of paper.

'Just a second Hawke!' The head disappeared. Ceun now had hold of a talon just as its partner was bearing down upon his neck. He caught the other claw easily and tied the creature's appendages together. The face reappeared followed by an equally ball-shaped body.

'Sorry about that.' The desk Sergeant said, giving the bounty hunter his full attention. Out of all the freelancers on the books, Hawke always intrigued him. Most of them were great muscular lumps with a mental capacity that limited itself to hunt, catch and deposit, sometimes even alive. Hawke didn't fall into that category. He wasn't excessively tall; in fact, some people might also be inclined to say he was quite short for his profession. They generally didn't say so twice. As far as apparent physical strength was concerned, he was wiry rather than the battering ram norm. Scorning the leather of his peers, he was always smartly dressed in an almost black suit and t-shirt, wearing his dark, shoulder-length, curly hair tied at the base of his neck. With a normally cheerful disposition, the Sergeant often wondered why someone so clearly educated would want to deal with the dregs of society. For whatever reason, Hawke was at the top of his profession a legend almost.

If a criminal knew Hawke was on his tail chances were, he would turn himself in rather than go to the trouble of trying to escape. Of course, not all of them were that bright.

'Doughnut?' Ceun asked amiably interrupting the Sergeant's thoughts.

'That's a filthy stereotype, and you know it!' He replied indignantly. 'My wife has me on a very strict diet. I'm this shape because it's genetic!'

Ceun leaned forward, pointing towards a large globule of jam clinging tenuously to the material of the Sergeant's jacket. The man looked down. 'Oh great,' he whined. 'And how am I going to explain this when I get home?'

'Jam monster exploded on you?' Ceun offered helpfully as the Sergeant took a handkerchief from his pocket, spit on it and began dabbing at the mess ineffectually.

'Ahem?' Ceun coughed 'I don't mean to be difficult, but I have a prisoner to book in who could be described as a little on the hostile side.' The Sergeant leaned over the desk and surveyed the knot of arms and legs.

'I wanth to complainth abouth policth brutalitith.' It spluttered. There did seem to be an interesting trickle coming from a part of it that may well have been a nose, but on the other hand, that could have been completely normal.

The Sergeant looked towards Ceun. 'You hear that? Brutalitith?'

'This gentleman attempted to escape as I was trying to apprehend him. I was forced to persuade him that this was not a good idea.' Ceun said with a shrug.

'Heth tied me in a knoth!' the creature squeaked.

'But on the plus side, he is no longer trying to escape.' Ceun added warmly.

The officer shifted through a pile on his desk. He found the sheet he was looking for and pulled it out with a flourish. 'Ah, here we are. Zweep let's have a look at the balance sheet. Assault with a deadly appendage, demanding services with menaces – I don't think I even want to know about that – extortion and blackmail using information you gained while in the guise of an aspidistra. It's not very pretty Zweep, is it?'

'It wasth all a mistake!' The creature moaned 'I've been frameth!'

'More potted if you were a plant! Eh? Eh?'

Ceun and the creature both looked at the grinning man blankly. 'Never mind,' he said, the smile fading, 'Right then, let's be having you.' He pulled a lever causing the front portion of the desk to slide away. 'In you go Zweep.'

Zweep however, had no intention of going quietly. He had managed to unravel part of himself and was currently changing into a green ooze. Ceun grabbed at the remaining solid parts of the prisoner and squeezed him into the hole. Just as it closed, a fountain of gloop shot straight up. The Sergeant pulled the lever, and the prisoner disappeared just as the gloop remembered a little thing called gravity and covered him from head to waist. Blinking, he cleared the goo out of his eyes.

'I think we've solved the problem of the jam mark.' Ceun said conversationally.

'Bloody shapeshifters,' The Sergeant complained. 'Why is it at the end of the day they always revert to ooze? They're frightened, they ooze. They're angry, they ooze. What is it with these things?'

'They're not very adventurous, I suppose. Ooze works.' Ceun replied, filling in the register.

'Not like polymorphs; now they are a completely different kettle of fish entirely.' The Sergeant said, looking at the ineffective handkerchief. Ceun paused almost imperceivably.

The Sergeant continued, his head disappearing underneath

the desk as he searched for something more absorbent. 'Morphs, they really do give me the eebie jeebies. As if it's not enough that they get into your head…'

'Get into your head?' Ceun said.

'Well not like your head as such, but it's freaky that they don't have a real 'them'. You know what I mean. Whoever you want them to be; that's just who they are. It's as if they don't exist unless you are with them. What do they see when they look in the mirror, that's what I want to know?' He popped up from behind the desk, brandishing a discarded towel in triumph.

'That is the question.' Ceun rested his elbows on the desk.

'There's got to be no good in someone who manipulates you like that. It's…'

'It's how they were created; not much they can do about it.' Ceun said.

The Sergeant shuddered, 'I know, I know they do their thing and can make people in Realitas happy, spending time with their loved ones and all that stuff, but that kind of power, it's got to warp a person. Do you remember that one went rogue last year? Now she was crazy, completely homicidal. Was in some bloke's dream and became completely obsessed. I tell you she'd have done for him and his wife too. Brought in here kicking, screaming and scratching like a little hellcat.'

Ceun still hadn't moved, a plastic smile plastered on his face. 'They're pampered creatures, used to getting their own way.'

'She certainly learned the hard way, elite or not. You can't go taking revenge on some human just because you don't get your way.' The Sergeant laughed. 'Hey.' His brow creased in thought, 'You brought her in didn't you[TT1]?'

'I did.' Ceun said. 'You deserved danger money for that one Hawke and no mistake.

'Thanks, now any chance that the state is going to pay me my bounty for Mr Zweep? How am I going to keep up my rock and roll lifestyle if I don't have the cash?'

The Sergeant leant forward conspiratorially, 'You mean the fast cars and the women, right? I've heard about you bounty hunters...'

'I couldn't even begin to tell you.' Ceun whispered. The Sergeant raised his eyebrows hopefully. 'No.' Ceun said, 'I really can't tell you.'

'Right, well, yes.' The Sergeant coughed. 'Of course, I'll just get it from the safe for you.' In a moment he was back with two envelopes.

'Did I earn a bonus or is it my birthday and you clubbed together?' Ceun smiled, unnerving the Sergeant.

'One is the bounty the other is a message left for you.' 'For me?' Ceun examined the seal.

'It hasn't been opened, the person who left it was very definite that it was for your eyes only.' The Sergeant said hurriedly.

'And who could that have been I wonder?' Ceun asked, taking a penknife and unsealing the note.

'Um, I'm not sure. I could ask around?' the Sergeant replied. Ceun waved a hand dismissively as he opened the letter and read it through slowly.

'Bad news?' asked the Sergeant. Ceun fixed him with a gaze of steel. 'I think we can safely say it isn't good.'

CHAPTER 3

In his chambers, the Chairman of the Committee of Morpheus sat behind his desk lost in his thoughts. A discreet tap on the door stirred him. 'Come in Winkworth,' he said.

The door opened less than an inch. Winkworth, his assistant, slid through. The Bogeyman coughed.

'Yes, Winkworth.' The Chairman said again.

In the league of toadying Winkworth could have taken gold, silver and bronze medals. He lifted the gold horn-rimmed spectacles that hung around his neck and surveyed the clip-board he was holding. 'All the delegates are assembled my lord chairman and awaiting your pleasure,' he said nasally.

'I would hardly call it pleasure Winkworth. Anyone decline my invitation?'

Winkworth managed to blow his nose and convey horror all at the same time. 'Decline sir? I hardly think that a personal invitation from the, sorry, The Chairman of the committee could be declined!' He gave a little laugh at the absurdity of the idea.

'Hmm.' The Chairman rested his head on his hands and looked at the little creature in front of him. 'Is it the right thing to do Winkworth, that's what I keep asking myself?' But what is the alternative?' He sighed.

Winkworth wound the toadying up a notch. 'It wouldn't be for me to say, your lordship, I wouldn't presume.'

'You must have an opinion?' The Chairman countered.

'It is not my place to have one sir.'

The Chairman sighed again. 'Very well, Winkworth, I suppose that place falls to me.'

'Indeed sir, which is why you are the Chairman.' His assistant said firmly.

Getting up from behind the desk, he crossed to the full-length mirror. From under the red curly wig, a troubled face looked back at him. Even the thick white makeup failed to hide the worry lines etching a map across his forehead. 'I'm looking tired Winkworth, very, very tired.'

'Yours is a great responsibility, sir.' Winkworth slipped silently across the room and placed the ceremonial gown across the Chairman's shoulders.

'Is this completely necessary? I could go as I am. After all, informality might be the thing?'

'No, sir. The ceremonial duck and goose down robe has been worn by generations of Chairmen, and I'm sure you do not want to be the one that breaks with tradit… Ahhh, Choo!'

'Bless you! I wonder you know with your, um how can I put it… allergies that perhaps it might be better not to be around it, for you, I mean?'

Winkworth sniffed. 'Your concern touches me, but it is quite unnecessary.'

'Oh of course,' the Chairman said hurriedly, aware that he might have inadvertently ruffled more feathers than those on his back. 'Of course, I understand that the whole mucus thing is very much cultural. I assure you that I was only thinking of your comfort.'

'I appreciate that, Sir.' He said, mollified.

'I meant I know Bogeymen take great pride in their traditions, just as I do in mine. Why I suppose you would no more be without your snot than I would be without my shiny red nose?' The chairman honked to demonstrate the point.

'Indeed sir, now if I may be so bold, I really would suggest given the circumstances you do not keep the committee waiting any longer than necessary?' Winkworth said, brushing down a few stray feathers.

The Chairman surveyed himself in the mirror. 'How do I look Winkworth, nose shiny?' 'The shiniest Sir!'

'Then let's get this show on the road.'

~~

The flop, flop, flop of shoes on marbled flooring could be easily heard from inside the meeting room. The Chairman knew from personal experience that there would be a flurry of activity inside as everyone tried to take their places. He slowed his walk, deliberately to prolong their anticipation. Not so long ago he had been on the other side of those imposing oak doors, and it had been a struggle to get where he was, but finally, he was the one who would throw them open and face the committee of Morpheus.

'All rise for the Lord Elect, High Sheriff, Bango, elected representative of the Clown, buffoon, farceur, fool, funster, gagster, harlequin, humorist, jester, joker, jokester, picador, pierrot, prankster, punch, Punchinello, quipster, ribald, wag and wisecracker party and Chairman of Morpheus!' The effort of announcing the chairman's arrival sent Winkworth into a coughing fit. Apart from the rasps behind him, the long table was utterly silent as the chairman flop flopped his way to his seat.

'Ladies, Gentlemen and Things,' He began, 'Thank you for taking the time to attend today's emergency meeting. Please take your seats.' Bango used the general flurry of activity to review his notes. 'My Friends...' He began before noticing a shadowy hand rise slowly. He nodded in acknowledgement. 'The chair recognises the honourable member for Chasing, lurking, surprising and throwing people off things.'

'I haven't received my agenda; we always have an agenda, and I haven't received mine!' The grey creature spluttered nervously.

'You won't have received an agenda. It was an emergency meeting, Fred.' Bango said. Another hand rose. 'The chair recognises the honourable member for Pirates, buccaneers, sea-rovers and marauders.'

'I assume we will still be having lunch. I know it is an emergency meeting as you said, but we always have sandwiches at least.'

'Cheese and ham! Cheese and Ham!' The parrot squawked from the honourable member's shoulder.

The Chairman took a deep breath. 'Winkworth, did you order some sandwiches?'

Consulting his clipboard, the assistant looked pointedly at the pirate. 'Refreshments for the emergency meeting have been ordered and will be available at the end.'

'Right!' Bango started again, 'is there anything that anyone would like to know about sandwiches or agenda's or anything else?' A hand started to rise, but its owner felt the full force of Winkworth's glare so swiftly put it down again.

'Good.' The Chairman leant on the table. 'Because the reason I have called you here is a grave matter, one might say it is a disaster in the making.' All eyes in the room were on Bango, in some cases more than two per person.

'So, what is it then?' Cried the honourable member for putting things in the way for humans to trip over and make them twitch in their sleep.

The Chairman paused for dramatic effect. 'It has come to my attention… that someone is at large in Morpheus… someone from Realitas. What's more, my sources tell me that it is very likely this human will soon be leading an invasion!'

The delegates looked at each other in confusion. 'I'm sorry.' Fred said, 'but you have dragged us all here to this essential emergency meeting because humans are coming from Realitas into Morpheus?'

'That's right,' replied the chairman.

Fred laughed. 'We realise you are new to this Bango...'

'Right honourable chairman.' Winkworth said automatically.

'Yes.' Fred snapped, 'I don't know where the honourable chairman has been for the last, ooh I don't know, five thousand years, but humans from Realitas are always coming to Morpheus. Isn't that normal? When they sleep, they cross dimensions and come here; they are an essential part of our economy. I fail to see the issue.'

Several other heads around the table were nodding in agreement, and there was a general muttering. Halfway down the table, a silver-haired grandmother was knitting a bed jacket, not an easy thing to do with both arms in plaster casts. 'I think there is a point that our illustrious chairman has failed to mention,' she said without looking up from her knitting.

'Yes, yes, indeed, thank you, Ethel... um, I mean the honourable member for Polymorphic services.'

'You're welcome, dearie.' Ethel continued her knitting.

'As Fred has pointed out.'

'Honourable member for Chasing, lurking, surprising and throwing people off things.' Winkworth muttered.

'Yes Winkworth, thank you, but I think in the circumstances we can dispense with that.' The chairman ignored the hurt look on his assistant's face. 'As stated, humans have been coming here for generations. But... they have always been visitors and abided by our rules. On the return journey to their own dimension, everything gets scrambled up, so they may remember this or that, but for the most part, they are no real threat, that is until now! It appears that one of them has developed a machine which not only stops the scrambling of information on their way home, but it also allows them to control every-thing that happens in their dormant state. They will soon be dictating our landscape; what we eat, what we wear, where we live, it is a complete violation of our freedom. My friends, we will effectively become the slaves and playthings of humans!'

'They can't do that!' The member for Things that go bang in another room cried out.

'It's outrageous!' wailed the honourable member for Angelic presences bearing messages. There was an uproar in the room as forty-seven voices all trying to be heard at the same time.

'Everyone! Please!' The chairman appealed for calm.

'Are we sure about this?' The Pirate called out.

The Chairman hung his head. 'Very sure, I'm afraid. Ethel, would you tell us your story if you think you're up to it?'

The old lady bowed her head slightly, as much as her ortho-paedic collar would allow. She knitted another line before she spoke. 'As you know my dears, it's not like me to make a fuss.' There was a general murmur of agreement as she continued with her stitches.

'Go ahead Ethel,' the chairman said gently, 'tell them what happened if it's not too upsetting.'

Ethel sighed. 'As I said, I don't like to make a fuss. I went to investigate one of these new-fangled dreams that have been popping up all over the place. One of my constituents, Rose, you know her with the veins, anyway, she had told me about this castle had just appeared. One minute it wasn't there, the next minute large as life and right overlooking her tomato plants. She said to me, Ethel, my tomatoes will never ripen with that dirty great building there, and you know she's right because if they don't get the full sun, then you have wasted your time. You can make chutney out of green tomatoes, but to be honest, I don't like it much; it makes my eye twitch...'

'Yes Ethel, but can you tell us about your accident?' the chairman said. 'Accident?' she spat, 'It was no accident I can tell you!'

'Can you tell us what happened?'

'I was getting to it,' she said indignantly. 'Anyway, as I was saying. Rose wanted me to investigate and as an elected representative of the comm...'

'What happened?' Several delegates shouted together.

Ethel pursed her lips. 'Do you want to hear about it or not?' she said crisply.

'We do; we do,' said the chairman placating her. 'Now if everyone could keep quiet for a moment, Ethel will tell us how she came by her injuries. Shall we go from when you were inside?'

'I went inside,' Ethel continued, 'and it was filthy. There were animals everywhere and their... doings. And the people! The people in there didn't look as though they'd had a bath this side of daffodil Sunday, and they were acting mighty peculiar as well.'

'Peculiar how?' asked the pirate.

She stopped knitting and fixed her gaze on the pirate. 'Like they hadn't got minds of their own.' There was some whispering around the table. Ethel let the news sink in. 'So,' she continued, 'I go up to this large chap. He's from Realitas, and he may have grown a bit, but I recognised him. Nasty little creature, he was when I knew him. Stealing pocket money, pulling the legs off spiders, kicking puppies, you name it, he was into it. In my official capacity as a polymorph, the little boy saw me as his great-grandmother, a woman who by all accounts was quite formidable, and the idea then was to persuade him back on to the straight and narrow.'

'Did it work?' A monster breathed from further down the

table.

'I believed it had.' Ethel continued, resuming her knitting. 'However, it seemed that the little boy had rather harboured a grudge against dear old great-grandma.'

'Tell them what he did Ethel.' The chairman prompted.

'I went marching up to him and demanded to know what he thought he was doing! Now, normally, he would look at his shoes and be very ashamed, but not this time.' Ethel's needles moved faster until her fingers were a blur. 'He laughed, a nasty, sinister evil laugh. It made the blood run cold; I don't mind telling you. Then... then he said... You ain't the boss of me great-granny and...'

'And...?' the whole room held its breath.

'He... he... he told me to walk outside... made me get into the bucket thing on the trebuchet and... and...' she sobbed. 'Had me shot over the wall into the moat.'

The whole room gasped.

'His own great grandmother!' Fred squeaked.

'Did nobody help you?' The monster asked horrified.

Ethel was unable to speak, so the chairman stepped in. 'The way she told it to me, Ethel was completely under his control, there was nothing that she could do except comply.'

'It was like being in a trance. I wanted to give him a good clip round the ear!' Ethel said bitterly.

Bango looked around the table, making sure he had everyone's full attention. 'This is what we are dealing with my friends; this is what happens when one of those things turns up in Morpheus. We're powerless. If this atrocity goes unchecked, we could be completely destroyed.'

The pirate got to his feet, dislodging the parrot which flapped around his head. 'It's an outrage!' He yelled. 'It can't be allowed to happen!' Other delegates were yelling too. Bango held his hands up.

'Order! Order!' Winkworth banged his clipboard on the table until order was restored. 'There is one solution,' the chairman said quietly, 'but I warn you all it is not something to be taken lightly, and I will need you all to agree.' The delegates waited.

~~

'We capture this human. Stop him before his plan for Morphean domination comes to fruition.' There was a general murmur amongst the creatures.

'You're suggesting that we… kill this person?' Fred said, shocked.

'We can't do that! It would be entirely unconstitutional!' added the Pirate. 'Unconsti…. Qwark!' The parrot decided not to bother. 'Bad Bango! Bad Bango!' It screeched instead.

'Silence that bird.' The Chairman growled. Recovering himself, the chairman continued. 'I know it is a radical step. However, as far as we know, there have been reports of up to three people who have now taken control of a situation. It seems to be localised around this castle. According to my intelligence…' There was a noise from the parrot muffled immediately by the pirate clamping its beak shut. 'According to my intelligence,' Bango said with a pointed look towards the parrot, 'the first invader was a human by the name of…?'

'Will Cooper, my lord.' Winkworth supplied.

'Will Cooper.' Bango repeated for effect.

'What about the others?' the shadow man asked.

'Is he the one that attacked Ethel?' said the Pirate.

Bango held his hands up again. 'We believe that this Will Cooper is responsible for the operation. The other two seem to be his staff, or scouts or whatever you want to call them. The one they call…?' Bango looked to Winkworth.

'We don't have a name your chairmanship.'

'Anyway, he appears to be fairly harmless, although some of the ladies may not agree...' Bango waggled his eyebrows suggestively but received only blank looks in return. 'Ahem, anyway, according to Ethel, her assailant was never intelligent enough to come up with something like this. So, it would seem Will Cooper is the man we need to stop.' Bango sat down as the committee argued amongst themselves.

'It really can't be the only solution. Perhaps we could talk to this person, explain what we are doing?' The honourable member for putting things in the way of humans to trip over and then twitch suggested.

'And confirm that to Realitas that we are vulnerable? We may as well put a big welcome doormat on ourselves.' Bango scoffed.

'But this could mean...it would be an act of war...!' A voice said quietly from the back. The whole room went silent. All eyes fixed on the chairman.

'It would be self-defence,' he said eventually. 'The way I see it, we have no choice.'

CHAPTER 4

The ceiling fan only served to move the warm stuffy air around the office, and half-drawn blinds barely let any light into this mausoleum. Behind the enormous desk, the Don of the Morphean Mafia sat watching the door, while adding cigar smoke to the general gloom. Finally, a pounding on the wood announced the arrival of an expected visitor. Without waiting for an answer, the door was propelled open by the face of Vinny the Snitch, assisted by four meat-like fists.

'Vinny!' The Don said, coming out from behind the desk, arms outstretched. 'So good of you to come and visit with us.'

On his knees, Vinny tried to make himself even smaller than his rat-like frame. He fixed his eyes on the shiny red shoes in front of him. 'You… you wanted to see me?' He stuttered.

'You make it sound like a chore, Vinny. Haven't we always been good to you?' The Don looked at the henchmen behind the shivering Vinny. 'Salvatore, Alfredo, we hope you have been looking after our guest?' A pair of sharp eyes darted around the room before settling once more on the unfortunate Vinny. 'Anyone would think you were reluctant to accept our hospitality?'

The two thugs looked at each other and smiled in the way of bullies who know they're on the right side. Alfredo, the younger, a hulk of a man in an ill-fitting suit and with a temper to match, always relied on his brother Salvatore to deal with being the smarter one in every sense of the word. This role was one that Salli had relished since they were children when he'd realised that, despite his own lack of muscle, as a pair, they could be very 'persuasive'. A hand was placed under Vinny's down-turned chin, forcing him to stand and face the dumpy woman standing in front of him. 'Nnnot at all.' Vinny spluttered, 'I am always happy to see you, Godmother.'

She leant back against the desk and took another puff on the cigar, flapping the smoke away with her wings. 'That's much better,' she said with a smile so sweet it would make your teeth itch. She proffered a hand, which Vinny stared at as though it may bite. A none too gently nudge from Alfredo reminded him of his manners, so he bent forward nervously and kissed the pale skin. Satisfied, the Godmother renegotiated the desk and returned to her enormous chair. 'A seat for our guest,' she said as Vinny was manhandled into position. 'Now then,' she began, 'a little bird tells us that something is causing the good citizens of Morpheus to get their tails in a twist. The same little bird, or possibly it might have been a different one; the trouble is they all look identical. You know how it is with our feathered friends?' Vinny nodded so hard he nearly dislocated his neck. 'The point being, something is happening, and that something is big. Now we are led to understand that you were there when the event took place?' Vinny's eyes had grown to the size of dinner plates, much as he tried, he couldn't drag them away from the silhouette in front of him. 'We think that as fine upstanding citizens, we are obliged to be up to date with all the latest news, to see how we can help. You understand?' said the Godmother. Vinny nodded harder. 'So, we would be very much obliged if you would tell us everything you know.' She finished, inclining her head that he should begin.

Once Vinny started talking, it was difficult to get him to stop. Silence would mean his usefulness was over, and his existence possibly along with it. Therefore, his only hope was to keep going and pray that his information was useful enough to buy him a reprieve. '...and then the morph went over the wall like a rocket, and there was nothing any of them could do. They were like puppets, just moving wherever this guy put them, it was crazy.'

'And you say that this human was talking about something, some gateway that was allowing him to control things?' the Godmother said.

'Yes, yes. A machine, a Vio he called it, he was getting excited and leaping around. He kept making people do things. He had one man on his knees barking like a dog, another one he made to walk into the duck pond. It was the weirdest thing I have ever seen. He was yelling things like 'this is going to make a million, we can write our own pay cheque', and 'those boys have done it. They have really done it!'

The Don ground her cigar into the ashtray. 'It's safe to say that the man you saw is not the one in control of this machine, that there is someone else behind it, perhaps more than one some-one, and they are the key to how it works?' she said slowly.

'It seems that way, Godmother.' Vinny said, hopefully.

'And how, pray, were you not affected by its power, we won-der?'

'I don't know.' Vinny frowned; it had been going so well. 'I was watching from the edge.'

'Just lurking and sneaking around?' the Godmother said un-pleasantly. 'You really are a little snitch, aren't you?'

Vinny laughed nervously, 'That's what they call me.' The Fairy Godmother laughed. Salvatore and Alfredo laughed. Vinny laughed. Suddenly they stopped, leaving Vinny chuckling on his own.

'Something funny, Vincent?' The Godmother growled. Vince gulped.

'But… err… no?'

'Good, because we would hate to think that you found us… amusing?' Vinny went back to the safety of shaking his head.

'Thank you,' she said eventually, 'you have been most... helpful. The boys will see you out. We are very pleased. You should come and see us again when you have recovered from your accident.' Terror gripped the little man along with the two thugs as he was dragged out of the room.

The Godmother lit another fat cigar. 'Did you hear all of that?' she said to the empty office. A partition opened in the panelling; a tall figure stepped out into the room. From the sunglasses on his snout to the curly tail peeping out of his overcoat, he exuded malevolence.

'I heard it.' he snorted.

'Someone in Realitas is behind this device. A device that could be very useful to us.' The hit pig said nothing. 'We want you to go and find that person or persons Porkio. We would hate to think of power like that in the wrong hands. If this device can be used across the dimensions, who is to say that it cannot also work in reverse? Now that would hold some exciting possibilities for us, very interesting indeed. We want you to find them, and we want you to bring them to us.' Porkio turned to leave. 'Oh, and Bacon Slicer...?' The pig turned back to face his Don. 'We would prefer them in whole pieces.'

CHAPTER 5

As Murray Leibowitz opened his eyes, his body was already half-way up from the couch. He virtually bounced into the kitchen, where Adam was dabbling on his laptop, and Will was busy pacing the floor. The American pulled his braces over his shoulders. As the pink chicken pattern settled over his massive frame, its owner struggled for words. 'Amazing!' was all he could manage.

'You liked it then?' Adam said, looking up.

'Liked it? LIKED IT! Are you guys kidding me? That has got to be the singularly most amazing experience I have ever had!'

'I think we could safely say he believes we can do it.' Adam said grinning at Will, who was more concerned with getting the precious device back into his possession.

Murray ran a hand through his receding hairline in an attempt to compose himself. 'The colours, the experience... what I was able to do, something I always wanted to do, but guys, guys you made it possible!'

'I think you can keep the details to yourself, Mr Leibowitz' Will said primly.

Murray grabbed him forcibly by the shoulders. 'What did I say boys... what did I say? Leibowitz, no need for the Mr, no need for that between partners, huh?' He held out a hand. Will stared at it. In a moment, Adam was on his feet and shaking the proffered hand, nudging Will to follow suit. 'I take it we have a deal. I'll get my people to crunch some numbers, draw up some contracts, and before we know it, we'll all be on the gravy train.'

'Just what sort of figures are we talking here M... Leibowitz?' Will asked.

'What he means is how much of a cut are you going to take?' Adam added.

'Hey, hey, guys!' the American held his hands up in mock surrender. 'I need to look at the investment required here. You courier me over your numbers, and I'll let my legal eagles work out the fine details. Don't worry though Willy boy you'll have more than enough to keep a pretty wife happy. Just remember, they get used to it. I have three Mrs Leibowitzs to help me spend my cash, and none of them is my Mom.'

Will was confused. 'What makes you think she's pretty?'

Murray laughed. 'Why would a genius like you marry a plain Jane? Come on, we don't marry them for their brains now do we? Now then, enough of the questions, we're celebrating! You got anything stronger than caffeine in this joint?'

'It's eleven in the morning!' Will said, glancing pointedly at the kitchen clock.

#'Yeah, but it's five o'clock somewhere, isn't that right Leibowitz?' Adam said, handing out some cans of lager from the fridge. 'And this is a celebration after all.' The three touched cans before pulling ring pulls.

'A toast gentlemen.' Murray held his can aloft, a huge grin on his face. 'To the future of the Vio. Today merry old England; tomorrow the world!'

The shrill, painful sound of a sonata being brutally murdered began somewhere in Will's trouser pocket. Embarrassed, he fumbled for the phone mouthing 'sorry' as he pressed the call accept button. 'Hi Honey-kins!' trilled a voice at the other end. Will smiled awkwardly and retreated to the hallway.

'I'm in a meeting, Cass.' He hissed, 'Can I call you back?'

'It won't take a minute, Sweetie. I was just calling to see how everything went. Is it all systems go?'

Will smiled despite himself. 'It does seem so.' He whispered, glancing back towards the kitchen.

Cassandra squealed in excitement. 'Who's a clever boy then?' she cooed. 'I knew you could do it!'

'Thanks… well… um… I'd better go…'

'Just a minute baby, while you're on the phone, and in such a good mood? I was talking to my personal trainer at the gym, and you will never guess…?'

'You're right, I won't ever guess, but now is not a really good time…'

'Don't be cranky William,' she snapped, before quickly switching to a more amenable tone. 'It won't take a minute, and it is important.' Will opened his mouth to speak, but she continued anyway. 'You know the old farm buildings out towards the river? Well, according to Ricardo, he knows a lady whose husband knows one of the builders, and they are developing the whole estate. It is going to be tres chic apparently, THE place to live!'

'And this has what to do with us?'

Cass' voice raised an octave in excitement. 'Because I have managed to get us a very exclusive invitation to view the plans and have a private chat with the developer.'

Will could hear her clapping her hands. 'Cass, why would you do that? They sound very expensive, and we are struggling to pay the mortgage we've got.'

'Don't be a cross puss,' she whined, 'we will have the money soon, now that my clever, clever husband has managed to sell his toy?'

'Not for a while, we have some potential finance in place, but the V10 will have to go through trials, then we have to source the materials, then there is the marketing and the focus groups not to mention hoping that people will want to buy it! Anyway, why would you want to live here? You are always saying you can't wait to leave this stinking small town and move to the city?'

'But I'm thinking of you sweetie,' she wheedled. 'Think of the image. House in the country and a chic apartment in town, it's the least anyone who is anyone would expect of a genius inventor like you. Do you think the inventor of the interweb lives in a two bedroomed flat?'

Will shook his head. 'We just don't have the funds...'

'It's always later, later, later with you.' Cass said petulantly. 'You have your game thingy. Why don't you go to the bank like a normal person, and borrow some money? When we got married, you told me I could have anything I wanted, and I am tired of waiting!'

'I know baby, and you have been very patient, but right now we need to keep an eye on the pennies, your credit card alone...'

'So, you want me to walk around naked now!' She squeaked almost bat-like. Will moved the phone away from his ear a millisecond too late. 'I buy a few essential items, and you don't even want me to have those!' she continued.

'Cassandra, you bought seventeen pairs of shoes.' 'I needed those, anyway, what would your American man think if he knew you wanted to keep your wife barefoot?'

Will couldn't quite give up, even though he was long since defeated. 'I had to clear out nearly half of my wardrobe space to accommodate them!'

Cassandra giggled, 'and it was so sweet of you to do that for me.' Will knew he had lost, and so did his wife. 'I've made an appointment for about three on Wednesday, so I'll pick you up about two, sweetie.' She cooed.

'Ok, I'll see you later, but...' The phone had already gone dead.

~~

Ethel nodded her thanks as the glass door was opened for her. 'Thank you, dearie,' she said sweetly. 'You're welcome Auntie Phyllis.' The officer replied before shaking his head slightly in confusion. Ignoring him, Ethel made her way carefully to the reception desk. With effort, she pressed the bell and waited.

'Just a moment,' came a voice.

Ethel dinged the bell again. 'I'm coming. I'm coming,' said the desk Sergeant irritably as he arrived buttoning his jacket. 'Oh...' he said, stopping short.

Ethel held up a finger. 'Before we start with the 'oh it's you, grandma so and so,' you should be aware that I am, in fact, the honourable member for polymorphic services. Should you care to examine it, I am wearing my credentials.' As a polymorph was nearly always confused for absolutely anyone other than the person they really were, it was a requirement, when not on assignment, to wear an identification badge. The badge was rarely noticed.

'Ah, yes committee member visit? I didn't think we were due one of those for another month or so?' The Sergeant said.

'We like to keep an eye on things, especially nowadays. My neighbour, Mrs thing, she had terrible trouble with young people in her orchards. The police were marvellous, absolutely marvellous. I won't hear a word said against you. You do a very difficult job.'

The Sergeant puffed out his chest with pride.

'If there is anything I can do to help you, in my capacity as an honourable member, I think it is my absolute duty to do so.' Ethel smiled.

'Well, I think there are a few items that might need some attention...I'll fetch the chief. He'll be able to...'

Ethel turned so her outstretched hand could pat the Sergeant's podgy fingers. 'Don't you worry him, dearie. As if he hasn't got enough to worry about without fussing around little old ladies. I don't want to be a bother.'

'No… but…' The Sergeant tried again.

'Really, you wouldn't want me to think I'd been a trouble to you, would you? With how busy you all are?' He rheumy eyes gazed into his earnestly. 'Well, no, you…'

Ethel allowed him another pat. 'I'll tell you what, I'll have a little wander around, have a look, chat to a few people, and then I'll be out of here in a wag of a baby lamb's tail. How about that? I have my credentials?' She proffered the badge.

'Weeeelll, I suppose so…' The Sergeant said uncertainly just as the door flew open and a duo of bounty hunters came in with something flailing between them. 'Just don't get in the way,' he said to Ethel as he left the desk to help.

'You won't even know I'm here,' she said, smiling to herself as she unclipped the badge and slid it carefully into her knitting bag.

CHAPTER 6

Morpheans tend to take their crime very seriously. For those unlucky enough to end up in the high-security prison block, it is the equivalent of being locked up and the key thrown away, melted down and sold for ornamental buttons. Not, of course, that a key would be required. The doors mould perfectly into place, sealing themselves instantly, and can only be opened from a separate secret location by prior arrangement. No windows break the sheer line of shiny white walls, and the single entrance/exit is continuously manned by three ever vigilant guards. Even the meagre food is delivered to the prisoners automatically. This jail is designed to thwart even the most determined escape artist, and so far, had been so successful that no-one has ever had the will to try. Ceun re-read the small document he'd received with his letter. Looking back towards the entrance, he folded the paper and placed it back in his pocket. He'd been on surveillance for some time and had yet to see a flaw in the security. Only one of the sentries changed at a time, so there was no opportunity to use the old, 'the other guards know all about it' routine. These were men who very rarely had anything happen to break the monotony, at moments of even the smallest activity their nerves were so taut they almost hummed.

For what seemed like the hundredth time, Ceun looked at the release paperwork. It looked genuine. Of course, he knew it wasn't. There was no way that this would be done so unofficially. He felt a long-forgotten thrill of excitement. If this went wrong, it was extremely likely that he would soon become a permanent resident behind those cold walls. But, he reasoned, why would someone go to all this trouble just to set him up? There were easier ways to get revenge. He'd heard enough rumours to corroborate most of the contents of the mysterious message, and the rest he could easily believe. Now he just had to have a little faith and hope for the best.

The guards watched the truck as it slowly approached the gateway. There was always a great deal of preparation to do before they received a new inmate, so this was definitely not a delivery.

'Not an official truck.' Guard Two-three-one said.

'Civilian driver,' said Guard four-two-three.

'Cool shades,' added Guard Eight-one-five. The other two looked at him sharply.

'What has that got to do with anything?' asked Guard four-two-three.

Eight-one-five shrugged, 'It was just an observation.'

'My observation is that this is trouble,' said Two-three-one.

Eight-one-five rolled his eyes. 'When that pigeon landed on the roof and slid off, you thought that was trouble.'

'It could have been,' said Two-three-one.

Ceun jumped down from the cab and strolled towards the entrance. 'That ain't no pigeon,' said four-two-three.

'HALT!' shouted Two-three-one, making Eight-one-five jump. 'STATE YOUR BUSINESS!'

Ceun took off his sunglasses, reached into his pocket and slowly drew out the release warrant. He waved it at the guards like a white flag.

'APPROACH!' screamed Two-three-one.

'Does he have to shout?' Eight-one-five asked Four-three-two. His colleague shrugged.

'I have here a warrant for the release of a prisoner into my custody.' Ceun called out as he walked towards the three men. By the time he reached them, Two-three-one was smiling unpleasantly.

'No one is ever released from here,' he growled, 'nice try though.'

'No skin off my nose.' Ceun said, turning to go, 'I didn't want the job anyway. Babysitting some freaky nut job just because the powers that be think she's the only one who can save us all.'

'We have received no instructions that a prisoner is to be released regardless of world-saving ability,' said Four-three-two.

Ceun read through the warrant. 'I brought her in here and, believe me, the last thing I want to do is take her out again. This warrant says that at three o'clock I am to collect her. It's five minutes to three, and I'm here. If it isn't happening, then personally I will be delighted, she was a pain in the arse. Some other idiot can come back and collect her once the committee has sorted out all the red tape.'

'What do you mean by that?' asked Four-three-two.

'There was an emergency meeting,' Eight-one-five said, 'perhaps it's something to do with that?'

'No one is ever released from here,' repeated Two-three-one doggedly, sticking with what he knew.

'That's what I like to see, unfailing devotion to duty. It matters not that the skies will be crumbling, the seas boiling, and we will all be enslaved for eternity, there is will always be someone is making sure everyone returns their library books.' Ceun smiled. 'It'll probably be safer in there. He nodded towards the prison.

'We are going to need to check this out,' Four-three-two said uncertainly. Ceun handed over the warrant and his identity card.

Eight-one-five looked at the image on the card and compared it to the man in front of him, who grinned manically. 'Ceun Hawke, Sandman, Bounty Hunter...'

'And an all-round good egg.' Ceun finished for him.

'I've heard of you,' Eight-one-five said staring at him. 'You have brought in all the dangerous criminals single hand!'

'Hardly,' Ceun said modestly, 'although, I have helped to fill up a few rooms in this little hotel of yours...'

'Ceun Hawke?' Four-three-two asked, 'what really? I used to read all the stories about you when I was little. You captured the smoke beast with only a slice of bacon and a balloon!'

'And the cavity fairy with a bowl of raspberries and a tooth-pick!' joined in Eight-one-five. 'We ate raspberries for months after that!'

'You shouldn't believe everything they read, should they Mr Hawke, *if* that is indeed your real name?' said the more cyn-ical Two-three-one as he examined the warrant. 'Just as I don't believe everything put in front of me. If you will excuse me, I have some calls to make.'

'Be my guest. I quite agree, and you two are making me feel quite old.' The bounty hunter leaned back against the cool wall.

'But you look younger than us?' said Four-three-two. 'The luck of Sandman genetics, but don't be fooled. I have been around a very long time. Perhaps that's why someone has sent me on this wild goose chase, some bureaucrat's idea of a joke?'

'Your paperwork seems to be in order Mr Hawke,' said the returning Two-three-one. It was clear that he took that very personally. 'I haven't been able to verify your particular au-thority in this matter, one way or the other. Everyone seems to think your name credential enough.' 'However,' he brightened a little, 'Unless the remote locks are activated, which even you couldn't achieve with all your considerable talents,' He used finger quotation marks around the word talents, 'your paperwork and credentials are… worthless.'

As the distant chimes marking the third hour faded, there was a faint whirring followed by a pronounced click. The main door slid silently back into the wall.' Three guards and one bounty hunter peered into the hallway beyond. 'I think we may have had a revaluation,' said Ceun.

If you bathed a man-eating tiger, tied a bell to its tail, bound all four of its feet tightly together, and sat just out of reach making ner ner ne ner ner noises, it would be a pussy cat compared to the venomous polymorph that was currently being expelled from the prison.

'What the hell?' Ceun exclaimed in surprise.

'It's my Janice,' said Four-three-two. 'My wife!' Two-three-one gasped. 'His wife.' Eight-one-five agreed.

'What I meant.' Ceun continued patiently, 'Is what is she…in?'

'Oh that. Prisoners are kept in a kind of shrink wrap; it keeps them compliant.' Four-three-two supplied, still staring in horror at the apparition.

'And fresh, I would have thought.' Ceun added.

'You'll need more than smart quips if you're taking this one away,' said Two-three-one. 'It's the solitude. If they weren't mad before they arrived, then it isn't long before they are completely homicidally insane. If you want my advice, under no circumstances remove the outer casing, this one is dangerous.'

The morph glowered with hatred as soon as she set eyes on the bounty hunter.

'She's pleased to see you then?' Four-three-two said nervously. The truck was soon loaded, and Ceun was driving away. He made sure there were many miles between him and the prison before he even considered stopping. A secluded copse seemed the perfect hiding place. He pulled a few branches over the front of the cab before moving along to the rear doors.

'Rise and shine!' he shouted, banging on the side of the truck. Unbolting the back doors, Ceun was knocked backwards two black figures in cowls exploding out of the back of the truck. He lay on his back cursing. Quickly scrambling back to his feet, the departing figures were followed by a charging poly-morph who leapt from the vehicle and pushed him back into the earth. She shook her matted head and screamed into his face.

'Hello Anaya,' he said.

'Hello Ceun,' she hissed. 'Did you miss me? I've thought about you... a lot.'

~~

Ceun hadn't become the supreme bounty hunter on Morpheus without learning a thing or two about the element of surprise. Despite her initial advantage, they were a short and violent wrestle away from the polymorph being once more secured.

Dusting himself off, Ceun watched as Anaya, the rogue poly-morph, struggled against the bonds now securing her to the back of the truck. 'Bloody monks.' He complained to himself as he rolled his shoulder.

'Let me go!' Anaya screamed, ineffectually trying to kick in his direction.

'So that you can try to claw my eyes out again? Hmmm, let me think...No.'

'I won't,' she said, trying to regain control of herself. 'Just untie me.'

'Biting, scratching, kicking, ripping out my entrails and stran-gling me with them. All not an option, you can stay there until you calm down.' He said, waving a hand at her in dismissal. The other nursed his ribs which had connected with the morph's foot.

Anaya began kicking and screaming again. Ceun squatted just out of reach as the polymorph vented her frustration. 'It may have escaped your notice,' he said as she paused for a moment's breath, 'but I have just broken you out of a maximum-security prison.'

'I was released!' 'No. You are currently free, there is a difference, and it is not going to be long before someone is wondering why you are sitting here instead of tucked up in your shrink wrap coffin so maybe pipe down before they come looking, on and while you're at it, perhaps a little gratitude should be in order?'

'Gratitude!' She spat. 'You were the reason that I was locked up in that plastic hell in the first place!'

'Now that is not exactly true, is it?'

'Don't you patronise me!'

'No, no, you're quite right. Of course, none of that was your fault.' Ceun stood up. 'I was the one who made you get attached to that human. What was his name?'

Anaya took a deep breath and struggled to regain her composure. She closed her eyes. As if of its own accord, her hair began to unravel and soon lay neatly to her shoulders. 'Robert,' she said quietly as if her tamed look was directly related to her temper.

'Ah, yes, Robert. I was the one who made you stalk his dreams night after night. I still don't know what you were hoping to achieve?'

'You wouldn't understand,' she said, staring at her knees. 'You have no feelings.'

'You're right. I don't understand. You're a polymorph, Ana. It wasn't even you he saw.' He paced the track.

'Don't you think I know that?'

'If you knew that why did you keep going back? Every time a different face, a change in voice, for what? So that he could indulge whatever fantasy happened to be top of his list that night? That is why you let others take over. You move on. You don't become obsessed, and you don't threaten them when they don't return your attentions!'

'I've heard all the lectures, Hawke. I was there at the hearing, remember?' She turned her face away.

'Yes, and so you will also recall me standing up and speaking for you? You promised me that you would leave Robert alone if I helped you. You begged me.'

'I did leave him alone,' she said petulantly.

Ceun slapped the side of the truck, making her jump. 'Do you take me for a fool?' he growled. 'You left him alone all right, oh yes. You left him right alone. You excelled yourself there. His poor wife, however, I bet you can't remember her name?'

Anaya shook her head.

'Sarah, that was her name. You hurt her; you tortured her Anaya. You couldn't get your own way so, like a spoilt little child, you attacked and bullied someone innocent, someone, who could not defend themselves.'

'I... I didn't mean...' she said.

'You didn't mean what? You didn't mean to drive her to the point you did? You didn't know that she was depressed already? You didn't intend for things to end up as they did?' She shook her head again, looking up into Ceun's face, the tears just starting in her eyes.

'Don't even try it,' he said, disgusted. 'You didn't care. All you could see is something you wanted, and when he didn't want you, then you wanted your revenge. You're a brat, a spoiled, pampered creature who lashed out when she didn't get her way. You fooled me once, but there is no way you are going to do it again!' Ceun was breathing heavily. He leaned on the truck and fought back the anger inside.

'If I'm such a terrible person, beyond all redemption, why did you go to all this effort to rescue me then?' Anaya said eventually.

Ceun sighed. 'Don't do that.'

'What?'

'Play the martyr card if you like but, it doesn't suit you and certainly won't make any difference to me.'

'So why am I here? Oh, and by the way, please let me know the very moment I manage to do or say something that reaches you on your moral high ground?' the morph said sarcastically.

Ceun ignored the comment. 'You're here because Morpheus is in trouble. Someone has broken through from Realitas, and they have discovered a way into lucid dreaming. It is already starting to cause chaos, and my information tells me that this is just the beginning.'

'What has this got to do with me?' She asked, arching an eyebrow.

'This is nothing to do with the police or the committee or anything official. This is a private commission.'

'Private? Oooh, so you're going a little rogue yourself these days?' She said, with glee.

Ceun glared at her, 'I am trying to do the right thing. My source tells me that the committee wants the inventor of this technology to disappear, quite literally. But my client doesn't believe that this is the answer. The man probably doesn't know what he's doing, or the damage he is causing. Even if he was removed, there will be others. We have to try and stop him before the committee does it more… permanently.'

'And who is this benefactor who cares so deeply for humans?'

Ceun said nothing.

'You don't know, do you?' she gasped, 'you're taking all of this on trust. Do I think you are a fool? Err… yes? How do you know it isn't just some giant set up?'

'Because, whoever it is, they arranged for you to be released. They organised the locks and the paperwork. They are not someone without influence.'

Anaya shifted her position, 'I was wondering about that. Lovely as this outing is, I ask again, what has all this got to do with me?'

'I need to get to this human, make him understand that what he is doing has greater implications. I need to tap into his dreams and have someone he trusts convince him to do the right thing. In short, I need you.'

'I see,' she said calmly. 'I thought I wasn't trustworthy. I'm a bad person? Use a working morph.'

'My client seemed to think that you would be willing to help.'

'That should have been your first clue that they are mentally impaired.' She snorted.

'They suggested they could help you regain your freedom.' Ceun threw the letter onto the ground so that the polymorph could see for herself. He paced as she read through the contents. Anaya thought for a moment. 'If this mystery person believes in me, it seems I don't have a great deal to lose, then, does it? But they must be crazy putting us together. Why would they think you would ever trust me?'

Ceun began to untie the ropes. 'That's easy. I don't, and I won't.'

Anaya rubbed her wrists. She glanced at the bounty hunter from the corner of her eye. 'I wouldn't even think about it if I were you,' he said simply without looking.

She smiled without humour. 'Can't blame a girl for murderous optimism… So, what's the plan? We walk up to this bloke and tell him to stop doing whatever, job done?'

'Not exactly. We have to tap into something that has already been placed in his subconscious; that way, it won't be affected by the thrall this machine throws over everyone.'

'When you say it… I am assuming you mean me?' Anaya said.

'Your morphy mojo actually, and when you have his attention, you have to use this.' He held up a small device a similar size and shape of a credit card. 'But,' he said, holding the object as if it was an unexploded bomb. 'And the instructions were very clear on this. It's experimental, and we only get one shot.'

CHAPTER 7

The warm sun beat down upon the park bench. It also beat on Will, who just happened to be sitting there. A couple of poodles cartwheeled past, followed by an Old English sheepdog backflipping in hot pursuit. 'That's just showing off.' Will called after the dog, but it paid him no attention. Will crossed his legs. It was then the concept dawned on him that he was completely naked. As the true horror of the situation was establishing itself, a six-foot, pink chicken sat down next to him, carefully took a newspaper from under its wing and began to read. Will covered his modesty as best he could. Although, as this was a chicken, he supposed it was technically naked too. However, as it was not Will's normal comfortable state of dress perhaps the chicken could be persuaded to part with some of its newspaper.

'Err, excuse me?' The chicken peered slowly over the top of its paper, revealing itself to be Cassandra in a convincing chicken suit. She looked Will up and down in disgust.

'Yes?' She snapped.

'Cass, Why...?' he began.

'Don't even think about finishing that sentence,' she growled, before retreating behind the paper.

'But...' A pair of murderous eyes stopped him again. He decided not to pursue the matter. They sat in silence for a few minutes.

'I wonder if I could borrow some of your newspaper, nothing vital, the classifieds or the financial section, anything really,' Will lowered his voice, 'I find myself a little embarrassed.'

The chicken slowly looked him up and down. 'You're right to be embarrassed.' She made a great play of sorting out some pages before handing them over with a dismissive flourish. With a snap of the remaining pages, she disappeared back behind the news.

'Thank you,' Will said as he arranged his new coverings over his lap. They sat there in silence as Will watched a battalion of penguins waddle past.

'This is all very odd,' Will said. Faux Cass just ruffled her feathers and turned slightly away. The minutes ticked by.

'Anything interesting?' Will tried again, 'I mean in the paper?'

'It's becoming a sad and dangerous world,' Cass the chicken tutted.

Will nodded his head sagely. 'So… you're a chicken now then?' There was an uncomfortable rustling of pages and feathers.

'As you see.'

Will glanced at the headline. 'BEWARE!' It screamed, literally. The words leapt from the page and exploded in the air before dissolving in a flurry of sparks. Will jumped. 'And… Err… how is that working out for you?' A shaken Will continued.

'What's that?' Cassandra replied, apparently not noticing anything out of the ordinary.

'Being a chicken?' Will answered, glancing around nervously in case anything else was considering shouting at him.

'It's not too bad. I'm only temping,' she shrugged.

Will dared another glance at the headline; perhaps he had imagined the whole thing. 'YOU ARE IN GRAVE DANGER!' The words launched themselves from the page and began dancing around his head like angry mosquitoes. Will screwed his eyes tight and batted them away with flailing arms. When he opened his eyes again, Cass was giving him the international look for 'you're a lunatic'.

'Are you having some kind of fit?' she asked eventually.

'Didn't you hear that?'

'Hear what?'

'Those screams? The words from your newspaper?'

'The 'beware' one, or the 'you are in grave danger 'one?'

'Either, both, it doesn't matter. You must have heard them, seen them? They were right here.' Will's voice was gradually getting higher.

'Nope,' she said, with something almost resembling glee.

'What do you mean, nope? You must have, you said it... I mean they were right here!'

'You are becoming hysterical. I didn't hear a thing.' The chicken got to its feet and tossed the paper into the air, where it dissolved into a shower of bubbles that popped one by one. Will could feel himself starting to gibber. The chicken began to walk away.

'Um, Cassandra?' Will called after it.

'I'm not Cassandra,' the chicken called back. 'I'm a chicken.'

'Oh, that's all right then.' Will said to himself, as he awoke in a cold sweat.

CHAPTER 8

'You look awful,' Adam said, opening the front door.

'Thanks very much, I feel it.' Will looked around. 'No company this morning?' He said snarkily.

'Michelle had to be at work early, and I know how prudish you can be.' Adam said with a false smile.

'Michelle? I thought you were seeing Louise?' Will asked.

Adam shrugged, 'I am seeing Louise, just I wasn't yesterday…?'

The eternal monogamist Will stood dumbfounded at his friend.

'Anyway,' Adam ushered him into the house, 'tell me why you are looking like someone just dug you up. I am guessing it is not because of your wild social life.'

'For one thing, Cass has decided we need to move into some luxury complex thing and won't stop talking about it.' Adam nodded his head in sympathy. 'And secondly, I think there may be something wrong with the console.'

The last statement grabbed Adam's attention. 'Define wrong,' he said carefully.

'Last night, when I finally got to sleep, I had the weirdest dream.'

'And you were using the console?' Adam asked.

'No, just ordinary dreaming, but Cass was dressed as a chicken and warning me about something.'

'But you weren't wearing the V10?' Adam clarified.

'No!' Will snapped, 'but do you think it's possible that the testing is affecting my sleep waves, that perhaps there could be side effects?'

Adam looked as if he had just been slapped. 'Side effects! Are you mad? There are no side effects! Don't go shouting about side effects.' He said, frantically looking over his shoulder.

'But how do we know?' Will whined.

'We know because we have tested and tested and tested. It is perfectly normal to have freaky dreams; it's probably all the pressure. The chicken could be a... a manifestation of the enormity of what we are about to do, and Cass, you said she was pressuring you about this house and the cost, and that is probably what your subconscious is warning you about. You know it would be a mistake to take on that kind of commitment.'

'There were an awful lot of noughts on that contract we signed?' Will agreed tentatively.

'Exactly, and you know how that kind of thing worries you.' Adam gripped Will by the shoulders. 'We are two unknowns about to revolutionise the gaming market. This is huge, and I can't have you going to pieces now. The design is sound. The V10 is safe as safe can be. it's your mind that's on the blink.'

'I do feel like this thing has taken over our whole lives.' Will said uncertainly, 'and I don't really want to buy that house.'

Adam slapped his shoulders. 'There you are then. You've answered your own question. Call wifey, tell her the trip is off and chill out.'

'Oh no!' Will coughed, 'I am going to have to go and see the thing. It will be easier, and then I'll tell her I don't like something about it.'

'Whatever. Just if I were you, I'd get some rest before you go into battle. Here, try out the modifications to the medieval joust, that'll get you in the mood.' Will took the proffered console. 'I've got to go out for a bit, so crash on the sofa,' Adam said, grabbing his coat.

'Michelle or Louise?'

'Debbie actually, she's taking me for lunch.'

'She's... oh never mind. Give me a shout when you get back.' Will plumped a couple of cushions and, with the console in place, lay back on the sofa. It was true, he thought as he drifted off, he hadn't been very settled lately. Adam was no help, and there was a lot of work still to be done. But not at this precise moment, now he would lie back and enjoy a little fantasy role play.

~~

Will opened his eyes to peer through the narrow slot. Little puffs of steam wafted through his limited field of vision as the powerful horse underneath him took great deep breaths. His iron-clad fist weighed the lance in his right hand. The updates had certainly enhanced the feel of everything. A roar from the crowd reached his ears. Although muffled through the helmet, he could sense the excitement. There was a sudden hush as the throng watched Will's opponent enter the arena. He strained to see through the visor. Framed in iron, parts of the black knight came into view.

'Classic,' Will murmured happily. Every part of his body was tense. He watched the starting maiden blush as she waved her handkerchief to the spectators. She held it high, causing the arena to freeze, until with a flourish, she threw it into the air. Will dug his spurs into the side of the horse, making the startled animal lurch forward at a terrifying speed. The image of the black knight grew larger and larger in the visor. Suddenly it was all black. Will thrust his lance to the side. His opponent veered out of range and careered on, unmolested. They galloped to the end of the arena and turned to face each other again. Steam now rose from the war horse's flanks. In seconds the charge was on again, the ground shaking, as the two laden beasts hurtled towards each other. Out of the corner of his visor, Will saw a flash of pink standing at the barrier. With limited visibility, he automatically turned his head to get a better look just as the black knight's lance slammed deep into his chest. With one motion, the horse continued on its way, while Will painfully changed direction and somersaulted backwards into the wet mud. The crowd groaned.

On his back, Will screwed his eyes tight shut and tried to concentrate on his breathing. The armour now felt like a ton weight pressing down upon his lungs. He tried to work his way up from the tips of his toes and assess if there was any other damage. The helmet was pulled roughly from his head. Will briefly thought of those in motorcycle accidents, and how it was a very bad idea to do that. Still, he kept his eyes shut. There was a gentle nudge to the rib area. Will decided to ignore it until he had finished his inventory of possible injuries. This time there was a definite kick. He looked up into the face of an upside-down Cassandra, framed by a beak and pink chicken head. 'I'm no expert,' she said, 'but I don't think that's how you are supposed to do it.'

'You're correct; you are not an expert,' he snapped before closing his eyes again. A surprisingly sharp chicken foot caught him between the gaps in his breastplate. 'Hey!' he shouted, 'Man lying on his back in the mud trying to decide if anything is broken, how do you think kicking me is going to help?' Will felt something cold pressed onto his forehead. He opened his eyes, and the world seemed to waver slightly as if out of focus. There was an audible fizzle. Will snapped his eyes open fully to see his chicken-shaped wife tucking something into her feathers.

'You're dreaming. When did you ever hear of anyone waking up with broken bones, idiot?' Cass the chicken snapped.

'Good point.' Will said as he struggled to an upright position. 'Hang on, how can you be telling me I'm dreaming in a dream?

What did you just do?' The crowd was looking around as if they had no idea where they were. One by one, they began to wander away. The chicken shrugged.

'You're the genius scientist, I, as you have pointed out, am just a chicken.' She flicked back her feathers in a very Cass like way.

'I meant to ask you about that. Cass, why are you dressed like that?'

'Who is Cass?' she said darkly.

'You are. My wife, you know, death us do part, love and honour and obey, all that?'

'Ah.' The chicken sat down next to him.

'Look, I don't mean to be rude, but you are not part of this scenario, so I command you to go away.'

'You command me? I think you're confusing me with your real wife… obey indeed! You see, I am not actually this person you think I am.'

'Well of course not, for one thing, this is a dream and for another Cass wouldn't wear a chicken suit unless it was made by Prada and had been the 'must-have' on at least four reality TV shows.'

The chicken nodded sagely.

'You're just a figment of my imagination.'

She turned her head slowly. 'I'm sorry, I'm going to have to stop you there.' she said through gritted teeth.

'You can't be anything else.'

'Let's get one thing straight,' she said, pointing a wing at him menacingly. 'I am not a figment of anyone's anything. I am my own person and you better not forget it.'

'Uh, ok. You are your own person, got it.'

'Excellent, now let us get to the point. Personally, I would have been more for the grabbing you by the ears and giving you a good shake approach, but some people seem to think that subtle hints are more appropriate when dealing with you humans.' She said conversationally.

'Humans?'

'Yes... what did you think you were, a marshmallow?'

'Uh, no but why...?'

'How hard did you hit your head?' she said sharply. 'Now listen carefully. You are in quite a lot of trouble. I am here to help you against my better judgement, but that is another story. The point is, you are making this machine which controls dreams, and now you have to stop doing it before somebody stops you more permanently.'

'Cassandra, what are you talking about?'

'Are you even listening? I just told you, I'm not your wife and you're in danger.' She gazed up into the sky and muttered. 'I told him this cryptic stuff never works, but no, appeal to his subconscious he said, you have to draw attention to yourself he said, it has to be gently done he said.'

'Who are you talking to?'

She seemed to notice Will once more. 'My name is Anaya. I am a polymorph, and I can be anyone you want me to be. He is a sentimental twit with very strange ideas about the human psyche.'

'And you had to be dressed as a chicken because?'

'Because it had to be something already programmed into your subconscious so that I wouldn't be affected by your little toy. Seen a lot of pink chicken's lately?' Anaya shimmered slightly and changed Cassandra into wearing a tunic and breeches. 'It wasn't my idea. I thought it was stupid, and it turns out, I was right.'

Will looked around. 'Where is everyone?'

'I'm afraid we had to break the connection a bit.' Will

frowned.

'You're telling me you broke the connection on the Vio from inside a dream?'

'Uh-huh,' Anaya said, 'a bit.'

'My dream had rebelled and decided that it doesn't want to do as it's told... that's it. I have finally gone insane.'

'Look. You are in a lot more trouble than losing a bit of sanity, and all you want to do is argue with me. I am trying to help you.'

'Dressed as a chicken?'

Anaya snorted and got to her feet. 'I give up!'

'Ok, ok, I'm sorry. I'll go along with it if it helps,' Will said, aware he had caused some offence. 'I suppose it was quite a big chicken.'

'Shut up. It was him. He probably found it funny. I think it says a lot more about his twisted brain than yours.'

'Why was it pink?'

'I don't know!' she sighed, 'perhaps he felt that it would humiliate me further, who knows? Probably wanted to teach me a lesson, there is no telling how his mind works.'

'But why, why do it at all and who is he?' Will pleaded.

'I refer you to the earlier part of the conversation when I was telling you how there are those who would like to see you disappear.'

'You are joking?'

'Do I look like I'm joking?' Anya said, arching an eyebrow.

'No, but up until a few minutes ago, you were a chicken.'

'Will you stop with the chicken thing? I knew this wouldn't work.' She said in frustration. 'Apparently, you don't have that much time. We are supposed to keep you safe until you see the light.'

'Who are we?' Will said exasperated.

Anaya folded her arms, 'It's time you met the supposed brains behind this little scheme, and perhaps he can talk some sense into you because clearly, I am getting nowhere.'

'Do I have a choice?'

'No.'

Will struggled to get up. 'Any chance of a little help then?' She looked down at the struggling knight.

'Not much.' Anaya started to stride away.

When he eventually righted himself, Will tried to jog after her, not the easiest thing in full armour. Finally, he caught up. 'I mean, it's not exactly intimidating is it?' He wheezed conversationally, 'You could have gone with anything, a lion, a tiger even a slightly irked koala, but a chicken? What were you going to do if I didn't listen, lay an egg on me?'

CHAPTER 9

Cassandra clicked the car remote control. From the workshop, she could hear an ear-bleeding rendition of something being vocally beaten into submission. Following the din, she walked along the path and opened the door. Being so engrossed in the dissected console on the workbench, Adam was mid chorus before he noticed her standing there, arms folded, with an amused smile on her perfectly made-up face. He clicked the off button on the stereo.

'There is such a thing as knocking you know,' he said tersely.

'Like you would have heard me?' She said with a sing-song voice.

'Like you would have knocked in the first place.' He mimicked her. 'Is there something I can do for you?'

Cass giggled and flicked back her hair, 'Now that is a loaded question.'

Adam rolled his eyes.

She eased herself onto a stool and crossed her legs. 'You are so clever. I don't know how you put together all those tiny little parts and make them into something that works.' Cassandra stretched out a leg, allowing the impossibly high heel to sway back and forth.

'It's nothing really, just a little patience and a lot of genius.' Adam said absentmindedly, as he continued to tinker.

'Does that apply to everything you do?' She smiled mischievously.

'Everything... that Will and I do regarding this project.' He said pointedly.

Cass had the grace to avert her eyes slightly. 'Where is Will? We're going to look at our new home today.'

'He mentioned it. In the house, I think he was testing out one of the role plays.'

'So, he's in there unconscious, and you and I are out here all alone. How inappropriate,' she said, leaning forward.

'I'm sure he will be awake; he could walk in at any moment.' Adam said nonchalantly.

'And what would he see?'

Adam blinked slowly. 'He's in the house, go ahead and wake him if the lazy sod isn't up yet.' He said, turning back to his work and flicking the switch on the stereo to signal she should leave.

Cassandra slid elegantly from the stool and strolled across to the door. 'You don't know what you missed, you know...' she turned coyly to look over her shoulder, but it was wasted. Adam was already engrossed in his micro world.

It was a matter of minutes before the door burst open again, crashing dramatically into the wall. 'I said you should knock, not demolish the place!' Adam shouted, switching off the stereo again. He'd never seen Cassandra looking even remotely ruffled; she seemed to sail through life completely crease-resistant. The woman who currently stood framed in the doorway had definitely been bent out of shape.

'Quick,' she gasped, 'It's Will.'

'What is? What's the matter?'

'It's Will.' She turned and tottered in the direction of the house.

~~

By the time Adam caught up, Cassandra was slapping Will

about the face; a red print was building on his cheek.

'Help me. I can't wake him!' Adam moved her forcefully out of the way.

'Will, Will! It's Adam, can you hear me? Time to wake up, buddy.' He was gently shaking his friend's shoulders when a cold shock of water hit him in the ear and trickled down the side of his neck. Will had taken most of the deluge straight in the face.

~ ~

Trudging beside Anaya Will suddenly felt a freezing blast from nowhere. He stopped short as the shock took his breath away for a second before the coughing began. Struggling for breath, he lurched sideways, barging into the polymorph.

'What the hell are you doing?' she snapped.

~ ~

'What the hell are you doing?' Adam snapped, turning his head on one side to remove the water from his ear canal.

'Trying to wake him up, I've seen it in the movies, you throw cold water over them.'

'Him possibly, not necessarily me! You could have warned me first!' He looked back at the patient who, besides being somewhat wet, appeared to be still sleeping peacefully.

'I'll get a towel,' he said, getting up. Cassandra was half crouched next to her husband. Adam couldn't quite make out what she was doing. As he peered over her shoulder, he saw a safety pin, with the sharp end jabbing into Will's hand.

~ ~

'OW!' Will screamed, grabbing his hand.

'What's the matter now?' asked Anaya.

'I don't know, ow, ow, OW!' Will clawed desperately at the metal glove. As he removed it, a small bead of blood began to form on the skin.

'What have you done?' Anaya took hold of his hand, trying to see the cause of damage.

'Nothing, nothing at all. It must have been something in the glove.'

~ ~

'Stop that! What is wrong with you woman?' Adam snatched the pin out of Cassandra's hand.

'It's how they tell if people are dead, if there is no reaction, then it's definite. I saw it on a detective show.'

'Did you?' Adam said slowly, 'And did they also mention any-thing about the fact that the person is breathing? Did they? Hmmm?'

'I was overcome with panic.' Cassandra replied, now the pic-ture of calm.

'Why don't you go and call an ambulance, that may well be the safest thing for Will before you move on from drowning and bloodletting.'

'So you do think there is something seriously wrong with him!' She squeaked, instantly hysterical again. 'I knew it; I'm going to be a widow!'

'Just call the ambulance,' he said wearily, 'I'm sure everything will be alright, but the sooner we get some medical help, the better, ok?'

'Ok.' She sniffed, picking up her mobile phone and walking out the front door.

'It must be a woman thing,' he said to the unconscious body on the sofa. 'They can't just make a phone call; they have to be all private about it.' The minutes ticked by. Adam could hear a muffled one-sided conversation outside, but not clearly enough to know what exactly was said. Eventually, the door clicked, and she reappeared smoothing her lipstick.

'Well? How long?' She looked confused for a moment. 'Oh, err, not long at all. How is he? Is he still breathing?'

'Just the same.' With a dramatic flourish, she threw herself across her sleeping husband.

'Oh, my poor darling, my poor baby, why, why, why!' Adam could hear Will spluttering as he pulled her away.

'I would give him some air if I were you, we don't want to confuse the paramedics by giving them cause to think he'd been smothered.'

'I am a very emotional person. You know I couldn't bear it if I lost my baby.' She picked up her handbag and in one easy movement, selected a compact. 'You don't think the press will get hold of it, do you? After all, with the V10, Will was going to be the next big thing.'

~~

'You went a very odd colour just then.' Anya said frowning at Will who was acting odd, even by human standards.

'I couldn't breathe! It was like something was being held over my head. What's going on here? Are you doing this to me?' He pointed his finger in accusation.

'It's not me.' She replied, holding her hands up. 'I told you you're in danger, although this does all seem a little peculiar. We need to see the bounty hunter, no time to lose!' Anaya grabbed him roughly by the elbow and dragged him on.

CHAPTER 10

'How long did they say they would be?' Adam whispered.

Cassandra was pacing up and down and doing her best to ignore Adam's question. She seemed to be carrying on an internal conversation.

'Cassandra? How long?'

She waved her hand, dismissively. 'They said they would get here as soon as possible.'

At the sound of the doorbell, Adam was amazed to find an agitated Murray Leibowitz on the doorstep. 'Leibowitz! What a surprise.'

'I was just passing, and I thought I'd drop in to see how things were going.' He forced a smile while simultaneously trying to peer around Adam.

'It's not a good time if I'm honest…' Adam began as the American pushed past him.

'Is that Cassy I see back there?' At his entrance, Cassandra suddenly became animated.

'Cassandra honey, how're you?' He kissed her once on each cheek. 'Oh Murray, I don't know what to say, it's all been such a shock.'

'What is honey?' he said pointedly, glancing at Adam.

'Will… look!' Cass sobbed into a tissue.

'He didn't look well when I met you guys last. We should have seen this coming. Some sort of break down, is it?'

'You mean the dreams, of course. I know. I blame myself.' She looked up at Murray, her eyes wet with forced tears.

'Not at all, honey. It's not your fault,' Murray patted her hand.

'There weren't dreams, there was A dream that he was a bit concerned about, that's all!' Adam said. His brow furrowed. 'Just a minute, I wasn't aware the two of you knew each other?'

Cassandra ignored the question, ploughing on with her distress. 'It's just he has been working so hard, testing, getting everything ready for production... It is ready, isn't it?' she asked.

Adam responded automatically. 'Yes, it was pretty much completed... so, hang on, when did you meet Leibowitz? Did you call him just now?'

'As I said, I was just passing.' Leibowitz snapped.

'Really!' He folded his arms.

'Ok, ok, Cassy called me. She was worried.'

Adam glared at Cassandra. 'As I said, I didn't realise you knew each other? By the way, did you call him before or after you called the ambulance?'

'Of course, I called the ambulance first.' She lied. 'Oh, Murray and I met a long time ago, it was just a coincidence that he recently found out I was married to Will.' She said dismissively.

'Oh, yes, very recently.' Leibowitz added, too quickly.

Adam frowned. 'Since yesterday?'

'Ha, ha, ha... just my little joke. I didn't want to put the fella off his game. He's a skittish one, like a colt I once had.' The American said with excessive brightness.

'It's all been a shock.' Cassandra interrupted. 'Anyway, as you were saying, you have finished the prototypes?'

'We still had a few more tweaks to do, especially after the dream. He was worried that the console was malfunctioning, but he wasn't wearing it. He was just being over cautious...'

Adam began.

Murray put his arm around Adam's shoulder, quite forcefully. 'Shhh, we don't want to be saying things like that. And we definitely don't want to be mentioning that this happened while the V10 was in situ, do we?'

'You don't mean that it could affect sales?' Cassandra gasped.

'It may well do… if it got out.' Leibowitz and Cassandra looked at each other, then towards the prostrate Will.

'Do you think we should…?'

Adam realised what was going on. 'You are not going to remove the V10!'

'It would just get in the way of the medical people…' Cassandra began.

'And it obviously does not have anything to do with his condition.' Murray continued.

'You don't know that! They may be linked. You have to leave it there.'

'And risk someone at the hospital getting the wrong end of the stick?'

'You know how gossip starts…'

'It only takes an idle comment…'

'These things get out of hand…'

'There are a few words to the press…'

'Next thing you know…'

'It's what he would have wanted…'

Adam was appalled. 'What he would have wanted? He's not dead; he's still breathing. And if this is connected with the machine, then we are going to want to know surely?'

'Weren't you the chief engineer and designer?' Cassandra fixed Adam with a cold stare. 'Wasn't it you who completed those extensive tests to make sure that it was safe? Wasn't it you that said there were no problems and his dream was just his mind? Are you telling us that you made a mistake and that you have turned your best friend into a vegetable? Is that what you are saying, that this is your fault?' Adam felt himself wilting under Cassandra's gaze.

'No, I...' He stuttered.

'Because who do you think they are going to blame?' Murray had joined in glaring at Adam. They began to close in on him. 'It won't be the financier. I didn't design the thing.'

'It won't be the wife.' Cassandra was saying. Adam watched her lips move. He began to panic.

'Will is... indisposed. That leaves only one person,' Murray shrugged, 'the engineer.'

'I may even bring criminal charges, loss of income.' Cassandra said.

They had advanced upon Adam to the point where the corner of the TV was wedged into his back. 'Ok!' he cried, 'Take it off!'

Murray patted his shoulder, 'You've made the right decision. Trust me. It's what Will would have done. But I think you should do it. You are, after all, the expert.'

Adam carefully removed the console. The offending arm flopped limply by his side as he stared at his friend.

'Why don't I pop that into my handbag where it will be safe?' Cassandra whispered. Sidling up to Adam, she deftly placed her hand in his, the hand holding the console. His full attention on Will, Adam let go.

CHAPTER 11

Will was starting to feel uncomfortable. It was something about the way the people were staring at him. He supposed he must make an odd sight trailing across the courtyard after Anaya like a robot puppy, but there was something in the way they looked at him. They barely concealed their hostility. Suddenly, he was yanked sideways into the cool dark of a doorway. Will instantly missed the protective properties of his helmet as the odour of stale beer, and the even staler clientele hit his senses. As his eyes adjusted to the darkness, Will was aware of the tableau caused by his arrival. Tankards stopped halfway to mouths, and conversations trailed off mid-sentence as though paused in a film.

He waved a hand uncertainly. 'Hello?'

'Sir William of Wordsworth, you must be here to refresh yourself after the tournament.' A voice said a little too loudly from behind his left shoulder. The voice obviously had access to two rather strong arms, which were now propelling Will and Anaya towards a shadowy corner. As the tavern regulars returned to the serious business of drinking, Will found himself pressed onto a bench.

'What the hell were you thinking to bring him here?' The voice belonged to a man, an innocuous man. Not a man that you could have picked out in a crowd. The dark curly hair framed a genial face, even though, at the moment, piercing blue eyes revealed murderous intentions towards the polymorph. Anaya seemed oblivious as she flopped onto the opposite bench.

'He wasn't listening to me. I told you hints don't work. I'm not even sure he's the right one. He doesn't seem very bright.'

'That's him,' The man hissed, 'and you have just brought him right into the nest of vipers.'

'Oh, don't be so dramatic Hawke,' she said dismissively as she inspected her nails. The man mimed strangling her, but she didn't even look up.

'Err, excuse me, but I am here!' Will said.

Ceun turned his attention to Will for the first time. 'That, my friend, is exactly the problem in a nutshell.' he said quietly. 'Because thanks to madam 'I can't follow a simple instruction' here now everyone and their horse know that, and word spreads very fast.'

'I don't understand what is going on. All Cass would say is that there is some danger, which is ridiculous really, this is only a dream.'

'Cass?' Ceun looked at Anaya questioningly.

'Wife.' She supplied 'See,' Anaya said triumphantly, 'Won't listen. I told him I wasn't her, but he won't believe me, about that or any of it.'

'Why did you do that? The whole idea was to be someone he trusts!'

'I don't like being other people, and wifey wouldn't dress like a chicken, which was a really silly idea, by the way, as that was all this idiot fixated on. She doesn't seem to be a very nice person anyway.'

'You both have something in common then!' Ceun snapped.

'He gets very irritable,' Anaya said to Will, 'and dramatic.'

'I do not. I get understandably annoyed. Why? Because you had a straightforward brief and what do you do, completely ignore it and do your own thing!'

'He's having some odd stuff happening to him too, but as I am so hopeless, I will let you sort it all out!' Anaya got to her feet. 'If you get really desperate and need me, I will be outside.'

'She seems nice?' Will said uncertainly, once she'd gone.

Ceun looked incredulous. 'Does she? I suppose she would if you married her?'

'She said she wasn't Cass.' He said, idly waving a hand towards the door. 'This is very weird, and if you don't mind, I'd really like this dream to stop now. How do I wake up?

'Not yet. Since you're here, I may as well explain things to you properly. I am… how can I put it? I suppose I am like a bounty hunter. It's my job to apprehend those elements that are unsuitable in Morphean society.'

'Wow, I seem to have some serious unresolved moral issues about the V10,' Will said to himself.

'Ah. Yes, you do. Now we are getting somewhere.' Ceun clapped his hands, making Will jump. 'It's wrong to produce this thing. It is very wrong, and when you wake up, you will destroy all copies and never allow it to be made commercially?'

'Of course not,' Will scoffed. 'I'm not *that* unresolved! I have simply been working too hard, and because of that, elements of my unconscious mind have crossed over into this scenario. It must be something to do with the brain waves. I'll have to get Adam to look at it.'

'It was worth a try.' Ceun said with a sigh. 'Let's look at this another way. What if this isn't just a dream? You are fully conscious.'

'I built this device.' Will felt more on home ground now. 'It allows the wearer to be fully in control of the whole interactive dream experience…'

'But what if all this…' Ceun indicated the dingy room, 'is not just in your head?' 'Of course it is. Morpheus indeed, what a ridiculous suggestion. You're trying to tell me that this is all real? Next, you'll be saying that my house, my work, my wife, all of that is just a dream!'

'No. That all exists, but so does all of this.' Ceun said patiently.

'You're trying to tell me that dreams are real.' Will scoffed.

'In a manner of speaking, the place is real, Morpheus is real. There are beings, real live beings, who live here all the time, and they are the ones your device is threatening.'

'My brain has fried, hasn't it? The V10 has malfunctioned and fried my brain. I'm probably in a coma.' Will said, throwing his hands in the air.

'You're asleep. Nothing more. Humans are not meant to be in control here. Try to think of Morpheus and Realitas as two sides of the same coin. When you sleep, you cross to the other side, but in the crossing, your memories are jumbled up, scrambled, things are forgotten or moved into different orders, this protects us all.'

'That's impossible. It's just as likely I've discovered a way to travel back in time... That's it, I haven't, have I? Oh my god, I've invented a time machine!' Will excitedly.

'No, you are still in your own time,' Ceun said wearily, 'but what I am telling you is true.' He paused. 'You think a time machine is entirely plausible, but what I'm explaining is impossible?' He asked, shaking his head incredulously. Before the inventor could answer, he continued. 'Never mind. Try to think of the two dimensions as one of those 3D puzzles before you put the glasses on. They're side by side but fuzzy.'

'I've had enough of this. I think it is time that I woke up.'

'No, no, don't do that, I need to explain...' Ceun said as Will pinched himself hard between his thumb and forefinger and squeezed his eyes tight shut.

'You appear to be still here,' said Ceun's voice after a few moments. Will pinched himself harder, then pinched his ear, pinched his neck and held his nose. 'I wouldn't keep doing that. You are going to go a very funny colour.'

Will opened his eyes. 'Why aren't I waking up? What did Cassandra do to me?'

'Nothing. She just broke the control link on your machine. You should be able to wake up normally?'

Will slapped himself across the face. 'Does this look like I am waking up?' He said, his voice tinged with panic. 'What is going on here?'

'That is an excellent question. Anya said some strange things that happened to you on the way here?' Ceun asked.

'There was an icy blow in the face and then a pain in my hand and some blood.' He held the injured hand up to be inspected. Ceun pushed in gently down again.

'That sounds like something happening to your body in Realitas. You should have woken. Something or someone is stopping you.'

'That's is not a good thing.'

'You're right. That means someone wants you to stay here, and I'm guessing it isn't for your health.'

'There are enough figments of my imagination to form a committee?' Will said in amazement.

Ceun sighed. 'Let us go back to the beginning. Neither they nor I are figments, we exist.'

'But there is a committee who run Morpheus, and you think they are the ones who have somehow prevented me going home.' Will said.

'Right.'

'And you think they have done this because they want to kill me?'

'Not necessarily kill…' Ceun looked carefully at Will. 'Ok, kill yes.'

'Because I have invented the V10 and they think this is dangerous to Morpheus? But it wasn't just me, what about Adam, he is just as responsible, more so actually, why pick on me?' Will whined, his voice rising an octave.

'Perhaps they felt you were the more dangerous of the two of you?' Ceun said with a shrug.

'Even you don't believe that!' Will snorted.

'I don't know, my information just said you.' The bounty hunter shrugged again.

'I still don't see why it would be such a bad thing. If this place does exist, and I have to say I'm still none too sure, we already come here so what's the problem?'

'Listen to the arrogance of you. What makes you think that you would be a great addition here? Look at what you've done to your world. The violence, the destruction of your environment, you're parasites that infect and destroy everything around you. You would come here in your hordes and wouldn't be content until it was as polluted and stinking as home.'

'That's harsh!'

'It's the truth. There have already been incidents that are making some people in high places very, very nervous. And of course, there will be some who want to use this to their own advantage.' Will looked surprised. 'Your world does not have a monopoly on criminal elements and greed.'

'This is ridiculous. It's a joke, isn't it? Adam's idea of being funny? He's programmed this into the scenario.' Will turned his face upwards. 'I DON'T THINK THIS IS FUNNY!' He yelled.

'Will you keep your voice down?' Ceun hissed as the other

patrons turned their attention to them. 'Can't hold his ale,' he said. This explanation seemed to satisfy the clientele. 'Are you trying to get yourself in even more trouble?' The bounty hunter asked.

'How much more trouble can I be in? Ok, ok, if Adam wants me to go along with this, I'll go along with it. What do we do now Mr bounty hunter?'

'That will do for the moment. We keep our heads down, try not to draw attention to ourselves and keep you safe until we can work out why you can't go home.'

CHAPTER 12

Will blinked in the sunlight.

'The first thing we have to do is stop you sticking out like a sore thumb. Can you do something about… that?' Ceun indicated the armour.

'I'm not sure what I've got on under this.' Will said uncertainly.

'This device of yours, did you build in something to allow you to change your appearance or your clothes?'

'No. It's all set up in the programme.'

'That's helpful then, isn't it? I think we are going to have to resort to the old human premise that you haven't brought your kit so you can play in your vest and pants… figuratively, of course.'

Will looked horrified. 'And how is that going to stop people looking at me exactly?'

'It was a joke? You're going to have clothes under that lot, aren't you? Armour against the skin? I don't think so. The stable is there; take the stuff off.'

'I think I may need some help.' Will said.

'You will manage.' Ceun said finally, as he lounged against the wall. 'Or I could send An to help you?'

'I can manage.' Will said hurriedly. After what seemed an age and sounded like a couple of rats playing tennis in a dustbin, Will emerged. It had been a relief to get out of the metal suit, although he did suspect he may have strained something vital.

'I think this looks ok?' Will said uncertainly as he sniffed at the sleeve of the hessian shirt he now wore over dun-coloured breeches. He pulled a face.

'Where's that bloody morph got to?' Ceun said, ignoring him. He began to walk along the edge of the square. Will hurried to keep up. 'She's probably sulking somewhere, expects us to run around looking for her.'

'You were quite rude?' Will said.

'Look,' Ceun stopped suddenly, 'whatever she appears to be, she is not your wife, she has none of the characteristics of what's her name?'

'Cassandra.'

'Do not imagine that she is going to react like Cassandra because just when you're convinced she's sweet... she will bite you.'

'Did she bite you?' Will asked innocently.

A dark shadow passed across Ceun's face. He was about to answer when they heard a loud 'Pssst!' The sound led them to a shadowy corner and dark steps leading into a black storage cellar.

'Has someone sprung a leak down there?' Ceun asked as another drawn-out psssssst emerged from below.

'Have woman,' came a gruff voice from the darkness.

'I'm sorry, I think you've mistaken us for someone else, we don't provide that kind of service.' Ceun said politely.

There was a silence as this information was processed. 'Your woman, have here,' it grumbled.

'Again, I think you are mistaken. We don't have a woman,' Ceun said cheerfully. A few moments passed as the thing considered. Suddenly the polymorph was thrust roughly into the light and then dragged sharply back again.

'That... that hand, it wasn't a hand, there was hair and... claws!' Will whispered.

'Thank you, yes I did see that.' Ceun whispered back. 'Sorry, that's not ours.' He said, his hand cupping his mouth as he shouted into the cellar.

'How can you say that? I might remind you that someone who looks like my wife is in there!' Will remonstrated.

Ceun grabbed his shirt and pulled him forward until they were nose to nose. 'Not your wife.' He hissed. 'and if you want to get her back, I suggest you shut up or go in there yourself and take your chances.'

'Your woman!' the voice insisted, 'you take woman, give that.' A gnarled finger pointed out of the gloom at Will who took a step back as Ceun released him.

'You're not going to send me in there!' He squeaked.

Ceun put a finger to his lips. 'No, thank you. It's quite all right. You can keep her.' Ceun called out as he turned and began to walk away, making sure that a firm hand took Will with him.

'You can't just leave her in there with that thing!' Will said, trying to look over his shoulder.

'Will eat woman... slowly.' The voice called after them, but there was a note of uncertainty to it.

'Good luck with that!' Ceun continued to walk, dragging Will with him. 'If it tries, it'll have the mother of all stomach aches. Don't worry. She'll work her way through eventually.'

'Can she do that, be eaten and be ok?'

'Don't be ridiculous. She'll have been digested. Just keep walking.'

In the darkness, a pair of green eyes glowered at the departing figures. Anaya twisted to face her capture.

'That went well then?' She said looking up into a canine face who's brows furrowed in confusion.

'You no talk will kill you now.' It said, uncertainly.

'And what do you think that will achieve? Wolf mauls a young girl, in town, in daylight? It will be pitchforks and torches after you, that's what. You'll be a head on somebody's wall before the end of the day.'

The wolf stared at his captive. Now that he looked at her... no, it couldn't be? He blinked. He knew this was wrong, she smelt different, but now that he looked at her properly, it was his mistress standing there. She was a bit younger, but it was *his* mistress without a doubt.

'You're a bad dog, aren't you?' She said. Despite every other sense in his body telling him to kill her now, there was something built into his very fibre. You don't bite the hand that feeds you. His ears flattened, she was right; he was a bad dog.

'I can help you. You stay here until it's dark and then slip away. I will leave now, and no-one will ever know that you were here.'

The wolf struggled to compute all the different messages his brain was receiving. A hand reached up and tickled him behind the ear, involuntarily his tail wagged. 'You're a good boy, really, aren't you? You're just misunderstood.' His tongue lolled out of his mouth as he fought the urge to roll on his back and have his tummy tickled. What did it matter that this mistress was strange and wrong? This was heaven. 'Who's a good boy, who's a clever, handsome boy then?' She cooed, scratching his ear. His left leg twitched. 'Now you stay here and wait for dark, and then you go home. There's a good boy.' She stopped scratching and began to walk away. Despite himself, the wolf moved to follow her. 'No, no,' she said tapping him gently on the nose with her index finger. 'You stay!' The wolf sat obediently. 'There's a clever boy. You stay. When the sun goes down, you can come home, and I'll give you a lovely bone.' The tail wagged faster.

Anaya walked out of the dark resisting the urge to run. The wolf watched the form of his mistress go, inside he howled.

As she rounded the corner, Will sagged with relief.

'You took your time,' Ceun said as she strode towards them. Will threw his arms open for an embrace. Barely breaking her step, Anaya marched right past him to stop, her hands on her hips, in front of the bounty hunter.

'You were just going to leave me there!' She spat accusingly.

'I knew you could handle it,' he said calmly, 'and here you are.'

'No thanks to you.'

'I'm, err, I'm glad you're ok. What was that thing?' Will asked.

'Wolf. I believe he calls himself T. B. B.' Anaya answered still glaring at Ceun.

T.B.B?

'The Big Bad Wolf?' Anaya supplied.

'The very same,' said Ceun. 'Luckily for us, he is not The Big Bad Intelligent Wolf. Now I suggest we get as much distance between ourselves and it before whatever spell our charming polymorph put him under wears off.'

CHAPTER 13

'Can't I just tell myself that I'm out of here?' Will looked around nervously, heartily wishing he was a million miles away.

'You can try, but we tend to find walking a more effective form of transport if you want to get anywhere…' Anaya stopped as Ceun came into view with two horses and a very depressed looking donkey. 'You have got to be joking!' She said.

'If I were joking, I'd have brought the goat, which was the only other thing he had. Would you like me to go back for it?' Ceun said.

Anaya hopped effortlessly onto the back of a horse. 'No, thank you.' She said with a fake smile.

'Err, I don't ride…' Will said.

'What was that large thing with a leg at each corner that you were charging up and down on earlier then?' Ceun asked.

'That's different. It was a simulation of a horse.'

'I don't think anyone told the horse because it seemed pretty convinced.' Ceun said with a shrug.

'And I fell off it.' Will said petulantly.

'Take the donkey, she's called Nelly. She's very gentle. If it helps, imagine she's a virtual donkey.' Ceun said, ignoring him.

'And she's little, so when she bucks you off, you won't hit the ground quite so hard.' Anaya added.

'Not helpful Ana.' Ceun shot in her direction as he climbed into his saddle.

Reluctantly, Will approached Nelly. She eyeballed him evilly. 'She looks like she doesn't want to be ridden.'

'It's a donkey,' Ceun said amiably, 'they generally don't, but we can't always have our way, now can we? If you would mount up, while we are still young?' Will grabbed the reins and the front of the saddle. He began to wish that the joust scenario had included mounting and dismounting. His foot slipped easily into the stirrup. Just as he was about to mount, Nelly took four steps sideways causing Will to hop backwards desperately. Ceun reached down for Nelly's reigns and held her still, while Will clamoured on to the beast's back, but she was not an animal prepared to submit to being transport without a fight. As soon as Ceun released her, she charged headlong out of the gates with Will clinging on for his life. Will, who had closed his eyes, opened them as Ceun shouted, a trough was coming towards them, fast. Nelly's legs which had previously been moving like a locomotive suddenly performed an emergency stop, her head dropped, and Will plopped neatly into the stagnant water. He emerged spluttering and, after wiping his face, found himself eye to eye with Nelly. He could swear she sniggered.

~~

To Will, it had seemed an age since, soaking wet, he had climbed back onto the donkey. His back ached, his legs ached, even his hair ached, His clothes had dried into a sitting position, and he suspected he might walk bow-legged for the rest of his life. The bounty hunter and polymorph had bundled him, protesting, back onto the animals back and she had since been content to move no faster than a gentle amble. Just in case, Will's knuckles, white with fear, refused to release their grip on the animal's mane.

Civilisation, such as it was, had been left far behind, now all there was in front of them was a wide expanse of damp heath. It seemed to go on and on and on. Will could swear they had passed the same forlorn bush at least twice. He tried to get more comfortable, but this only served to remind the donkey he was there. She eyeballed him over her shoulder. Her look said if he wanted to avoid another swim, he had better sit still. The moor began to break up into a little scrub here and there until eventually, they descended into woodland. The side of the track began to fall away, leaving the path balanced with difficulty on the edge of a deep ravine. Will was afraid to even breath.

'We'll camp here for the night.' Ceun said as they finally, and thankfully reached safer ground.

'Out here?' Anaya said incredulously.

'I'm sorry I can't provide the four-poster bed and wall to wall running servants that her majesty is accustomed to, but, until we work out why mi-lado can't go back, I suggest we stay away from people.'

'It's lovely,' Will said wearily. 'Anything that doesn't constantly jolt up and down would be wonderful.'

Ceun threw them each a bedroll. 'Make yourselves comfortable, and I'll get some wood to build a fire.'

'You're enjoying this, aren't you?' Anaya stood looking at the bedroll at her feet.

'Yes, fresh air, the countryside, all very exhilarating,' Ceun said as he wandered off whistling cheerfully.

'What about you? Is this bringing out your inner boy scout?' She said to Will was as he was busy trying to lower his aching body to the ground without screaming.

'What?' He asked.

'Never mind. I'll go and get some water.'

Will shifted in the bedding. He wasn't the most comfortable he had ever been, but he was so exhausted he felt like he could have slept on Nelly. As he drifted off to sleep, he briefly wondered how it was possible to dream about sleeping and would he dream within a dream. Familiar voices were talking. He couldn't make out what they were saying, but he certainly recognised them. He was sure that was Cassandra and a man. Adam? No, the accent was wrong, it was American, Leibowitz! Will tried to speak, but it felt as if his mouth was glued shut. He tossed and turned in his Morphean sleep, completely failing to notice the small shape that skittered across the grass. The little creature sniffed at the restless figure. As Will turned, the creature hopped sideways chittering in protest, a small indignant puff of smoke escaping its nostrils. It eyed Will carefully. Content that the movement had stopped, it shrank to the approximate size of a newt and quickly wriggled down between the folds of cloth.

The next morning seemed to start even before the previous evening had ended. Will was rudely awoken while it was still dark. 'It is possible to get someone's attention without kicking them,' he muttered.

'Is it?' Anaya said innocently. Her stance, the way she moved, everything screamed Cassandra to Will. It seemed unreal that she was an imposter.

'Did you go to look at the house?' he said with exaggerated innocence. He could feel her watching him in the gloom. 'Don't do that,' she said, turning away. 'Do what?' 'Try and trick me or drag me into whatever fantasy you happen to be having about what's her name.'

'I wasn't. I just thought…'

'You just thought what?' Ceun asked as he approached. 'Breakfast?' He indicated two hands filled with eggs.

'Do I even want to know what creature they are from?' Anaya asked.

'Probably not if you want to eat them.' He smiled.

In the growing light, Will spotted a movement in the trees

above them. 'What was that?' he asked, trying not to panic. 'I saw someone up there.'

'Don't look at them,' Ceun snapped.

Will squinted to see them clearer. 'They look like holy men, or monks, perhaps they can help us?' Will began to feel a bit more hopeful. 'They could offer us sanctuary?'

'Ignore them. They are a bloody embuggerance.'

'Look,' Will persisted, 'I appreciate that you are probably not a religious man but still, that's no way to talk.'

Ceun turned sharply from cooking the eggs. 'It is nothing to do with my beliefs, and they have a very odd idea of what constitutes helpful. Just don't look at them and they will hopefully go away.'

'I've always found them extremely helpful.' Anaya said happily.

Ceun harrumphed. They began to eat.

'One of them is waving.' Will said quietly.

'Which part of 'ignore them' isn't clear. Just don't look.'

'I can't help it. They seem to be tap dancing.'

'Let them.'

'Now one is balancing on the other one's shoulders!' Will laughed incredulously.

'If you are not looking, how do you know?' Ceun said through a mouthful.

'It's difficult not to.' Will said, still staring.

'Try harder. In fact, sit over here where you can't see them.' Ceun indicated a space.

'He seems to have something against the Brothers of Chance.' Anaya said gleefully.

Will poked at the eggy mess in front of him. 'Brothers of

Chance? Is that a religious order?'

Anaya was about to answer, but the bounty hunter was already whipping their plates away.

'Time to get moving, I think.' Ceun said firmly.

'I don't see why we can't just talk to them?' Will murmured.

'He's just testy because they tend to make things happen. If something happens by 'chance', then the chance is probably down to the brothers.' Anaya supplied.

'So why don't we just ask them to 'chance' a way for me to get home?' Will asked.

'Because they are more trouble than they are worth, and that is all you need to know.' Ceun snapped. 'Come on, let's get moving.'

As the riders disappeared behind the trees, the two cowls looked at each other and shrugged. The sad excuse for a track took them far too close to the edge of the river for Will's comfort. The water pounded past, oblivious to the smooth boulders in its path. Each time Nelly's hooves slipped, Will could imagine himself plunging into the icy depths. Despite his fears, and in the spirit of self-preservation, at least three of Nelly's feet remained consistently true. It was just not necessarily the same three at the same time. As a watery sun struggled into the sky, a narrow bridge came into view.

'Why are we stopping?' Will asked.

'Just checking for a welcoming party.' Ceun replied. 'We wouldn't want any nasty surprises, would we?' Ceun looked pointedly at Anaya.

'What?' she said. He nodded towards the bridge. 'Me?' Both eyebrows threatened to leave her head in amazement. 'You do it.'

'You don't keep a horse and wear your own saddle.' Ceun said sweetly. 'Now get on with it, unless of course, you are too scared?'

'Does that kind of reverse psychology rubbish ever actually work? Think what you like, but I'm not doing it, send him.'

'We are trying to keep him safe.'

'And I fully intend to keep me safe!' Anaya folded her arms across her chest. 'Not going to happen.'

Ceun raised his hands in resignation. Dismounting, he pointedly handed the reigns to Will before carefully approaching the bridge.

 'It's not very chivalrous trying to send a girl.' Will said.

'Do you think I'm weak?' Anaya snapped, glaring at him.

'Um no?' Will replied.

'Are you sure?' The glare sharpened.

'Positive.' He said.

'Good. Then shut up.' She said, turning back to face the bridge. Will let out a breath.

Ceun took a few tentative steps, pressing gently on each board and listening intently.

'Does he think the bridge isn't safe?' Will whispered.

'Not exactly...' Anaya was focussed on the intricate dance taking place on the bridge.

Eventually satisfied, Ceun began to walk towards the shore. He was almost back when the river started to gurgle before exploding into a six-foot swirling vortex of water, which now engulfed the whole area where the bridge and the bounty hunter had been moments before. The water boiled and gushed then subsided as quickly as it arrived leaving the scene untouched and uninhabited.

Anaya stood in her saddle, straining to see. 'Ceun!' She called out. 'Ceun! Where are you? Can you see him?'

'It's as if he was never there!' Will said.

A splutter from above revealed a very wet bounty hunter clinging to a branch. 'This wouldn't have happened if you'd gone.' He coughed.

The flash of relief on the morph's face was quickly replaced with contempt as she remembered herself. 'No, it would have been me hanging from the tree.'

'What the… was that?' Will's eyes were bulging.

'Gorgonian.' Ceun replied as he hung from the branch, before dropping neatly to the ground. 'This area is infested with them. They like to take over bridges and convert them into nice little traps for tasty morsels to drop in.'

'Like the Billy Goat Gruff?' Will said.

'What are you talking about?' Anaya asked. 'What is he talking about?'

'It's a children's story, about a troll that lives under a bridge and the Billy goat travels across it…' Will began. 'A Gorgonian was probably where whoever wrote it got the idea from.' Ceun interrupted. 'We're going to have to kill it, aren't we?' Will asked.

Anaya snorted. 'How exactly are you planning on killing something you can't see, can't touch, and only come into contact with as it eats you? Anyone going anywhere near it will be sucked into oblivion.'

'It is theoretically possible to attack it if you could find immunity to drowning, your body being dashed against the rocks and your brains leaking out of your ears.' Ceun added.

'Ok, I get it. It can't be defeated by conventional means. But it must have a weakness? Come on. These things always do, plucky hero saves the day?'

'No-one has ever seen one. Correction, no-one has ever seen the outside of one.' Ceun said.

'In the depths of the ocean, there are sometimes creatures that live in the dark constantly. Sometimes they wash up in nets, or they send cameras down and… Will noticed the blank expressions. You don't care, do you?'

Two heads shook simultaneously. 'We'll not get past here.' Ceun said. 'Not in one piece anyway, they're sneaky, if it has a web here there's a good chance there are others.'

'Can't you do your freaky 'look at me, I'm what you want' mojo then change into something vicious?' Will asked Anaya.

'I won't even justify that…' She said in disgust.

'We'll cross the river further up where it's shallower.' Ceun interjected.

Further along, the river seemed just as hazardous to Will, as Anaya turned her mare into the strong current. 'This is shallower?' He exclaimed.

Ceun urged his animal into the torrent. Despite their differences, Will could not believe he was asking Nelly to do this. The horses struggled against the current. Will could feel Nelly's feet struggling to gain purchase on the stony riverbed. She fought on, finding less to stand on she was having more difficulty in keeping her head above water. But as they were swept along with the current, she seemed to be winning the battle. The other shore seemed finally within reach. Exhausted, the donkey hauled herself out of the water, but the bank was treacherous, and her feet began to slip, to lighten the load and save herself, she reared. Will scrabbled for a hold on the saddle. His searching hands managed to grip the bedding roll, which ripped free from the saddle. From nowhere, a column of water appeared. As it grew Will was dragged backwards into the icy vortex, the bedding roll still in his clenched fists.

CHAPTER 14

The pressure of the water coupled with the icy shock knocked Will into unconsciousness. Deep within the bedding roll, a small creature was roused by the sudden unusual swirling sensation. It was not impressed. While it circled, it is worth taking a moment to investigate the visitor further. 'It' is what humans would know as a dragon, fully loaded, fire breathing sulphur farting, horns, tail, teeth dragon. That is, however, only its generic name. Common on Morpheus, they usually have the good sense to stay out of sight. However, depending on its breed, temperament and, if they feel like it, they have an uncanny ability to watch and provide an accurate record of events for anyone brave enough to attempt to train one, and his one was paying particular attention to Will.

For a dragon of any persuasion, the sensation of being unimpressed is not necessarily the same as being concerned. To its credit, its current predicament appeared to be nothing more than an interesting distraction.

At the heart of the vortex, the gorgonian was waiting for its meal; unfortunately, for the creature, it had not realised there would be an additional side order. Its great slobbering tongue tasted the water as Will, and his passenger passed its lips and headed straight into the stomach of the eating machine. The dragon was generally content in most environments because when you are at the top of the food chain, it is hard to get excited about other animals eating habits, but one of the few things to attract its undivided attention is when it becomes the thing that something, however misguidedly, is trying to eat.

With a small puff of smoke from its nostrils, the dragon began to grow from a small, cute lizard and very soon it had reached alligator proportions. It became larger still until it was definitely in the dinosaur category, its talons gently gripping the still unconscious human.

Meanwhile, it was beginning to dawn on the gorgonian's limited brainpower that it had bitten off considerably more than it could swallow. It fell back on the only thing it could, digest and digest as fast as possible. However, this only caused the swelling in its stomach to increase further until a tiny spark dawned deep within the creature that it was now trying to ingest something almost larger than itself. Full to capacity, the vortex which supplied its web was unable to vent causing the twister to turn inwards. The pressure inevitably became too much. As the creature had its final thought, best described as the interspecies equivalent of 'uh oh', its stomach contents were breaching the surface of the water in a violent fountain of tentacles, jelly and gastric juices.

By the time the waters had stilled, and Will was dragged to safety, the dragon had sufficiently diminished, so all that was rescued from the debris was a battered inventor and a rather soggy bedroll. Darkness surrounded Will; he could hear voices, distant, as though underwater. He was aware that in some way, they were talking about him rather than to him. He tried to speak, just as a slap stung across his cheek. There was a sensation of not being able to breathe for a second before his lungs rejected their watery contents, and he was emptying them, and his stomach, onto the grass.

'I told you not to stand so close.' A female voice scolded.

'I didn't know he was going to do that did I?' Will opened his eyes to see Ceun wiping vomit splashes from his boots. 'I think we'd all be very interested to know how you managed that.' Ceun said, crouching down.

'I didn't mean to. It was the water.' Will said weakly.

'He means how you managed to kill the Gorgonian.' Anaya said.

'I didn't kill it. Perhaps it just wasn't hungry?' Will said, struggling onto his elbows.

'Given there are assorted bits of it all over the place I think we can be fairly certain you killed it.' Ceun said. 'You must be the only edible thing that a gorgonian has ever spat back. I'd hate to think what you taste like.'

Anaya said grinning. 'What he means is, well done.' Will felt an involuntary blush rising to his ears. Despite the fact he knew this wasn't Cassandra, the idea of impressing this version did appeal. 'It was nothing,' he said modestly.

'That's what we thought.' Ceun eyed Will carefully. 'What aren't you telling us? It certainly wasn't luck.'

'Whatever it was, it seems to be on our side, and that is all we need to know.' Anaya said pointedly.

'Hmmm.' Ceun said, scratching his chin. Anaya held out her hand and helped Will to his feet.

'Pay no attention; he gets like that when it's not him playing the hero,' she said quietly.

~ ~

Their journey continued under an uncomfortable silence. Exhaustion was becoming a real concern for Will, coupled with the second soaking in less than twenty-four hours, and he felt things couldn't get any worse. This could only be described as a nightmare, and deep down, he didn't believe in any of it.

'You're very quiet.' He hadn't realised Anaya was watching him.

'I'm just trying to make sense of it all.' He said with a shrug.

'And how are you getting on?' She asked.

'Figments of my imagination are asking me to destroy my potential future, all my work and Adams, based on what? I am in a place that I don't believe exists outside my mind where other figments are trying to kill me. I think perhaps I need some therapy.' He said with a snort of humourless laughter.

'You don't have faith in your own mind?' She asked with her head on one side.

'It plays tricks and makes you see things that aren't there. Take you, for example, you are exactly what I'm talking about.' Will gestured towards her.

Anaya flinched as though slapped. 'Meaning?' She glared through cold eyes.

'Um, well no offence obviously.' Will added hurriedly. Nudging her horse into a trot, Anaya gave Will a final glare before catching up with Ceun.

'If I didn't know better, I'd think you almost cared I might have drowned?' He said with a glint in his eye as she drew level.

'It's a very good thing you do then isn't it?' She growled and carried on past him to take the lead. By the time they made camp, the silence had become oppressive. Will sat by the fire, trying to rub some feeling back into his hands as a gentle steam rose from his warming body. He didn't notice the small dark shape slip out of his baggage to forage.

A little way off, Anaya stood with her hands on her hips. It incensed her further that Ceun continued petting that damned horse when it was obvious that she was upset.

'What is the point of this?' She demanded eventually.

'He likes it.' Ceun answered.

'Don't be obtuse, you know what I mean, what we're doing, what is the point?' She snapped.

'He sees the error of his ways, destroys the machine, and all is well with the world.' Ceun said.

'He is as bad as the rest of them.' She said, gesturing towards the human.

'Ok.'

'Just like that, Ok?' Anaya paced backwards and forwards, desperately trying to put into words her frustration.

'What do you want me to say? I'm sorry that you are angry. I'm sorry that you are in this position, is that what you want from me?' He asked.

She paused for a moment. 'No, I just don't see why one man is worth risking our lives for.'

'This is not about us, can't you see it's bigger than that, even you can't be that self-absorbed? This is a disaster waiting to happen.' Ceun said irritably.

The morph tapped her foot angrily. 'Why is it your decision to make? We don't even know who is behind it. It could be a trap. When they realise what we've done there will be some very unhappy people, the kind that you don't want to make enemies of? Let the committee deal with it.'

Ceun folded his arms. 'We can't hand him over, knowing what they will do to him? I would have thought you would be the last person to suggest that. They will torture him. They will find out everything they can about this machine, and then they will kill him. The next thing you know they're finding a way to exploit the technology.'

'So? That's not my problem.' She said stubbornly but without conviction.

'If this gets into the wrong hands, it will be everyone's problem. We have a chance to stop it. He's a good man. He'll do the right thing.' Ceun was gentler now.

'And you are such a great judge of character?' She snorted.

'I used to be, once…' He said quietly.

'What's that supposed to mean?' Anaya snapped.

'It wasn't supposed to mean anything. I was expressing an opinion.' He said.

'An opinion about me. Don't say it wasn't, and don't give me all that I was disappointed, and you let me down malarkey because I didn't ask for your help.' She retorted.

Ceun faced her properly for the first time. 'You did actually. You begged me to help you.'

'I didn't think you'd actually do it!' Anaya yelled in frustration. Ceun patted the horse a final time. 'Then you shouldn't have asked,' he said before walking away, leaving the morph blinking away tears.

The little stowaway pattered away from the camp, at a safe distance it increased to the size of a small dog. The dragon proceeded to munch its way through an exciting selection of minerals, and as many rocks as it could cram into its mouth at a time. The problem generally being solved by slightly enlarging the mouth, soon it had cleared the surrounding area. With a happy belch, it waddled back to its charge.

As Will huddled under his blanket, rest refused to come. Dream or not, this was complete madness. He turned over again, trying to get comfortable on the damp ground. His exhausted mind tried to process all that had happened logically, but he could no longer see through the dark clouds of fear, so paranoia began to set in. How did he know these people were even on his side, just because one of them looked like Cassandra? What if that was their plan? He had a nagging feeling that something wasn't right here, why would they want to protect him, what was in it for them? They wouldn't be doing this out of the goodness of their hearts. Ceun, he'd managed to evade the river monster, hadn't he? Why then was Will sucked in, and how did he escape? The thoughts rolled around and around until he thought his head would explode. 'This is ridiculous!' He said suddenly. Realising saying such things out loud was not the best escape plan, he peeped cautiously over the edge of his blanket. To his relief, Anaya appeared asleep. Ceun stared intently at the fire oblivious. 'I have to get away from these people.' He thought. 'There must be someone in charge that I can speak to, ask them to send me back... no demand that they send me back. I am a British Citizen; I cannot be held against my will.' The inventor peeped over the blanket again. Ceun looked up vacantly as he felt Will's gaze. 'I'm just going to check on the horses,' he said as, trance-like, he walked away. Alone with just the sleeping morph, Will realised he might not get a second chance. He slid out from the covers and quickly gathering his things. The bedroll seemed incredibly heavy; Wills knees buckled under the weight. Balancing himself as best he could, he crept silently away. Just over the ridge two cowled sleeves high fived.

~ ~

Anaya stretched. Finding herself alone, she wandered over to where Ceun was standing with the horses.

'For goodness sake, leave the horse alone or get a room!' she said. Her approach roused him from his reverie.

'Back for round two?' he asked genially.

'Why didn't you wake me?' Anaya asked.

Ceun looked confused. 'Wake you? What are you talking about?'

Anaya searched his face to see if he was teasing; all she saw was honest confusion.

'For the second watch. You do know it's morning?' She asked.

'Very funny.' He laughed.

'No really, look at the sun.'

Ceun glanced up. 'But we were talking only a few minutes ago?' he said, but his tone was less sure now. 'Where's the human?' They ran back to the makeshift camp and the bed space where Will ought to have been.

'Why the hell weren't you watching him?' Ceun shouted.

'Because as I just said we agreed, I would sleep and you would take the first shift!' Anaya shouted back.

'I don't remember that,' Ceun rubbed his temples. 'Something has been messing with us.'

'Really, you think so?' Anaya was so angry how dare he blame her?

'Bloody monks!' he spat. ' We have to find him.' Ceun was already packing.

'Why!' She almost stamped her foot, 'you're taking too much on yourself, you're not a one-person police force. Let the committee deal with it, that's why they're there Or leave the stupid man to it if he doesn't want our help. What do we care what happens to one human?'

'You suddenly seem to have a lot of faith in the people who locked you up and threw away the key? This isn't a matter for bureaucracy, this is a life, and who knows how many others. You think when they discover Morpheus is real, they are just going to say, oh that's nice? No, they are going to want to explore, discover, and conquer. And then there will be war. It might be our fault he's stuck here, it's our responsibility.' He said, grabbing her arms.

'Who knows who else is looking for him? Let's just tell whoever sent us here that he got away and that we don't know where he is?' She said, mirroring the gesture.

'Why are you still here?' Ceun pulled away. 'Your part is done. You caught him, now why don't you go and get on with your life?'

'Let's get this straight. I'm here to get my pardon, that is it, but I don't want to die in the attempt!'

'Then leave!' Ceun said exasperated. 'Go! I won't try to stop you. It could be years before anyone thinks to look for you. I certainly won't be coming after you!'

Anaya was stung. Ceun mounted his horse and had a good head start before she finally caught him. They rode in silence, neither wanting to be the first to speak. 'Drama queen!' She said eventually.

CHAPTER 15

'I think that went quite well, Winkworth don't you?' Bango said as he rested his large shoes on the desk.

'Very well, Sir, everything according to plan.' Winkworth replied, handing the chairman a large tumbler of whiskey.

The clown twirled the glass, gazing into the liquid. 'This will be the making of us. Can you imagine the opportunities that will arise, the technology itself…?' He took a sip, a small smile of satisfaction on his lips as he savoured the liquid.

'Indeed, Sir. You persuaded them the human was a threat, and now they will accept anything that happens to him. Masterly.'

The Chairman gave a hollow laugh. 'There is always a downside. But, the fate of one cannot outweigh the need of the many.'

'So, he will not be killed immediately, Sir?' Winkworth asked.

Bango allowed his lips to stretch into a smile that almost matched his make-up. 'Not until we know exactly how this device works and how it can be used to our advantage.'

'You will go down in history as the chairman who took Morpheus to new levels Sir, new frontiers, an empire!' Winkworth clapped his hands in delight.

'But, of course, that will simply be a by-product of protecting our personal safety. This is purely about self-defence.' Bango said pointedly.

'As you say Sir.' Winkworth bowed his head in deference as the smile returned to his boss's face.

~~

'You are an idiot! You were so close you could smell him, and you let him get away!' The wolf's ears flattened to the side of his head.

'Mistress angry?' He whined.

'Angry? I wonder why? Here you are minus the thing I sent you to fetch? I thought even you could manage 'fetch'!' She raged.

The wolf cowered.

'You'll have to do it yourself. I am just too annoyed!' She snapped as her arm extended, index finger pointing towards a newspaper. Reluctantly a hairy paw took the paper and thwacked it down across the wolf's own nose.

He whimpered in confusion. 'You say me come home; you promise me bone?'

'I said no such thing you stupid animal, what makes you think you deserve anything? You were tricked. This woman, you say she was me, and there was a man with her?'

TBB emitted a low growl. 'Two man, one, Bounty hunter, me know, Hawke.'

'So, Ceun Hawke is after our prize as well, that is very interesting. And he had a polymorph with him? I can't think of anyone who would take that risk.' She rubbed her chin, 'polymorphs out in the world without their paperwork. I wonder if he's working officially.'

'Mittee find man, me take then?' The wolf sat up, ears pricked, his tail flicked hopefully.

'And how do you think are you going to do that, flea boy, after your resounding success today?' She nodded towards the newspaper. With tail between his legs, the wolf smacked himself again. 'No, we have to be clever, difficult for you, I know. They're out in the open now. We just have to make sure we get to them first, when I say me of course I mean you.'

'Yes, mistress.' The wolf said miserably.

'You have to try to understand what this means.' She bent down so that her face was close to a furry ear. 'They have to learn their lesson. They have to be trained. They are bad, and we know what happens to bad things, don't we?'

The wolf swallowed nervously.

'They are destroying everything they have. They need someone to take them in hand, show them the error of their ways, and I am that someone. All I need is…'

'Will get man.' The wolf growled.

His mistress turned away. 'Just see that you do, now get out of my sight.'

~ ~

Anaya was trying to keep her patience, but it was becoming increasingly difficult.

Ceun squatted on the ground staring intently at a rock here or a mark there and then, discarding it as irrelevant, would move on to the next.

'You have absolutely no idea what you're looking at, do you?' She said eventually.

'I will know when I see it.' He said, 'But my concentration is not helped by your constant fidgeting in my peripheral vision.

'Oh very cryptic, what are you expecting to find exactly, a big arrow and a message saying 'he went thataway'?' She said, her arms sweeping into a big arc off into the distance.

'How many people have you ever tracked?' He snapped, staring up at her.

Anaya just tapped her foot impatiently.

'Well? How many?' He insisted.

'None.' She muttered reluctantly.

'As I thought so shut up or at least make yourself useful and look for some tracks.'

A while later as the polymorph was kicking sulkily at a shrub. Ceun suddenly called out. 'There's our arrow.'

~~

Anaya stared at the ground in confusion.

'Look, the marks here and here.' Ceun patiently pointed out the slight tracks in the dust. 'You can also see there are some broken brambles here and up here where he got caught up, and he was dragging something, something heavy by the look of it.'

Now that she knew what to look for, there was indeed a vague indent along the ground. She smiled in comprehension, catching the bounty hunter staring at her, also smiling, she looked away, embarrassed. It was awkward for them both, and by the time she'd mounted her horse, Ceun was already riding off through the wood.

~~

Will was lost. Not just lost as in, he didn't know where he currently was, but so lost that he didn't even know where he was supposed to be. Nevertheless, it was a relief to have some time to try and make sense of everything. If the console was malfunctioning, then he needed to find a way to wake up and fix it. He had to get away from this insane place. He had to find the wizard or the king or this Committee.

With an everlasting faith in the great and the good and their ability to make everything right, he continued onwards, dragging the bedroll behind him.

Finally, the woods began to thin out, presenting him with a steep incline. With the heavy weight on his back, the grassy slope in front of him may as well have been Mount Everest. His calf muscles were screaming before he'd even reached halfway.

'What about keep-fit while you sleep,' he said to himself absently. 'I wonder whether it does tone the muscles in your body. If we could find a way to exercise while sleeping?' He mused. 'Now that is a good idea. I must remember that.' As he reached the summit, he was suddenly aware of being engulfed in silence. No birds, no insects, his movements seemed deafening as though he was the only living thing for miles around.

The gigantic upright stones ahead could not be described as living, although they radiated an almost tangible presence. They were arranged in a circle, some vertical, with the others balanced across to form arches.

'Stonehenge!' he breathed. Except this monument looked like the builder had just finished the pointing and had gone off for a cup of tea before the opening ceremony. The stones glistened with a newness their Realitas counterparts had not presented for millennia. From behind one of the larger stones, a soldier appeared, followed by another, and another. Will wondered with so many, how he hadn't seen or heard them coming. More sets of identical armour joined the throng, and soon the hapless inventor was staring at a semi-circle of steel.

'Can I help you?' Will asked, sincerely hoping that he couldn't.

Sergeant Simpson unrolled a scroll and made great play of clearing his throat. 'Are you the inventor William Cooper, human?'

'Depends who wants to know.' Will said cautiously.

'I will take that as a yes.' The Sergeant said with a shrug. Clearing his throat again, the soldier continued. 'By the order of Lord Elect, High Sheriff, Bango, elected representative of the Clown, buffoon, farceur, fool, funster, gagster, harlequin, humorist, jester, joker, jokster, picador, pierot, prankster, punch, Punchinello, quipster, ribald, wag and wisecracker party and Chairman of the elect committee of Morpheus, I hereby...'

'Who?' The soldier looked over the scroll at Will.

'You trying to be funny sonny?' He growled.

Will held his hands up in a gesture of surrender. 'No, no, not at all, whatever you just said sounds perfectly reasonable to me.'

'Good.' Simpson cleared his throat again. 'I hereby advise one William Cooper, human... that's you.' He nodded at Will.

'Thank you?' Will said uncertainly.

'William the human, that he is under immediate arrest and will accompany the squad... that's us.' There was a nod, but this time towards the assembled squad. 'For his protection and to uphold the law of Morpheus.'

'That's marvellous!' Will said enthusiastically.

'It is?' The Sergeant seemed genuinely interested. 'Are you sure you understand?'

'Yes. You see there appears to have been a bit of a mix-up, and if I could just speak to the person in charge, I'm sure I can get everything cleared up.' Will said, clapping his hands.

'I see.' Simpson looked at the scroll to hide his confusion. 'You're saying you want to be under arrest and taken to the chairman?'

'I do!' Will said cheerfully.

The Sergeant leant forward conspiratorially. 'Are you quite sure?'

Will nodded. 'Yes, let's get going shall we?'

'I don't think you understand. You are under arrest. You do know what that means?' Simpson had been prepared for kicking or screaming, hopefully, both, he had not been prepared for happy acceptance.

'You did also say it was for my protection.' Will said.

Simpson scratched his head under his helmet. 'I did say that, didn't I? How about are to be taken under arrest so that the committee may punish you for your crimes.'

'Hey, wait a minute. No-one said anything about any crimes!' Will protested.

Satisfied that everything was now going to plan the soldier rewound his proclamation. 'Take him away!' He yelled.

'Hang on, don't I get a say in this?' Will said.

The Sergeant bent down until his nose was inches from Wills. 'I don't think so.'

The whiskers on the dragon pinged with Will's fear. A curious reptilian snout popped out of the bedroll and sniffed. 'Now gentlemen, there is no need for force.' Will tried to back away from the men and their shiny sharp swords.

'I think there is.' Simpson was smiling now he was back on familiar territory. 'Every reason.' As the soldiers advanced, the little dragon slipped from its shelter and began to grow.

'Now look here!' Will started, 'you can't treat me like this. So far I have been knocked from a horse, ambushed, nearly drowned and now you want to take me captive in my own dream. Well, I tell you, I am not having this, and you can jolly well...' The squad stopped in their tracks, their eyes as big as saucers. Utterly oblivious to the monstrous beast behind him Will continued. 'Yes, I thought that would make you think twice. I just took on a river monster, and I won so just you think about that!'

His head on one side, the dragon looked on curiously as the soldiers began to slowly back away. Simpson stood with his mouth gaping. For good measure, the dragon grew by an extra ten per cent and snorted a blast of hot air in the Sergeant's direction. This was enough to persuade Simpson that in some cases, discretion is the better part of valour, he turned and fled after his men.

The immediate danger now passed, the dragon deflated like a balloon and scrambled back to his original place. Will blinked at their retreating backs in surprise before the enormity of his victory reached his ego. 'So stick that in your pipe and smoke it.' He yelled after them, but not too loud that they might come back. 'Who said I couldn't look after myself!' Will crowed to no-one in particular. He lifted the weighty pack and strode positively towards the circle. Just as he was about to step through, one of the keystones moved.

'Tricky situation there, John. I heard it all.' On closer inspection, the stone was in the shape of a small, slightly square man. It winked a coal eye.

'They realised who they were dealing with and thought better of it.' Even as the words came out of Will's mouth, he couldn't quite believe he was saying them.

'Hmmm, ok, mate. Are you on the list?' The man said pleasantly.

'Um, list? List for what?'

A stone thumb pointed to the structure.

'Errr, not really, I was just going to have a look around.' Will replied, not sure what to believe any more. The little man hissed through diamond teeth.

'Wouldn't do that if I were you, John. Remarkably dangerous places your average outcrop. Don't want to be poking around in there. Plus, if you're not on the list, technically you're not getting in.' The man shrugged. 'Not my rules I just work here.'

'Don't be silly, I can just take one step, and I'm inside.'

'True, true.' The gatekeeper nodded his head. 'But then you see you would a problem taking the second step on account of me hacking your other leg off. Nothing personal, you understand?' From nowhere the man heaved a sharp-looking stone axe which he now tossed from hand to hand.

Will hastily took a step back.

'You shouldn't take everything a face value. I mean, take that for example.' A stone thumb indicated the circle. 'To the naked eye, it's a bunch of dodgy-looking rocks standing around. Am I right, or am I right?'

Will looked at the circle. 'And that's not what it is?'

'Now you're getting it sunshine! Surrounded by magic and mystery, they are.' He lowered his voice. 'The things that go on in there, I tell ya, it would make your moss curl.'

'You mean like naked virgins being sacrificed under the rising sun?' Will breathed.

The little man made a noise like a car speeding over gravel. It took a while before Will realised he was laughing. 'No mate, nothing like that. Oh granted, days gone by you couldn't spit a pebble without hitting a virgin on a warm midsummer's day, but not these days, defunct they are, no call for them.'

'Virgins?' Will asked, his brow furrowed.

'No.' The gatekeeper snorted. 'That lot in there. Druids they call themselves, but they're nothing on the old lot. See this here was a portal.'

'To where? My world? Do you think they can maybe get me home?' Will began to hope.

'Depends where you've come from John. Personally, I'm surprised if they could get themselves home. Retired they have, more into having a good time than anything else.'

'I'm willing to take any help I can get, and magic just might be the answer, and if this is a portal, it makes about as much sense as anything else that's happened today.' Will said.

'I wouldn't hold your breath. Tell ya what. I'll let you in coz you look like you've got an honest face, but I won't be responsible for anything that happens to you in there. Kapeesh?' In a flash, the stone axe vanished, and the man was holding out a stone hand.

Will took it instinctively, before asking. 'Like what exactly?'

'Your guess is as good as mine sunshine? But if one of them

thinks it's funny to turn both your legs into lava, don't come running to Rox. That's me.' He said, pointing a thumb at his chest.

'Pleased to meet you Rox.' Will said, eyeing the circle nervously.

'You have to step through, don't ya, John.' Will passed through the arch, and then hastily backed out again.

'That was quick,' said Rox.

'It's a… it's a disco. Circa nineteen seventies I'd say. It had a glitter ball and everything!' Will squeaked.

'Is that what it is this week then? It's pan-dimensional.' Rox said proudly.

'You said it was a portal.' Will said, eyes wide.

'It used to be until they got all progressive. Now it does the best cocktails this side of the equator.'

'Right.' Will took a deep breath. 'I'm going in.'

He stepped into the circle with the words 'be lucky' ringing in his ears.

~~

Will could barely hear himself think above the sound of the music, and it was only once his eyes adjusted to the flashing lights, he became aware of the people. The clientele was mostly men wearing long flowing robes of different hues with matching facial hair masqueraded as hairy chests, complete with medallions of varying sizes. The dance floor was filled with a group, all wearing different shades of blue, who were executing an intricate dance involving some fancy footwork and lots of clapping.

Will worked his way across to where a sleeping druid sat with his face lying on the bar and his beard over his head. 'Excuse me?' Will said tentatively.

'Private Party.' The beard muttered.

'Um, sorry. Rox sent me.' Will replied, shouting above the din. A pair of green eyes peered out from behind the beard.

'Rox? He's supposed to keep you people out of here.' The druid complained.

'I was hoping that someone would be able to help me, you see...' Will began.

Before he could finish the sentence, the Druid sat bolt upright and was straightening his attire. 'We're the ones for help. Oh yes, you've come to the right place, don't you worry about it. You name it, and we can help, yes, indeedy.' He got up excitedly and began running around collecting his colleagues. Music was switched off, and all eyes were on Will.

When they were finally assembled, the Druid said, 'Go on then. What do you need? What's the job?'

Will coughed nervously. 'I'm stuck. I'm having this dream, and I can't seem to wake up. Rox said this was a portal and I was hoping that perhaps you could help me get home?'

'Ah.' The Druid said, rubbing his beard. 'Can't do much about that. Sorry.' He raised his arms to the crowd. 'False alarm guys, sorry.'

The others wandered back muttering as the dancing resumed.

'But... but... that's it. You don't even know where I want to go... What's the point of having a portal? Surely you can do something?'

''Fraid not. You're from Realitas, yes? Can't be done, we closed all links to that world aeons ago. It was too dangerous. Too risky that you people would cross over permanently. Is it true you lot eat puppies?'

'No!' Will was shocked. 'Well some people maybe do, but they're really, really bad people, and the rest of us are appalled about it.'

'But you don't do anything about it?' The Druid said, raising an eyebrow.

'I signed a petition online.' Will said primly. 'How did you hear about it?'

'Uh-huh.' The man responded sceptically. 'So, it is true.' I knew a druid who knew a troll who spoke to a faery whose sister once met a human in Realitas. Word gets around.'

'You people came to my world?' Will asked in surprise.

'All the time. It was backwards and forwards in the old days. Humans came here, we went there, and everyone lived together perfectly happily. We were the gatekeepers. We lived in both dimensions. It was bliss.' The man's eyes darkened. 'Then it became too dangerous. You people began to question everything, especially us. You wanted to explore, to conquer, and to convert everyone to your new religions. You stared to say we were make-believe, or worse, emissary's of this new devil you'd invented, so, the old Druid Master, Tiberus ordered all the portals to be closed. We couldn't stop you coming here, but we could make sure you were all mixed up by the time you returned. It was the last real magic we ever did.'

'That's terrible. What am I going to do now?' Will wailed.

'Beats me.' The Druid chirped. 'I'm Moonstone. They call me Moonie, have a drink.'

CHAPTER 17

A dark shadow descended over Rox. It seemed attached to a pair of enormous trotters. His eyes moved up and up and up until, way in the distance, they met a pair of sunglasses, which were studiously ignoring him.

''Ere John, you're in my sun.' Rox shouted.

The head rotated downwards as the glassed turned their attention to the little rock man. The snout sniffed a deep inhalation of scent.

'I'm going to need you to move. I could be covered in moss in seconds, the slightest bit of shade and its five o'clock shadow all over.' Rox said, conversationally.

The pig took a length of straw from the pocket of his overcoat and began to chew.

'That's a filthy habit. You want to give that up. Why don't you go over there and think about it?' Rox glared at the stranger's kneecap. Bending down, the Pig picked Rox up by his head to get a better look. 'Hey, put me down you big pork pie! What do ya think ya doing?' Rox wriggled angrily. Porkio chewed on his straw.

'I am looking for someone,' he said eventually.

'If the someone you're looking for is trouble you overgrown sausage, then you've found him!' Rock fists swung at the snout missing completely.

'Do you think we should help him?' Anaya whispered to Ceun as they watched the scene.

'You want to help someone? There won't be anything in it for you.' Ceun said pettily.

Anaya feigned shock. 'It hardly seems fair. I thought you were all about helping the little guy. And for the record, will you just get over yourself already.'

'Ah, so what you mean is you're looking for a fight?' Ceun said, arching an eyebrow.

The morph smiled. 'Of course not. I just thought perhaps you'd been playing the good guy so long you've forgotten what it's like to have a good scrap.'

'You want *me* to get into the fight?' He added.

'If you insist. Who am I to stand in your way?' She said, extending an arm as an invitation to join the fray.

'Who indeed. But I think I might sit this one out.' Ceun said, crossing his arms.

Rox's body was swaying dangerously from side to side.

'Do you want to think about that because I'm reasonably sure that the neck is supposed to hold the head on the body, not the other way around.

'I am looking for a human. You will tell me where he is.' The pig said.

'I will tell you nothing, treacle.' Rox grunted. Finally, the crack gave way, and the Pig was left holding just a head. The body rolled twice before performing a perfect back lift and landing on its knees. It immediately began hurling pebbles in the general direction of the pig. 'That's it! You got 'im a corker there, right on the snout! Get 'im!'

Porkio shook his head in irritation. Still grasping Rox's head he charged at the stone man's body, knocking it flying. As it flailed, a great trotter stamped down upon the little body causing it to break up into torso, arms and legs. His attention turned back to the head. 'You will...' He began before the barrage started again. This time, the arms held one leg like a bat. The other leg used the torso as a platform to launch stones, which were thwacked accurately at the pig. 'Don't like it, do ya drippin' breath? There is no human here, but you can be sure I wouldn't tell ya even if there was. Go ahead smash me up some more. I can do some real damage once you turn me into grit, ever got grit in your eye... I will drive you insane.' Rox goaded.

A sneer passed the pigs mouth. 'I don't think you know anything. Perhaps I should smash you up anyway.'

'Go for it, you overgrown... chop... Even if I'm dust, I will irritate you until you can stand it no more, everything you eat, I'll be in there, and once I get in your stomach... oh, momma, we're going to have us a party!'

Porkio snorted. Dropping Rox's head in disgust, he kicked it under a bush. Even after he'd walked away, Rox was still shouting. 'Come back here you coward. Come on, what are you going to do to me? Nuffin' that's what!'

~~

'Help me gather up the bits.' Ceun was busily piling what remained of Rox into a pile of rocks.

'You could have helped him, what about defending the weak and all that stuff you're supposed to believe in?' Anaya picked up the little silent head and placed it on the top. She blinked, she could have sworn it winked at her.

'Defending the weak yes, but when criminals fight between themselves, then there is one less of them to have to take in.'

'Who are you calling a criminal John? And watch what you're doing wiv them, they's bits I'm fond of.' Both Anaya and Ceun looked at the pile which had recently been Rox, with Ceun rapidly dropping the two large pebbles he held in his hand.

'If the lichen fits? How long is your rap sheet at the moment? Few breaking up and entering? Bit of bodily assault, your body being the one doing the assaulting?' Ceun said, wiping the palm of his hand down his trouser leg.

'I've done my time Hawke.' The pebbles and rocks were gradually moving around, pilling up and assembling until they re-animated as the stone man.

'Another one of your fan club Ceun?' Anaya smiled sweetly. 'Oh, I think you may have that on the wrong way around.'

Rox looked at his right arm and after flexing his elbow somewhere in the region of his buttocks, did concur that things weren't quite right. 'Thanks, Doll.' He said as the arm reassembled correctly. 'I did ten years of hard labour.' Rox continued.

'Breaking rocks?' Anaya asked sympathetically.

'No, being the rock that was broken as it happens, I used to be seven foot two.' He said with a solemn expression which dissolved immediately at Anaya's look of horror. 'Im only pulling your leg Doll.' He said with a wink. 'But I bear Mr Hawke no ill-feeling, made me what I am today. He did me a favour. In the security business now. Straight as a die. I'm a self-made man.' He glanced up to see if the morph would notice the pun.

'Very funny.' she said.

'So what was with your friend?' Ceun asked.

'No friend of mine. Shady character and no mistake. One of the faces I reckon, am I right or am I right?'

'Is he right?' Anaya asked. 'What's a face?'

'Porkio, otherwise known as the bacon slicer. Morphean Mafia… nasty piece of work.' Ceun supplied.

'Tole ya. A proper face.' Rx said nodding.

'Now what would he want here?' Ceun looked pointedly at the rock man. 'From you?'

Rox inspected his fingers. 'Sure I can't say.'

'You can't say or you won't?' Ceun asked.

'Don't know anything, John, you're barking up the wrong wossname.' Rox replied as he swapped two fingers on his right hand.

Ceun was staring at the archway.

'Nothing to see there.' Rox said.

He took a couple of steps forward, resting a hand against the stone. 'So it's not the entrance to a pan-dimensional portal, all of which were outlawed years ago?'

'You're right there. It's not.' Rox said, none too subtly moving between Ceun and the gap.

'So it's been deactivated and is now completely dormant?' Ceun said, stepping to the side.

'Weeeeel... not exactly dormant, not if I'm being completely honest.' The stone man said, sucking air through his teeth.

'And when have you ever been that Rox?' Ceun said with a snort.

'Now fairs fair. Violence and a bit of redistribution of wealth perhaps, but I've never been dishonest!' Rox said, holding out his hands in entreaty.

Ceun smiled. 'I apologise.' Ceun said with a bow of the head, 'So, if say, you saw someone coming this way, perhaps some-one from Realitas. And, if just, for example, they happened to be hiding in this, not exactly a portal, you couldn't, in all honesty, deny it?' Rox scratched his head as he considered the question, his face contorting in thought.

'It's not a portal.' He concluded.

'But the rest would be somewhere near the truth?' Ceun prompted.

'You're confusing him.' Anya said accusingly.

Indecision was etched all Rox's face. 'I don't want to get in-volved.'

'Look Rox, the bacon slicer is looking for this man, and who knows who else.' Ceun said. 'You're not doing him any favours by keeping quiet.'

'There were soldiers here earlier.' Rox volunteered in an attempt to change the subject.

'When?' Anaya asked, glancing over her shoulder.

'I noticed them coming and made myself scarce, you know, like just another pebble on the beach.' Winking at Anaya, he continued, 'When I opened my eyes they were running past like all the bats in hell were behind them, that was just before your man came along... oh bugger!'

Ceun grinned.

'Where is he now?' Anaya asked.

'Now how about a date and maybe I'll tell ya, beautiful?'

Anaya rolled her eyes. 'How about I take up where the pig left off?' She said.

'I like a woman with grit.' He said.

'Oh, for goodness sake. Of course, you don't, no man does!' Anaya scoffed.

'Touchy ain't she?' Rox said nudging Ceun's knee.

'You don't know the half of it.' Ceun replied, shaking his head.

'Listen.' Anaya interrupted. 'This human is being hunted, and not by him for a change. We are probably his best shot. You'd prefer someone else got to him first?'

Rox scoffed. 'You're the law's trained monkey. You'll just turn him in any way. A nice big fat reward is there?'

'He's gone freelance.' Anaya said. 'Hey, I don't suppose there *is* a bounty in this?' She said, turning to the bounty hunter.

'No bounty.' Ceun was getting impatient. 'Is he in there or isn't he?'

'Search me, treacle.' Rox said with a shrug. It was against his nature to be too helpful to the authorities.

Ceun was still looking at the portal. 'So if we go in here, we won't find anyone remotely human.'

Rox answered completely honestly. 'You could find anything, John. You could find any

thing.'

CHAPTER 18

'So you're stuck, and you think people are trying to kill you?' Moonie asked conversationally. 'That's heavy, man.'

'That's about the size of it yes, hic.' Will took another sip from the green, smoking cocktail glass. 'These are really very good. I'll have another when you're ready.' He waved his glass in the general direction of the bartender, a young druid with dread-locks in his beard. 'Why can't you open it up again, this portal thing, then I go through, and you can close it?'

Moonie hissed through his teeth. 'It's not like unlocking a door and then bolting it again. There are rituals to be performed.'

'Like what?' Will asked, taking an unsteady sip of his refreshed cocktail.

'Well, you know.' Moonie waved his hands expansively. 'Then there is getting enough power together, need the juice, and there's making sure that no-one notices this portal's been opened, that again will be some more rituals.'

Will nodded, 'Rituals.' He agreed.

'Very very complicated, rituals' Moonie said.

'You don't know how to do it, do you?' Will said wearily.

'Oh yes, in theory, we could do it, it's the practical application that we may have some problems with.' Moonie said expansively.

'Such as actually knowing how to do it?' Will said doggedly.

'That would be one of them, yes. But it will be in the archives, and I'm sure for a good cause we could get hold of them.'

Moonie said, raising a glass, only to find it empty. He stared sadly into it.

'I'll drink to that! Two more here, barkeep!' Will gestured to the bartender as two glasses appeared on the counter.

'You remind me of my best mate.' Will said, waving a finger at the younger druid. 'He's got those little knotty things.'

'You sure he should have any more. That's his fourth dragon's breath.' The barman asked, ignoring Will and addressing Moonie.

'Sure, why not. If a man can't drink when he's on a hit list, when can he?' Will said in resignation.

'If he has many more, you'll be saving them the job.' The bartender scoffed.

'I'm a marked man.' Will gurgled into his drink. 'They'll never take me alive!'

'How about unconscious?' A familiar male voice said behind him.

'Ceun! Anaya! Pull up a stool,' He waved the glass in their direction, green liquid slopped over the top and sizzled on the bar top. 'These green dragony things are great!'

'You look surprisingly pleased to see us considering you ran away.' Anaya said, taking a seat and gesturing with one finger to the barman.

'I'm going home, hic! And I've had a lot to drink. Shhh!' Will giggled.

'Are you some of his assassins?' Moonie asked. 'Do you normally pop in and say hello first? I have to say, that is really very civilised.'

'What does he mean, going home?' Ceun wanted to know. 'This place can't still be active?'

'Not at the moment. But I believe we can get it operational

again. Recently we have been experimenting with the existential properties of a funky disco beat in the cosmic production of trans dimensional navigation of the astral plane. But it can wait. Opening the portal will be much more exciting.'

'And you can do that, get it working again just like that?' Ceun asked.

'Not exactly. I mean when old Tiberus wanted something shut, it was done properly, but in theory, everything we need is here. What's the worst that could happen?' He said with a happy shrug.

'Why are you letting this happen?' Anaya hissed into Ceun's ear.

'Do you have a better idea?' He said with a grin. 'Aren't you curious to see what the worst is going to be?'

~ ~

A veritable vat of coffee had appeared, and most of the druids seemed now to be at least reasonably sober. There had appeared a stream of chests filled with parchments, scrolls, and stone tablets. The druids had become madly animated in their heated discussions, and it seemed there were a few schools of opinion when it came to which rituals and in which order. Finally, the preparations concluded in a flash of robes and knees in full flight.

'But shouldn't you be hauling them in, isn't this technically illegal, and if I recall, you tend to be generally against that type of thing?' Anaya asked.

Ceun held her gaze. 'In this case, it is for the greater good. If we can get him out of here and back to his people, then he will be safe, at least for the time being, and at least until we can find out who and what is after him.'

'But we'll have to find him all over again when he comes back!' Anaya said, throwing her hands in the air.

'It could be a while before he dreams again. By that time, perhaps he will have destroyed the device, and the whole thing will be forgotten.' Ceun said.

'Do you honestly think he is going to give it all up?' Anaya said incredulously.

'You're delusional.' She scoffed. 'There is no way he's turning down fame and fortune. He doesn't even believe we exist!'

'We have got to try, and I told you, no one is making you stay.' Ceun said, turning away.

Anaya sighed. 'Someone has got to stop you from getting yourself into real trouble. You're operating on the wrong side of the tracks this time Hawke.'

Ceun smiled 'Thank you.'

Anaya was exasperated. 'And you can stop looking so smug! You may like these creatures, but you have no idea how their mind works.'

She stomped across the room, nearly colliding with a charging druid. As if someone had blown a whistle, the activity stopped. The dance floor was now replaced with a spiral of stones, and in its centre, a pedestal which, until recently elevated a spider plant, but now held the unsuspended glitter ball. At seemingly random points within the spiral, runes were etched which matched those uncovered from the monoliths in the stone circle. Will watched in wonder as a few blades of grass began to creep through the carpet.

'It's reverting to its natural state.' Moonie volunteered. 'Ah, it feels good to flex the old magicks again.'

'And this is going to send him back, is it?' Anaya nudged a stone with her foot.

'There is a fair to middling chance.' Moonie fussily placed the stone back in position.

'This antiquated thing? It will probably blow up and turn him into chopped liver.' Anaya said.

'Whoa!' The effects of the dragon's breath were wearing off, and Will was no longer feeling invincible. 'This could blow me up?'

'Of course not; well, not much.' Moonie soothed. 'Now come and stand in the middle, placing your hands on either side of the globe.'

'That's the glittery thing.' Anaya added.

'I know that.' Will snapped. He turned to Moonie. 'This is safe, isn't it?'

'There is no danger. This device has been used for centuries.' Moonie gently tried to direct Will towards the ball. He wasn't moving. 'I'd say I'm cautiously optimistic.'

Will shrank back in horror.

'Look at it this way. If you stay here you'll be toast anyway, so you might as well go with a bang!' Anaya shoved the reluctant human into the spiral.

Will looked entreatingly at the druid. 'Don't I even get to say goodbye?'

'You just did. Now come along, we don't have very much time. We could all be locked up for this anyway so the sooner you're gone, and it's safely disassembled the better. Now stand still with your hands upon the orb, when the door appears you simply push through it and you will be safe in your own bed.'

A hand appeared on Will's shoulder. 'You have to destroy the device.' Ceun said, squeezing slightly.

'But…'

He was cut off. 'Don't prove me wrong. You can't forget this. Your invention is dangerous. Please don't make me have to find you again because next time I won't be so… polite?' The hand squeezed harder.

'Um right.' Will said.

'If you've finished intimidating the subject, can we get on?' Moonie asked petulantly.

Ceun backed out of the circle as Will shouldered his backpack and braced himself against the ball. The druids formed a circle and began to chant, quietly at first, then rising in volume until the first standing stone began to glow a pale blue. In quick succession, the corresponding spiral rune matched its colour. One by one the stones and runes began to glow, marking a trail towards Will. As the final light appeared, the spiral began to turn slowly, then gradually faster and faster until Will's stomach began to feel like he was on a very unpleasant fairground ride. The spiral started to rise through the ball until it was indeed a revolving door. Will's hands were all ready to push, and that's what he did.

Unfortunately, the door didn't move. He tried the other side, but that didn't seem like a door at all, it was too solid. Will tried again, he barged the door with a shoulder, but all that achieved was potential bruising. Backing against the door, he pushed as hard as he could with his feet.

Meanwhile, the druids were trying to maintain power. Finally, there was nothing for it. Will took a run up and charged full pelt towards the door, just as the power failed. The door folded in on itself and disappeared as Will flew headlong out of the circle, tripped on a stone and slid dramatically across the floor until he collided with the edge of the bar.

Deciding it was best not to move until he could work out which way was up, Will stayed where he was. 'What happened?' He gasped.

Moonie was shaking his head. 'You did push the door?'

Will glared at him. 'Push, kicked, barged. You name it. I did it. It would not open.'

'That is very unusual.' Moonie scratched his beard. 'They're usually hair-triggered.'

'Are you sure you did it right?' Will asked, struggling upright.

Moonie drew himself up in offence.

'But something was stopping you getting through.' Ceun interrupted. 'There is definitely something that doesn't want you to go home.'

'Something or someone.' Anaya said.

'You can do that here, stop me waking up?' Will asked.

'It isn't necessarily being done in Morpheus.' Ceun said thoughtfully.

'Um... gentlemen?' Moonie was tugging gently on Ceun's sleeve.

'You're sure it was working correctly, that everything was set up?' Ceun looked towards the druid, but the other man's eyes were fixed firmly on the centre of the circle.

The commotion had woken the dragon. It had been twirled most uncomfortably and was feeling quite dizzy and sick. Enough was enough. Residues of magick sparked from its scales as the steadily expanding dragon stretched its wings and looked for the source of its discomfort.

'Is that a...?' Will gasped as he got to his feet.

'Dragon.' Ceun supplied. 'That would explain how you have been so easy to find.'

'No, it doesn't?' Disappointment, coupled with this new threat, was taking their toll on Will's nerves. 'It explains nothing!' The dragon turned towards the noise and let out a half-hearted puff of smoke.'

'You've been dragooned' Ceun said.

'Now you're just making things up.' Will wailed.

'Someone has planted it on you to keep track of you. How can I explain? They have a psychic link to their master and will have been reporting on your whereabouts until they decide to collect you. Very clever, really.' He explained.

'You mean like a bug?' Will asked.'Don't be ridiculous.' Anaya said. 'What possible good would a bug be?'

Will ignored her. 'So who sent it?'

'Do you want to go and ask it?' Ceun indicated the beast, now all twelve foot of teeth and claws. 'Be my guest.'

The dragon shifted position. It was watching Will with its head on one side as if listening.

'Pfft, I would have noticed if that was following me around!'

'It wouldn't have been that size. They change to fit their surroundings. It could just have easily been in your pocket.' Ceun said.

'Or my pack? It seemed to get very heavy after I left you. Is nothing as it seems in this damn place?'

Ceun patted him on the shoulder. 'That would have been where I'd have hidden if I were, you know, a dragon. It would probably explain the gorgonian too. Nasty tempers, dragons.' He said, rubbing his chin. 'It has its assignment, but it still needs to eat. My guess is it fed, and that's when you noticed the difference.'

'What does it eat, rocks?' Will snorted.

Ceun stared at him. 'Really?' He said with a frown, 'Well it can get me off its to-do list right now. It can have whatever it wants as long as we can leave it here.'

'It might not be that easy to explain to the dragon. They are very single-minded. You can't reason with it, can't argue with it, can't kill it. It will keep with you until it is called off or you die, whichever happens first.' Ceun said.

Will digested the information. 'But it likes a full stomach?'

'Yes. Rocks, minerals, anything it can get really.' Ceun agreed.

'And we are in a circle full of rocks?'

Ceun pursed his lips. 'We are indeed.'

Will picked up a stone from the outer spiral and tossed it towards the dragon. 'Nice dragon, good dragon, have some nice mineral.'

'Hey, what are you doing?' Moonie hissed. The dragon sniffed the rock suspiciously, before swallowing it with a flick of the tongue.

'Here's the plan. We are going to back away very slowly and hope that it doesn't take rejection too badly.' Ceun hissed back.

'And if it does?' Will asked.

'Once I start running, I would suggest that you try to overtake me.' The bounty hunter replied with a twinkle in his eye.

'You can't leave that here!' Moonie said, his eyes never leaving the dragon. 'I'm sure it will just get bored and wander off.' Ceun said unconvincingly as he, Will and Anaya inched towards the exit. 'Eventually.'

'That dragon is going to destroy the place.' Anaya said.

'At least we know the portal will be closed for good this time.' Ceun agreed, 'Now I suggest we move.'

'You found him, and in one piece too?' Rox said as they appeared outside.

'For the moment.' Ceun patted the little man on the shoulder. 'I would suggest you take a break. Possibly quite a long one.'

There was a roar from inside. 'Is that what I think it is?' The sheen on Rox's face paled. The others didn't wait for an answer. When you are made of stone, and therefore on the top of a dragon's snack list, you have an incentive to produce an impressive turn of speed in the opposite direction.

As far as the Dragon was concerned, events had taken a fascinating turn. Its nostrils twitched. On the one hand, its charge was out of sight, on the other he was in Dragon heaven, the equivalent of a human being trapped in a big sticky bun and having to eat their way out. The temptation! Licking its leathery lips, it nibbled delicately on the central column. Deciding it was indeed delicious, he swallowed it whole as the glitter ball smashed to the ground. The crash seemed to wake the druids from their shock. Still weak from trying to open the portal, their powers were no match for the creature who found itself suddenly showered with miniature cheeses, a small aubergine, a collection of pocket lint and a blue plastic bucket which bounced off its nose. The Dragon let out a belch with just enough fireball to deter any further interruptions to its meal. The Druids put their heads together. Perhaps given the number of them, they might have just enough juice left to send the beast away.

'Ok, everyone. We need to think of the thing we most need, all together now!' Moonie shouted. Eyes tightly shut, as one, they began the chant. The air shimmered with power as into being came a deluge of gin and tonic. It hit the Dragon square in the side of its face. Turning, the creature bellowed with rage sending a sheet of fire singeing beards.

'You were all thinking of having a drink?'

'It's the thing I need most!' One of the Druids shouted back.

Moonie sighed. 'There is only one thing for it now... RUN!'

CHAPTER 19

The hospital corridor echoed to the clip clip of Cassandra's heels. Things were working out better than she could have possibly hoped. Not only had she managed to sell her story to a national magazine, titled 'My Genius Husbands Coma Hell', but she had also been on two morning television programmes, had a slot on local radio and was officially trending, albeit behind the Prime Minister's new haircut. No longer was she merely the glamorous wife of a geek who no one had heard of outside of those boring technology outlets, now she was a celebrity in her own right. As far as she could see, there was no way she could lose.

Before long, she would be making her own money from her own career. Not that she would ever admit it to a living soul, but it would be much more convenient if Will never woke up. She was fond of him of course, but it wasn't going to work out long term. A divorce would be terribly difficult to arrange, and her public wouldn't accept her leaving him while he was comatose, that was far too melodramatic. A much more palatable image would be the long-suffering widow, standing by her man until the inevitable finally took him from her side. There might even be a book deal in it.

Cassandra stopped to check her reflection in the glass, not a hair out of place. She may be acting the devastated wife, but there was no need to let standards slip. The clip clip resumed. It was just a happy coincidence that should Will actually die, she would get the whole of his half of the company, not only the quarter via the divorce, and those assets were not inconsiderable.

She had to admit, Murray was a genius. The publicity REM-CORP was squeezing out of Will's illness was unbelievable. As soon as the news leaked, press releases were flying out of the American's office like a flock of very well worded seagulls. Murray was right; you couldn't buy that type of coverage.

His publicity department had been very careful not to reveal the exact details of what the V10 could do but gave enough hints to send the industry into a whirl of interest and, to think, Adam wanted to leave the console in place. But that would be just like him. Cassandra let out a sigh. Not that the machine could be blamed, Adam was a phenomenal engineer, a craftsman, a perfectionist. But for the time being, it wouldn't hurt to keep a little doubt in his mind, for insurance purposes.

Fixing an expression of serene suffering onto her face, Cassandra pushed the door, it faded as soon as she realised Will was the only one there, and he was in no position to appreciate it. Settling herself into the comfortable chair, she picked up a celebrity magazine and began to flick idly through it. The Doctors had mentioned that chatting to Will might help, that the sound of her voice might be enough to bring him back. Cassandra tried at the beginning, but somehow she just felt silly, so she stopped. Now she just glanced through the exploits of the B listers and dreamed of the day when she would be one of their number and beyond.

Time in a hospital seemed to drag. Sighing heavily, she threw down the magazine and wandered over to the flowers carefully arranged around the room. Picking up random cards, she committed each message to memory, noting that many were from competitors of REMCORP, distributors, suppliers, pretty much everyone who could smell a gravy train. There were so many people wanting to pick up where her husband had left off, even if most of it was rumour and conjecture so far, the possibility of what he and Adam had done made a bunch of flowers a minimal price to pay.

Lost in her thoughts, Cassandra jumped as the door clicked.

'How is he?' Adam whispered.

'You don't have to speak so quietly. It's not as if you are going to wake him up.' Adam ignored the barb. 'It's just hospitals, they do that to me, like church for sick people.'

Cassandra tossed her hair. 'It's a daily trial, but someone has to do it.'

'What have the doctors said?' He asked, 'Did the MRI show anything?'

'No and no change, but then they can't find anything wrong with him, so I'm not really surprised.' She said.

'So what do we do now, get a second opinion, bring in some specialists? For goodness sake, he's in a private ward. You'd think they would be doing something!' Adam said, pacing the room.

'They are doing something, siphoning as much money out of the situation as possible. I think we may have to face facts that this may be as good as it is ever going to get.' Cassandra said bitterly.

'Is that what they said? They told you that he's never going to get better?' Adam asked, visibly shocked.

'Not exactly,' Cassandra looked at her nails, 'they are running some more *very* expensive tests, but you can see it in their eyes.'

'We have to stay positive. How is talking to him going?' Adam said with some relief.

'Oooh great. I was having a long chat with him before you arrived. It hasn't seemed to help very much.' She lied.

'Remember, think positive!'

'Ok, I will,' She gave a fake smile. 'Anyway seeing as you're here, I will be getting along. You know how it is a million and one things to do.'

'More important than being with Will?' Adam asked.

'Of course, not silly. But you're here now, and I can take a well-earned break. I appreciate this.' Cassandra patted him on the arm and was out the door before he could reply.

Adam perched next to his friend. 'I know you love her and everything, buddy, but... still, we'll have that conversation when you're up and about.' The expressionless face said nothing. 'That's it, give me the silent treatment, see if I care.'

Suddenly Will began to splutter as if having difficulty in catching his breath. 'What's the matter? Will? What's wrong? Nurse! Someone!' Adam shouted as he frantically pressed the red call button.

CHAPTER 20

'There must be another way,' said a bush.

'Hmmm?' A small copse of trees replied. 'I'm working on it, give me a minute.'

The bush rustled. Another bush just wheezed asthmatically.

'So you're agreed that he needs to go back?' The bush responded.

'I'm not saying anything of the sort. You said you thought he should go. I was very clear, in my opinion, and I don't believe in talking to plants.' Anaya stepped out of the copse and brushed a few stray leaves from her tunic.

Ceun climbed out of the bush. 'You can't be too careful with Dragons.'

'I thought you were the great Ceun Hawke, a righter of wrongs, apprehender of evildoers?' Anaya said with a laugh, 'Surely you should have it in custody by now?'

'You did see the size of that thing!' Ceun said, pointing back the way they had run. 'Also it's an animal, not a sentient being. Therefore it has no concept of right and wrong and is out of my area. Oh, and it's a Dragon.'

'So, a technicality?' Anaya said, grinning.

Ceun dragged the still wheezing Will out of his hiding place. 'A solid fact.' He said, narrowing in eyes at her before turning his attention to the inventor. 'Better?' Will, still unable to talk, nodded, before going back to the serious business of remembering how to breathe.

'Tech-ni-cality.' Anaya teased in a sing-song voice.

'There must be another way.' Ceun repeated, ignoring her.

'You said that, any closer to discovering *technically* what that might be?' She replied.

'What you want me 'ole china's is someone who can cross over into both dimensions. You can piggyback our friend across that way. Am I right, or am I right?'

Both Anaya and Ceun looked around. The voice had not come from Will, but there was no-one else to be seen.

'Down here.' The moss under Anaya's foot began to move. A hand appeared, then an elbow, as the adjacent rock levered itself from the ground. 'I'm with Hawke, and you can't trust those lumps of flying handbag as far as you could chuck 'em.' Rox shook himself, sending clumps of moss flying in all directions.

'You were saying?' Ceun asked, picking moss out of his mouth.

'The geezers who cross over. The tooth fairy, Santa Claus...'

'The Boogeyman!' The three said together.

In the tree above a bluebird squawked involuntarily.

'What was that?' Ceun said. The bird wedged a wing into its beak and kept perfectly still. They all listened. 'Must have imagined it.' Ceun said eventually.

'I'm... not...sure...I... like the... sound... of... boogeymen!' Will managed.

'It's perfect. We need a being that exists in both dimensions. They travel on dream waves all the time.' Anaya said.

'Do you think he would help us?' Ceun directed the question straight at Anaya.

'How should I know?' She shrugged.

Ceun folded his arms. 'I wonder. Someone who would help someone else to get across to Realitas. Hmmm, how could you possibly know?'

With the group being distracted, and already armed with some dangerous information, the bluebird saw its chance and fluttered away through the trees.

'I have never been to Realitas.' Anaya said petulantly.

'But you were planning to? Did you think I didn't know?' Anaya glared at Ceun.

'So it is possible to… do it this way?' Wills comment broke through the icy wall between them.

'It is possible. But it wasn't anything to do with the *Boogeyman!*' Anaya replied.

'If you say so, and with him being such a fine upstanding member of the community, I couldn't possibly imagine him breaking the rules, the very idea!' Ceun retorted.

'That is just speciesist. Just because you don't like him and if you had any real proof you would have locked him up with me.' She growled.

'So this person could… Hang on a minute. You were locked up?' Will stared at Anaya in amazement.

'It was a crime of passion.' She said primly.

'Ha!' Ceun laughed. 'That's what we're calling it these days is it?'

'What did you do?' Will asked.

Anaya produced her best wheedling Cassandra smile. 'We don't want to go into that just now do we? The point being, if I was guilty, would I be here helping you, now would I?'

Ceun coughed.

A warm hand cupped Will's face gently but firmly until he was looking into a perfect facsimile of his wife's eyes. 'You have to trust me, Will, there is absolutely nothing to worry about. You do trust me, don't you?'

Will was hypnotized. 'Where do we find this Boogeyman?'

'There's the thing, my sweet William.' She cooed. 'We need to find him where you last left him in your nightmare.'

~ ~

'I'm not sure about this.' Will murmured. The forest was straight out of a classic fairytale, dark, desolate and dangerous. Gnarled trees shook their bare branches, and golden or red eyes watched from every crevice.

'What were you expecting, sunshine and rainbows?' Anaya asked. 'It's a nightmare.'

'No, but...' Will said, tripping on a root which he could swear slithered away afterwards.

'Relax, it plays to the tourists.' Ceun said, clapping Will on the back. 'It is worse than it looks.'

'What!' Will spluttered.

'Sorry, I meant it's not as bad as it looks. Silly mistake.' Ceun said with a wink.

Will did not look convinced.

'What we need you to do is try and focus on that nightmare, preferably the point where you remember the Boogeyman appearing.' Ceun said.

'Do I have to?' Will whined. 'Can't we just send him an email or something?'

'If we can get you back into that dream, then we can ask him to help us send you home. Now you'd like that, wouldn't you?' Anaya said.

'Please don't talk to me as though I was five!' Will snapped.

'How old were you when you last had a Boogeyman dream?' Anaya asked.

'Five.' Will mumbled.

'Then it will help you get back into character.' Ceun said brightly. Rox already regarded the group critically.

'And I am here why?' He said eventually.

'It was your idea.' Ceun replied.

'Dunt mean I had to get mixed up in your caper, though does it?'

'You're here now, and you're unemployed, so do you have anything better to do?' Anaya asked as she shoved Will none too gently towards the first arch of trees.

'Fair enough.' Rox said with a shrug.

~ ~

The foliage became thicker as they pushed on until it was little more than a dark curtain, virtually impregnable. As Will fought through, he tripped and plunged forward into the darkness. Fighting for breath he tried to pull the smothering blanket of leaves from his face, but it was no longer the forest holding him down, and with stomach-churning familiarity, he realised that it was a feather down duvet covering his head. Gripping the edge of the cover, Will pulled it down slowly. He was in his bed. Not exactly his bed, more his five-year-old bed in the old house that his parents had been renovating at the time. Listening in the darkness, he could hear the old property groaning and creaking as unknown terrors crept towards him.

'This is ridiculous,' he said to the shadows in the room. 'I am not a child anymore.' To prove the point he pulled back the covers and tentatively felt with his foot for the floor, his imagination sensing all kinds of tentacles and talons ready to grasp at the vulnerable appendage and pull him to his doom. Unmolested, his other foot joined the first, and he levered himself up until he stood beside the bed, his hands on his hips, defying the dark.

Shivering with the numerous drafts, Will looked towards the mirror and to his horror saw his superman pyjama staring back at him.

'Hmmmf.' He muttered, climbing back into the bed. 'At least they are not the same size as the ones I wore when I was five. If this is my dream, then I should be able to choose what I wear.' Fixing his eyes shut, Will focussed all his attention on an outfit suitable for Boogeyman hunting, something rugged and manly, possibly with thick boots and a whip.

So intent was his concentration that it was some time before his bladder managed to attract his attention. Suddenly, the memory of all those nights in the darkness came flooding back to him. Flooding probably wasn't the best image at this precise moment. He squirmed uncomfortably, willing the pressure to go away, but his body was insistent. He needed to pee. There was nothing for it. He would have to run the gauntlet to the house's one bathroom.

Technically his room was above the bathroom. The convenience had been tacked on to the back of the house by a previous owner, and his bedroom was added at the same time. However, to get to said inappropriately named convenience, it was necessary to cross the next room, negotiate a narrow and winding staircase and finally run for your life across the gaping void which constituted the old wash house, complete with the boarded-up boiler. It was this room which caused the dread to rise up in his throat.

In daylight the home of various pieces of harmless junk the washhouse was nothing, but by night it became the lair of creatures ready to pluck out your eyes, disembowel you and rip off your arms to give you a round of applause with your own flapping limbs. Will shuddered. His bladder shuddered even harder. He vaguely considered the idea of wetting the bed but remembered the last time he had used this solution and the subsequent conversation with his mother.

'Big boys are not afraid of the dark. Big boys do not wet their bed, or have accidents before they get to the toilet!' He may have been terrified of the things in the washroom, but they were nothing compared to his mother when she had yet to have a washing machine installed, and soiled bedclothes in desperate need of a wash.

Reluctantly, Will got up and approached the bedroom door. Everything in the room seemed much smaller, but that didn't make it any easier. He crossed the next room, keeping a hand on the wall to steady himself against his shivering. He reached the end and stared into the dark abyss which passed for the staircase... He reached for the light switch but, as usual with the random wiring, it just clicked and illuminated nothing. Will belatedly remembered the torch left by his bed for such eventualities and cursed. As his hand guided him downward along the wall of blackness, Will decided to give himself a good talking to. 'It is just a nightmare. I am an adult, and there is nothing here that can hurt me. It is just in my mind. Whatever I may see or hear, I am in control of the situation.' Feeling anything but, he slowly descended into the pitch landing below. Straining his ears, Will could swear that something slithered away just ahead. With each step, he believed tentacles to be just inches from his ankles as his imagination performed cartwheels and backflips.

To his amazement and relief, he reached the bottom safely. Taking a deep breath, he pushed against the hated door into the washroom. It crept open. The room seemed to stretch into infinity. On the other side, the sweet bliss of the toilet bowl, but first he had to get past that hideous copper boiler. He began to creep across the flagstones. The cold biting into his bare feet seemed to have a direct line to the increasing insistence of his bladder. He tried to keep his attention on the sanctuary of the bathroom, but from the corner of his eye, he could feel the great round copper watching him eyelessly from behind its prison of boards. Shadows lunged. Keeping his pace steady and trying to control his rising terror, Will moved across the room. A shadow detached itself from its companions and placed a hand on Will's calf. Will screamed.

CHAPTER 21

'Are you insane?' Will screamed again. He had narrowly avoided wetting himself, although he had no idea how. He was now curled up in a ball on the floor trying to stop himself bursting into tears.

'Sorry John, they said to stop you before you got to the, you know, wossname.' Rox said apologetically.

'But by grabbing me in the dark! What would have happened if I'd attacked you?' Will sobbed.

Rox squared his shoulders. 'I expect you would have had a lot more to worry about than the Boogeyman unless those jammies are accurate.'

Will tried to cover up the giant S on his chest. 'Where are they anyway?' He hissed.

'On surveillance, for when you know who arrives.' Rox hissed back.

'So why are you in here?' Will asked.

Rox looked almost embarrassed. 'They said out here I'd pass for a...' The words trailed off.

'For what?' Will asked as he got to his feet. 'Was it something ornamental?' With the little rock man here, Will didn't feel so vulnerable. He had even forgotten about his desperate need to pee.

'So what if it was. I was the man for the job.' Rox said, dusting off his shoulder.

'One of my mothers gn....' Rox placed a rough hand over Will's mouth. 'I wouldn't say it if I were you, sunshine. The last person who made that crack had a little visit to the bottom of the river to meet the fishes. I made sure he got good and acquainted before I let go of his ankles,' he growled. 'Now I am going to let go of your flapping gob. I suggest it does not start again. Do we understand each other, treacle?' Will nodded, aided by the stone gag. 'Good.' Rox removed his hand. 'Now, where does this geezer normally appear?'

'From under the copper, just before I get to the bathroom door.' Will said, peering at the boarding dubiously.

'Well, best you run on along there. Just remember I'm right behind you.' Rox said encouragingly.

'Can't you be in front of me?' Will squeaked.

'But it's not me he's come to see now, is it? I am not, as it were, the main event. Am I right, or am I right? Just remember, they're more afraid of you than you are them.'

'That's spiders.' Will said.

'Same principle. Now quit stalling and get on with it.' Rox replied.

This was it, the final moment when that thing would jump out in front of him. Mucus would hit him in the face, the thing, that horrible thing, the eyes, the teeth. The result would always be bone freezingly terrifying and inevitably messy. He squeezed his eyes tight shut and waited. Nothing happened. His eyes were still shut, and his pyjamas remained unsoiled. Will felt a tug on his left leg and dared to open an eye.

'Well?' Rox demanded.

'Well, what?' Will replied, daring to look around the room. 'This is where it is supposed to happen. This is where it always happens.'

'Just here. This exact spot. Are you sure? This is where he jumps out and...' Rox said, scratching his head.

'Yes ok, I know what he does. But I am telling you, it's here. Unless…'

'Unless what?'

'Perhaps because I am bigger I frightened him away or perhaps because you're here?' Will said.

'Psst, what's happening?' Will jumped again at the sound coming from a crack in the bathroom door.

'Anaya? What are you doing in there?' He whispered back.

'It's a bathroom, what do you normally do in a bathroom?' She replied.

'Now?' Will asked incredulously.

'Of course not. I'm hiding. What's going on, where is he?'

'Dunno. Boogey hasn't shown up.' Rox was approaching the copper.

'Don't go near there!' Will called out as yet another shadow unravelled from the wall.

'You do all understand the concept of hiding and waiting? We may as well have hired a marching band, it would have been less obvious!' Ceun brushed the brick dust from his sleeve.

'He's a no show.' Rox supplied redundantly.

Ceun ran a hand over his hair. 'Yes, I think that is fairly obvious given that this washhouse has more people than a…'

Anaya waved him into silence. 'Shhh. Did you hear that?'

'Wha…' Rox began but was quickly waved down again. There was a low groan, barely audible. They all listened hard. There it was again, just on the edge of hearing.

'That's where he normally comes from, where the fire is at the bottom.' Will said, still not daring to approach.

Ceun kneeled and inspected the boarded-up fireplace. 'Pull those curtains back, let a little moonlight in so we can see what we're dealing with.' Giving the board a push Ceun opened a decent size hole. A trickle of dark goo oozed onto the floor. Will took a step backwards.

'Give me a hand, will you?' said Ceun, his head inside the hole.

Rox began to pull the remaining boards away. 'Stone the crows?' He exclaimed as they hurriedly pulled bricks away from the crumbling mortar until there was a space big enough to expose a vague body shape. Overall it was lumpy. The big square head had growths wandering off in directions all of their own, which was good because that distracted the viewer from the yellow canines protruding from its mouth. Out of that same mouth ran a trickle of green mucus, the same mucus that was also pumping from beneath the knife still protruding from the gaping hole in its chest. The creature groaned.

'You don't look so good, mate.' Rox said.

'Who did this to you?' Ceun asked, awkwardly cradling the creatures head.

'I...' The Boogeyman coughed sending splatters of mucus to join the rest on his chin.

'I know it's hard to talk, but if you can try to tell us what happened.' Ceun said gently.

The Boogeyman half shook his head.

'So that's the Bogeyman?' Will whispered to Anaya. 'He doesn't look so scary in the light.'

'Boogeyman.' She corrected. 'They get the extra o for being in the field. It reflects the shape you humans make with your mouths when you see one.'

'They? You mean there are more of these things lurking around.' Will said, surprised.

'So many people to jump out on, how did you think one creature could manage all in one night? Who do you think he is, Santa Claus?' She said.

Will pondered the remark. The Boogeyman was trying to speak again. In the end, he gave up and slowly raising an arm pointed towards Will and Anaya.

'Will did it?' Anaya said as all eyes fixed on the human.

'I did not!' Will began indignantly.

'Well, I certainly didn't.' Anaya added defensively.

The Boogeyman shook his head. 'Looking for…' he croaked.

'Looking for him, they had the same idea as us. Can you tell us who?' The stricken creature lifted his head to speak, but all he could manage was a cough. He tried to clear his throat, but as his eyes glazed over his body began to fold in on itself with eyeball churning speed, the creature became smaller and smaller, even hoovering back the pool of goo until all that remained was the chink of a knife hitting the stone floor.

'Is it dead?' Will asked warily.

'There were large amounts of stuff coming out of it, and we just saw it implode. What do you think?' Ceun snapped.

'I'm sorry, just that thing plagued me for years, I can't say I'm sad to see it destroyed, and you didn't like it either so don't have a go at me!' Will said.

'I may not have liked him, but it doesn't mean I wanted him dead. Something else that had happened because of you. Now I suppose it's up to me to find out who is doing this and why.' Ceun said.

'They were looking for us. They didn't get what they were looking for so let's just get out of here before they come back.' Anaya snapped.

'Don't you see? They are one step ahead of, every time, and next time they might succeed!' He said in frustration, trying to explain.

The standoff between the two was almost tangible as they stood nose to nose in the dim room, daring the other to back down first.

'I hate to break up this little love in but…' Rox began.

'What!' The two said together glaring at the little man.

'As I said, I hate to break things up, but I think we've got company!' He said, nodding a head to the left. After what seemed like an age of silence, four pairs of eyes turned towards the window just as the top of a cowl disappeared below the sill.

'It's those bloody monks!' Ceun cried.

'Do you think they did… this?' Will indicated towards the now clean knife lying on the floor.

'Unlikely, they don't mean any harm; just some people have an irrational dislike of them.' Anaya said pointedly.

'Irrational or not, I'm going to have a little word with our robed friends, and whatever mischief they're up to, I intend to put a stop to it.' Ceun strode towards the back door. Yanking it open, he stepped outside and stopped. 'No-one here.'

'Did you expect there to be. You know the minute you get near them, they disappear.' Anaya leaned against the door frame. 'Hardly surprising, the way you went charging out. I'd have run away too.'

Ceun kicked at a bush. 'If I ever get my hands on them…'

'You'll what? Lock them up? For what, getting on your nerves?' She said.

'It's a start.' He grumbled.

From above, a pair of golden eyes watched with interest. The Dragon knew its charge was around here somewhere, very close. And these two creatures, they had been nearby before. It shifted slightly, there was no concept that it had eaten too much, there was no such thing, but just at the moment on top of a full stomach, the exertion of catching up had made it feel ever so slightly uncomfortably stuffed. There was gas to be released, but at the moment its instinct told it to stay unseen.

It wasn't the only creature watching.

'So what do we do now, no Boogeyman?' Will asked.

'I suppose we could try to find another one?' Anaya suggested.

'It won't have the same connection with Will. We're going to have to find another way.' Ceun said, pacing up and down.

'How many other ways can there be?' Will said petulantly.

'As you people have been coming here since the dawn of time, it follows there must be lots of ways to get back. We'll just keep trying until we find one that works!' Ceun said patiently.

'In the meantime, what? I just wait for the next person to attack me. I'm beginning to think I should have stuck with the Dragon.' Will said.

Someone was creeping towards Will with a large brown sack. Silently, he stalked an inch at a time through the overgrown garden, taking great care not to attract attention. Will, oblivious, stood with his back to the danger and continued to sulk. The Dragon observed carefully, this most definitely looked like a threat, but at the moment, it was just interested to see what was going to happen.

It all unfolded in slow motion, or that was how it appeared to Will. Ceun had shouted and leapt forward pushing Will out of the way and into Anaya. Simultaneously, the world had become filled with leathery wings and warm sulphurous air which buffeted him sideways. There was shouting, a lot of shouting before a hand grabbed him roughly and dragged him away. His legs were running on autopilot as Anaya hauled him after her. Feeling his lungs were about to burst, he finally collapsed on the ground, not caring that he was still dragged a little further until the polymorph stopped too.

The Dragon was annoyed. Not only did it have indigestion, but its charge had run away again.

Ceun was also annoyed. In the confusion, the sack was thrown over his head, and he was currently being carried unceremoniously away. It then occurred to him that this was the perfect way to meet whoever was behind this so with a slight smile on his lips, he made himself as comfortable as possible and waited. When they found out who they captured, things were going to be very interesting.

'I think you got your wish. Return of the Dragon as it were?' Anaya said, panting.

'I didn't think it was supposed to want to hurt me!' Will still lay on the ground. It seemed the safest place.

'It was protecting you. Someone was trying to capture you. I imagine they were going to put a large brown hessian sack with potatoes written on the side, over your head and kidnap you.' Will looked up.

'That's oddly specific?' Will said.

'I only mention it because it seems to be what is happening to Ceun at this very moment.' She said, pointing in the direction of the disappearing assailant.

'We have to help him!' Will said, scrabbling to his feet.

'For one thing, they don't know they've got the wrong person, and we don't want to alert them to that, and we definitely don't want to deliver the person they do want. For a second, I only saw them for a glimpse, and now they appear to have vanished, and for a third, he's a big boy, he'll be fine, what we have to do is make sure we get you home. Right now, I'm in charge. OK?' Anaya said decisively.

Will nodded daring to say nothing else.

'Oh gods, I'm in charge.' She said to herself as the realisation hit her. 'Everyone's depending on me?'

~ ~

Rox ran out of the back door just as the commotion was ending. Everyone seemed to have gone. He didn't know whether to be relieved or annoyed.

'They might have said cheerio.' He muttered. He was suddenly aware of leaves floating on a warm gust of air as realisation began to dawn.

'Uh, oh!' He turned slowly only to find himself face to nostril with the decidedly wrong end of a Dragon. 'Nice Dragon. Good Dragon. He's not here, you see. So why don't you toddle off and find him?' Rox attempted to shoo the elephant-sized creature as it regarded the frantically waving thing with interest. It took a step back. Rox felt hope begin to grow.

'Go on now, find him. Where is he? Good Dragon, find him.' The Dragon turned his head from side to side. It even managed a half-hearted glance in the direction the little Rock man suggested it 'fetch'.

For some reason, the thing kept shaking its arms around. It wasn't attacking or scared. This was no fun. Considering its options, the Dragon came to a decision. It raised its enormous head and sniffed the direction Will had gone. Then with one sweep bent its neck towards Rox and swallowed him whole. There was no such thing as eating too much.

Rox did not share this opinion. From deep within the ancient animal's stomach, there was a rumble which sounded a good deal like 'Oh Bugger!'

~~

The metal lid on the old boiler began to turn. It lifted slowly as a porcine head emerged. Not caring, he demolished the rest of the brickwork and, brushing off his overcoat, picked up the knife. Porkio wiped it carefully on his sleeve, a grim look of irritation etching his snout which sniffed the air. So the little feathered freak had been right. Porkio did not necessarily approve of the network of bluebirds employed by the Godmother, but he had to admit they had their uses. The human should have been on his own. That's how nightmares work.

They are not scary if you have a whole gaggle of people with you. Secreting the knife in his overcoat, Porkio snorted. It annoyed him when people didn't play by the rules. There had to be rules, of course, they didn't apply to him, but how was he supposed to work if other people started breaking them. It was now time to start playing dirty. With one last look around the room, he shrugged the coat further onto his shoulders and moved out into the night.

CHAPTER 22

'I just want to go home!' Will moaned.

'You may have mentioned that at least four times in the last hour.' Anaya said irritably.

'It just proves how badly I want to go home then doesn't it?' Will realised he was being petulant. 'I miss *my* Cassandra.'

Anaya looked at him sharply. 'And what am I, chopped liver!'

'Why do people say that? Chopped liver?' Will asked, 'Why not, what am I, a microwave oven, or what am I, a bag of cheese and onion crisps?'

Anaya stared at him for a long moment before deciding she couldn't be bothered to get into that conversation. 'The point being, for all intents and purposes, I am Cassandra, so you should be happy.'

'But you're not, and I know you're not. You could try and act a little bit more like her?' Will brightened a little.

Again Anaya stared for a long moment. 'No,' she said finally. 'But you may have hit on an idea. What was it Ceun said, the blockage may not be in Morpheus? If we can somehow contact wifey, at the very least, she may be able to help us find a way to send you back using that machine thing?'

'It wasn't designed with that in mind. You see...' Will began.

'Is this about to involve a very complicated and boring lecture about the capabilities of your machine?' Anaya asked.

'Um, an explanation perhaps.' He said.

'Am I likely to be in the slightest bit interested?'

'Possibly not.'

'Is it likely to have any relevance on what I am suggesting?' She said.

'Well, it might because I don't know...' Will tried.

'Up until recently, there were many things you didn't know. Most importantly, that we existed and that you were going to cause all this trouble. So, I would say that you don't really know what you have created and therefore you do not know if it is in some way be able to pull you back.' Anaya said with a smile.

'But...'

'Then we are agreed.' She said cheerfully. 'You want to see your actual wife and I want that very much too, so we'll try anything necessary, yes? Yes.'

~~

The offices were all cool, clean lines, bordering on the clinical. Cassandra strode purposefully towards the wall-sized double doors at the end of the corridor. She had just reached the reception area when a woman barely out of her teens blocked her path.

'Can I help you, madam?' The blonde Barbie doll asked, eyeing Cassandra suspiciously.

She felt a hundred years old. 'I've come to see Murray.' She said as she tried to continue on her way.

The receptionist blocked her path. 'Mr Leibowitz is in a conference at the moment and cannot be disturbed. I am his personal assistant, Gina. Can I help at all?'

Cassandra took in the designer clothes, the perfectly coiffured hair and immaculate make-up and hated this creature even more.

'No, I don't think an *assistant* will do. My business is with him, and I believe he will want to see me. Tell him it's the lady with her husband in a coma. He'll know who you mean. Of course, if he is too busy to see me in my hour of need, I understand many of his competitors will be happy to give me the time of day.' Cassandra said with exaggerated sweetness.

The girl's mouth made a perfect O. 'Of course, madam. Do take a seat, I will tell him you're here.' She wandered back to a floating desk and glancing back only once, pressed a button and had a hurried conversation into her headset.

'Mr Leibowitz will see you in a moment. And here at REM-COR are all sorry to hear about your husband.' Fake sympathy washed from the girl in waves.

Cassandra sent back a suitably insincere smile in response. 'Thank you so much. You are too kind. But I believe I will go in NOW.' Before the receptionist could stop her, Cassandra had marched down the corridor, pushed open the door to Leibowitz's office and was watching Murray and presumably another young female assistant adjusting themselves.

'Cassandra, honey! What a pleasure to see you,' he gushed while simultaneously ushering the assistant through a side door.

'Murray. I'm sorry, was I interrupting something important?' She asked sweetly proffering a cheek.

'Not at all.' Murray adjusted his tie before kissing her lightly and perching on the edge of his desk. 'Now what do I owe the pleasure of this visit? How is Will, is he… is there news? Take a seat.'

Cassandra settled herself into the leather upholstery. 'I have been thinking…'

'That sounds dangerous.' Murray joked.

Cassandra gave a quick acknowledging smile before continuing. 'As Will's wife, I have been extremely helpful to you.'

'Very co-operative, yes. And I think you will find we have

been more than generous, we have after all provided for all the medical expenses for your husband, and ensured that you have been generously cared for, financially.'

'Indeed, you have. However there are a few additional expenses I have incurred, incidentals and that sort of thing, so I was wondering if I could have an incey wincey advance.'

'Surely you've been well provided for?' He asked guardedly.

'To a point, yes, but there are like I say, a few unforeseen expenses. I wouldn't ask unless I needed it. You said yourself, when this V10 goes on the shelves it is going to be enormous, the cash is just going to come rolling in. Need I remind you that I am the almost widow of the brains of the operation?' She said, smoothing the skirt down on her thigh.

Leibowitz snorted. 'Hmm. One of the brains, my dear, only one of them. How incey wincey are we talking here, and remember I have three ex Mrs Leibowitzs.'

'I was thinking about a million.'

Murray choked. 'Dollars or pounds?'

Cassandra smiled. 'Pounds, of course.'

'Not that it matters. A million! Have you gone out of your freakin' p-brained mind?' He spluttered.

'Not at all. I think it's fitting that I should be compensated, given Will's genius. I would hate for any nasty rumours to upset things, with the launch. Even the slightest rumour that Will's illness is connected to the V10 wouldn't do its sales much good.' She said, with an exaggerated sad face.

'What is it you English say? Wouldn't that be cutting off your pretty little nose to spite your face?' Murray growled.

'Ha, ha, funnily enough, a nose job was on my shopping list.' She said gleefully.

'So just the essentials then?' Murray said bitterly.

Cassandra smiled. 'So we have a deal?'

'It is going to take a helluva long time before you see any more money after an advance like that. For the love of God woman, can't you wait until we go into production?'

Cassandra waved a hand airily. 'I'm sure you haven't forgotten how I helped with your exclusive rights, how I influenced Will, right from the beginning. I'm certain you could put it down as a sundry consultancy fee. No-one needs ever to know.'

'Blackmail is a very nasty business to be in.' Murray said.

'Who said anything about blackmail?' She said innocently. 'I am just protecting my interests, in the same way, that you would protect yours. Need I remind you who persuaded Adam to remove the V10 from Will? Think of it as insurance.'

Murray muttered under his breath. 'Give me some time; I will have to see what I can arrange.'

Satisfied Cassandra got up to leave. 'Don't take too long now. Oh, and by the way,' she said, turning back. 'I'm not happy with the name. The V10, it sounds like something you should be smearing on a rash. I want the name changed to the Daydream Believer. I think it has a better ring to it, don't you? It's more romantic and more exciting?'

Murray was incredulous. 'You do remember that you are merely the wife of one of the inventors? You have no decision making powers. You don't have a say in how it's marketed, what it does, or what its freaking called!'

'I do love my new celebrity status, Murray. It's amazing what media door it opens. When I talk, people listen.' She pointed a finger into his chest.

'Your fifteen minutes of fame?' He snorted. 'As if anyone is going to listen to a ghoul like you!'

'I think they'll listen, Murray. Even Adam listens to me. Remember when the ambulance arrived, who got him to see sense? You should take my advice and keep me on-side.' Cassandra said.

'And how much is this going to cost us for your advice?' He spat.

'Oh think of that one on account. I'm sure you can arrange it, you're a powerful man.' She said.

Leibowitz smiled as a thought struck him. Cassandra looked at him questioningly.

He grinned wider. 'That's what I like about you, Cassie. You always do the right thing.'

'I have no idea what you're getting at Murray. If you're thinking of getting out of paying me the money...' She said suspiciously.

The American held out his arms expansively. 'It is the very least you deserve honey. It's a negotiation. I can't just hand over cash without a little tussle. It's the businessman in me.'

Cassandra crossed her legs. 'So you will give me what I ask for, everything I asked for?'

'How could I refuse?' He said.

'Just like that?' She looked at the American suspiciously.

'You're going to be taking a more active role in the project. All I ask is that you don't distract the hippy too much.'

'Distract the hippy... Adam?' Cassandra said in confusion.

'You're a good looking broad by anyone's standards, and he does like the ladies. I've seen the way he looks at you sometimes...' Murray leant in conspiratorially.

'The way he looks at me?' Cassandra asked uncertainly.

'Yeah, the way he looks at you. You women, you're all coy, play hard to get, I understand. You're a married woman, a classy woman, married to his best friend no less, you're not going to encourage an alley cat like him.'

'He's not interested in me.' Cassandra said uncertainly.

'Sure, he is. Why wouldn't he be, he's got eyes ain't he? I tell you, honey. I've seen guys like him before. They find the dumb ones easier to handle, pretty and dumb. A smart, sophisticated broad scares them. You scare him, but that doesn't mean he don't want you all the same. You're like the forbidden freakin' fruit. I hear it in his voice when he talks about you.'

'You do?' Cassandra felt her stomach flip.

'Sure. So all I'm saying is try to keep the little smucks mind on the job and not on you. Ok sweetheart?' Murray said, patting her hand.

'Ok.' Cassandra got up and began to walk towards the door, slightly bemused. 'You're being very understanding...' she began.

'Of course.' Leibowitz said, moving from the desk to show her out. 'Understanding is my middle name.' He closed the door, narrowly missing a little fluttering shade at Cassandra's shoulder. 'Just like yours is gullible,' he smirked.

CHAPTER 23

Despite her show of confidence and her potential new-found wealth, Cassandra was feeling decidedly low, low and confused. Everyone told her how beautiful she was. She had the perfect figure, the perfect hair, and the headshots she'd had taken were marvellous. The magazine and television people had all said so. But she could see it, what they were really thinking, she was thinking the same, when she looked in the mirror and when she looked into their eyes. There were signs and seeing that… that child today hadn't helped. Cassandra had to face it. She was getting older. She could see little tiny wrinkles beginning around her eyes. She could swear that her jowls were starting to sag. She had to wear underwear to push things up and suck things in and smooth things out. No matter how little she ate or how much she exercised, there were lumps where lumps had never been before. She pulled and prodded at them, but she couldn't make them go away. It was all so unfair. And then there was Adam.

Cassandra remembered the first time she saw him. Murray had arranged for her to be at one of the American's meet and greets as a pretty face to distract the potential money-spinner long enough for him to get a signature on the dotted line. Mostly they were geeky little no-bodies who blushed, stuttered and stammered and talked to her cleavage. Adam had been different. There was something almost animal about him. He oozed self-confidence, it was mesmerising. Unfortunately, though, he hadn't exactly been forthcoming with any inside information, that had to come from his far less magnetic friend. A few fluttered eyelashes, a couple of glasses of wine and Will was eating out of her hand and telling her all about the project. She liked what she heard, and it was too good an opportunity to miss. The downside was by the time she had the full story, Will was wholly besotted, and Adam never gave her another glance.

She took a long gulp from her wine glass and kicked off her high heels. At one time she would have worn them all day and danced in them all night. Now a couple of hours and her feet felt as though she'd been walking over hot coals. It had been an exhausting couple of days. Cassandra leaned back into the sofa and closed her eyes.

~~

'I don't feel right about this.' Will said.

'Again, do you always have to repeat yourself?' Anaya said.

'It feels like spying.' He added.

'She's your wife. How can it possibly be spying?' Anaya replied.

'It's private, the things that go on inside a person's head.' Will said petulantly.

Anaya smiled. 'Sounds like someone has a few guilty secrets of his own?'

'No, no,' he said hurriedly.

'Then go and talk to her.' Anaya began to push the door.

'But what about you, won't there be some kind of explosion if the two of you meet? And what about me, if you're right and that is my hospital room, then I'll be in there and won't that be just...?' he tailed off.

'Only you see me as Cassandra, and there can be more than one of you in her dream, in fact, it happens more often than you'd think, but that's another story. If it makes you feel better, tell her it's an out of body experience.' Anaya said.

'But what if I'm awake in there?' Will said, stalling for time. 'I won't know what to say to myself.'

'You will be you, this you,' she prodded him in the chest, 'but if there is another you in there, then it won't be you will it, because you're you.'

'I think I'm getting a headache.' Will said, rubbing his forehead.

'Your head is fine.' She said, rolling her eyes. 'Just try not to think about it.' She added before pushing him into the room.

The room was not how he imagined. There was no bed, no sheets, and no hospital, full stop! If such a word existed, then this room would have a very dungeonesque décor. Large imposing walls in dark grey surrounded a small cage. Inside the cage curled up, hugging her knees was Cassandra. She was rocking slightly backwards and forwards.

Will was shocked. He opened his mouth to speak, but then he arrived. Not the real Will but a facsimile, a caricature almost. This creature danced and capered manically, ignoring the genuine article entirely. It circled the cage, then like a magician flourishing a bunch of flowers, from behind its back it produced a pair of shoes. As Cassandra grasped for them, the beast threw them into a wood chipper that Will could have sworn wasn't there a moment before. Cassandra howled. That seemed to push dream-Will to an even more frenzied performance. He pulled a string of diamonds from his pocket and dangled them invitingly just out of Cassandra's outstretched hands. The more desperately she grabbed for them, the more he taunted her. For a finale, he leaned over backwards, something which made the real Wills backache just watching, and swallowed the necklace whole as Cassandra screamed. Happy with this result, the creature pranced past its doppelganger.

'Just a minute,' Will began.

His other self seemed to notice him for the first time. 'Buzz off mate,' Dream-Will hissed as he hopped past, 'I'm working here.'

'Now just a minute,' Will was not to be put off, 'I demand that you stop this immediately!' He moved towards the cage.

Cassandra became almost hysterical. 'No… no… not more… please no more…' She wailed, shying away.

'You're upsetting her,' Dream-Will said.

'I'm…. I'M upsetting her!' Will coughed in amazement.

'Yes. Look I don't know who sent you but this ain't your gig so sod off!'

The real Will was genuinely speechless. Here stood the embodiment of everything that Cassandra despised in him, and it was telling him that he was the problem. Confused, he backed out the way he came.

'What happened?' Anaya asked. Will shook his head. 'Hey! What happened? Tell me!'

'I'm torturing her…' Will said tears welling up in his eyes, 'She thinks I torture her.'

'She thinks what? Oh, for goodness sake, I'll look for myself!' Sticking her head around the door, Anaya was silent for a few moments. Suddenly she sighed. 'Oooooooh!'

'What? What's happening now?' Will demanded shaken from his stupor.

'I understand why you're upset, don't look any more.' Anaya said hastily, blocking the space between him and the gap in the door.

'How can it be any worse?' He said in despair.

'It can be, trust me.' She said.

Will pushed her out of the way and pressed his eye to the gap and immediately began to wish he hadn't. The tormentor was now wedged into the cage. Cassandra was free, her blonde hair flowing in an inexplicable wind. She was wrapped around what Will rightly assumed to be the engineer of her escape. In this case, it tuned out to be someone very familiar. Adam, naked to the waist, his blonde dreadlocks blowing dramatically in the same breeze, had his arms around Cassandra. Will went unnoticed as his wife's knees visibly buckled under the weight of his best friend's crushing kiss.

'The bastard!' Will yelled before Anaya's hand arrived to yank him backwards by the scruff of his neck.

'Listen to me!' Anaya said, holding Will tightly by the shoulders. His eyes still watered as her features swam before his eyes.

'Whatever you are seeing, remember this is her dream, not his. He is not part of it. He is not real. He's just an actor playing a part!' Will blinked.

'What's happening to you?' Will said, blinking quickly.

'Me?' Anaya looked unusually confused for a moment before realisation dawned. 'I'm the person you care for most in the world remember. Let's just say you're having a bit of a crisis of faith. Try to stay with me.'

'But you're, you're melting, changing.' Will said, his hand reaching out to touch her face.

Anaya batted it away. 'Trust me. I'm not.'

'Are you ok, did it hurt?' Will asked as the polymorph's form settled.

Where Cassandra's willowy frame had been, but a moment ago, there was now a woman who could kindly be described as dumpy. She wasn't fat, but if she had been six inches taller, it would have helped with the perspective.

Suzie/Anaya pushed the thick glasses up her nose. 'Now try and stay with me,' she said, 'I may look like someone else for a while, but I'm still me. I'm Anaya, say it with me.'

'I'm Anaya.' Will said hypnotically.

'Close enough. Good boy. Now, if I let you go, you're not going to do anything silly, are you?'

'Like what?' Will said, still staring in amazement at the new person standing in front of him. He tried hard to picture her as Cassandra. It just wasn't working.

'I do love a lack of imagination.' She said with a sigh. 'What do you want to do now, should I get rid of him so you can talk to her?'

'You're Suzie,' Will said dreamily, 'you always had such a lovely personality. You were steady and reliable. You never demanded anything.'

'Fantastic! I'm Suzie, I'm ugly, and I have all the charm and sex appeal of a labrador.' Anaya rallied, 'Suzie says do you want to go and talk to Cassandra?'

'I'm sorry I didn't call you Suzie that was a mean thing to do.' Will said dreamily.

'It's all right. I forgive you...' Anaya said hurriedly, 'Now about going back in there...'

'It's not all right. I was terrible to you.' Will cut her off. 'Let me explain.'

'No need.' Anaya began, but he had such a pitiful look on his face she couldn't refuse. 'Oh go on then but make it quick.

Will took her hands in his. 'You see I met someone else, and I didn't know what to say to you,' Will pleaded.

'You someone else, ok, got it. It doesn't matter, now shall we go and talk to your wife, your wife that you love?' Anaya pulled towards the doors, but he held her hands tight.

'I never want to speak to that... that Jezebel again. Now I know what she wants, what she dreams about!'

Inside, Anaya sagged. 'I think we had better go and rethink

things,' she muttered as she dragged the dazed Will away.

Not looking where she was going, halfway along the corridor Anaya crashed into a fluttery shape. 'Careful, you idiot!' They both snapped.

'Anaya!'

'Lily!'

Will blinked. He was rapidly beginning to feel like his brain was too big for his head. The person now standing in front of him could, at its kindest, be described as colourful. Sunbed orange it or rather *she* was dressed in a bright pink velour tracksuit. Barely covering its contents, the top distortedly tried to spell out the word juicy. It may have been down to deliberate under-sizing or something to do with the two enormous gossamer wings protruding from her back. The trousers barely covered the diamante encrusted thong peeking from underneath. Every other inch of spare flesh sported a piece of gold jewellery. Minimal was not in this girl's vocabulary. Manicured fuchsia talons flicked a hair extension from her eyes.

'Oh, my god! Oh my god, oh my god!' She squealed excitedly. 'Hey, girlfriend! Imagine bumping into you here!' Anaya allowed pumped up lips to plant air kisses into each ear.

'Lily! It's been a long time?' Anaya responded less enthusiastically.

'I'm surprised to see you... on the outside?' She leaned in close and whispered theatrically. 'Are you supposed to be, you know, outside?' Large eyes looked Will up and down. 'Who's your friend?' Lily held out a large incredibly sparkly wand and waved it experimentally across Wills bodyline. It crackled. 'Whoa. It's a live one!' The faery said, checking a dial on the handle.

'You're here for Will?' Anaya asked.

'Hell no. I've just been to the gym.'

'You don't look like you've been exercising.' Will said slightly dazed. The faery laughed. 'Exercising! He's a funny one. I haven't been exercising sweetie. I've been harvesting.'

'Harvesting?' Will repeated.

'And you're here because?' Anaya asked.

'I might wonder the same thing about you. Purely business. I've got one I've been working on for months, and she is like about to blow!'

'Is her name Cassandra?' Will wasn't sure whether he was happy or distraught at the prospect. 'You're going to blow her up?'

'Is he all right, you know in the head?' Lily whispered loudly to Anaya.

'He's fine. He's just had a nasty shock that's all.'

'I am here, you know.' Will said.

'So how's business?' Anaya asked, ignoring the human.

'So, so.' Lily looked at her wand coyly. 'OK!' She said suddenly animated as she splayed her fingers in front of her. 'I can't lie to you, girl. It is like amazing. I am getting every quota and beyond. I tell you, it's a gold mine. The more these people get, the more unhappy they like become, it's awesome!'

'What is it you do?' Will asked.

'Oooh isn't he formal, like a queen or something?' Lily gushed.

'Lil here is what you would call a…' Anaya paused. 'What are they calling you guys these days, since the rebrand?'

Lily directed her answer straight to Will. 'I'm a Paranoia faery hun, you must have heard of us?'

Will shook his head. 'Ok, perhaps you haven't.' The faery seemed vaguely put out. 'You know when you get up in the morning, and you feel a bit fat, even though you weigh exactly the same as you did the day before?'

Will shook his head again.

The faery looked to Anaya for support. 'Ok, let's try this,' the morph said, 'You have a vague suspicion that your wife is having an affair?'

Will snorted. 'There is no suspicion about that is there!'

'Right, right. Bad example.' Anaya grimaced. 'What I'm trying to say...'

'Very badly.' Lily interjected.

'Very badly, apparently, is there are some things that touch a nerve, it might even be as simple as an irrational belief that everyone is talking about you?'

'Paranoia?' Will supplied.

'Exactly.' Lily said happily. 'Now he's getting it.'

'Lily is a faery who collects that paranoia.' 'I help it along a little bit. The odd whisper here, pointing out a little flaw there but for the most part, the humans like do it to themselves.'

'That's horrible!' Will gasped.

'Why?' Out of keeping with the rest of her, Lily managed a surprised look which was halfway genuine. 'The way your world is run, these thoughts and feeling are there anyway; all I do is harvest them. You'd be amazed the wattage you can get from a simple pimple. This place alone could be like powered for a month, and it's entirely environmentally friendly.' She finished.

'But you're profiting from peoples misery!' Will said.

'No I'm not, I'm recycling.' Lily said primly.

'And you're here for her?' Anaya indicated the room where Cassandra was presumably still mid clinch. 'I have to say, she didn't look very paranoid a moment ago.' She added with a grimace.

'We have time. It's a recurring dream. The thingy will beep

when she's ready. Anyway, more importantly, girl, what about you? Last time we met you had big plans, how did that work out for you?'

'Long story short. It wasn't great.'

'I heard,' Lily looked thoughtful, 'And the dreamy Mr Hawke took you in, I heard all about that too.' She nudged Anaya with an elbow. 'I kinda thought he'd be coming along to like question me?'

'I kept you out of it, Lil.' Anaya said.

Lily giggled. 'Spoilsport. I was looking forward to being thoroughly interrogated. If I remember rightly, he has a very persuasive manner.'

'He does? I didn't know you knew him, you know, personally?' Anaya looked surprised.

'You don't know a man like that, that's part of the fun, but oh we had a time!' Lily tapped Anaya playfully with the wand, it crackled.

'You and Ceun, I mean Hawke?'

'Ooh seems you're giving off a bit of juice yourself there Anaya. You can't mind, from what I heard you didn't take too kindly to the gentleman's attention?' The faery said innocently.

'He was arresting me.' Anaya replied indignantly.

'Yeah, that's got to put a downer on things... Don't know what you're missing though.' Lily winked a heavily mascara's eye at the morph just as her wand began to beep. 'Anyway looks to me like someone is just about working herself up to an emotional meltdown.'

'What's wrong with her?' Will asked.

The faery took out an electronic notebook and opened it with an unnecessary flourish. 'This one thinks she's got wrinkles, a spare tyre and having got herself into a steamy clinch, has now been rejected because she's imagined herself to be a hag. All in her head, of course, it generally is.' She snapped the book shut. 'Best get on. I have a timetable to keep. Oh Anaya, when you see that dreamy bounty hunter, tell him I'm available for questioning… any time.'

'Will Cassandra be all right?' Will asked ineffectually.

'No time for that trollop now. We have to get out of here.' Anaya grabbed Will roughly by the arm and was dragging him away from the room.

'But… but now that she's alone…Or perhaps your friend could help us?' He said, looking over his shoulder.

'Don't even think about it. You can't trust them. You have faith. You meet someone who you believe is a decent person, and then you find out that they're tonsil wrestling with every alley cat that slinks by in their designer outfits that they just threw on and nearly missed. Who needs them? No, we're better than that.'

'Are we still talking about Cassandra?'

'Of course, we are. Now come on.' Anaya tried to push the double doors at the end of the corridor, but they resisted. They resisted to the extent that they began to open inwards. Will felt his eyes trying to leap out of his head, to his mind, they seemed to have the right idea.

'Back away, very slowly,' Anaya hissed in his ear.

'I'd much prefer the turning around and running like hell option,' Will hissed back.

Porkio cracked his trotters and advanced.

'Can we run yet?' Will asked, desperately.

'When I say go.' They backed along the corridor.

'GO!' Anaya turned and ran towards the doors at the far end. It was a few moments before she realised she was on her own. She turned back to see Will staring hypnotised by the hit pig's sunglasses.

'Will!' She shouted.

'You know when you are trying to run away, but your legs refuse to work? How do you stop that happening because I would really like to know just about now?' He called over his shoulder.

'It's mind over matter. You just have to want to run.' She yelled.

'Believe me, I want to, I really, really want to.' Still Will remained frozen to the spot.

Porkio had produced a knife from the folds of his raincoat. He held the blade under Will's chin and grinned.

Will whimpered.

Anaya tried to move, but she also found her feet frozen.

'Hey, Anaya! You're still here girl.' Lily wandered out of the room. 'I tell you that was some good stuff…'

'Oooh!' Lily waved the wand. 'There is some serious panic going on over here too.'

'It's the pig.' Anaya said out of the corner of her mouth.

'No. I think it's coming from the human. I think that smell is too.'

'Never mind that. Help him!'

'Why?'

Anaya looked at the faery in amazement. 'Why? You're asking me why? Do you not see the large pointy object held at his throat?'

Lily wandered up to Will completely ignoring Porkio. 'Wow, these readings are off the chart. You, my friend…' She said tapping Will with the wand, 'Are under a great deal of stress.'

'You think?' Will squeaked. The faery turned her attention to Porkio. 'You, on the other hand, seem remarkably calm. I would go as far as to say cool and calculating. What's your secret, is it yoga, meditation?'

Porkio now distracted found his eyes involuntarily following the waving of the wand.

'This is good… this is very good,' she said.

'No, I think I can safely say it's quite bad.' Will said, trying not to move.

'Lily! Do something… This human needs to be protected… I'm protecting him for Hawke!'

The faery turned to Anaya, her head on one side. 'You and Hawke working together? Pfffft pull the other one it's got bells on!'

'No, really. It was an accident, but Hawke is in trouble, and I need that human to get him out of it.' Anaya fibbed.

Lily considered this for a moment. Finally, she came to a decision and twiddled with the settings on her wand. 'I just know I am going to regret this.' She muttered. 'But you had better make sure that Hawke knows I helped.'

'I will. I will!' Anaya said.

'Me too.' Will agreed, nodding as much as the blade would allow.

Porkio's attention had now wandered from the faery, that is until she took the wand and smacked him sharply on the end of his snout. He blinked, and the blade dropped a few centimetres. The pig tried to recover, but the lapse was enough, Will took the opportunity and ran.

Lily looked sadly at the wand just as a great trotter came to sweep it away. The faery twitched and narrowly missed the swipe.

'Uh, uh uh!' She said, waving the wand admonishingly. 'That wasn't like very polite. I think you're going to have to pay for that. Let's see how lacking in hang-ups you really are Mr Pig.' She pointed the wand at Porkio and pressed the discharge button. 'You owe me, Anaya, this is going to put me back days. Now get the hell out of here!'

Anaya didn't need telling twice as she dragged Will backwards through the door. There was nothing on the other side. Suddenly they were falling, and Will could have sworn he heard a despairing oink of 'I sometimes think nobody understands the true me.'

CHAPTER 24

It was just occurring to Will that he had run out of scream before he ran out of fall. Even from the highest rise building, there should have been the inevitable splat by now, but they just continued falling. If he was honest, you couldn't even say it was falling. It seemed to Will that he was stationary, just a lot of wind seemed to be going past his head very quickly. He had long since moved through blind panic and was currently experiencing an odd curiosity about the situation. It did not, however, extend to looking down.

'Anaya!' he shouted, trying to get her attention.

'What?' She yelled back.

'I'm just asking, and please don't think I'm being over critical or anything, but was there a plan when you decided to throw us to our doom?' He screamed over the rushing air.

'Plan as in?' She asked.

'As in how we were going to land. Incidentally, if you hit the ground when you're falling in a dream, is it true you die?'

'Does it work that way in your world?' She said.

'Yes!'

'Then I think you have your answer.'

'Oh.' Will didn't feel that was the answer he'd hoped for.

As it happened, there wasn't going to be time to consider the problem any further as the ground was approaching at an alarming rate. Unfortunately, this was the point Will decided to look down. As his final words, Will decided to go for the ear-splitting scream. It was, after all, a classic in an imminent death situation. It started well but was soon nothing more than a muffle as he landed in a cart carrying the universe's largest and, apparently, deepest cargo of hay. There was a faint thump as Anaya landed close by.

Will lay on his back panting heavily. 'That... was... lucky...' He managed.

'Hmm. I very much doubt somehow that luck had much to do with it. Don't you think we are going a little fast?' She responded.

Much to Will's annoyance Anaya seemed entirely unfazed by their adventure. 'I don't... care what... you call it... my organs are... on the inside where... they belong... I am not about... to question... speeding... violations.'

'It might be a case of out of the doorway and into the haystack.' She said, sitting up.

'Frying pan... fire...' He gulped.

'That's just silly.' Anaya murmured. She was trying to stand up and see who was driving, but the rocking of the cart kept knocking her over. 'We could be in big trouble,' she said after her fourth unsuccessful attempt.

'I know this is... inappropriate, but... at the moment... I don't...' Will gasped.

The cart abruptly lurched to a stop sending both passengers spinning into the front board. Before they could untangle themselves, the cart began to tip backwards. Anaya hung on to the side as Will started to slip past with the hay. He grabbed her ankle, and the additional weight was enough to cause her precarious finger hold to fail. They both slid unceremoniously out of the cart, and because they were buried in hay, neither of them saw the cart continue on its journey nor the jolly wave of an arm in a dark robe.

The gates could not merely be described as huge. Huge was

far too small a word. The comparison would be more akin to standing a slightly oversized ant next to an elephant. Will squinted, trying to see the top, but the cloud cover made it impossible.

Anaya was busy picking bits of hay out of her hair. 'I am going to be finding these for weeks.' She complained.

'Look how ornate they are, just look at the workmanship.' He said in awe. 'I wonder what all those symbols mean.' The gates were a mass of pictograms, swirls and markings as if the carvers had not known when to stop. Each story merged into the next, some pictures being used to tell several stories, so much information it made the observer's eyes water.

The gates began to open. 'Where are you going?' Will asked as Anaya was already halfway through. 'How do we know there weren't warnings of impending death up there, like on electricity substations?'

'I would say security would be a bit better, wouldn't you?' She said, looking upwards.

'It could be a trap.' Will said, following cautiously.

'Now he worries! I thought you didn't care. Come on, what's the worst that can happen?' She said, waving him through.

Will already imagined that and worse as he stepped through the gate and followed her into the rain forest beyond.

'What was that?' Will asked in a hushed voice.

'What did it look like?' Anaya looked back.

'On the ground, long, slithery, brown and very snake-like.' Will said, his eyes darting around his feet.

'I'm guessing a snake then,' she said matter of factly. The cicadas chirruped unseen in the surrounding undergrowth as they continued single file along the narrow track.

'Loud, isn't it?' Will said eventually.

'What?' She asked with a grin.

'I said… oh very funny.'

'Oldest joke in the book.' Anaya said, laughing. 'Where's your sense of humour?'

If Will didn't know better, he'd have said she was enjoying this. 'I have trouble keeping it in a snake-infested jungle!'

'I don't think one snake counts as an infestation.' She said as from far above there was a flurry of activity, something dropped into the ferns close by Will's feet. Then another one, and another, and another until it was raining objects. They ran for cover.

'What was all that about!' Will asked, looking back.

'Birds in the canopy I expect. They're not dangerous, just meant to scare us away from their nests.'

'If it's not dangerous, why did you run?'

'I didn't say it didn't hurt! As a tactic it generally works,' she said, simply continuing on the path.

Will caught her up. 'I didn't think you liked the great outdoors?'

'Hmm? Oh, when you can't go outside, you appreciate it when you get the opportunity.'

'From when you were locked up?' He enquired.

'Don't want to talk about it.' She replied in a sing-song voice. 'Oooh, I wonder what's in here.' Anaya had climbed a small outcrop of rocks and was peering into a dark hole. 'It looks like a cave. Let's see.'

'Explain to me why I would want to go into a dark, smelly cave no doubt filled with all manner of creepy crawlies.' Will asked.

'Because otherwise you get left out here alone with the snakes.' She said, her head bobbing out of the hole.

'Fair enough.' He replied scrambling after her as she was already halfway through the hole. Immediately the ammonia smell caught in the back of his throat. He just knew it was going to stink. That wasn't the worst part. Above he could hear rustling, the rustling of lots of pairs of wings settling together. As his eyes adjusted to the gloom, Will dared to look up. High above his head stretching out and filling the whole roof space was a mass of writhing bodies.

'Bats,' he said, trying not to breathe, 'we're in a cave full of bats!'

'Shhh!' She said, holding a finger to her lips.

 'What if they're vampire bats?' He whispered.

'I'm not worried. They only feed on human blood.' She chuckled softly.

'What?' He exclaimed.

'Only kidding.' She nudged him with an elbow and moved on.

Will decided now was a good time to shut up and persuade his body that breathing was optional. The bats moved restlessly but seemed in no hurry to go anywhere, and that suited him fine. Underfoot the ground crunched interspersed with the odd squish where something was very fresh.

'Can we go now?' Will gasped.

'There's something a bit further on. I'm going to have a look. It looks like a chest. It could be treasure.' She said.

It was a large brown chest. 'Open it and have a look.' She said.

'Me?' Will momentarily forgot himself. There was a flurry above and a rain of something unpleasant, but aside from that, the occupants seemed to settle down. 'Me?' He whispered,

'You wanted to come investigating chests in caves. You do it.' Will could just about make out Anaya pointing to him and then the chest, the international symbol for 'you do it.' He responded by pointing back at her and then at the box. Anaya poked him hard in the shoulder and pointed at the box, he could tell without even seeing her face that she was not in the mood to argue. Will reluctantly crouched and felt for a catch. He prayed it would be locked. It wasn't. Cursing whichever idiot had left an unlocked box just lying around for anyone to open, he flicked the catch. Holding his face away in case anything decided to leap, fly or slither out at him, he gingerly opened the lid.

When nothing attacked, Will decided to be bold and peer into the chest. It was too dark to see properly, but there was something nestling in the far corner.

'What is it?' Anaya whispered.

'You want me to stick my hand in there and find out, I suppose.' He asked. He took the lack of response to mean, yes. Carefully, he reached towards the shape. His fingers found something soft. It didn't appear to have a heartbeat or teeth, so he continued with the investigation. To his knowledge, very few creatures outside children's television possess zippers; therefore, he felt confident enough to grasp the thing firmly and pull. 'It's something in a bag.' He said.

'Well take it out then, let's have a look.' She said.

Will pressed his fingers to his lips and pointed towards the entrance. Anaya nodded. About a minute later a wandering gust of wind decided it would be a marvellous wheeze to pop into the cave and have a good blast around. From behind came an ominous creak. They turned to see the lid of the still open chest wobbling dangerously. Will's eyes widened as the realisation dawned. Before he could react, the lid of the chest succumbed and closed with an earsplitting crash. The echo ripped through the whole cave.

There was a moment of immediate quiet after the explosion, and then it began. The air filled with ultrasonic squeals of alarm. Will and Anaya sprinted towards the opening, but they were soon overtaken by a mass of black bodies, thick furry bodies with claws and wings. The animals surrounded them. In a vain attempt to repel the onslaught, they waved their arms frantically. That only served to cause more panic as the bats veered into each other to avoid a flailing limb the smell of fear almost overpowering the guano. At the worst possible moment, Will tripped, sliding forwards through the contents of the floor. Without stopping Anaya grabbed him by the collar and fought her way through to the fresh air. They dived through the entrance and lay still until the deafening sound of wings passed.

'You ok?' Anaya asked poking Will with her foot. He was laying face down with his arms protectively covering his head. 'Will?'

Raising his head cautiously Will looked around. 'OK?' He squeaked, sounding very bat-like himself, 'I've just been on the wrong end of a bat stampede. How do you think I am?'

Anaya moved into a sitting position. 'Bat's do not stampede. But, if some idiot had closed the chest after them, it wouldn't have happened. No bang equals no bats.' Will put his head back under his arms. 'So, what did we get?'

'Mmmmf?'

'In the bag. Where is it?' She asked.

Will dared a look around. 'I must have dropped it,' he said before hiding his head again.

'Well go back in there and get it.'

The astonishment was enough to make him sit up. 'Me? Go back in there? You must be joking!'

'What are you worried about? All the bats are out here now,' She said logically, 'and it's not as though you're going to get any dirtier. Chop chop!'

Will didn't have the energy to argue. His shoulder hunched, he climbed back into the cave and soon returned with the bag. He held it out to the morph.

'You open it,' she said, waving it away. 'It's all covered in stuff.' Sagging even further, Will opened the zip and pulled out what seemed to be an upside-down mesh umbrella.

'What is it?' Anaya asked.

Will shrugged. 'It's going to be no use against the rain. The prongs seem particularly well reinforced.' He opened and closed it a few times to demonstrate.

'So it's useless then?' Anaya said.

Will raised his shoulders again. 'It was important enough for someone to hide.' 'Or throw away.' 'I'll take it. It seems weirdly familiar. I think I should know what it's for. I can't place it.'

~~

Anaya strode on through the undergrowth with Will following behind swinging his brolly in what he hoped was a suitable fashion. Not quite paying attention, he barrelled into the back of a now stationery Anaya.

'Any ideas?' She said indicating the three paths ahead.

'You haven't watched many films, have you?' He responded as Anaya gave him a long stare.

'No, I thought not. Well, in the film, the right and the left paths normally lead to a safe place. The straight-ahead path is generally the quickest but also the most dangerous. That's the one people take, and that is when they usually die horribly.'

'Straight ahead it is then.' She said.

'Whoa! You did hear what I said about it being the most dangerous?' He said, grabbing her arm.

'Have you forgotten? There seems to be a multitude of people trying to capture you. We have no idea where we are, Ceun is missing, and you have your little doo dangle there. How much worse can it get?' She responded.

'Um...'

'Good. You can go first,' Anaya said, pushing him ahead.

The track seemed deceptively quiet. Still, Will managed to jump at even the slightest noise.

'I do wish you would calm down,' Anaya said from the rear.

Will mouthed her words parrot-fashion, confident that she couldn't see what he was doing. It was eerie. There was hardly any noise at all. Even the cicadas had given up. He felt uncomfortable as all the hairs on the back of his neck stood to attention. He could feel his eyes trying to swivel in opposite directions to increase his field of vision. The mesh umbrella weighed heavily in his hand. He gave it a perfunctory swing to show he meant business. He just wasn't sure what that business was meant to be.

High above in the trees, two pairs of beady black eyes were watching the couple's progress. The silver swishing fascinated them as it glinted in the mottled sunlight. The animals moved silently from tree to tree, barely raising a leaf movement as they tracked the intruders barging through their forest. Will stopped suddenly. The creatures stopped too, barely twitching a hair.

'What's the matter now?' Anaya asked.

'Stupid thing is caught in this creeper. Give me a minute it's almost free.' He yanked the umbrella just as Anaya was bending to untangle the thing. Will opened his mouth to yell as the mesh sprung upwards at the same moment the bears decided to take a much closer look.

Spreading its arms so that the flaps of skin allowed it to glide, the first bear sailed through the air towards Will. It collided with the now fully unfurled mesh with an unmistakable 'oof!' The speed of descent caused the brolly to act as a deflecting trampoline onto which drop bear bounced and was immediately catapulted sideways into the ferns. The bear's mate launched herself a second later from a different tree. She was repelled not only by the mesh, but also the momentum of Will turning suddenly to try and see what had hit him the first time. The she-bear was bounced sideways and landing on the track where she rolled to a stunned halt at Anaya's feet.

The creature immediately righted itself onto four stumpy green/grey legs. To all intent and purpose, the small bear would have passed for a koala, if the koalas had a commando division. It looked small and sweet if you discounted the ferocious claws and the teeth which it now bared in Will's direction. Her pitch-black eyes darted back and forth, searching for a means of escape, or the best method of attack, Will couldn't be sure. With her back to Anaya and a bit shaken, the bear wasn't aware the morph was standing right behind her. She growled menacingly, but before she could make good her threat, she'd been scooped up in the brolly bag, and the zip had been snapped firmly shut. Anaya held the bag at arm's length as the bear struggled and mewled.

'At least we know what your little doo dab is for now,' She said. 'There is just one thing though, what happened to the other one?' They both inched around until they were standing back to back under the safety of the mesh. Upon scanning the foliage, there was no sign of the bear's partner.

'I think it landed over there.' Will said quietly pointing to a gap in the vegetation, which did look at though it had recently received a missile. They shuffled a little closer to the spot but could see nothing. 'Perhaps it hurt itself in the fall?' Will whispered hopefully.

'Judging by the speed and precision these things applied, I would think hurling themselves out of trees is a fairly routine occurrence. That involves some form of landing or, in this case, crashing. It will be around here somewhere.'

A small movement caught Anaya's eye. About halfway up a

tree, she thought she caught sight of something. She squinted. The paws gripping the tree, easily blended in with the bark. However, the round fluffy face peering around the trunk was definitely not vegetable.

'There!' She said out of the corner of her mouth. Will followed the direction of her nod. The bear was staring at them but seemed to be more curious rather than aggressive. Realising he was spotted, he moved around for better concealment.

'This all seems so familiar.' Will mused.

Anaya glared at him. 'Go on.'

'Adam told me about these stories when he was in Australia. The locals would tease tourists about being on their guard for the drop bears when they were out walking. It was a kind of joke.'

'Adam? The one that your wife was, um, thinking about?' Anaya asked innocently.

Wills's eyes narrowed. 'Yes that one,' he said through gritted teeth, 'and now we are experiencing them first hand.'

'So how do we get rid of them?'

'How should I know? They don't exist except in stories.' Will said with a shrug.

The male drop bear seemed perfectly content to stay in his tree. He clung to the trunk and peeped out at them periodically. By now, even the captured bear had calmed down.

Anaya sniffed. 'I think our friend may have had a little accident, mind you, so would I if someone shoved me into a bag.' She held the bag further away. 'So, here's the plan, these things bounce, right?'

Will nodded. 'Yes.'

'And they do seem attached to each other, or the other one would have run off?' She added.

'That would seem to be the case.' Will agreed.

Anaya held the zip and began to swing the bag.

'But...' Will began.

'No buts... run!' Anaya pulled the zip and at the same time hurled the bag as far away from them as possible.

Anaya and Will took off at full speed in different directions, zig-zagging on the theory that if the male attacked, it would be harder to hit a moving target. Will planned to make it very hard indeed. Without looking back, they crashed on, straight through the curtain of vines now blocking the path. Will skidded to a halt in front of a large glowing sign which looked completely out of place. 'Level Two'.

CHAPTER 25

'Excellent!'

The wolf's ears stood to attention. Praise was the thing he loved most in the world. 'Get man,' he said happily, his tail wagging so hard it was in danger of falling off.

'So it appears. Just one thing, why isn't it moving?' A foot nudged the sack gingerly.

'Stairs.' The wolf said with a grin from ear to ear.

'Stairs?'

'Take sack upstairs, and head go bong, bong, bong, bong, bong, bong, bong, bong, bong, bong, bong, bong, bo...' He added with a hairy claw bouncing on each bong.

'Yes, I think we get the idea. Let's hope that it didn't go bong once too often.' The voice said wryly.

'Now man sleep but still breathe. I hear.'

'Good. Now let's have a look at him.' A hairy hand grabbed the top of the sack and pulled it upwards with a flourish. It was a few minutes before his tail stopped wagging once he noticed the fury on his mistress's face. 'What,' she spat, barely able to speak, 'or rather *who* is this?'

TBB looked into the bounty hunter's unconscious face. 'Is not man,' he said miserably. 'Is another man.'

'Is it? Well, thank goodness I have you to solve these terrible mysteries for me. You idiot, you captured the wrong one!' She wailed.

'Was dark.' The wolf murmured wishing that he could run and

hide. 'Was big lizard too.'

'Was big lizard too!' She mimicked, 'that explains everything if there was a big lizard too! Why do I keep you? Explain it to me? You'd be of more use to me as a rug.' The wolf cowered. 'Get out!' she screamed. 'No, don't take him with you, just leave him and get out of my sight!' The Big Bad Wolf slunk out. After he'd gone, she looked at the bounty hunter for a long time. 'There must be a way I can use this to my advantage.' She thought.

~~

The room was in darkness by the time Ceun eventually woke up. He blinked, but it didn't seem to help. A smell of acrid smoke hit his nostrils. He coughed, making the egg-sized lump on the back of his head throb.

'Nice of you to join us, Mr Hawke.' A voice chuckled. 'Please don't get up.'

Ceun realised the joke was his wrists were bound to the chair. From his point of view, it wasn't particularly funny. He tried to rise anyway, but it was impossible. Somewhere behind him, there was a low growl.

He slumped back into the chair. 'I suppose it is too much to ask that you are going to tell me who you are, what you are doing, that you have now seen the error of your ways, and you're going to let me go?' Now that his eyes were adjusting to the dark, Ceun could just about make out the shape of a large swivel chair. It seemed to contain the voice.

'Oh, yes, that's what is going to happen. How did you guess?' Ceun waited. 'Bu...' started a second voice behind him which was immediately silenced by the sound of something landing with a thump. 'I was being sarcastic!' The chair snapped.

'I did get that.' Ceun cheerfully said as he tried to reach the knots.

'I am not a patient person Mr Hawke so please don't try to be clever with me.'

'I wouldn't dream of it.' He replied.

'Do you have any idea why you are in your current… predicament?' The voice asked.

'Nope.'

'Come now, Mr Hawke. I did advise you not to play games.' The voice admonished.

'You advised me not to be clever, and I am not clever at all. If I were, then I would know why you smacked me over the head and brought me here. You should make your mind up.'

'Not smacked, bon…' came the voice from the rear but was immediately silenced.

'Don't make me throw the other shoe!' Ceun could have sworn he heard a whimper.

'Let me make it simple for you then Mr Stupid. I want the inventor.'

Ceun thought about this for a moment. 'The question would then be, why am I sitting here instead of him.'

The chair hesitated. 'That was… unfortunate. He was spirited away before I could take possession as it were. Really, it is your own fault that you are here. All those unnecessary heroics.'

'I'm very sorry to have inconvenienced you,' Ceun said. 'You only had to ask, and I could have delivered. After all, he's a valuable commodity. I would have been prepared to negotiate. What did you want him for?'

'Don't take me for a fool bounty hunter. We both know you have long since given up caring about just the money. I know, for example, that this is not an official assignment. You also seem to have developed some silly ideas about making a difference. We only need to look at the polymorph.'

'What about her?' Ceun's voice was cool.

'Ah, I seem to have struck a nerve. Yes, I know about her too. I know you tried to save her, do you honestly think she's changed, that you can trust her?' A hollow laugh trickled from the chair. 'Considering your chosen occupation bounty hunter, you can be incredibly naive.' 'So enlighten me.' Ceun said.

'Don't you think it was a little odd that she was released into your care? And for what, why?'

'She was needed.' Ceun said.

'She was? Honestly? Out of all the morphs in Morpheus, the only one that could help was a notorious vicious felon. Perhaps it had more to do with getting you on board, a little reward for your services, hmm?' The chair goaded.

'You don't know what you're talking about.' Ceun said feigning disinterest.

'Not to mention, you are the method of her release. Oh, it's just too perfect, the power, what were you expecting, that she'd be grateful?' The voice mocked.

Ceun scrabbled furiously with the knot. He wanted to get his hands on this creature.

'I'll enlighten you, Mr Hawke. Someone is controlling her and through her is controlling you. The question you are asking yourself is whether she's in on the game.'

Ceun refused to be drawn any further. Instead, he focussed his attention on the rope.

The wheedling voice continued. 'What if our little Anaya isn't feeling all rescued. She may have had different allegiances all along.'

'I suppose you're going to tell me she's working for you?' Ceun's fingers slipped on the rope. 'If that were true, and it's a big if, why would I be here? She would have just delivered the inventor to you, and that would be it.'

'Perhaps our little jailbird was enjoying her freedom a little too much and forgot her loyalties.'

'Or perhaps you were wrong about her.' Ceun couldn't keep the smugness out of his voice.

'I am an excellent judge of character.' The tone was offended now. 'I just think that perhaps... she needs to realise playtime is over.'

'Your agent has gone off the rails, and you want me to rein her in? I think you may be barking up the wrong tree.'

'I will catch up with them sooner or later.'

He could tell the voice was getting annoyed, and that suited him fine. 'Then you don't need me.'

'Need you? No. But it would make my life so much easier. Much as I hate to say it, you are the best there is, and I would like to protect my investment. You bring the inventor to me, and you will be well paid.' The voice explained.

Ceun scoffed. 'You said yourself, I'm not interested in money and don't give me that 'everyone has their price' stuff because I don't.'

The chair chuckled. 'Ah but you do my dear Mr Hawke. There are more forms of remuneration than mere money. I know that while you may not care for your safety, and you may only marginally care for the inventor. But when they are eventually caught, and they will be caught, what if anything were to happen to the polymorph... hmm, I wonder. The only difference being if you bring them to me, then you will be paid when I don't take my frustrations out on the girl.'

Ceun said nothing; he was thinking.

'I meant the morphs life would be the payment.' The voice added as if needing to clarify the point. 'As in, I won't kill her.'

'I understood what you meant.' Ceun said.

'Do we have a deal, Mr Hawke?'

'Do I have a choice.' Ceun asked.

'Indeed, do as I say she lives, refuse, and she dies.'

'How do I know you're not bluffing.' Ceun asked.

'Can you afford to gamble with her life?' The voice asked reasonably.

Ceun considered, 'Ok.'

'Excellent.' There was the sound of hands clapping. 'Oh, and just in case you change your mind, I have set up a little insurance policy.'

Ceun lifted his head. 'What insurance?'

'You'll see. You have three days before the brains hit the fan. I will be watching.' Ceun would have asked more questions, but something substantial made contact with the already painful lump on his head. Once again, everything went black.

CHAPTER 26

The red earth stretched out in front of them as far as the eye could see. And it was hot. Not a pleasant, sitting by a pool with a nice cold drink, but the retina scorching kind that prickled on the skin as the rays tried to bore through the bone.

'It's a game!' Will said excitedly, 'I knew it seemed to be familiar. Adam was working on it. He asked me an odd question or two, but I said I didn't want to see it until he was finished.'

'There's nothing here,' Anaya said watching the shimmers on the sand.

'Don't you understand? This is Adam's game. He dreamed it up, literally.'

'So he is likely to be here somewhere?' She said, looking around.

'Probably, and I want a word or two with him!'

Anaya sighed. 'You still don't get it, do you? It wasn't him. He can't be responsible for your wife's fantasies.'

'He must have done something to encourage them!' He said doggedly.

She sighed in a way so like the real Suzie that Will stared at her in amazement. 'Let's try this again. Your friend is not responsible for your wife's dreams. Your wife is not responsible for her dreams. That is entirely the point. It is your funny little human subconscious. You should not be able to control them.'

To Will, Suzie's light brown eyes bulged over slightly chubby red cheeks. 'But more importantly,' she continued, 'if we can find your friend, then we have our link with Realitas... you could go home?'

'Ok, ok, there is that.' He conceded eventually. 'But where is everyone?'

'Morpheus is a big place, infinite you could say. There might not be another person for a thousand miles.' Anaya said.

Will inspected the sign. At the bottom hung a whistle next to a small neatly printed notice with the words 'Please call for assistance'. He picked it up. 'There is this?'

Anaya read the sign, then looking around she shrugged. 'We are in the middle of nowhere getting sunstroke and heat exhaustion, plus we have no idea where we are supposed to be going. I would say that qualifies as needing assistance.'

Will wiped the end of the whistle on his shirt, lifted it to his lips and gave a good hard blow. There was no sound. '

Try again.' Anaya urged.

He tried again, and a third time, by now Will's cheeks ached purple with the effort. 'It doesn't work,' he said eventually.

'Keep ya hair on mates. I was coming as quick as I could!'

Anaya and Will jumped. Where there had previously been miles of nothing but sand now a sizeable red kangaroo was standing in front of a rickshaw.

'Howayagoing?' The kangaroo said amiably.

'Sorry. We didn't think it was working,' said Anaya as Will walked around the rickshaw scratching his head.

'No worries.' The kangaroo winked at her. 'I normally work nights, but you know how it is when you have a Joey on the way.' It winked again. 'Hey, what's blue doing back there?' The kangaroo craned its neck to look at Will.

'I was just looking at your cart.' Will said hurrying to the front.

'Bonza, isn't it?' The kangaroo said, patting the shaft fondly.

'The wheels are a little...unusual.' Will mused.

'Really, how?' The roo twisted itself around to try and see. It seemed genuinely curious.

'Shouldn't they be round?' Will asked.

The animal considered this for a moment. 'Na mate. That wouldn't work.'

Will still wanted to push the point. 'But they are oval?'

'Yes, I know.' The kangaroo seemed satisfied that it had answered all questions. 'So, you getting in or what?'

'But it's...' Will began.

'Yes, we are getting in.' Anaya pushed Will into the rickshaw and climbed in after him.

'Off we go!' They hastily sat as the kangaroo set off at a surprising pace. Each leap coincided perfectly with the higher point of the oval, each descent in precision with the lower, altogether this resulted in an unlikely but remarkably smooth ride.

'This shouldn't work, you know.' Will shouted over the creaking.

'I'm not sure he knows that. So let's not enlighten him just in case it stops working, huh?' Anaya gripped his knee tightly to reinforce the point. All of a sudden, the kangaroo stopped. There was no slowing down, no skidding, one moment they were speeding along and the next they were stationery.

'You fellas in some trouble?' The roo called over his shoulder.

'Of course not,' Anaya called back.

'You're sure?'

'Quite sure,' Will said, a little too high pitched.

'So the large column of blokes on the horizon dressed as guards would have nothing to do with you?' The Roo asked.

Anaya stood in the cart squinting ahead. 'Perhaps they might have a little bit to do with us,' she conceded.

'There's nowhere to hide. There's nowhere at all to hide!' said Will.

'Don't panic. I'm sure we'll think of something, with the aid of our new friend here.' Anaya said, hopefully.

The kangaroo considered this for a moment. 'I don't want any trouble. The missus would kill me,' he said eventually. He considered it a little more. 'On the other paw, she'd kill me if I get another speeding ticket, I come home late, or I breathe too loud. Her hormones are all over the place at the moment. Oh to heck with it, I'm in. What do you need?'

'We need to get out of here,' Anaya said urgently. She could see the dark mass getting closer.

'No worries.' The kangaroo turned to the right and was off again at top speed. Will and Anaya hung onto the sides of the cart as they rocketed along.

'They're gaining on us,' Will said straining to look behind. Indeed the column had wheeled left and was following.

'Let's see them rozzas catch this.' The kangaroo shouted. He lowered his head and redoubled his efforts. The cart began to rock to the point that Will wondered if it could take the strain as they were engulfed in a cloud of dust. It was impossible to see anything, they just had to hope the guards couldn't see them either. Suddenly the rickshaw stopped. Simultaneously, the kangaroo ducked pushing down the handles. Anaya and Will catapulted into the air and sailing over the trees, landed with a thump in the sand beyond. Spitting sand out of his mouth Will surveyed the scene. In front of them, surrounded by trees was the most perfect pool of clear water. The sun shone from it as if it was crystal glass. Anaya was already on her feet. The pure white sand under her feet crunched like icing sugar.

'Oh.' Will whistled through his teeth. 'It's beautiful.'

'What's the use of beautiful, we can't exactly hide here can we?'

'I can't understand how this can't move you. It's amazing. It's... it's heaven!' Will said, awestruck.

'I wouldn't be so keen to get to heaven if I were you. I'm going to have a look around. Don't go away and try not to draw attention to yourself!' She said.

The sun was unimaginably hot. Will had retreated to the shade of the trees. Anaya must have stalked the shoreline at least five times. She stood now staring out into the desert. 'They're coming.' She hissed. 'All around us is nothing but desert. If we try to run, they will spot us from miles away.' She chewed her lip thoughtfully. 'There isn't even anything we can use as weapons. The wood is too brittle. There aren't even any rocks. I could always bury you in the sand?' She said. Will looked doubtful. 'Do you have any better ideas?' She snapped.

'We could hide up in the trees?' Will said, squinting upwards

'Thought of that. They're not strong enough. Can't even duck under the water it's too clear, they'd see us. I can't think of anything else.' Anaya began to dig. The soft sand fell back into the hole as fast as she was removing it. 'You could help!' The morph snapped.

Will began to scoop sand. It was so dry after a few minutes frantic digging it was as though they hadn't started. 'It's hopeless.' Anaya moaned, collapsing back onto her haunches. Restlessly she got up and looked out towards the approaching soldiers. 'They're gone!' 'Gone?' Will said, shading his eyes and staring out into the sand.

Anaya scanned the horizon. 'They must have gone straight past. I don't understand.' She flopped down onto the sand next to Will. Now that the immediate danger had passed Anaya had to admit it was idyllic. Of course it would be better if they weren't miles from anywhere, and of course, Ceun still hadn't turned up. She picked up a stick and began to stab at the sand.

'Penny for them?' Will asked.

'What?'

'You're worried about him, aren't you?' Will said gently.

'Who? No, of course not. I told you he's a big boy. He'll be fine.' She said, tossing the stick aside.

'You thought he'd have found us by now.' Will said.

'Don't imagine you know what I'm thinking.' Anaya said sharply. 'He always comes up smelling of roses whatever he happens to fall in. I just think it's pretty poor that he's just left me to deal with everything.'

'You don't believe he'd do that, and you seem to know each other pretty well.' Will said.

'He doesn't know me. He's a pretty open book. Always doing the right thing, it makes you sick.' Anaya muttered.

'Is that what he did before? The right thing?'

Anaya glared. 'Nice try, but I told you. Not going to talk about it now, or ever. Got that?'

'But you've known him for a while? There's history.' Will persisted.

'Hell's bells, what's with all the questions? I have known him for a while, ok? We have a history, now leave it alone.'

'But you're close, friends, maybe more than friends?'

She stood up. 'I'm going for a swim, it's too hot,' she said before striding off towards the lake.

Standing with her back to him, Anaya blinked back the tears threatening to well up in her eyes. 'Stupid.' She scolded herself. 'Stupid, stupid, stupid.' The water was so clear and inviting. 'A nice cool swim will get everything back into perspective.' Stretching, she prepared to dive low. Her knees bent, she pushed forwards, left the bank and skidded to a halt in a mound of sand. She sat up coughing.

Will ran over to her. 'Are you all right?'

'Apart from a lung full of hot sand, I'm fine. What happened?' She said, wiping her face.

'I'm not sure. You were about to dive into the water and then you kind of... missed.' He said with an apologetic laugh.

Anaya looked at him doubtfully. 'Explain how I could miss an enormous great pool of water right in front of me.'

'Look at the facts. A large pool of water over there, swimmer lying in a furrow of sand over here. You missed.'

The morph got to her feet and brushed herself down decisively. Pushing Will out of the way she headed to the water's edge. Bracing herself, she jumped and landed up to her ankles in the sand. Will could not believe his eyes, mainly because his eyes had not registered there was anything unusual they should be paying attention to. The water hadn't moved. He was certain of it because he would have seen it. It was just never there.

'That's weird.' He spluttered after a few seconds. Anaya nodded leaping sideways into the now innocent-looking pool. As she landed the lake immediately wasn't there. After a few more exploratory jumps, Will began to feel as though his eyeballs were trying to turn themselves inside out. 'Stop doing that!' he shouted. Anaya stood by the shoreline her hands on her hips.

'I think what we have here is a mirage. That would explain why the guards disappeared. I don't think they were gone, we were.'

'Great.' Will said, flopping onto the sand. 'So we are left in the burning sun with a terrible thirst and a wonderful cool looking lake which we can't catch. The guards couldn't have tortured us any more than that.'

'Don't take this out on me!' Anaya said crossly. 'I'm beginning to think you weren't as nice to Suzy as you should have been!'

Will had the good grace to look slightly embarrassed.

'Listen.' Anaya said. 'I'm sorry, I shouldn't have said that. I'm still Anaya, remember that.'

Will nodded. 'So, how do we get out of here and find Ceun?'

'I'm not sure.'

'That doesn't sound like much of a plan.' Will said.

'It gets worse. If this is a mirage, it should be impossible to get in, so imagine how easy it is going to be to get out again.'

CHAPTER 27

With a grunt, T.B.B. heaved the dead weight from one shoulder to the other. 'Take this here, take this there, always take this, do this, don't this. I The Big Bad. I the one to tell what should be done...' He muttered to himself. The sack over his shoulder began to wriggle. Stomping over towards a tree, the wolf smacked what he presumed to be the head end against the trunk. The wriggling stopped. 'Mmm.' The wolf grumbled. 'Me smart, me know how things get done. Others no play fair, not my fault.' The muttering and moaning began to fade as the wolf trudged off into the night with his burden.

~~

No matter how many times they tried, the lake managed to outsmart them. They both tried jumping together in different directions. Then Will would leap up only to have Anaya jump past to where the pool should have been. There were attempts with eyes closed, half-closed, they jumped backwards and sideways. They tried one jumping and the other sidling in when they hoped the water wasn't looking, all a complete failure. Flopping on the sand Anaya glared at the water. If possible, it tried to give the appearance of complete innocence.

'What about...' Will began.

'No, we already tried that one.'

He sat down heavily next to the morph. 'You don't know what I was going to say.' He turned his head to one side and banged his upper ear a few times.

'I could throw you in?' Anaya said, brightening. 'That's how we got in here?'

Will looked sceptical. Suzie might well be built for brute strength, but Will didn't fancy being on the receiving end of it. 'It's hopeless. The thing is mocking us,' he said.

'Wait, I have an idea.' Anaya was on her feet. Will lay back in the sand, folded his arms and closed his eyes.

'I am not letting you try to throw me in,' he said firmly.

Anaya crouched next to him. 'Perhaps that's the point? If you didn't want to go into the water, you would? That may be the key?' She had been whispering.

Will opened an eye. 'Perhaps someone has been out in the sun too long.' He closed his eye again.

'No.' She hissed urgently tugging his shirt. 'It would make a warped kind of sense. We are here… hot… thirsty…'

Will groaned. 'You had to mention thirsty. I was trying very hard not to think about thirsty.'

'Shhh! I meant it would be very difficult not to want to go into the water. I bet that's the secret. That's our way out.' She glanced suspiciously at the pool. The shoreline seemed to have crept closer as though it was straining to listen.

'To not want to go into the cool lush water?' Will would have drooled had his mouth not been so dry. 'Sounds sick and twisted. You could well be right.'

'What are you waiting for?' Anaya prodded his arm.

'Oh yes, me right, of course.' Will reluctantly got to his feet. 'I don't want to go into that pool. I don't want to dip my feet in that water that looks so cool and inviting. No, I absolutely do want to paddle in the sand.' Closing his eyes, he approached the lake. After a good few minutes walking and still dry toes, it was apparent the lake was on to them.

~~

The wolf grumbled in the sudden heat of the day. He seemed to have been walking for hours and minutes all at the same time. This alone would have confused a creature with more capacity for thought; however, in his case, it just meant he panted more enthusiastically. The burden was laid on the dusty earth. The wolf sat next to it and idly scratched an ear with his back foot. He waited.

~~

'That didn't work.' Will said, collapsing back onto the sand.

'You weren't very convincing!' Anaya said accusingly.

'I wasn't convincing because I do want to go into the water, I know that, you know that, even the bloody lake knows that. I want to go in there more than anything else in the world. I want to swim and cool down. I want to drink until my stomach explodes!' He exclaimed, his arms flailing wildly.

Anaya kicked him. 'Try another tack. Imagine that the water isn't cool and lovely. It's warm, and it's stagnant. It has crocodiles and floating things of dubious origin. It's foul and smells disgusting. You're supposed to be an inventor, invent that image.'

Will nodded, trying to get the picture into his head. Anaya grabbed his collar and began dragging him backwards towards the pool.

~~

T.B.B. pricked up his ears. It was coming. There is something about an animal's ability to sense the unseen. They know when a storm is brewing, an earthquake is coming or a biscuit tin is about to be opened. They also know that when something technically isn't there. There's the adage. You shouldn't believe everything you can't see. Lifting his nose, the wolf inhaled deeply, followed by three short sniffs. Dragging the bundle left for four paces, he looked to the left and the right then sniffed again. Satisfied, he turned and padded away. Around the sack, a small storm of sand appeared to cover it from view, and then it was no longer there.

~~

'I'm going to throw you in with the crocodile. The murderous reptile with large pointed teeth!' Anaya shouted. 'Your nose is going to be filled with rank mud. You'll be choking on rotting leaves.'

Will tried to keep the swamp image in his head, but the image of floating on his back in the fresh, clear water kept appearing in his head. He began to choke from the shirt being pulled up under his chin. His hands grasped at the material as he tried to shout and more importantly breathe.

'You're going to be ripped limb from limb. There is nothing that you can do. I'm going to throw you into that fetid pool, and you are going to sink in slime!' They were almost at the water's edge. 'Errrgh! It's disgusting. Can you smell that, the stench of death, it's in your nostrils, it's...? Mmmmmfw!' The grip was suddenly released from Will's collar. Ceun had appeared from nowhere. He was still groggy, but seeing the struggling Will and the shouted threats and fearing the worst, his instincts took over. Throwing himself at the polymorph, she let go of her victim. Bounty hunter and morph were propelled forwards by sheer momentum. Surprising both themselves and the lake they landed in the water with a satisfying plop and promptly disappeared.

CHAPTER 28

With a 'whoomph' two soaking wet people landed heavily on the sand.

'Ow!' Anaya croaked. 'What the actual hell?' She tried to move, no mean feat with an enraged bounty hunter pinning her to the ground. 'You decided to put in an appearance then, where have you been?'

'Just as well given what you were trying to do!' Ceun growled.

'What the hell are you talking about? Get off me, you idiot!'

Ceun refused to move. He leaned closer, their noses almost touching. 'I had a very interesting little chat with someone who seems to know you very well. I didn't believe it until I saw it with my own eyes.'

'Again, very cryptic,' she said evenly as a drip landed on her nose.

Ceun's face was a mask of fury. 'I didn't want to believe it. In fact, after I was told about your involvement, I tried to convince myself it was a mistake. But after what I've just seen I think that's all the proof I need, don't you?'

'You're dripping on me.' Anaya said, blinking as another drop landed close to her eye.

'Is that all you can say!' Ceun exploded. 'Your loyalties have been exposed. Your lies and deceit not to mention murderous intent and you're worried about a few drops of water. I should have told them where to stick it when they wanted to saddle me with you!'

'I beg your pardon! While you've been off on your little sabbatical, I have managed to keep the inventor safe. Without me, he'd have been captured by a whole army of guards, a whole army, and I managed to get us here…' Anaya trailed off becoming aware of her surroundings for the first time. 'Speaking of which, what happened to here?'

'Don't try to distract me. I know you're in on it.' Anaya's head flopped back into the sand.

'You do realise you are surprisingly heavy?' she said. Ceun unconsciously moved so that he was supporting most of his own weight, but he wasn't letting her go. 'Thank you,' she said, 'now would you like to start from the beginning? Who have you been talking to?'

'I was hoping you could tell me that.' The morph rolled her eyes. 'You're making even less sense than normal. Did you hit your head as you were assaulting me?'

'You're working for more than one master then?' Ceun sneered.

'I'm not working for anyone!' Anaya shouted in frustration. Ceun sat up, taking care not to give her too much space to escape. 'We hid in the mirage. The damned lake kept moving. We decided if we didn't want to go into the water, then we might be able to find a way out. That's what I was doing before you came charging in.' She glanced to the side again. 'It appears to have worked. Apart from the fact that now the little human is nowhere to be seen!'

Ceun still glared at her. Eventually, curiosity got the better of him. Wary that this might be a trick he carefully looked around. They were on a beach but not the white crystal sand of the mirage. This sand was golden and contrasted beautifully with the brilliantly blue ocean. A couple was walking cautiously towards them along the shore. Ceun scrambled to his feet. Instinctively he held out his hand to help the morph. She ignored it. The man stopped short of them, his companion a few feet behind.

'Cool appearance, man,' he said amenably. 'You just appeared from out of the sky!' The newcomer stared at Anaya, then back to his companion, then at Anaya again. 'Twins, cool!'

Ceun had the decency to hide an involuntary smile by glancing at his feet. As a result, he didn't see the slap coming. Anaya caught him hard across the side of the face. Ceun, recovering his balance, looked at her questioningly. 'That's for thinking I was betraying you, for leaving me to deal with it all on my own and for what you are just thinking,' she said accusingly taking another swing.

This time Ceun was ready for it and caught her wrist. 'You only get one free shot.' He warned.

'Identical twins!' The man was oblivious, too busy staring between Anaya and his companion. The latter now had folded her arms with an expression of venom on her face.

~~

It had taken Will a few moments for the realisation of his situation to sink in. One second he was being dragged backwards trying, quite unsuccessfully he thought, to imagine unknown terrors in the water, and to avoid blacking out. The next, he felt as though he had been hit by a train. The attack had been entirely unexpected, the force and speed terrifying. In an instant, the hands that had been pulling him towards the water had been ripped away, and Will had been propelled roughly face-first once more into the sand. Once he had righted himself and dusted the sand from his eyes, Will realised that he was now completely alone. He could have sworn that he heard a splash just after the assault, but no matter how many times he scanned the water, there was not even a ripple to confirm that his hearing was accurate. The terror of recent events, together with this sudden abandonment seemed to allow something to snap in Will's overheated brain. His head clicked worryingly to the left. His right eye began to twitch furiously. He began to yell. No particular rhyme or reason was attached to the rant that poured forth. He just let go of as many vowels and consonants as he could think of. The yelling, although satisfying, didn't quite allow him to fully release the stress and frustration threatening to make him explode. He added a kind of dance to the performance. Turning in angry dusty circles, he stomped in a circle, as if putting out an imaginary ring of fire, his arms outstretched and beating up and down. Eventually, he began to tire, his throat aching with the effort. Expelling one final sob, he crumpled to the ground and looked around him. This oasis, once so beautiful and inviting, now seemed cruel and full of unknown dangers. He distractedly wondered at the wisdom of having drawn so much attention to himself, and then decided he didn't care. Curling up, he held his knees close to himself. What unimaginable shapes could be lurking in the trees? As he listened, his ears strained for any other sounds, his skin recoiling when he imagined unseen lips whispering threats.

Clouds had gathered, taking the shine from the scene and bathing it in an eerie half-light. Sitting out in the open seemed the worst position to be in, considering this, Will moved to an area where he felt he could at least have an advantage against any threats. His back firmly against a tree trunk he scanned the horizon for any sign of life. Concentrating as he was, there was a heart-stopping moment when he thought he felt the tree trunk move. His imagination was getting the better of him. The knowledge didn't help. There was no way of knowing what had happened or worse still what was likely to happen. He was in a world made of dreams, so perhaps his desperate imaginings of water dangers had manifested themselves from his mind and into the world. In this place, there was no way of telling. His terror meant that movement was impossible. If natives of this place, Ceun and Anaya could be taken, so easily, what chance did he have when he couldn't begin to comprehend how this place worked? He didn't have their familiarity with life here. It was only a matter of time before he would be picked off.

The dangers he had so recently scoffed at now seemed very possible. As the clouds thickened, Will understood for the first time the real concept of nightfall. It fell, with an almighty thud, even the sudden moonlight, as if a light had been switched on, seemed to perform a sinister dance on the water. Will glared at the lake that had taunted and teased, refusing to give up its secrets until it had the chance to steal Anaya away. There was no way that he was going anywhere near it. Of course, the morph could have been wrong. The lake wasn't necessarily the gateway out of here. There must be another option, preferably one that did not involve the terror of attack and abduction. If he stayed put perhaps, she would find her way back to him, assuming of course that she was still alive and assuming he didn't die of thirst or hunger first. But, worryingly, in the meantime, there was no way of knowing what else may be looking for him. Images of crocodiles charging out of the water made his spine try to crawl up into the safety of his skull.

Curling into the foetal position, Will tried to get comfortable on the rough ground. The once welcoming sand now felt damp, cold and hostile under his terrified body. Eventually, despite his terror, fatigue got the better of him, and he fell into unconsciousness.

From their vantage point, two dark shapes had been watching the events unfold. They had been observing Will and Anaya's progress with satisfaction. Barely had they shrugged when the polymorph and bounty hunter disappeared. They watched the remaining figure ran around in a panic, yelling, screaming and trying to perform a kind of ancient rain dance. There may have been a hint of shaking shoulders. As the man retreated into the shadows, it became apparent that his fear had enveloped him almost completely. The monks put their heads together. After much arm-waving, and gesticulation, they came to a decision.

~~

'Men!' Anaya spat, very clearly including all of those present in her disdain.

'Hardly surprising is it? This is my job. You shouldn't even be here!' The other polymorph complained.

'Don't blame me for his twisted mind!' Anaya countered.

'Debbie...Other Debbie... there is plenty of me to go around.'

'Wait a minute. I know you!' All interest in the other polymorph forgotten, Anaya looked at the man properly. Under her intense gaze, he puffed out his bare chest a little more.

'You know her?' Debbie asked.

'Well yes, she's you, isn't she?' The man replied.

'Perhaps a bit skinnier than when I last saw you.' Anaya narrowed her eyes. 'It's you!'

'Much as I hate to break up this touching reunion, haven't you forgotten something? You need to explain yourself, and then we have to find a certain inventor,' Ceun said quietly, but apparently not quietly enough.

'You've found him. What do you need?' Adam said.

'What about me!' Morph Debbie chipped in.

'Baby, what can I say? When the call comes, it comes. I'm brilliant. I can do anything.'

'Does that include putting a shirt on any time soon?' Ceun sniped. 'Sorry, wrong inventor.'

The bounty hunter took hold of Anaya's arm to pull her away. She turned to face him, snatching her arm back angrily.

'Listen. Before you so brilliantly managed to lose Will, this was who we've been looking for. This is the other one.'

Debbie was shouting at Adam now, but he waved her into silence. 'Will? What about Will. He's in a coma.'

'No, he isn't. He's stuck here.' Anaya said, barely glancing at the man.

'But this is a dream?' Adam said.

Ceun gestured towards the inventor. 'Here, we go again.'

CHAPTER 29

Moving silently, the monks glided across the sand. Not even a footprint appeared to show they had passed. They stood for a moment, either side of the sleeping Will before exchanging a nod. With one monk at his head and another at his feet, they carried him carefully down to the water's edge. Together they heaved him back and forth, building a good momentum. On the second outward swing, they let go, and his body flew through the air. Unfortunately for Will, he regained consciousness just after he hit the water.

Registering the shock of the cold water before his brain even had time to consider what was happening to him, Will thrashed around, expecting his lungs to be filling with liquid. It eventually occurred to him that although he was indeed soaking wet, equally he was not in the water, ergo, his battered consciousness decided, he was not about to drown.

Poor Will wasn't sure what was real any more, but judging by the ache in the base of his back, he had landed on something hard, and that was undoubtedly real enough. Considering the options, he didn't know whether he dared to open his eyes but judging by the inside of his eyelids, he wasn't in the dark anymore, unless he included the dark shadow that was standing over him. Lying still, he wondered how long he could get away with pretending outside didn't exist. He decided to err on the side of caution and kept his eyes closed for the moment. If he was fortunate perhaps his assailant, or worse, assailants would think that the fall had killed him. The thought briefly popped into his head that maybe he had been a possum in a previous life when such pleasantly diverting meanderings were sharply shaken away by hands that belonged to the shadow and a voice which sounded somewhat familiar.

'Wake up and tell this moron that I was not trying to kill you!'

Eventually, the threat of dislodging his teeth overcame his fear, and he opened his eyes. Suzie was kneeling over him, shaking him hard. Standing behind her was also Suzie. Will decided to close his eyes again until the concussion wore off. The shaking resumed.

'If I say what you want will you leave me alone? You weren't trying to kill me. Will you stop trying now, please?' Will managed.

'Hey man! You're here. These guys have just been telling me the weirdest stuff.'

Will recognised the voice. Within a second he'd pushed Anaya/Suzie out of the way and was throwing himself at Adam. Ceun caught him mid charge.

'You bastard. I am going to beat the living daylights out of you!' Will shouted. Ceun held on to the struggling inventor.

'Calm down! What is wrong with you?' The struggling stopped with Anaya delivering a stinging blow across Will's face.

'You're getting a little too good at that,' Ceun observed.

'Thank you,' she said, rubbing her hand. 'Now look. William, how many Suzies do you see?' 'Two?'

'You mean Debbie?' Adam interrupted.

'Hang on, who is Suzie?' Ceun asked.

'Long story,' Anaya said, 'there are two Suzies because this person here is also a polymorph.'

'This person is Lara actually,' The other Suzie complained, 'not that anyone bothered asking.

'Don't confuse things anymore, there's a dear.' Anaya said.

'Well, I like that...' '

Shut up!' Ceun said forcefully.

'Now. Lara, who appears as Suzie appears to Adam as Debbie, and so do I.' Anaya said in exasperation, 'The person you saw with Cassandra was a male version. It was not your friend any more than I and Lara here are really Suzie. There is no reason for revenge. It is not his fault. It's not her fault. It's not the polymorph's fault, now will you please get over it?'

'Wait. If what you're saying is right. Cass had a dream about me?' Adam preened.

'Not helping.' Anaya said, holding her hand out. 'Stop talking now.'

Will swallowed his indignation.

'Bossy, isn't she?' Adam muttered, earning himself a look of disapproval from the she in question.

'So this Adam, the real Adam, wasn't there, knew nothing about it until you fed his ego. Ok?' Anaya said. Will nodded. 'Now Ceun is going to let you go. You are not going to attack anyone are you?'

Will shook his head. 'But it...'

'Not real!' Anaya held a finger up to his nose and tapped it lightly. 'Not real!'

'Oh and I escaped from my kidnappers, thank you for asking,' Ceun said, releasing his captive.

'You were kidnapped.' Will said, trying to massage some feeling back into his arms.

'Yes, held against my will if you pardon the pun.'

'Oh poor baby, were you in a maximum-security cell?' Anaya snorted.

'You were in maximum-security?' Will asked.

Anaya laughed bitterly. 'Yes, I was in prison, maximum security, where all the really nasty ones go. Why don't you ask Mr

Bounty hunter here how I got there?'

'You want to do this now?' Ceun said, running his hand over his hair. 'Ok, you might want to ask her how she got out too!'

'I got out because you needed me. It's all about you and your little causes. I wouldn't have been there but for you!'

Will gaped. 'You put her in prison?'

Ceun turned on Will. 'It wasn't a travesty of justice or anything. A bit more complicated than that. Don't imagine little miss innocent here was the victim of some cruel plot whatever she may tell you! And now she'd up to her old tricks. Manipulation. Why you? Why did they pick you?' He said, accusing her.

'How am I supposed to know? You were the one who came charging in and busted me out. I thought you said they needed me.'

'To get to me!' Ceun exploded.

Will backed away. 'I think I'll go and explain things to Adam while you two kill each other if that's ok.

'Fine.' They both said breathing heavily.

'How many times do I have to say it? I did what I had to do. You gave me no choice.' Ceun said, trying to regain his composure.

'There's always a choice... What did you mean, to get to you?'

'Nothing.' The bounty hunter looked uncomfortable.

'Why would dragging me into all this get to you?' she asked again.

'You should know you're the one with all the answers!' he snapped.

'Will did say I was innocent!' she sniped back.

'You do tend to pick a person's blind spot.'

'It's like I told you, why couldn't you just believe me?'

'Because when it comes to telling the truth, honesty and integrity, your track record isn't all that great, now is it?' Ceun finished.

A genuine look of hurt crossed Anaya's face. 'This time I am telling the truth,' she said quietly. 'I know I haven't always been the most trustworthy person, but this is different. I don't know what you're talking about. I have been trying to... help. I don't know what else I can say to make you believe me.'

Ceun caught the desperation in her voice. Her eyes filled with tears. Despite himself, his temper began to melt. 'If I have reached the wrong conclusion. I'm sorry,' he said in a tone that suggested he wasn't in the slightest bit sorry. 'But you must see how it looks. You must know who the woman was. She certainly knew you.'

'I don't know. What woman? I am certainly not working for anyone. If I were, the pay and the hours would be better, not to mention the company.' She tried a small smile, 'truce?'

'Truce? You think that's it?' Ceun subconsciously fingered a thin golden wire around his neck.

'What is that?' she said, staring as if she'd never seen the bounty hunter before.

'It's nothing.'

'Let me see...' The morph reached for his hand, but he pushed her away.

'I told you its nothing. Now leave it alone.' Pushing her aside, Ceun stopped for a moment. 'I don't trust you,' he said before striding off after the others.

CHAPTER 30

'What do you mean you haven't been able to find him, Captain Todd?' Bango said quietly.

The Captain stared at a spot just above the chairman's curly red wig. 'We haven't been able to locate the fugitives as yet.'

'Your lordship.' Winkworth said pointedly.

'We are supposed to have the best force in the universe, but they are unable to find one human who must stick out like a sore thumb?' Bango pressed his fingers together. 'You said fugitives... plural?'

'Intelligence has it that the human is being assisted.' The Captain said in a monotone.

'Your lordship!' Winkworth added more forcefully.

'By citizens of Morpheus! But that's treason!' The Clown exploded.

'Hardly your lordship.' Winkworth gulped as the furious Chairman rounded upon him. He continued hurriedly. 'The charter does state that knowingly harbouring an enemy of Morpheus is a treasonable offence. However, if indeed the target is being aided, it may be that said citizens are unaware of his status.' Winkworth said, blowing his nose.

'But the captain here seems to be under the impression that these people have foiled attempts to capture them?' Bang said, gesturing a white-gloved hand towards the officer.

'The target has as yet not been neutralised.' Todd agreed.

'Your lordship!' Winkworth added through his handkerchief.

The chairman waved his assistant down and turned his full attention to the Captain. 'Do we know who these helpers are?'

'A Rogue polymorph that recently escaped from high security, we believe that she may be involved.'

The chairman sighed. 'What is it your not telling me captain. Apart from the fact that our high-security prison doesn't seem to be that highly secure?'

Todd looked to Winkworth for support, but the Bogeyman was no steadfastly refusing to acknowledge his existence. 'Your lordship?' The man tried hopefully.

'Please don't let the make-up and nose confuse you captain. I am not a fool. Well. I am a fool, but I am not stupid.' Bango growled.

'The person we believe assisted the polymorph in her escape.' The Captain hesitated.

'Yes!' Bango said, bringing his hands down on the desk with a thump.

'We believe it to be one of our own operatives. A bounty hunter by the name of Hawke.' The Captain finished miserably.

'Hawke... Hawke... Should I know that name Winkworth?'

The Bogeyman blew his nose noisily. 'One of our freelance operatives your lordship. Excellent record, highly decorated.' He said evenly.

'Oh well, that's all right then. This Hawke will bring him in, and that will be that.' Bango said, sitting down heavily in his chair.

The soldier's eyes flickered for a moment.

'That's not all right?' Bango said, catching the movement.

'The bounty hunter does not seem to be working within our parameters,' he said hopelessly.

Bango's eyebrows nearly disappeared into his wig. 'I'm sorry?' Bango looked from his assistant to Captain Todd and back again. 'Will one of you please tell me what is going on here?'

'What he means your lordship is that the bounty hunter appears to be working for himself. It is alleged that he is assisting the fugitive.' Winkworth supplied.

'Why is he doing that? Whose side is he on?' The Chairman yelled, banging the desk again.

'We... we don't know.' Todd replied.

'I suggest you and your so-called intelligence bloody well find out. I want that inventor before he does any more damage. Understood!' The Clown shouted.

The captain nodded his head once and remained at attention.

'What are you waiting for? Get on with it!' Bango screamed.

Todd turned smartly on his heels and double-timed out of the room. Never had he been so grateful to be dismissed.

~~

'I really am sorry, man.' Adam said for the fifteenth time.

'You weren't to know.' Now that Will had grasped the fact his wife and his best friend weren't having an affair, he was prepared to forgive the removal of the console.

'The important thing is that you don't forget once you wake up,' Ceun said. 'You have to remember. It's going to be difficult because your dream will be scrambled. Repeat it again.'

Adam sighed. 'I've got it.'

'I'm sure you have, but let's just be sure.' Ceun insisted.

'Console will bring Will back,' he said parrot-fashion.

'And again.' Ceun said, rolling his hand to encourage repetition. 'I want you chanting that as you wake up. It might be the only thing you remember.'

'That's a shame.' Adam grinned at Lara, who had her arms folded and was staring steadfastly in the opposite direction.

'Do you mind?' Anaya asked the other morph.

'I'll leave, shall I? It's not as if I'm wanted or anything now that you've crashed my job.' Lara tried again.

'It's nothing personal.' Ceun began.

'Of course not, why would it be. I'm working here, and madam turns up, and muscles in like she owns the place. I'm going to make a complaint.'

'No...' Ceun began.

'The honourable member is going to hear about this.' She said, wagging a finger.

Anaya shrugged and looked at her fingernails. 'Complain away. Go for it, run off to your little master, get a treat and a pat on the head.'

Ceun shot her a warning glance.

Lara got to her feet. 'I'm going and don't think you're going to stop me!'

'Wouldn't even think about it. You still here?' Anaya dared the other morph to comment. Instead, Lara just turned and walked away.

'Console will bring Will back,' Adam chanted in the background.

'What was the point of that? Now every bounty hunter, guard and soldier are going to be here in seconds!' Ceun was incensed.

'She was going to complain anyway, might as well let her get on with it.' She said with another shrug. 'You wanted her staying here and listening to our plans.'

'We have a plan?' Will interjected.

'Just a minute.' Adam said, getting to his feet.

'Stay here and continue chanting.' Ceun said.

'In a minute.' Adam replied before running after the departing morph. The others watched in amazement. Lara stopped her arms folded defensively, everything about her screaming anger. Gradually, as Adam talked, she began to relax. One hand came up to her hair, twisting a strand distractedly. She soon appeared to be smiling and then giggling.

'What is he doing?' Ceun asked.

'Probably persuading her not to go talking to anyone.' Will said. 'It's like his superpower… it's infuriating.'

'What is?' Ceun asked.

Will just shook his head.

'It's called having charm and charisma.' Anaya said with a smile. 'You might want to try it sometime.'

'I have charm and charisma!' Ceun said, a little hurt.

'Console will bring Will back.' Adam said happily sitting back down in the sand.

'I take it your friend is now perfectly happy?' Will said almost bitterly.

'Yeah, all explained, no problem.' Adam said. 'Console will bring Will back.'

'Are you going to tell us about the collar then?' Anaya said sidling up to the bounty hunter and whispering in his ear. Ceun's hand subconsciously came up to his neck.

'It's nothing.' Ceun snapped.

'It's something, why won't you tell me what it is.' Anaya cooed as she stroked his arm.

'I don't know.' Ceun said, finally.

Anaya laughed musically. 'You are a terrible liar. You know exactly what it is.'

'If you're so clever then you don't need me to tell you.' He said, pulling away.

'I've never seen one, but I have heard of them.' She said, her hand gripping his arm firmly.

'Console will bring Will back.' Adam chanted.

'What is it?' Will asked, looking from one to the other. 'What are you two plotting?'

'Are you going to tell him?' Anaya said, raising an eyebrow.

He removed the hand from his arm. 'You go ahead.' Ceun said crossly. 'After all, it's a gift from your friends!'

Anaya frowned. 'My friends?'

'Look!' Will shouted. 'I am getting completely sick of this constant bickering. You tell me what it is.' His finger pointed directly at Anaya.

'It's a control collar,' she supplied automatically, 'they are used to contain prisoners.'

Will turned to Ceun. 'Why are you wearing a control collar.'

Ceun shrugged, 'Present from my kidnappers.

'So you're being tracked? Someone knows where we are?' Will asked.

'I doubt it they are more for...' Ceun started.

'Control and torture.' Anaya said quietly. 'How long?'

'Three days.' Ceun replied.

'Three days, now what are you talking about? Will said.

'If I don't show up with the human, you, in three days then she is going to come after you, both of you. We need to get Will home. We may have to send An with you.' Ceun said, running a hand through his hair.

'Who are you to make that decision for me?' She said. 'I don't want to go. I've seen what it's like over there remember. We just have to find a way to get that thing off you.'

'You know there's no way to do that Anaya.' Ceun warned. 'There is no other way. I can't hand Will over, and I doubt this is a person true to her word.'

Will frowned. 'If you don't turn up with me, we all go back to my world, right?'

'He won't be coming with us, will you?' Anaya said.

'Keep chanting,' Ceun said poking Adam, who was now engrossed in the conversation.

'Console will bring Will back.'

'Why won't he?' Will asked.

'Because I have another appointment.' The bounty hunter looked meaningfully at Anaya.

She just shrugged and pulled a face.

Ceun suddenly looked around. 'Where's the hairy guy, Adam?'

'He must have gone back, woken up?' Anaya said.

'Just like that? Do you think he'll remember?' Will asked.

'We'll have to hope so. In the meantime, we need to find somewhere to hide. You're becoming just a little bit too much of a tourist attraction. Anaya, any ideas?' Ceun said.

Anaya had been strangely lost in her thoughts. 'Hmm?'

'Ideas, where we can hide while we wait for Will to get out of here.' Ceun continued. 'Anaya. Morpheus to Anaya, Morpheus to Anaya, are you reading us?'

'Yes!' She said irritably. 'I'm thinking.'

'What about the dream scenarios we set up. The joust was real enough. Surely the others must be here too?'

'First place they'd look.' Anaya said, tapping her chin with her forefinger.

'But if they've already looked there?' Will continued.

Ceun shook his head. 'They'll be under surveillance. We go in at the beginning, and they'll be waiting for us.'

'Do we have to go in at the beginning?' Will asked. Anaya and Ceun stared at each other. 'I mean, I'm not sure how these things work, but...' Will persevered.

'It could work?' Anaya conceded. 'We could buy some time until Adam gets the machine back on Will.'

'No-one would be expecting it?' Ceun conceded.

'What? We can hop in halfway?' Will cut in.

'Better than that.' Anaya said, smiling. Ceun matched her grin. 'We can go through backwards.'

CHAPTER 31

The girl didn't even blink as Will waved a hand in front of her face. Her clothing would have considered the term 'rag's an upgrade. She clung to the broom as if it was the only thing she could fully depend on. 'What's wrong with her?' He asked.

'This is what your machine does. She's playing a part, but it's not her in control. We aren't supposed to be here, so she is just awaiting instructions.' Ceun said, trying to guide the raggedy creature through the kitchen door. 'Anaya, I doubt she'll fight you. Get changed, and we'll put her somewhere safe.'

'Me?' The morph said, looking at the creature with some distaste.

'You think Will to be the heroine? Just do it. We'll go and find roles for ourselves.' He said.

'Surely she should be getting married. That's how the story ends?' Will asked.

Ceun shook his head. 'You want to try gate crashing a royal wedding? They have a nasty tendency to lop bits of you off.'

Will shook his head.

~~

No sooner had Anaya emerged dressed in this season's scraps than suddenly a bony hand caught her under the elbow and propelled her towards the drawing-room. Will and Ceun meanwhile had wandered in different directions. Will found a footman standing idly gazing into space as he headed towards the kitchen. The struggle was unequal, and soon Will was fastening the buttons of his uniform and heading towards the sound of an urgent bell.

Ceun wandered around outside. There had to be a place for him somewhere, but there didn't seem to be anyone else around. He sat down and fingered the collar idly. Closing his eyes, he tried the think of a way out, something smart, something cunning. Suddenly, he felt a rush of air, as though he had been caught in a small whirlwind. His eyes snapped open, then opened wider as he looked down at himself. 'Oh, no!' He breathed.

~~

Will blinked at the scene in front of him. Anaya was sitting on a humble scrap of paper on a rather grand chair in an even grander parlour designed by someone who believed taste was nothing more than a five-letter word. Her clothes were filthy, covered in coal dust and ashes, making her look even further out of place. Hovering behind her seat were three ladies of indeterminate age. On one side, nervously stood two particularly plain-looking women. The first had been squeezed into a cerise dress, comedically designed for a much smaller woman, which bulged unpleasantly where one wouldn't normally expect lumps and bumps to be. She had a round, slightly stupid face, topped off with puffy red, piggy eyes.

The other did not fare much better. She was as thin as her sister was fat. The lime green dress hung from her bones, making her skin appear even pastier than it really was, it now bordered on the translucent. Her hair hung in rat's tales framing a sharp triangular face with prominent front teeth.

On Anaya's other side, glowering over the scene was an enormous shrew faced, older woman, a perfect amalgamation of her daughters had they been put into a genetic blender. She was draped in layers of yellow and purple, making her look something like a bejewelled easter egg. Her eyes darted back and forth as her hands constantly washed each other.

The reason for the trio's discomfort was apparent. Kneeling in front of Anaya proffering an exquisite glass slipper was a man that even Will had to admit was beautiful. This young man could have walked straight out of an international advertising campaign for aftershave or underwear, pausing only to have seraphim dress him in the finest silks. From his strong, handsome jawline to his tousled blonde locks, he was every inch the Prince Charming. As Anaya proffered her grubby foot the Prince placed the dainty slipper upon it, it fitted perfectly.

A beautiful smile crossed the Prince's face, and he leant forward to kiss his bride to be, whose hands gripped the side of the chair and who's eyes had become rather wide at the prospect. From nowhere, a large grey cat leapt into her lap, breaking the spell. It turned and hissed at the Prince ominously, flexing its claws, causing the prince to shie away.

Removing the shoe, and with a brow furrowed in confusion, Anaya was shoved roughly from the seat, and prince assumed the position kneeling in front of the bony foot being pushed into his face. It was evident that the slipper was not going to fit, it was never going to be flexible enough to fit over her knobbly toes. That aside, the foot was just too long to accommodate the dainty glass.

Seeing that her sister hadn't passed the test, the fat girl shunted her roughly out of the way and squeezed her ample bottom into the resisting chair. Prince Charming looked to Anaya, begging for help. His plea went unheard, and despite having found his Princess, he was still inexplicably asking unsuitable maidens to try the slipper. This did not fit in his pretty, but simple mind very well. The fatter sister had no chance of even getting a little toe into the shoe. She squeezed and squeezed but still, it refused to budge.

'I have been walking a lot today, and it is hot, but it is definitely my slipper...' she whined.

The Prince stood up and scratched his head. 'There is something not right here.' Will heard him mutter under his breath.

Anaya, still cradling the cat in a kind of headlock, gestured discretely with an inclination of her head that Will should show the prince out. Their Royal visitor was quite reluctant to go but found himself herded towards the door and eventually persuaded to return with his aides to the waiting coach. Will felt quite sorry for him; all he was doing was playing out the story. It wasn't the prince's fault that it wasn't going the way he expected, and now the poor man had to spend goodness knows how long looking at a constant stream of unsuitable feet. Will shuddered. As he returned to the parlour, the sounds of great excitement reached his ears. All three women were squealing at a pitch that made Will's ears ring. Anaya had slipped away. Once the three women had vacated the parlour like a pair of galleons in full sail followed by a kayak, Will crept down the steps to the kitchen door, which surprisingly was locked fast. 'Anaya!' He hissed glancing behind him in case he was followed.

'Will?' Her voice came back. 'I can't unlock the door?'

'Well, there are ugly sisters, a glass slipper and I'm locked in a scummy kitchen with a blanket in the ashes. What do you think is going on?' She said.

Will glared at the door. 'There is no need to be snippy!'

'Snippy! I didn't even get to do the happy ever after thing. No, he brings us into the bit that is… rubbish. I suppose he would find that very amusing.'

'Speaking of which where is the bounty hunter?' Will asked.

'Who knows? You didn't see him. He wasn't one of the guards or something?' She asked.

'I thought he was going to be Prince Charming, didn't you?' Will said innocently with a silent chuckle to himself. The door shuddered with a vicious kick.

'No I most certainly did not, and you should think yourself lucky that there is a very heavy thick door between us or I would be pummelling your head for that remark.' She growled

Will chuckled. 'Fine! Have it your way. I'll be back in the morning. When they let you out or lock you in, or...something.' Will, hadn't quite managed to clarify the order in his mind, but that seemed about right. Anaya muttered something indistinguishable back at him.

Inside the kitchen, Anaya had to admit things looked bleak. The fire had almost gone out, and the thick stone walls gave off a damp aura. A swift scan of the cupboards revealed that there wasn't anything to eat apart from a few left-over scraps. She couldn't find any candles, and the light was fading rapidly, which left only the embers to cast a faint eerie glow. Anaya shook out the threadbare blanket to remove most of the ashes. She wrapped it around herself to keep warm. The cat clambered onto her lap, mewling to be allowed into the cover. Its warm fur and soft purring were surprisingly comforting. She stroked its ears as the animal rubbed its head up against her hand.

'This is a miserable turn of events hey puss?' The cat meowed in agreement. 'Shut in a cellar with no-one but you for company. I wonder what has happened to that idiot. I don't know how he ever managed without me, always getting himself lost or captured, leaving me to sort everything out!' Two sharp blue eyes blinked at her in the rapidly darkening room. 'I mean it's ridiculous to suggest that I had been hoping he was Prince Charming. There is nothing whatsoever charming about the man... ow! Puss watch those claws!' The cat circled her lap until it had managed to wind itself down into a soft grey ball with ears and eyes. 'I am a bit worried as to what has happened to him though puss. What with that collar...' she gasped, 'what if moving states made the collar explode? His head could have gone poof, and I would never know!' Anaya's voice had risen. She took a deep breath. 'Would serve his stupid self right,' she said, stroking the cat a little too hard. It wriggled in protest. 'Do you know he accused me of being a traitor? He thinks that

I am working with whoever is trying to get the inventor.' The cat blinked at her. 'Yes,' She said, rubbing its head. 'I know. Ok, so perhaps I haven't always been entirely honest and trustworthy, but that was just unfair. I haven't done anything wrong! Is it too much to believe that I want to help?' The cat stretched and rolled onto its back as Anaya began to tickle its stomach. 'I wouldn't do anything to hurt him,' she continued. 'He's annoying and bad-tempered and did I mention annoying?' Briefly, the claws flipped out but were retracted rapidly as she went on. 'But I wouldn't want anything to happen to him. I guess I feel safer when he's here.' The cat's eyes winked several times. Anaya wrapped her arms around the little creature noticing for the first time that it wore a simple collar. 'You are a domestic cat after all?' She whispered into its fur, before curling them both up in the blanket and lay down to sleep.

Anaya was half awake at the sound of the door unlocking. The cat nuzzled against her neck, making her stir slightly. The cold stone hearth hadn't been the most comfortable of beds, and it had taken some time before Anaya had fallen asleep. Of course, now that it was time to get up, she could have slept forever. Seeing she did not intend to move the cat sat up. Lifting a paw, claws safely tucked away, he smacked her sharply across the nose. Anaya jumped as the cat bolted for the safety of the kitchen table. Forced to rouse herself properly, Anaya rubbed her eyes and tried to get a sense of time. It seemed to be what passed for late on in the evening, time running backwards was going to take a little getting used to.

Outside the door, Will was having an encounter with the lady of the house. 'She is to have nothing but bread and water, do you understand?' Will nodded slowly. This woman was even more terrifying up close! The mother slipped the key into her ample bosom. Will shuddered at the thought. 'No one goes in or out. Forget the bread and water. The insolent chit can starve!' The voice grated along Will's nerves, but he found himself still nodding in ascent. Once the hateful woman was out of sight, he made a run for the kitchen door, finding it unlocked, he pushed it open to see Anaya sitting huddled in the blanket.

'How are you doing? He asked.

'Fine,' her neck clicked as she moved her head, 'nothing that a team of doctors and a year in traction couldn't solve. Any sign of Ceun?' Will shook his head. 'Do you think…?' Clearly he had the same thought as Anaya.

She shook her head, vigorously, 'No. He will be around somewhere.' The bell for the parlour began to ring so hard it looked ready to leap from the kitchen wall.

~~

The arrangement of their outfits could be described as nightmarish or possibly genius. Stepmother had chosen a dress of vivid orange and purple, which disturbingly matched her skin tone. On her head, pinned precariously, was a brilliant white wig, only just visible through a menagerie of combs and feathers. Her daughters were looking for a bolder statement. Fatty chose a layered white creation, which, from a distance, could be easily mistaken for a wedding cake, the subliminal message approach perhaps? Her bouffant was raven black and taller than her mothers.

But if subliminal messages were being sent, who could imagine what skinny was trying to say? The dress was black, completely straight up and down, back to front with no danger of a curve to mar its line. In a possible homage to her mother, her 'do' was a brilliant orange giving her the overall image of a matchstick.

'Now Cinders, bring us something to eat.' Mother's voice, like nails on a blackboard, made Will's eye twitch.

'Did you clean my room?' Fatty squeaked.

'And my room too,' Her sister agreed. 'And mended my stockings,' 'And mended mine too.' 'And rethread my corsets,'

'And...' eyebrows furrowed across the thin nose, 'you might just have had your work cut out with those.' The fat sister harrumphed in indignation as the three women then climbed the stairs.

The grey cat curled itself around Anaya's ankles. As she moved to pick him up, the creature ran just out of reach. 'What's the matter puss?' Anaya took a step forward only to have the cat move again just out of reach. 'What is it with the stupid thing?' She muttered.

'I think it wants us to follow it,' Will began to move towards the cat who ran a few steps then looked back over its shoulder, 'Someone probably needs rescuing from a well or something.'

Anaya gazed incredulously at the inventor. 'Don't worry about it,' he said.

The cat led them to one side of the house where they found an enormous pumpkin smashed and broken on the gravel driveway. From above a tornado of sparkly white lights engulfed the vegetable. As they shielded their eyes, the lights subsided, and the wrecked pumpkin transformed into a beautiful glass carriage. Four white mice ran unbidden to the front and were whisked instantly into four magnificent horses.

Will saw the column heading his way. He immediately decided that sparkly lights and things turning into other things was not something he wanted to be a part of. With surprising speed, he dodged the magical spiral. It immediately doubled back, heading towards the reluctant man with even more gusto. A few sharp corners later, the swirling sparkles had Will trapped against the wall. He dodged right, he dodged left, and both times the column anticipated his move. It waited, to Will it seemed to be watching him. Finally, out of desperation, he jumped to the left again, only this time to be engulfed in a swirl of fairy dust and magic. When the sprinkles subsided, Will looked down to find himself in a smart footman's livery, all dark-blue knickerbockers suit with shiny buttons. It could have been worse.

Satisfied, the sparkly white lights moved on to Anaya. This time it was broaching no nonsense. The gown was exquisite, a delicate eggshell blue, from the fitted bodice right to the gentle curve of the skirt, the gown gave off an iridescence of its own. Her hair was piled upon her head in a creation of auburn curls and diamonds. A few tendrils had been left to cascade down her back. She held an elaborate mother of pearl mask, which fitted her exactly as she moved it into position.

'Wow!' Was all Will could manage to say. Even Suzie could be turned into a princess.

'Wow indeed.' A voice from the shadows made them both jump as Ceun stepped forward, dressed in the same livery as Will. They both stared at him in amazement. He grinned back. 'You two don't scrub up too badly.'

'Where have you been?' Anaya snapped.

'Why?' He raised an eyebrow. 'Were you worried?'

'Of course not!' She said, a little too quickly.

'Then we had better go.' Ceun opened the carriage door and offered his hand to Anaya to help her inside. She looked at it for a moment as though it might explode. 'Aren't you even going to give us an explanation?' She asked.

'No time my lady, you have a ball to abandon.' He said with a smile.

Reluctantly, she took his hand and allowed herself to be helped into the coach. Will was about to join her when Ceun stopped him. 'What do you think you are doing?'

'Getting a lift?' He replied.

Ceun prodded him in the chest. 'You're a footman. You ride on the back.'

'What about you?' Will resisted the urge to prod him back.

The bounty hunter grinned devilishly. 'I drive.'

CHAPTER 32

The coach started on its journey at some speed. Will did not really know much about the vehicular qualities of fruit, but he was beginning to understand they did not extend to suspension. He tried to bend his knees against the jolts and judders of the road, but each rock and pothole send a shudder through him. By the time they got to the palace, he felt as though at least three teeth had been shaken loose. The conviction wasn't helped by his head hitting the back of the coach as the vehicle lurched to a halt. By the time he had assessed the level of concussion, Ceun was already lowering the delicate steps for Anaya's descent.

'Time for your grand exit Milady.' He said with a low bow before pausing to smile up at her.

Anaya paused.

'What are you waiting for? Time to go in there and find your prince charming.' He said, smirking.

Anaya negotiated the steps as best her dress would allow. 'Prince charming. Hmm.' She straightened the dress. 'Do I look ok?'

Such an unusual lack of confidence was a surprise. 'You look lovely.' He said honestly. 'Perfect, the prince is a lucky man.'

Placing her mask on her face, the morph scanned him for any trace of sarcasm. Not finding what she was looking for she simply muttered. 'Thanks.' Then hobbling as best she could in one slipper, she was up the steps and into the ballroom.

Will felt his head begin to swim. The ground seemed to be

churning under his feet. The world winked out for a moment. Instinctively he reached out and grabbed something soft and velvet. As everything reasserted itself, he looked to see what he was clutching. Clearly, it was an unfamiliar arm. As Will's eyes travelled upwards, they met another pair looking back. Fully masked the man glanced briefly at his arm then back to Will's face in silent question.

'Um sorry.' Will said hurriedly removing his hand. He wasn't sure what happened when the help molested people, but he didn't think it would be good.

'Don't worry about it, time shift will do that to you.' The stranger said winking.

Will glanced around. One moment he'd been outside reassembling his skeleton, and now he was standing in a ballroom filled with extras from a historical novel. He looked back to the stranger. 'What did you mean...?' But the man was gone into the crowd.

The ball gowns and tiaras glittered under the light of a hundred chandeliers. All around masked women fluttered their fans provocatively, and popinjay men pretended to be provoked. A little way off Will located Ceun standing by a pillar with a tray of drinks looking for all the world as if he was meant to be there. Anaya was nowhere to be seen. As discreetly as possible, Will made his way across the space between them.

'Someone knows we're here,' he said from the side of his mouth.

'Stand next to me and pick up a tray,' Ceun hissed. 'Don't draw attention.'

Will awkwardly held the other side of Ceuns tray. The bounty hunter rolled his eyes.

'Did you hear what I said? I was just winked at and something about a time shift?' Will said, glancing around nervously.

'That'll be because we're going backwards; the dream tries to reassert itself. You'll get used to it.' Ceun said.

'I was wondering about that. If we're backwards, how come we are for all intents and purposes going forward?' Will said, frowning.

'We are going through the story backwards. We're not backwards. Don't be ridiculous!' Ceun snorted.

'How can you be so calm? Someone knows!' Will said seriously.

'Who?'

'Male. About the same height as me, posh clothes, mask.' Will said, glancing once more over his shoulder.

'So that rules out about half of the people in this room.' Ceun added with a raised eyebrow.

They were interrupted by a small commotion at the top of the stairs. The crowd turned to stare. Anaya ran across the landing lightly, if a little off-balance. The reason for her slight list became apparent as she paused briefly at the top of the staircase and slipped her foot into a carelessly abandoned glass slipper. With considerable more grace, she began her descent to gasps of admiration from the audience. Even Ceun seemed transfixed.

'I never thought I'd see her looking like that.' Will said wistfully.

'No.' Ceun agreed.

'I suppose I'm used to seeing her in misshapen cardigans mostly.' Will said.

Ceun's brow furrowed slightly. 'From what you've said, I didn't imagine your wife to be a cardigan sort of person,' he said.

'Cassandra? God noo... that's Suzie.' Will snorted.

'Suzie..?' Was all Ceun could manage.

'Anaya changed when I thought Cassandra and Adam... it was the weirdest thing.' Will explained.

'It would be.' Ceun said still slightly confused.

In the centre of the ballroom, almost engulfed in gowns was the outline of a young man. Judging by the ripples of fawning, this had to be Prince Charming. The prince was also mesmerised by this beautiful, mysterious woman who'd just floated into the room. He dismissed the grovellers and with a wave of his hand parted the crowd. This allowed everyone an excellent view of his purposeful stride to meet the masked beauty. She curtsied low as he took her hand and led her onto the dance floor. As they glided with the music, most of the ladies fluttered in agitation at this usurper, their fans hiding the less than complimentary things they had to say. In the corner, the ugly sisters flanked their mother, the three looking almost ready to explode with rage.

'Do you think we're going to have problems with them?' Will asked.

'You know the story.' Ceun said.

'Anaya said. It just gets worse for her from here. She thinks you've done it on purpose.' Will said with a slight accusation.

'I did not do it on purpose. It is the end of the story. It was going to get worse regardless if we're going backwards.'

Will nodded as he absently observed the guests. They had started off relaxed and fuelled with party cheer, but as time regressed, they appeared to become less refreshed and more jittery.

'How long do we have to stay here?' He said eventually.

'Until the grande entrance. If you're bored, how about you go and find your own tray?' Ceun hinted with a slight tug on the tray they both still held.

'I'm not bored. It's quite entertaining watching you make

puppy eyes at our heroine.' The tray was suddenly snatched from his hands. The bounty hunter opened his mouth to speak but was interrupted.

'Psst.' A voice sounded close to Ceun. He looked around, but there didn't seem to be anyone there. 'Pssst! I thought you should know. Soldiers are on their way.'

'Who are you?' Ceun hissed back.

'A friend,' whispered the voice.

'Yes, but who's friend?' But the voice was gone.

'Not that I am surprised. I mean she is genetically designed to look like the person you most desire, right?' Will continued, utterly oblivious to the separate conversation.

'Exactly.' Ceun said absently, still trying to see who the friend could be.

'So who is it for you?' Will asked but Ceun remained silent, still scanning the crowd.

'You don't have to tell me. I'm only making conversation. It's a bit dull.' Will continued.

'I have a feeling it won't be soon.' Ceun said mysteriously.

'But in the meantime? Ok, who was the one on the beach, is she like Anaya?'

'What? Oh. She's not the same level as Anaya, just a junior really,'

'So who do you see? I'm guessing it's a certain faery who feeds on paranoia? Now that is creepy. Am I right? No offence!'

'None taken.'

'So the faery, huh?' Anaya had left the prince and was now leaving for her entrance.

'That's our cue.' Ceun said, ignoring him.

CHAPTER 33

Adam half woke up as the second elbow caught him in the back. 'Mmmmf!'

'You were talking in your sleep!' Louise said, thumping him again.

'Mmmm?' He murmured.

'Who is Debbie?'

Adam's eyes shot open. 'No idea. You must have imagined it.'

'I don't think so. You were talking about Debbie, and then you started talking about Will and a console. But I'm more interested in Debbie!' Louise said, sitting up and folding her arms.

'The console!' Adam leapt out of bed and was halfway to pulling his trousers on.

'Wait a minute. Where do you think you're going? I want to know who the hell Debbie is!' Louise cried.

'It doesn't matter now. I had the craziest dream. Will won't wake up until we put the V10 back on. I should have thought of it before!' He said hurriedly.

'What about Debbie?'

'Who?'

'Debbie!'

'No idea. Sorry, I have to go and see Cass!' He said as he hopped on one foot while he put a sock on the other.

'And who the hell is Cass?' She said, throwing her arms up in exasperation.

'Long story, got to go. I'll call you later.' Kissing the speechless Louise briefly on the cheek he hopped down the stairs.

~~

Arriving at the house, Ceun helped Anaya climb down from the coach. 'You seemed to enjoy yourself?' he asked.

'I was just doing as I was told. No need to make it a chore.' She smiled and began to take off her gloves. 'And he's very nice to look at.'

Ceun pulled a face behind her back.

'What happens now, another one of those time shift things?' Will asked.

'No, now we need a little outside assistance.' Anaya cleared her throat. 'Fairy Godmother!' she called.

'You're calling THE fairy godmother?' Will asked.

'Of course, how else are we supposed to change everything back? You do know this story?' She replied with a raised eyebrow.

'About that…' Ceun began. He was interrupted by a blinding flash of pink sparkly lights and a faint waft of cigar smoke. There indeed was a kind of fairy, although this one looked incredibly annoyed.

It might have been the fact that she was dressed in a bright blue tracksuit, or that she had a napkin tucked into the top. It might even have been the fork of spaghetti halfway to her face, either way, had it not been for the hovering and broad wings, it could well have been a wrong number. The other hand patted a tightly wound lilac perm. Obviously surprised to have been summoned, she looked at the three of them with a mixture of amazement and incredulity. 'You called us here?' she said evenly.

'Is this a bad time?' Will asked.

'You…called…US?' The fairy godmother said again.

'Um, yes?' Will said.

'Do you know who we are?'

'If you're the fairy godmother, then yes we called you,' said Ceun. 'Is there a problem?'

The creature assessed the three of them carefully. Suddenly, she seemed to come to a conclusion. 'Of course, we are. You just caught me at an inopportune moment that's all. I'll be back in a second.' She waved the fork experimentally and vanished.

Anaya crossed her arms and tapped her foot in annoyance. 'What are we supposed to do now?' she said. 'Time is of the essence.'

'That is the fairy godmother?' Will said, trying not to laugh.

One costume change later the fairy was back. Either this dress had not been used in a while or had shrunk in the wash because it was clearly designed for a much lesser fairy. The sparkles stretched across the bodice like shooting stars captured in slow motion, and the way one sleeve slipped down her arm, it was clear that the fasteners on the back had long since given up trying to meet. 'Right then,' she said, hitching the dress back onto her shoulder. 'Would someone like to tell us what is happening here?'

'This is Cind...' Will began.

'You,' she said, pointing the wand at Ceun is a very unfairylike manner. 'It's time for you to turn everything back into pumpkins and ca...'

'We haven't done that kind of thing for years. Plus, we didn't manifest them in the first place. This is all wrong.' She tapped the wand in her open palm crossly.

'It's just a little out of order, that's all.' Ceun said.

'Hmmm. We think we understand. And who is this handsome young man?' The godmother pressed her wand under Wills's chin to get a good look at his face. To Will's mind, it was a little too forceful.

'I'm Will.' He said.

'A human, if we're not mistaken?' She said, raising both eyebrows and staring intently into his eyes.

'Yes, and we seem to have had a little problem with the authorities if you must know.' Anaya said hurriedly pushing to wand away.

'An...' Ceun warned, but the morph continued.

'So we are trying to stay out of the way, YOU understand how it is.' She said pointedly. ' So, if you could wave that thing and change things that would be a big help.'

'We like to help. What sort of problem?' The fairy godmother said, still studying Will.

'Let's just say there is a large contingent of guards on their way here to make our acquaintance.' Ceun said.

'Guards! How do you know?' Will demanded.

'Your friend from the ball. You're right. Someone does know we're here.' Ceun supplied.

'And you didn't say anything because?' Will said, pulling away from the fairy's grip.

'I didn't want you to panic.' Ceun said.

'Too late, I'm panicking.' Will replied.

The Fairy godmother smiled a smile which didn't quite reach her eyes. 'We wouldn't want you to be captured by the guards now, would we? We shall have to see what we can do.'

'About that...' Ceun began. But it was too late. With a wave of her wand, the coach turned instantly into a pumpkin, the four horses into somewhat confused white mice and Anaya's finery into rags and tatters. Last but not least, Ceun turned into a very guilty looking grey cat.

Anaya stared at him in surprise before bursting out laughing. 'You're a cat.' She wheezed as Ceun cleaned his paws disdainfully, only occasionally giving her a sideways glare. It was only a few minutes later that she remembered confiding in a feline. This feline. 'You sneaky little...' Anaya shouted grabbing the feline roughly by the neck. 'He could have told me he was the damned cat!' She held the creature up to eye level. 'You better explain yourself mister!' Ceun the cat growled in reply, taking a half-hearted swipe with a paw.

'He's a cat, he can't tell you anything,' Will said.

'He could you know if you wanted a talking cat. Personally, we find them most unsanitary, but the choice is yours.' The Godmother said, hitching her sleeve back onto her shoulder.

'I'm sure he would love to be able to communicate with us, wouldn't you puss?' Anaya said sweetly keeping her gaze firmly on Ceun, who unable to shake his head, was definitely wriggling his body in the negative. The godmother waved her wand nonchalantly and the stream of growls and hisses emanating from Ceun began to change into words, they were not very nice.

'Language puss!' Anaya said giving him a shake.

'She did it didn't she? You can understand me.' He said.

'Oh, yes. And I think you and I need to have a conversation.' Anaya said, shaking him again.

'I want to be a non-talking cat!' Ceun said miserably. '

We wish you would make your mind up.' The Fairy godmother said irritably.

'We need you. If there are soldiers on the way, then we will need to be able to communicate with you.' Will said.

'Communicate? COMMUNICATE! Well here is my first piece of communication, PUT ME THE HELL DOWN!' The cat yowled.

Anaya reluctantly released the angry cat who proceeded to

wash himself in agitation.

'Do you have to do that?' Anaya asked crossly.

'Yes,' he snapped back. 'It helps me think.' '

'So you are all done, no further need for us in this story, I think?'

'I think there might be. I need to be back, person-shaped.' Ceun said.

The godmother regarded him as she tapped her wand on her chins. 'We cannot do that. You are a cat and a cat you must remain. They are the rules, and we cannot break them.' And with a flourish, she disappeared.

'WHAT? You mean I have to spend my last days as a bloody cat!' Ceun hissed, showing bright white fangs.

Will opened his mouth in a question.

'I'll tell you, Will,' Anaya said, 'You may as well know. It is because at the end of three days if he does not appear, captives in tow, then that funky new collar will do things to his head.'

'What sort of things?' Will asked.

'Mainly separating it from his body. There is, of course, the advantage that he will only feel it frying his brain for a minute or two before his head comes off.' She said pragmatically.

Will tried to take this in. 'You have to hand us over, or your head explodes?' He asked the cat. What sort of people are you?'

'Don't be so dramatic.' Ceun added.

'Oh, do be dramatic, because that is what is going to happen.' Anaya said.

'Let's get it off then?' Will leaned towards the cat.

'Leave it alone. If you try and tamper with it... kaboom!' Ceun said hurriedly. 'Three days is three days.'

'Let him play the martyr if he wants to Will.' Anaya said.

'Yes that's right,' Ceun said through gritted teeth, 'I'm only doing it for attention.'

'Then let the inventor try and help.' He's good with gizmo's sort of.'

It was interesting to see a cat try to wave its front paws when clearly they were not designed to bend that way. 'Now you know, I'm a cat complete with collar. May as well stick a bell on it and complete the humiliation.'

'Oh stop feeling so sorry for yourself!' Anaya snapped. Ceun looked as insulted as his feline features would allow. With a flick of the tail, he turned and strolled out of the room towards the barn. He felt the need to murder something, and as long as he was stuck in this shape, they may as well be rodents.

A coach appeared over the horizon. 'Here come the sisters and their mother back from charm school' Anaya muttered. 'I suggest we make ourselves scarce.'

CHAPTER 34

The good thing about being a cat, Ceun decided, was that it was relatively easy to stay out of the way. There were so many more places for a small feline body to squeeze. However, given that he was likely to be losing a life fairly soon, he wasn't so keen on spending his final days in a permanent fur coat. Rolling over in his hiding place under the kitchen cupboard he wondered briefly if it was true that cats had nine lives, but even if that was the case, he doubted even they could withstand the removal of an entire head. It wasn't as if he could grow it back. He could hear Anaya working in the kitchen and was grateful that she hadn't managed to find him. The likely conversation was not one that he felt he would come out of well.

This whole new body was a revelation. It intrigued him how his knees now bent the wrong way. In fact, he was far more flexible all over, he twisted and rested his rear leg behind an ear, just because he could. And the tail, that thing seemed to have a mind of its own. He flexed experimentally, watching twitching up and down and fought the urge to bat at it with a paw. If this was how Anaya felt every time she changed shape, even slightly, then he could see how things could become confusing. He was finding himself trying to do normal human things without thinking and he really, really missed his opposable thumbs. It was a depressing thought, infamous bounty hunter, feared throughout the realm, very likely to end up as a furry hat. His thoughts were interrupted as a broom swept smartly into his hiding place, applying momentum to his bottom area. Unable to stop himself he shot across the stone floor smacking squarely into the wall headfirst. A little giddy, he sat up and shook himself.

'There you are! I knew you would be lurking around somewhere!' Anaya, from the other end of the broom, was looking at him accusingly.

'I was thinking.' He said indignantly, tail twitching in annoyance. When she didn't respond, he continued. 'Ok, so you found me!' He began to clean himself to unruffle the fur that had been mussed up.

'I found you! So you admit you were hiding?' She picked him up before he had the chance to run away. 'You're not very nimble for a cat, are you?'

'You try having two extra legs to deal with. It is very confusing!' He said squirming.

She held him up under his front two legs and sat so that his back feet were resting on her knees. 'You could have mentioned who you were?' She accused.

Ceun tried to look away, 'How exactly was I supposed to do that? I was a cat? Do you speak cat? No!'

'You could have done if you had wanted to. Or you could have gone away and not listened,' Her cheeks were beginning to redden.

'As I recall you had me in an iron grip. I couldn't go anywhere even if I wanted to.' He knew he was being petulant. Forcing himself to look at her face, he noticed the blush. For a second, he imagined how it would be if situations were reversed. Yes, she would probably have taunted him mercilessly. But hey, where he was going, he may need all the brownie points he could get. 'Look,' he said sighing. 'The whole not being able to communicate thing, it works both ways, I don't know what you said, couldn't understand a word.' The relief on her face was slightly disappointing, but he'd obviously made her happy.

'That's fine then, good cat,' she said, patting him on the head. There was only so far his good, about to die, nature was going to take him.

'Why?' he added mischievously, 'what were you saying? Something you wouldn't want me to hear?'

'No, nothing, not at all!' The blush which had begun to recede shot right back up to the roots of her hair. She was rescued by a violent banging on the back door, to their joint relief, she dropped Ceun onto the floor and went to answer it. She met Will on the way.

'Technically I think it's my job to answer the door. Give me a break from cleaning all those shoes,' he quipped.

'I don't think so. I'll get it.' Anaya countered. They ended up trying to open it together until Will finally wrenched it open.

A raven-haired woman with very pale skin and ruby-red lips stood glaring at them over the threshold. This in itself, did not appear to be particularly unusual. However, what was strange was an entourage of companions? Around her head flew a blue-bird chirruping loudly, and each shoulder had a squirrel clinging on for dear life. Around her feet clustered various woodland creatures, but the central core of the party were dwarves dressed for battle, of sorts. Each looked as though he had rummaged in cupboards for anything that would do for armour. Will was sure one of the helmets was customarily used as a collunder, it even had a piece of cabbage still attached. Most of the small men had beards and all everyone, including the dark-haired woman, looked extremely annoyed, however with the squirrels, it was hard to tell.

'You must be Snow White?' Will asked cheerfully. Snow White looked him up and down with disdain, then pushed him out of the way, sending the bluebird flying in the process.

'Dispense with the niceties. Where is she?'

'Who?' Will tried, but the angry woman had already spotted

Anaya. She charged towards her. Anaya stood her ground, her hands on her hips.

Snow White stopped when they were almost nose to nose, 'You the mystery dancing bint?' She demanded.

'I don't know. Are you the 'I didn't realise it was a poison apple, even though it was so obvious, ooh I'm choking' bint?' The two women glared at each other. Ceun crept out from under a chair where he had been watching proceedings. This was going to be interesting.

'Now, now.' Will stood in between them, 'No need to be like this ladies. Now Miss White, what appears to be the problem?'

'She is the problem.' Snow White jabbed a finger towards Anaya. 'She is attempting to steal my Prince, and I am here to tell you, lady, it isn't going to happen. You stay clear, you understand?'

'Excuse me? Your Prince? When did he become yours, I understand that he is fair game.'

Snow White was even more furious. 'How would you like it if I took your man away, that would make us even, you have the prancing ninny, and I'll have this one?' Grabbing Will by the arm she pulled him towards her.

'Back off missy, if you know what's good for you!' Anaya growled grabbing Will's other arm.

Will found himself as the rope in an impromptu game of tug of war. Both women were surprisingly strong. He looked at the dwarves as an appeal for help, but they merely stood back a little way, ominously brandishing their strange array of weapons. Was that a rolling pin?

'A little assistance fellas? Surely you would prefer it if Miss White here stayed with you? You don't want some Prince coming and taking her away?' He smiled at them hopefully.

'Are you kidding?' One of them said scornfully.

'The sooner he arrives the better,' said another.

'You think this is bad?' said a third. 'You want to try living with her full time,' said a fourth, or perhaps it was the first one again. Will found it hard to keep track, especially as now he was the only barrier between Snow White and Anaya.

'Why don't you just let go?' Anaya shouted, 'then we can sort this out woman to woman.

'Not likely,' Snow White shouted back, pulling even harder.

Ceun leapt nimbly onto the table. 'Right!' He yelled at the top of his voice. 'You Snow White. You stand over there.' He pointed a paw towards one side of the room. 'Anaya, you stand over there... both of you letting go of course.'

Anaya opened her mouth to argue but was cut off with a look. With extremely bad grace, the two women released their grip and retired to opposite ends of the room.

'Assorted creatures and mythical folk, you can wait outside. Scoot off you go!' The crowd milled about uncertainly. Ceun raised a paw. 'What did I just say?' Reluctantly, they left.

He turned his attention back to the two camps. 'Now Snow White. Who told you that An... I mean Cinderella was trying to snatch your Prince?'

'It's all over the forest!' Snow White exploded.

Ceun kept his tone calm. 'I see, but who actually told you?'

'A little bird,' Snow White replied through gritted teeth. All of them looked towards the door, where the bluebird was peeping around the door frame. It withdrew its head quickly.

'You! Get your little blue feathered tail in here?' Ceun growled. The bird reluctantly entered and fluttered nervously in front of the cat. 'Did you tell Snow White about this?'

The bird began to chirrup excitedly. Even to those who didn't speak bird, it was clear that it was trying to worm its way out of the situation. Ceun gave every appearance of listening intently to the bird. The human part of his mind was trying to gain control, but he couldn't help himself, it was just so fluttery. His feline taste buds watered in anticipation. The bird finished its speech and then seemed as though a sixth sense was alerting it to a new danger. It squeaked in fright as Ceun pounced. He barely missed the bird, who was now hiding behind Snow White.

Anaya scooped the growling Ceun up in her arms. 'Bad cat!' She scolded out loud. Then added under her breath. 'You should have pulverised the little squealer!' Ceun's inner cat mewled in annoyance. 'If you do not start telling me the truth, I am going to let that pussy cat go. How long do you think you would last?' Anaya said. The bird eeeped then began its chirruping again.

Ceun appeared to be listening intently, his head on one side. Every so often he licked his lips, which only made the bird chirrup faster.

'What did it say?' Anaya asked.

'Haven't got the faintest idea.' Ceun hissed under his breath. 'All I could think about was sage and onion stuffing... just agree with me.'

'The bird was told to tell both Snow White and the rest of the forest by a shadowy gentlewoman, probably in order to cause this kind of scene.' He announced to the room.

'So princess wannabe isn't going after the prince?' Snow White said and seemed disappointed that the episode had not come to blows.

'Far more complicated than just that Snow White, but you can rest assured, Prince Charming is all yours. So you won't be needing Will.' Ceun said sweetly.

Snow White scratched her head as if wondering how she got into this situation. Eventually, she walked towards the door and was just about to leave when Anaya called after her. 'I could have had him if I wanted to!'

Two dwarves restrained their own fairytale princess and dragged her away, explaining how there were dishes to be done before she had her poison apple and nap. 'But he isn't going to want a princess with dishpan hands is he?' She whined.

'Oh, for goodness sake.' A dwarf exclaimed. 'The woodland creatures do them anyway.'

On the roof, the bluebird was listening in glee. So engrossed was it in the drama unfolding it didn't notice the small, cat-sized dragon slinking silently towards it. With a barely audible eep, a single blue feather drifted sadly to the ground. It was followed by a muffled voice. 'That's all I need, bleedin' company.'

~~

Adam crept carefully into the Wills room in the hospital. He wasn't exactly sure why he was creeping, only that it seemed appropriate. Fortunately, the room was empty. Taking the prototype console out of his pocket, he checked for the fourth time that there was no-one around. He'd charged the battery, and double and triple checked that the thing was working correctly. 'Here goes nothing,' he said, placing the V10 in position and pressing play.

CHAPTER 35

'Girl! Where is that stupid lump?' Even from the depths of the kitchen, Anaya could hear the stepmother bellowing for her. Anaya threw down the cloth on top of the half-finished pile of silver and reluctantly trudged towards the door. A grey blur shot between her legs, rapidly followed by Will who leapt inside dramatically shutting the door behind him, he leant against it panting.

'We have a big problem.' Ceun said.

'We have quite a lot of big problems. Big mean looking problems in rather unpleasant uniforms.' Will added.

'Guards? But how?' Anaya said, glancing nervously towards the ceiling. By the sound of it, the soldiers were busy taking the house apart piece by piece. The crashing of furniture was more than audible above the screams of the three women upstairs.

'Will they be all right?' Anaya asked.

'I'm more concerned as to whether we will be,' Ceun said. 'Is there another way out of here?'

Anaya shook her head. 'Unless we are planning to sprout wings and fly up the chimney, this place is solid. They didn't want their little slave to escape, and they did a good job.'

'There must be a window, a secret passageway... anything?' Ceun said.

'Escape proof. Trust me.' Anaya said. 'I've checked.'

'Fairy Godmother!' Will shouted. The others stared at him.

'You have any better ideas?' He said. 'Fairy Godmother!'

A small pink cloud appeared. 'Your call is important to us. However, we are unavailable at the moment. Please hold.'

'What!' Anaya shouted. 'You cannot be serious!' The sound of large boots began to descend the stairs towards the kitchen. Anaya scooped Ceun up in her arms. The three backed across the room until the stove prevented any further retreat.

'Looks like this is it.' Will said as the door handle began to rattle. Instinctively, he took Anaya's hand. They waited as a massive shoulder hit the door, splintering it into pieces. The world lurched sideways. It righted itself then lurched the other way nauseatingly. It bent, it wobbled, it squiggled, squirmed and turned itself inside out. And then it was gone.

~~

Adam double-checked the console. The little red light was flashing just as it should be, but still Will was motionless.

'Hey, buddy! Will!' Adam hissed. There was no movement. From outside came the unmistakeable clip clip of heels along the corridor. Adam panicked. Removing the V10 quickly, he stuffed it into the pocket of his combat trousers. Cassandra breezed into the room but stopped as soon as she saw Adam sitting there nonchalantly.

'Oh, it's you,' she said coldly.

'Yes, it's me. Just came to see if there was any change really. Have a chat to him, the usual.' 'Hmm,' she said non-committally throwing her bag on the end of the bed. 'I'm here now, so there's no need to keep you.'

'Right.' Adam got up to leave. 'I was wondering whether returning the console would help, you know, to bring him around?'

Cassandra looked at him coldly. 'I don't think so. Surely you've done enough damage.'

'So you think we should postpone production?' Adam asked.

'The daydream believer is a marvellous invention. Will was a genius, and it is going to make a fortune. Everyone is going to want one of these. You probably just made a mistake with that one, a faulty connection or something. I'm sure when we get proper engineers on it, there won't be any issues.'

'Daydream believer? Engineers? You can't seriously be expecting to go ahead as normal with this. It could be a disaster!' Adam said incredulously.

'Hardly, there was just a small teething problem with that one. And yes, I have renamed the product and will be taking over in Will's absence to make sure that nothing else goes wrong.'

'You can't do that!' Adam yelled.

'I think you'll find I can. Who is going to stop me? After all, it was you who removed the thing.' Cassandra glared defiantly, but Adam was already thinking elsewhere.

'What happened to it the original console?' He asked.

'I have it safely locked away where it can do no more damage,' she said, folding her arms.

'I just thought that perhaps I should take a look at it, make sure that if it is responsible, then it can't happen again?' Adam said.

The woman gave a hollow laugh. 'Destroy the evidence you mean?' She poked Adam in the chest. 'Do you think I'm stupid? I hold you personally responsible for what happened to my Will, and I intend to make sure his interests are protected. I'm holding on to that console as insurance, and you better start to be a bit nicer to me in the future.' Grabbing her bag, Cassandra flounced out of the room, leaving Adam to begin work on a plan.

CHAPTER 36

The world stopped spinning butt took a few moments for Will and Anaya to catch up. Coming to their senses, they were no longer in the kitchen. On each side were trees, lots and lots of trees.

'Where are we?' Will asked.

'Where's Ceun?' Anaya said, looking around. 'I definitely had hold of him. Here puss!'

'Shhhh. We don't know who's around and he may not even be a cat any more.' Will said, glancing nervously over his shoulder.

'True,' she said, biting her lower lip.'

I hate to say it, but I think we should go on.' Will said. 'I'm sure he will find us.'

Anaya nodded reluctantly.

The further they ventured into the woods, the more the trees seemed to close in on them. Will began to shiver as the wind whipped around them. They had only walked a little way when Anaya stopped.

'Were you skipping?' She said accusingly.

'No!' Will was defensive.

Anaya raised a sceptical eyebrow but motioned for him to continue. A few yards down the track she halted again, grabbing Will by the arm.

'You were definitely skipping!' She said firmly.

'No, I wasn't!' He said.

Anaya wagged a finger at him, 'Don't skip! Skipping in fairy tales never ends well. No skipping!'

'I wasn't!' He muttered to himself as they moved off. Before long Will began to get the uncomfortable sensation that his walking involved rather more hopping than he was accustomed to, he was also aware that Anaya appeared to be bobbing right along with him.

This time it was Will that halted them. 'Ok! I admit it. I am skipping. I can't help it, but you'll notice I'm not the only one, and when did you put your hair into plaits?'

Anaya's hand went up to the side of her head and found, to her surprise that she did indeed have two long plaits.

She was distracted by Will laughing at her, 'Nice pinafore dress and apron combo!' Looking down at her gingham outfit.

Anaya winced outwardly, 'You can talk, Peter, the goatherd.'

It was then that the horrible truth dawned on Will. He was, in fact, wearing lederhosen and worse, a jaunty little hat with a feather in it. 'This is bad. I swear I would never have programmed anything like this, and I'm darned sure that Adam didn't.'

'I think Ceun was right. Someone is manipulating things, and I don't believe it is because they want to make our life easier.'

With no other choice, they continued into the forest at a half skip half walk, trying to suppress the urge. 'I'm hungry.' Will moaned, 'all I have is this mouldy old piece of bread in my pocket.'

'Lederhosen, going into the woods, bread. This all sounds horribly familiar. If I'm not mistaken then very shortly, we should see a solution to your hunger problem.'

Sure enough, they came to a clearing with a beautiful little cottage in the centre.

'Hmmm! Can you smell that?' Will could feel his mouth-watering.

'How could I not?' It was Anaya's eyes that were watering rather than her mouth.

Will hopped up and down with delight, 'This is the best thing ever. I would say tell me I'm not dreaming, but the point is redundant. Even so, dream or no dream that is the best thing I have ever seen!'

'You really do have an extraordinary mind.' The morph said, shaking her head.

The house was made entirely of garlic bread, aside from the roof which was tiled with pizza slices. If Will's keen sense of smell did not deceive him, the roof had his two favourite toppings, mighty meat feast and bar-b-que chicken. 'Oh my god! I have died and gone to heaven!'

'You may get there before you think.' Anaya muttered as she watched Will run towards the house and grabbing a handful of the warm moist bread, he began stuffing it into his mouth. Reaching up he pulled off a pizza tile slice and tried to stuff that in too. He presented a charming sight with most of the pizza sauce smeared around his face and garlic butter dripped down his chin.

'Hwarf sumph!' He encouraged Anaya, both his hands full of food as well as his mouth. 'Frow Hungfry!' From inside the house there came a soft muffled voice calling out. 'Nibble, nibble, gnaw, gnaw, Who is nibbling at my little house?' Will froze mid mouthful.

Anaya rolled her eyes and answered. 'The wind, the wind. The heaven-born wind,'

'The what?' Will whispered, spraying garlic bread crumbs all over Anaya. She brushed them off irritably. Silently, the door to the cottage opened to reveal an elderly lady with beautiful silver-white hair, tied up in a bun framed a cheerful brown face and two dark-brown eyes that twinkled mischievously.

'Cara mio. This one, he is hungry one,' the old lady pinched Will's cheek between two surprisingly strong fingers and shook it, 'He likes his food no?'

'Yes, he likes it very much.' Anaya said. It was evident to her at least why the woman had a house like this.

'You come with me. You remind me of my boy Alfredo. He like his food too. He especially like Mama's cooking. Inside the house, I have fresh meataballs. My own special recipe.' Will found himself ushered into the house.

Anaya grabbed his other arm and tried to pull him in the other direction, 'That's a lovely offer really, but we must be going.' The lady looked crestfallen,

'Ees ok, I understand. My boys, they don't come to see me, the young they are so busy with their lives, they are in business, you know? They don't call; they don't write. Ees fine, don't you worry about me. You go on your way. They are only suc-culent Italian meataballs in a fine Neapolitan sauce with gar-lic and rosemary roastie potatoes?' She looked at them slyly. Even Anaya had to admit it did sound good, and it had been an awful long time since she had eaten anything other than stale bread. The old lady lowered her voice, next to Will's ear, 'I think I may even have some beer from when my boys were last here?' That was the clincher. Will was already halfway through the door before Anaya could stop him.

'We'll just stay for a little while,' he said, seating himself at the table, 'It would be rude not to.'

'And you cara mio, you young girls never eat enough. The men, they like a bit of meat on the bones.' The old lady pinched Anaya cruelly around the waist. 'You a just a bag of bones. I giva you nice meal, yes? Then you find a nice husband.'

Anaya reluctantly followed her into the little cottage and sat down at the big wooden table. The old lady was already fill-ing an enormous bowl from the hob. Although, that wasn't the item that caught Anaya's main attention, almost taking up the entire end wall of the kitchen was a gigantic pizza oven. She felt a shudder go down her spine. This house may not be gingerbread, but it looked to be the adult equivalent. Will was already tucking into the bowl of pasta that had been placed in front of him, noisily slurping the sauce and licking his lips. The old woman seemed to have lost her doddery gait and was now moving around the kitchen at quite high speed. A bottle of Italian lager was placed by Will's right elbow while Anaya had a steaming bowl of meatballs clattered under her nose. 'Eat, eat!'

Anaya picked at it nervously. Somehow Will seemed oblivious to the danger they were in. The old woman hovered nearby watching Will eat with delight. 'You want I should make you some carbonara? I maka de best carbonara in de world!'

Will nodded excitedly, chugging another mouthful of beer. The woman's gaze came to rest on Anaya. The eyes didn't seem quite so mischievous, more malevolent. 'Was wrong wiv you? You don't like my meatballs?'

'Mmmm, yes, yes, they are lovely.' Anaya hoped she sounded more convincing than she felt. She took a large mouthful to reiterate her point.

The woman nodded her approval then went back to her hob, 'Gnocchi? You like gnocchi?' She moved further away.

Anaya leaned across to Will. 'You have to stop eating!' She hissed.

'Are you mad? This stuff is amazing. You should try the lamb.' he waved a fork at her.

She pushed it to one side. 'Doesn't any of this seem familiar? A house made of food, old lady wanting to feed you up?' Will shook his head, and then realisation began to dawn, 'Are you saying that you think she wants to eat us?' he squeaked.

'Shhh! I think there is a very good chance of it, don't you?' She said, gesturing at the décor.

'But she seems so…' Will hissed before he was interrupted.

'You stop eating! Why do you stop eating? I have lots of food for you to try. You want another beer?' Will looked like a rabbit caught in headlights until he realised that Anaya was eating once more and decided to follow her example. As soon as the old woman's back was turned, he stopped, strangely his appetite seemed to have gone.

'I wonder…' said Anaya. 'If perhaps we could have one of your wonderful pizzas?'

The old lady's eyes flamed momentarily. 'You wanna pizza? I make you all this wonderful pasta, and you wanna pizza?'

'Um, I would like one too. If it isn't too much trouble? Pizza is just my favourite, and I can't imagine that anyone would make it as well as you?' The old ladies face changed immediately, an almost beautiful smile crossed her lips, 'for you, my darling boy, is no trouble at all! What do you want, pepperoni, anchovies?'

'You surprise me!' He said with a wide smile.

The old lady began to sing as she prepared the pizza dough, tossing and twisting it in the air. Her dough prepared, the elderly hands were a blur as cupboards were opened and toppings sliced and chopped.

'When I give the signal be ready.' Anaya hissed.

After what seemed an age, the old lady opened the oven to light it Anaya shouted 'Now!' They rose together and rushed the old lady, pushing her head first into the unlit pizza oven slamming the door behind her. Before she could escape they made a bolt for the door, Will pausing only to grab a large piece of garlic bread on the way.

~ ~

Later that day a large black limousine stopped outside the garlic bread cottage. Two men got out wearing sunglasses and smart black suits. They looked either way before entering. Once inside they heard the banging and, after some searching, they opened the pizza oven door to find a slightly dishevelled little Italian lady inside.

'Mama!' They both exclaimed together.

'Salvatore! Alfredo! The most terrible thing!'

'What happened Mama? Who did this terrible thing to you?' asked Alfredo, the elder.

The old woman recounted her ordeal to her sons who shook their heads and exclaimed at each twist and turn of the tale.

'But I don't understand Mama, why did they shove you in the pizza oven?' Salvatore wanted to know.

The old woman shook her head, 'I donna know. I was here feeding them, you boys know how I love to cook and now the familia is all gone, I don't get the chance. Then crash they push me in the oven!'

'You're too trusting, mama! I tell you, don't open the door to strangers, don't build your house from garlic bread, but do you listen to Salvatore, no!'

'But they looked so hungry!' The old lady was almost in tears.

The two boys exchanged a hard look.

Alfredo cracked his knuckles. 'No-one does that to our Mama. I think we should explain how things work around here.'

~~

Anaya and Will did not stop running until the cottage was miles behind them. If the witch escaped, then there was no doubt that she would be upon them pretty quickly. The trees were getting closer together, the leaves rustling ominously.

Will was eventually forced to stop for breath. He was bending with his hands on his knees, trying to dislodge the stitch under his ribs when he noticed a cloak hanging over the bough of a tree. It was a fantastic shade of red and clearly velvet, judging by the way the fading light danced across the material, all the way up to the fur-lined hood.

Anaya, several metres in front, did not realise what he was doing until it was too late. Will reached out to take down the cloak, he cradled it next to his cheek, feeling the softness of the material.

Anaya stormed back to him, 'Are you a complete idiot?' She shouted, 'Of course I realise that is obvious but don't you think we are in enough trouble?'

'I thought you might be cold!' Will answered, sheepishly holding out his prize.

'Thank you, but red cloak with a hood in the woods?'

Will glanced at the cloak 'What's your point?'

'Let's see. What does a red cloak remind you of, no rush, take your time?'

'Ah.' He grimaced.

'That's all you can say... Ah? You may as well put a large sign above our heads with the message 'Come and get us.'

'Ah.' Will said again.

'I think this time you may have well and truly done it.' The morph said, throwing her arms up in exasperation.

Will looked sheepish. He hung the cloak back on the tree, giving it a few friendly pats for good measure.

'A little late for that, I think,' Anaya said, grabbing the cloak with one hand and Will with the other. We've already picked it up. I guess we're on our way to grandma's house, do you want to be red or shall I?' Within the woods, a pair of glittering eyes watched with interest.

CHAPTER 37

'Leibowitz. I need to talk to you about Cassandra.' Adam said, bursting into the office.

'How did you get in here?' The American asked. 'I'm supposed to have my visitors screened. I may as well get a revolving door!'

'Don't blame your sweet little receptionist. She was made an offer she couldn't refuse.' Murray raised an eyebrow. 'I'm taking her out on Friday. Anyway, I need to talk about Cass, and I know now is a perfect time.'

Murray made a mental note to hire a new assistant, preferably one who could block the door bodily if necessary. 'What about her?'

'For one thing, she thinks she's in charge of the project and, for another, I think she may possibly be some kind of homicidal maniac.'

'Don't hold back will you fella, say what you mean.' Murray said, leaning back in his chair.

'I want to know why she thinks she's the controlling partner? Oh, and she also seems to be attempting to blackmail me.'

'What can she possibly have on you?' Murray said with a smirk. 'I mean, given your reputation.' He tailed off.

'I took the V10 from Will. Now she won't give it back. Holding it for what you Americans would call collateral.' Adam said.

'She's a piece of work all right.' Murray agreed.

'Now I am assuming that given your approval of what she's

doing she has something on you too?' Adam said, leaning across the desk.

Murray pursed his lips against his fingers. 'Of course not, what on earth could she have on me?' He said with an unconvincing laugh.

'That's what I'm asking you. Let me put it another way. I need to get hold of that console. If it is responsible for Wills condition, you don't want a lawsuit on your hands now do you, terrible publicity. I need to check it.'

The American laughed. 'And you think she is gonna just hand it over to me? I think you may have underestimated the little lady.'

'You could at least try.' Adam said in frustration.

Murray smiled, opening his hands. 'I have nothing that she needs. You, on the other hand...'

'I, on the other hand, what? I have something?' Adam asked, his brow furrowing.

'You may have a certain... influence.' Murray said with an amused shrug.

'I don't think so. Last time I saw her, you could say there was a definite chill in the air.'

Leibowitz watched him over the pyramid of his fingers. 'How can I put this delicately? Whatever you have done to make her pissed at you, undo it. I know for a fact that she harbours a certain fondness for you.'

'Huh?'

'Oh, don't be such a moron. It's cards on the table time.' He paused for a moment as if considering his words carefully. 'You could say Cassandra was something of a freelance operator.' Adam said nothing waiting for Murray to continue. 'It's standard practice. Like a scout.'

'What, like a boy scout?'

Murray let it pass. 'An Indian scout. They are out looking for talent. The idea is they make the necessary introductions to the right people.'

'In this case, you and us?' Adam said.

'Indeed. But our lady is no fool. She saw a meal ticket right there and wanted in on the ground floor. However, the object of her intentions, you, were apparently oblivious to her charms, at least for anything long term so,' Murray clapped his hands. 'being the ultimate professional she went for the backup option.'

'Huh?'

'Oh come on baby, you can't be that clueless! She went for the next best thing?'

'Will?'

'Will.' Murray got up and walked around the desk, slapping a hand on Adam's shoulder. 'So, if I was twenty years younger, a coupla hundred pounds lighter and in your position, I would be using that to my advantage.'

'The bitch!' Adam said with a look of horror.

'You got that right. I've been in this game a long time buddy, and I have to tell you she is one cold-hearted...'

'I'm not sure I can do that to Will. For some reason, he is besotted with her.' Adam said.

'You want the gizmo back or not?'

Adam considered the options. 'It doesn't seem right. Will's a mate.'

'A mate who would want you to protect his interests.' Murray said, patting his shoulder again.

'Are you sure about this?' Adam asked suddenly.

'That's what you came here for wasn't it, my help? At the same time, you will be getting rid of a rather uncomfortable thorn in my side and protecting the thing I care about most.'

'Your reputation?'

Leibowitz laughed. 'Hell no! That ship has long sailed my friend, no, something far more important. My money.'

As Adam left a look of satisfaction grew across the American's face. He pressed the intercom button. 'Put me through to research and development.' After a few minutes, the intercom buzzed with a metallic voice. 'Have some of the boys collect up the prototypes for the V10 project. I want everything, every scrap of paper, piece of metal, the lot, and I want it here by the end of the day.' The voice crackled. 'No, no need to bother them, they will be far too tied up for the next few days, just get me that stuff ok?' Murray listened for a moment to the response. Slamming a hand down on the desk, he shouted into the box. 'What do I pay you for? I don't goddamn care how you do it, just do it!' He hit the disconnect button furiously. 'When did everyone grow a goddamned conscience?'

~~

'I'm guessing this is Grandma's house.' Anaya said as they approached the tumbledown cottage nestling in the trees.

'How can you tell?' Will asked.

'This is where the path ends, there are large wolf prints up to the door, and there was a sign back there saying Grandma's house.' The morph smirked.

'Wolf prints?' Will turned around and began to walk back along the path. Anaya grabbed his braces. 'I don't think so 'Mr you got us into this with your I've just found this cloak in the woods' we have to see it through.'

'Why?' The braces twanged hard. 'You make a good point,' he said, rubbing his chest. Will knocked softly on the door. 'Oh dear, no-one home,' he said, turning back along the path. Anaya grabbed his braces again and pulled them back. 'Ok, ok,' he said.

Releasing him gently, Anaya knocked on the door loud enough to alert anyone in the surrounding area.

A shaky voice answered. 'Come in.' Will lifted the latch and pushed the door open cautiously. Inside the cottage was in semi-darkness. The curtains on the small window had been drawn, shutting out any sunlight. In the gloom, they could just about make out a shadowy figure hunched up under the bed-clothes. 'Come closer, my dears, and shut the door, there is a terrible draft.'

'Is it the wolf?' Will whispered.

They crept closer to the bed. 'Come along dearies. I won't bite.'

'Can we have that in writing?' Will asked before Anaya elbowed him in the ribs.

The bedding chuckled. 'I do like you young people with a sense of humour.' There was not much to see. Where the blankets ended, the giant nightcap began. All that peeped out at them was a pair of pale eyes.

'Now look here, play fair. Are you or are you not a wolf!' Will demanded, dodging quickly to avoid any torpedo elbows.

The bedclothes shook with another chuckle. 'Goodness me no.' The voice quivered. 'Whatever will you think of next, a wolf in bed, how unhygienic.'

'Then why don't you show yourself!' Will asked.

'I haven't been very well, my dears. I've had a little accident. It's best to stay in bed. Tell me who are you, young man.'

'It doesn't matter who we are. It's who you are that is under discussion.' He countered.

'You are in my cottage. Therefore, I think I have the right to know who broke into a defenceless old lady's home.' She said, quite reasonably.

'We didn't break-in, you invited us in, and it is still to be proved that you are, in fact, a lady, old or otherwise.' Will said pedantically.

'It's your word against mine sonny Jim.' The alleged grandma snapped. 'Now dearies.' She tried a more wheedling tone. 'I'm thinking you might be this human gentleman that we have heard so much about and you may be a naughty little girl on the run?'

'Who told you that?' Anaya asked.

'It's the word around the forest.' The bedclothes shrugged.

'That bloody bluebird!' Anaya said.

'So it's true.' The voice said triumphantly. 'How very alarming, two desperate fugitives in my own home. What is a poor grandmother to do with no – one to defend her.'

'But you're a...' Will began, but the bedclothes were no longer paying attention to him.

'I said.' She began again. 'What is a poor grandmother to do with no-one to DEFEND HER?'

They waited. 'Oh, for goodness sake!' With one sweep the bedclothes were thrown back revealing a little old lady with both arms in plaster. 'What?' She said with a shrug. 'You were expecting Santa clause perhaps?'

'We weren't expecting you!' Anaya said.

'Do you know her?' Will asked bemused.

'I should say so. This is Ethel, our representative on the committee. Morph representative.'

'Honourable member for polymorphic services if you don't mind!' Ethel added. Walking across the room, she stood in front of a cupboard and gave the bottom a hearty kick. She said again. 'No-one... to... DEFEND HER!' With difficulty, she struggled with the catch.

'Would you like some help with that?' Will asked eventually.

'Could you dearie?' She said with a sweet smile.

Will lifted the latch and opened the door. Inside the cupboard, the wolf was waking up from a refreshing nap. Yawning and stretching, he flolloped sideways, looking up at the upside-down face of a furious mistress.

'Having a nice rest, are we?' Ethel asked, the tone of her voice could have cut diamonds. The wolf rolled onto his back his tail banging uncertainly against the back of the cupboard.

'He doesn't look very dangerous.' Will commented quietly into Anaya's ear.

'Looks can be deceiving.' She replied, beginning to back away.

'You idiot!' Ethel aimed a foot in the Wolf's direction. 'I said, and believe me if I have to repeat it, someone is going to be taking a visit to the rug factory, poor old lady etc. etc. no-one to DEFEND HER!'

Within seconds the Wolf had come to his senses, leapt to his feet and was snarling at the visitors.

'My, what big teeth you have.' Will said involuntarily.

'No. Not teeth, first ears, or eyes...' The wolf looked to his mistress for confirmation. All he received was a kick in the tail.

'Get on with it.' She snapped. 'The only important thing is that they are all the better for eating with.'

'Yes,' said the wolf, returning to his attack position. 'Eating better.' Licking his slobbering lips, T.B.B began to advance.

'You can do what you want with the morph; all I want is the inventor. I don't mind if he's a bit mangled, but I want him alive.'

Will and Anaya began to back away. They retreated towards the door.

'Quickly! Get them before they escape! Cut them off, cut off the door!!!' Ethel screamed. As they reached the door, Will and

Anaya turned to run. They didn't get past the threshold as coming the other way was Ceun. Dressed in checked tunic and breeks, he was every inch the storybook woodcutter, including the hand which held a rather large, sharp-looking axe.

He strode into the room and, swishing the blade dramatically, said. 'Somebody order some wolf kebabs?'

CHAPTER 38

Adam toyed with the mobile phone. It seemed to be mocking him. 'How hard can it be?' he muttered, 'she's just an ordinary woman like any other.'

A little voice inside chuckled nastily. 'She's not just any woman though is she? She is a barking nut job who happens to be married to your best friend.' Adam paced the kitchen again, trying to ignore the internal monologue.

'This is for the good of Will,' he said out loud.

'Like he's going to see it that way.' The voice added.

'Oh, shut up.' Adam said addressing the microwave, which happily obliged.

Nervously, Adam called up Cassandra's name on his phone. He was just about to press 'voice call' when the voice piped up maliciously. 'What if it doesn't work? Perhaps you don't want it to? With Will out of the way you can have Cass and the whole company.'

Adam ran a hand over his dreadlocks. Putting down the phone, he tied his hair back. 'This is ridiculous. Will is a mate, and I don't even like the scheming cow. But, I am going to be charming, and I am going to be nice, and I am going to get that console back. Then I'll deal with the fallout.' Adam snatched the phone and pressed call before he could change his mind. As it connected, there was an invisible flutter of wings and an inaudible sigh of disappointment.

'Cassandra? It's me.' There was a pause on the other end of the phone. 'Adam.' The silence continued. 'Are you there? It's

Adam.'

'Yes, I know,' she said eventually. Adam could picture her looking at her nails in that bored way. 'What do you want... Adam.'

'I was just wondering how you are.' He said.

'You saw me earlier, and you didn't seem too concerned as to my welfare then. I suppose you think you can sweet talk me into giving you that console? Well, it's not going to happen, so don't even bother.'

Adam paced the floor. 'Look, I'll get to the point. I know that you're upset with me, and I don't blame you.'

'You don't?' Cassandra said uncertainly.

'No. You have every right to be upset, really angry even.' Adam crossed his fingers. 'Here we are, friends, close friends, and all I've been worried about is Will. Who has been worrying about you, hmm?'

'Worried about saving your neck, you mean.' Cassandra huffed.

'What's to worry about? If the console is responsible, then I'm sure you having it locked up safe is the best place for it. With you looking after the project, there is no way it could screw up. We should have got you involved before.' He said as sincerely as he could manage.

'You should. I have excellent organisational skills.' She said, mollified.

'You do, not to mention some fantastic ideas... the new name, for example?'

'You hated it.' Cassandra said sharply.

Adam paused. 'Only because I hadn't really thought about it. But now I see...' he swallowed hard, 'daydream believer is an excellent name. I can see it on the shelves now.'

'I'm glad to see you have come around to my way of thinking,' Cassandra said, her voice thick with suspicion. 'So was there something else that you wanted?'

'No, no, nothing. I just wanted to tell you I am sorry for not being more supportive and if there is anything you need, then I am there for you. Anytime.'

'This sudden concern. It wouldn't have anything to do with the console then?' She said suspiciously.

'You keep it. I don't want it. All I ask is that you get one of your so,' He paused, 'your expert engineers to give it the once over, just to make sure. I am just sorry I've not been a good enough friend.'

'I...' Cassandra tailed off.

'Just say you forgive me.' Adam wheedled.

'I... suppose so.' She said. Adam could hear the confusion in her voice.

'Thank you. I mean it, anything you need. I am there for you, babe.' Adam thought he might be pushing things a little there.

'Ok. Thank you.' She said.

He breathed a sigh of relief. 'I'll see you soon. You take care of yourself.'

~~

The wolf immediately reversed direction and was trying to climb back into the cupboard.

'What are you doing, idiot!' Ethel screamed.

'Axe means bad!' T.B.B. said, trying to squeeze himself into a shoebox.

'Not as bad as it's going to be if you don't stop being a spineless wimp and take control of the situation.' Ethel growled.

'Talk about the nick of time!' Will said. 'I could hug you!'

'Suppress the urge!' Ceun replied quickly.'

'You're not a cat?' Anaya said.

'Yes, I know. Do you want to hug me?' Ceun asked with a smirk.

'I think I can hold it in.' She replied. 'Why aren't you a cat?'

'I suppose different story, different part to play. I passed out and woke up with this baby lying next to me.' He adjusted the axe so the light glinted from the razor-sharp blade.

'Boys and their toys.' She sighed. 'What about the collar?' She pulled at his tunic.

'Still there.' Ceun removed her hand gently. 'I see you two have been making friends?'

The wolf had succeeded in burying most of his head in the box and covering the rest with a blanket. His rear end quivered in fear.

'Will you get out of there you mangy mongrel!' Ethel shouted. The only effect was for the wolf to squeeze further into the corner.

'Aren't you supposed to be afraid of him, wasn't he going to eat you?' Anaya asked.

The older morph looked guilty for a moment. She seemed to shrink in stature to perfect frail old lady proportions.

'Indeed,' she said her voice quavering with effort. 'Thank goodness you young people came along when you did.'

'You were trying to get it to eat us!' Will said.

'And you're not being very nice to the wolf either.' Anaya added.

'You must have been mistaken. I was trying to distract it while you escaped!' Ethel insisted.

'You were telling him to cut us off at the door!' Will shouted indignantly.

'That's what I heard.' Ceun agreed.

'You were trying to serve us up for hors d'oeuvres.' Anaya said.

'No I wasn't.' Ethel said petulantly.

Will couldn't believe what he was hearing. 'Yes, you were!'

'No, I wasn't. I have never seen this mangy mutt before in my life.'

'Why did he call you his mistress then?' Will asked waggling a finger at her accusingly. 'Ah-ha!'

'He didn't.' Ethel said, sitting as primly as possible on the edge of the bed.

'Ah-ha!' Will tried again.

'He didn't you know.' Anaya said thoughtfully. 'I didn't hear it either.' Ceun added.

Will stared at the two of them in disbelief. 'You can't honestly tell me that you think she's telling the truth!'

'No.' Anaya conceded. 'But the wolf didn't say it.'

'Dmftwd!' Came a muffled voice from in the cupboard.

'That's a good idea. Let's ask him.' Will strode across the room and tapped the quivering rump. 'Is this or is this not your mistress and wasn't she instructing you to eat us?'

The wolf tried to crawl further into the cupboard.

'Put the axe down.' Anaya said to Ceun. 'But!' Ceun's eyes opened wider in protest.

'I know it's nice and shiny, and you're very proud of it, but he...' She indicated the cupboard with her thumb, 'is not going to come out while you are standing there cuddling it.'

Reluctantly, Ceun placed the axe outside the cottage door.

'The axe is gone,' Anaya said. 'We just want to talk to you, I promise.'

Carefully the mound began to move. A sizeable hairy ear appeared followed by a yellow eye. The eye surveyed the room, paying particular attention to the bounty hunter. Will backed hastily away. It was one thing to approach a terrified tail end, quite another to be close to the sharp, pointed bit. Slowly the rest of the wolf crept from its hiding place, his head low.

Anaya knelt beside the embarrassed animal. 'It's all right,' she said, 'no-one is going to hurt you.' The cottage suddenly darkened. His nostrils twitching wildly, the wolf lifted his head. His eyes blazed momentarily as the axe spun across the room. T.B.B ducked just in time as the blade landed with a thwack in the wall behind him. They turned to look towards the doorway. Filling the frame was the unmistakable silhouette of the hit pig. 'There you may be wrong,' he said.

CHAPTER 39

'Cass?' Adam called. Cassandra turned slowly. 'Fancy seeing you here?' He said, catching up.

'Shouldn't you be tinkering in your little workshop?' she said, her hands on her hips.

'Leibowitz is talking to some people about going into production, so I'm playing hooky. What about you…? You look different; did you change your hair?'

Instinctively, Cassandra patted her blonde locks. 'I have a meeting this afternoon,' she said simply, 'I'm surprised you noticed.'

It wasn't so much his powers of observation, but the fact that Adam had been wandering around outside the hair salon waiting for Cassandra to emerge. It did not serve his purpose to share this particular piece of information.

'Some of us do pay attention, you know! Who's the lucky man?' He said with a wink.

Cassandra smiled slightly and dropped her eyes. 'For your information, it's not a man. It's with a magazine if you must know.'

'I hope it's for the fashion pages because you are looking hot.' He said as Cassandra struggled not to smile. 'But before you go and storm the pages of Vogue, I don't suppose you feel like catching a quick drink?'

Cassandra glanced at the thin gold watch on her wrist, her lips pursed in indecision. 'Don't worry.' He said, waving a hand dismissively. 'I know you're probably on a tight schedule, only I rarely get the opportunity to make an entire pub jealous?'

She tapped a manicured nail against her lips. 'Ok,' She said finally, 'A quick drink, but only because I'm feeling charitable.'

'Would there be any other reason?' He said, with a small bow as he gestured towards the nearest pub.

~ ~

The tiny dragon watched from the rafters. It belched uncomfortably. Something wasn't right. It hiccupped and felt its whole body quiver with the repercussions. It was not feeling well at all.

Hackles raised the wolf arched his back ready to pounce. 'So... It's the little lap dog,' Porkio sneered.

'Pig!' T.B.B. spat through bared teeth.

'Well done, someone give that puppy a bone, he needs one where his spine should be.'

'You two know each other?' Will asked.

'Yes, clearly you're old friends,' Anaya said hurriedly, 'you obviously have a lot of catching up to do. We'll get out of your way.' She tried to usher Ceun and Will towards the door, but it was filled with 18 stone of rippling pork.

'I don't think so. You have caused me a considerable amount of trouble. I have taken it very personally.' Porkio said, taking off his sunglasses. They gazed into the black pits where his pupils should be.

'We're very sorry for any inconvenience.' Will said safely hidden behind Anaya.

The wolf let out a low menacing growl.

The hit pigs head snapped back to focus on the wolf. 'Shut up Fido.'

'No shut up,' T.B.B. snarled. 'No need shut up. How house building?'

'HA!' Porkio spat. 'Good enough for any huffing and puffing you can do, you pathetic excuse for a chimney brush.'

'And how are brothers... Oh, I remember... Bar-b-qued.' The wolf said with a huge lick of his lips.

'Why you...!' Porkio lunged forward but not quite enough to clear a path to the door.

'Can't you voodoo yourself into whatever passes for pig passion?' Ceun whispered to Anaya.

'It's not something I can just switch on if he doesn't see it then...' she replied in the same hushed tone.

'Hey! Hey!' Ceun shouted, waving his arms. Porkio turned his head slowly as if operated by gears. 'Look who we have here?' Ceun said, pushing Anaya forwards slightly.

Porkio regarded the polymorph for a moment. 'So?' he said eventually. 'Don't you want to talk to her, make up for old times?' Ceun tried again.

He stopped short as a sharp elbow hit him in the stomach. 'Stop trying to pimp me out!' Anaya said under her breath. To the pig, she managed a half-smile.

'No.' The clockwork neck turned back to the wolf.

'Great... are your powers on the blink or something?' Ceun said into Anaya's ear.

'Me?' She almost shouted then looked hurriedly to see if the pig was watching them. He wasn't. She started again, several octaves lower. 'This is a creature who probably loved his sweetheart, mother, grandmother and sister... would happily send them to a watery grave but loved them none the less... in his own way. I'm not likely to send his pulses racing in any form, am I?'

'Settle this pig...' The wolf was beginning the circle to the left. They only needed Porkio to move in sync, and the route to the door would be clear.

'It's already settled. I won.' The pig didn't budge; he just watched the wolf who was now moving back to the right.

'Bricks... bricks in a wood... you cheat!' The wolf spat.

'I still won.' The wolf chose his moment to spring. Porkio caught the snarling creature, nearly as big as himself. They staggered backwards into the doorway where they struggled, cutting off all chances of a distraction allowing their escape. Jaws snapped within inches of snout as the two wrestled to gain the advantage. With a mighty roar, sheer brute strength overcame agility, and the wolf was propelled backwards against the wall. A fine film of dust showered gently from the rafters as the wolf slid to the floor. Porkio stood teeth bared, his eyes glowing with rage in a rare loss of control.

'I have to live here, you know!' Came a petulant voice from the bed.

Remembering himself, Porkio turned his attentions back to the three potential escapees. 'Enough pleasure, back to business. If I didn't know better, I would say you three had been trying to avoid me?' The pig seemed genuinely upset if not entirely sure why.

'It's nothing personal.' Ceun said, slightly confused. 'It's just you seem to have an aura of wanting to kill us?'

'Kill you? When have I tried to kill you? If I was trying to kill you, you would know because you would be dead. On this occasion, there is someone very anxious to make the acquaintance of our human friend. I am just trying to make the introduction.'

'So, you don't want to kill us?' Anaya asked.

'Oh, I want to.' Porkio replied simply. 'But my desires cannot be allowed to interfere with business. I'm not a monster.'

'Leaving brothers... make you monster.' The heap that was T.B.B said quietly.

'Shut up, dog!' Porkio snapped.

The wolf began to hitch himself up onto his elbows. 'Wee, wee, wee, wee all the way home!'

'Isn't it time you slunk away to lick your wounds you mangy flea-bitten...' Porkio growled.

'Wee, wee, wee, wee, weeeeeeeeeeee!' Porkio's eyes flashed as he turned his full attention back towards the wolf.

'Wee, wee, wee, wee, weeeeeeeeeeeeeeeeeee!' The wolf giggled.

'Shut up!'

'All... way... home!' He finished triumphantly.

'I'm warning you mutt!' The Pig once more turned to face his nemesis.

Ceun tapped Anaya lightly on the arm and pointed towards the door. The morph, in turn, touched Will and nodded in the same direction. Porkio was now advancing on the wolf who seemed in no condition to defend himself.

'We can't just leave him!' Will said quietly, as they crept towards freedom.

'I think you will find we can, and we will. Don't forget a few minutes ago he was going to eat you.' Anaya replied firmly grabbing Wills arm and guiding him towards the door.

They had only just stepped into the sunlight when an elderly voice called out. 'They're getting a...'

The rest was drowned by an almighty explosion of snarls and squeals plus what sounded like a one-man band falling down a moving staircase.

'Now seems a good time to be somewhere else.' Ceun said. But he was already talking to himself Anaya and Will were already disappearing into the woods.

~~

Adam was surprised to find he was actually having a good

time. If he forgot the fact that his companion was married to his best friend, was utterly self-obsessed and had leanings towards murder, blackmail and world domination, her company wasn't too bad. He reminded himself that even Hitler had been described as charming on occasion.

The first drink had, in fact, turned into several. His had been a beer for Dutch courage, and hers a mineral water with just the faintest slither of lime, something to do with detoxing. Now she had to go to her meeting, Adam noted with a touch of pride that she seemed a little reluctant.

'How about something to eat later? You must be bored eating on your own?' He asked innocently. 'You could have a proper drink. You must need one with all the stress?'

'I should really visit Will at the hospital,' she said almost sadly.

'No problem, another time.' He said.

Cassandra seemed to deflate slightly. 'Unless,' Adam said, as if the idea had only just occurred to him, 'you wanted to go see him together, and we could go for a bite afterwards?'

'We could do that...' She said.

'I can book a table at that restaurant you like... Le something.' He suggested.

Cassandra smiled. 'La Grenouille Gaie. That would be wonderful.'

'Great. I will pick you up at six.' Adam tried to close his mind to what he was doing. He had to be insane, not only was he taking Cassandra to dinner, but stopping off to rub Wills nose in it on the way.

Ok technically Will would not know and was not conscious anyway, but who knew what he could or could not hear in his current state. After all the research they'd done together in the dream state, all the research and field trials, they never could've have imagined this would happen.

That first time, when Will met him on his dream beach, Adam had been sceptical. It was a dream, after all. But then what was the point in developing lucid dreaming if you didn't have faith in what you were seeing. It had all made sense at the time. Now it turned out, it was a whole other dimension, and they'd gone crashing into it completely blind. Will was stuck, and Adam wasn't sure how long his friend could hold out. Adam needed that console by any means necessary. He would just have to deal with the consequences later.

CHAPTER 40

'There doesn't seem to be anyone following us.' Will said for the fourth time as he peered over his shoulder.

'Lucky for us that they are too busy killing each other.' Ceun said. The bounty hunter nudged Anaya. 'You're very quiet?'

'I can't believe she would do that. Ethel of all people,' she said half to herself.

'You think you had the monopoly on being the bad morph?' Ceun joked.

Anaya grimaced. 'I just remembered the lecture she gave me before I went away. How I had brought disgrace upon the whole of our kind, that she was ashamed of me... ashamed, that's the word she used.'

Ceun shrugged.

'And all the time...' Anaya seethed. 'She was the sort of person who would have someone eaten by a wolf. I would never have done that... not actually eaten.'

Ceun stopped suddenly. 'Shhh!' 'Don't shush me! You asked me what was wrong. I am telling you, then because it doesn't fit in with your idea of a mwwwwwwphf!' Ceun slapped a hand over her mouth and dragged the struggling polymorph backwards towards the undergrowth. A slightly bemused Will followed. They crouched in the bushes silently. The air almost crackled with the lack of sound.

'Wh...' Anaya began as he released her. Ceun immediately placed a finger on his lips. He pointed in the direction of the path. Anaya was about to speak again when they heard it. The faintest of sounds, just on the edge of hearing, like a millipede in hobnailed boots dancing on a leaf. Ceun raised an eyebrow and. indicating that they should stay where they were, he crept forward, barely disturbing the shrubbery. A rustling from behind indicated that the others had taken absolutely no notice of him. He rolled his eyes and without looking gestured with the flat of his hand that they should stay still.

The sound was getting louder now. It was the tramp, tramp, tramp of many heavy feet that have walked far too far for far too long and are really getting rather fed up with the whole idea. The squad rounded the corner. There weren't that many of them in the grand scheme of things, just what there was filled a remarkably large amount of space. They did not look to be happy men. Immediately in front of Ceun's concealed nose, the Officer stopped and consulted with his Sergeant. Ceun held his breath.

'Let me have another look at that map old chap.' The Officer said nasally.

The Sergeant gave a long-suffering look and passed the map book across to his superior.

Taking off his hat, the officer scratched his head. 'This should have been a short cut. You see Simpson. You see there?' A finger jabbed at the map book.

Simpson obliged by looking. 'Indeed, Sir.'

'And yet we haven't the faintest blithering idea where we are?'

'No, Sir.' The long-suffering NCO agreed.

'This is really not going to go down terribly well with the people upstairs. We should have rounded up that damned human and have been home in time for mess. I'm telling you this damned map is wrong.' The Officer continued.

'Yes, Sir,' replied the Sergeant dutifully.

'We nearly had them at that damnable house, but they disappeared into thin air. I'm telling you, Sergeant, there is something seriously amiss here.' He continued.

'Yes Sir,' the Sergeant agreed miserably.

'And that blithering compass. Never shows the same direction two minutes on the bounce. It really is the most terribly bad show. Someone is for the high jump on this one, and it isn't going to be lieutenant Fotherington-Smythe-Willowby-Smith!' The Lieutenant looked expectantly at his subordinate.

'No, Sir.'

'No Sir, yes Sir. That's all you ever say. I want answers, man! I want results!' He slammed a fist into his open hand.

'I recommend we stop here for a short while, Sir. The men have been marching almost constantly for two days. Perhaps some rations and rest will clear our heads?' The Sergeant said.

Ceun shook his head involuntarily. 'No, no, no.' He mouthed.

The Officer stared at the man in front of him for a few minutes. 'Stop, you say? Rest? The men have been walking for two days. Have I not been walking right alongside them?'

'Since your horse ran away in the night, Sir yes.' The Sergeant said, suppressing a grin.

'Ran away Simpson? Did it run away, or was it the work of saboteurs?'

'I don't think you tied it up, Sir...' Simpson began before noticing the look on his superior's face.

'Perhaps that's why this map is leading us around in circles.' Willoughby-Smith continued regardless. 'We don't give in to saboteurs Simpson. They want us to give up, and so we are going to do exactly what they don't want.'

'I was simply suggesting a short rest, Sir,' said Simpson dejectedly. 'For the men's morale.'

'Precisely! And what better for morale than to complete our mission? We cannot rest. We will not rest. Get the men together Simpson. We have marching to do.'

Inwardly, Simpson sighed. 'Yes, Sir.' He turned to the platoon and shrugged. 'Squad! By the left... quick... March!'

'Let's have a rousing tune to help us on our way.' The Lieutenant said as Simpson fell into step beside him.

'Sir... I don't think...'

'A rousing anthem to lift our spirits.'

Sergeant Simpson cringed. 'Squad...By the right... four rousing verses...'

'Six,' interrupted Willoughby-Smith

'Ahem... six rousing verses of The Army is a Mother. On my mark...Mark!'

As the singing gradually faded away, Ceun allowed himself to breathe out. 'That was close,' he said. It was a few moments before he realized that there was no sound from the others. Not only was there no reply, but they didn't appear to be breathing either. Ceun turned slowly. The place where Anaya and Will should have been was strangely vacant. 'What the...?' he said to the empty space. Standing up cautiously the bounty hunter scanned the area. 'Anaya?' he hissed. 'Will?' He listened carefully. 'How on earth can they get themselves lost in a relatively small shrub?' he said crossly.

At a loss for where else to begin Ceun began to retrace their steps towards the cottage, but this time he kept to the cover of the woods. Every so often he would stop and listen, just in case, he could hear them blundering around. He was poised, listening, when the thing came out of the trees.

Some sixth sense told his body to duck before his brain really had time to register, he was just aware of the whoosh as the thing sped past missing the top of his head by inches. He stayed crouched, trying to see who or what was attacking. As he raised his head slowly, the thing took another swoop. It was coming so fast that he had time to register wings, but that was about all. He felt around for something to defend himself. His fingers touched a fallen branch. Not exactly as reassuring as a sword, but it would have to do for now. Ceun waited and watched the canopy; suddenly, the creature appeared almost on top of him. He raised the branch, but before the swing had even started the wood was plucked from his hands. The branch and its abductor swept off through the trees, leaves clattering in its wake. Within seconds it had returned but on a much lower trajectory. Ceun watched frozen as it passed directly over him throwing down the branch. It was directly on target smacking the bounty hunter squarely on the head. Ceun sat up rubbing the lump as the creature landed in a tree to look at him. He could have sworn it was grinning a big dragon grin.

Ceun stepped from his hiding place. Keeping his full attention on the owl sized dragon, he edged forward until he was standing in front of the tree. The dragon watched with its head on one side.

'Aren't you supposed to be protecting Will?' The dragon turned its head to the other side. 'How does dropping woodland on me look after your charge, or was that just for fun?' The dragon yawned. 'Have you lost him too?' A half-hearted flame shot out from the tree landing short of Ceun by a few feet, but he got the general impression that he'd asked a rude question. Stretching out its wings, the dragon flew to a tree in the direction Ceun had just walked. It stopped and turned to look at the bounty hunter.

'I see. You want me to follow you.' Ceun began to walk towards the new tree. 'Here's an idea,' he said, 'Why don't you just get larger and we'll fly there?' Despite the lack of expression, the dragon still managed to convey a look of utter disgust before flying on to its next perch. Ceun shrugged. 'Or I'll just walk.'

CHAPTER 41

Cassandra bit her lip thoughtfully as she ended the call to Adam. There had been drinks, there had been dinner, and she had to admit she was enjoying the attention.

'He's after something.' A little whiney voice piped up in her head. She put the mobile phone down and checked her hair in the hall mirror as a distraction. 'When was he ever this nice to you before? It's the console he wants, not you.'

'But.' Cassandra answered herself. 'He never had the opportunity before.'

'HA!' Squawked the voice. 'There were plenty of chances before you got together with Will.'

Unseen on her shoulder Lily, the paranoia faery was tapping a fuchsia talon on the edge of her wand. The readings were off the chart, and this was far too easy. She wouldn't have to work for months after this haul. Settling down the faery took off an impossibly high aquamarine slingback and rubbed her foot.

Even as flying for a primary mode of transport, these shoes were killing her, but they were worth it for all the envious looks she'd had in the office. No-one said being a fashion icon was painless[TT2].

'He's had a chance to get to know me now. He realises what he's missed.' Cassandra told herself. She inspected her eyes, turning her head this way and that.

Lily smiled. 'You're developing a few crows' feet around your eyes.' She whispered, 'I bet lover boy notices them. He's not going to want an old woman!' Lily didn't feel malice towards the people she whispered to, and she didn't feel pity. It was just a job, and the more she could get out of it, the better. 'Remember the dream you had. Adam came to you and then what happened?' Cassandra shuddered involuntarily. 'That's right. You held out your arms to him, and what did he do? Hmm? He looked at you in horror. Do you remember how your upper arms wobbled as you lifted them? And he laughed. Remember how he laughed at you, why would he want you!'

'It was a dream!' Cassandra said to her reflection.

'Was it? Or was it that your mind knows he doesn't really want you. You see him with different women all the time, flirting and charming, but when has that ever been directed at you? You're not good enough for him.'

Cassandra could feel tears welling up in her eyes. 'I like him,' she said to herself. 'He wouldn't spend time with me if he didn't want to.'

Lily checked the dial on the wand. It was in the red zone, try getting any more in there, and it could overload. Turning it off, she slipped on her shoes and got unsteadily to her feet.

'You're probably right,' she whispered into Cassandra's ear, and with a slight poof, she vanished.

~~

The dragon had been flying gradually further away before stopping meaning Ceun had to run to catch up.

'I hope this isn't just a wild dragon chase,' he said to the disappearing wings and tail as he watched them take another long glide through the treetops. This time as he approached the dragon didn't move. Perching perfectly still, it levied its full attention on a clearing ahead. Silently Ceun moved closer for a better look. Back to back in the centre sat Will and Anaya, with their hands bound together. Judging by Anaya, who was facing towards him, they were also gagged. Ceun noticed with a spark of pride that her feet were also bound tightly. Clearly, she had managed a trademark kick at some point in her capture. There did not seem to be anyone else around.

'Pssst!' Ceun said, barely showing himself behind the foliage. Anaya seemed to be focusing most of her attention on trying to wriggle out of her bonds. 'Pssst!' Ceun said again, risking a little more exposure. Still, she did not see him. Picking up a small stone, he weighed it for a moment in his hand. Checking there was still no new company, he tossed the stone in front of the polymorph. She froze at the sudden movement. Anaya scanned the undergrowth for the source of the missile. Her eyes opened slightly in recognition as the bounty hunter revealed his location. She began to shout incoherently hindered by the gag. Ceun put his finger to his lips for her to be silent.

'Who did this to you?' He mouthed. Anaya rolled her eyes and chuntered something muffled. 'Ok. Stupid question.' Ceun said to himself. He mouthed again. 'Are you hurt?' Anaya shook her head. 'Will?' Anaya slumped sideways with her eyes shut. 'Unconscious?' The morph opened an eye and looked questioningly. 'I said unconscious.' Ceun mouthed. She thought for a moment, then nodded. 'Where are they?' Anaya shrugged.

'Helpful!' muttered Ceun taking care not to be facing her as he said it. The morph seemed to be listening. With a sharp nod of her head, she indicated the trees to her right. Whoever they were, they were coming back.

~~

Will was aware of being back in his own body, his real human body. Even though he half knew it was hopeless, he attempted to wriggle his toes. It occurred to him after a few minutes that this was perhaps ambitious, if they were moving, he couldn't see it anyway. He concentrated on his left eyelid. 'If I can just open that eye, then I will be back.' He thought. So engrossed was he in this monumental task that he didn't notice the door open. Only when he felt rather than heard the chair move closer to his bed did Will concentrate on the person in the room. There was a long sigh, followed by prolonged silence. 'Who are you?' Will screamed in his head, eyelid aerobics forgotten. A hand touched his. Will wanted to jump with surprise, but his body stayed in its same catatonic state.

'Buddy?' A voice said eventually. 'Adam! Adam's here!' Will tried to move. He wanted to scream in frustration. 'It's getting crazy here man. I must admit I have my doubts. What if I just wanted you to be there so badly that I made you up in my dream?'

'No!' Will shouted internally. 'You have to get the console. Don't give up!'

'I'm trying to get close to Cassandra.' Adam continued. 'But I wonder why I'm doing it. I told myself to get the V10, but what if I'm just...' He sighed again. 'Will, buddy, if there is any way that you can give me a sign. I need to know I'm not going crazy! If, when you wake up, you're going to go mad when you find out how I've been playing up to Cass. What if I imagined that dream? If you're in there man, I need some help here before it goes too far.'

~~

Crashing through the undergrowth, Salvatore brushed the foliage from his suit. He turned as something hit the ground behind him and rolled. Reaching into the ferns, the thug grabbed his brother by the scruff of the neck and hauled him into the clearing. Alfredo tried to regain his composure.

'Something tripped me!' he said petulantly.

'The only thing that tripped you was your big clumsy feet!' Salvatore snapped.

Ceun watched as the big man walked towards the captives. Anaya was slumped with her eyes shut.

'They still haven't come around.' Salvatore nudged Anaya with his foot. Ceun thought he could see the faintest glimmer of movement in her face, but she kept still.

'I used the recommended dose...' Alfredo said petulantly.

'They were supposed just to come quietly, not be completed out of it for hours. That second dose was unnecessary.' Salvatore said.

'It wasn't you she kicked in the meatballs!' Alfredo winced at the memory.

'Well we can't move them until they're able to walk, that is unless you fancy carrying a couple of dead weights back to Mama's?' Salvatore asked.

'Why don't we just get rid of them here? A shallow grave, no-one would ever know. It'd be easy while they're out of it?' Alfredo reasoned.

Salvatore slapped his brother around the head. 'What's the point if they don't know what they've done? They wake up dead and think... why are we dead, hmm must have been an accident or something... Think! They need to know why.'

'Mama isn't going to like it. You know she hates us to bring work home!' Alfredo earned another slap.

'This isn't work, this is personal. Do you remember what they did to Mama? You think she's going to have any pity for them?' He spat angrily on the ground. Alfredo followed his brother's example.

'You're right,' he said, wiping a stray drop of spittle from his chin. 'I say we wake them up and get them moving.'

Ceun wriggled silently backwards until he was out of earshot. The dragon fluttered lightly down to the grass beside him.

'Can't you just go in there and incinerate them?' Ceun said quietly. The dragon yawned and looked at a talon as though it had only just noticed it had them. 'I'm guessing that's a no then. Which is why you need me.' Ceun answered his own question. 'How about causing a distraction while I pull them clear?' The dragon scratched its ear thoughtfully, using the newly discovered claw. 'You go into the trees over there, start a fire or a commotion or something, and when they come to see what's happening, I'll rescue Anaya and Will?' The creature flopped sideways and lay prone on the grass. It was changing colour to a rather unpleasant shade of puce. 'I'm not sure whether you understand me or not… what's the matter are you sick?' He asked, then added to himself. 'More importantly, I'm having a conversation with a dragon!'

'You think that's bad. You should try it from my angle. Am I right, or am I right?' Said a voice, it sounded a very long way away but close by at the same time. Ceun jumped back. He looked around there was no-one he could see. By now the creature was lying on the grass with its forked tongue hanging out of its mouth. Its chest heaved.

'Was that you?' Ceun asked the prone creature. 'Dragons can't talk, can they?'

'Too bloody right and they don't have any bloody manners either. Otherwise, they wouldn't go around eating people!' The voice complained.

'Rox? Is that you?' Ceun asked, 'where are you?'

'Where do you think I am? I'm in the bloody dragon. I'll teach the soddin' thing to watch who it goes around eating with neither a by nor leave.' Rox replied.

'You're doing something to it?' It occurred to Ceun that talking to a Dragon was one thing, talking to its presumably partially digested lunch was entirely another level of insanity.

'Only gone into its bloody bloodstream, haven't I? I wasn't going to be flushed out in assorted turds spread all over the bloody countryside. I may never be myself again! Plus, it was a bleedin' liberty. It needs to learn who it's dealing with!'

'You're going to have to stop it. I need snappy here to rescue the others.' Ceun said.

'Tough mate! This little bugger needs a lesson.' Rox said as the dragon gave another groan.

'Do you really want to spend the rest of eternity inside a decomposing dragon? Because from out here, the way it looks now, it isn't going to last the day.' Ceun argued.

'How long can it take for one of these sods to dissolve? Then I reform, and Bob's your uncle,' said Rox. 'Easy peasy lemon squeezy.'

'Try centuries! In the right environment, they can last even longer, possibly even forever, and believe me, you kill that dragon, and I'll make sure it is preserved in the most boring place I can find!' Ceun reasoned.

Rox hesitated. 'You wouldn't!' He said eventually.

'Oh, believe me, I would. You think prison was bad. You try being trapped in there for the rest of existence. Nothing to break the monotony, no-one to talk to just stuck there forever and ever and ever and...'

'Ok. Ok! I get the bleedin' picture!' Rox grumbled.

'At least this way you'll get to see a bit of the world?' Ceun reasoned.

'Bloody marvellous!' Rox was not convinced. 'I feel so much better now...'

Ceun risked a bob up to peer over the shrubs. He could make out the thugs milling around Will and Anaya. 'How long will it take... for you to flush yourself out?' He asked.

'I'm doing it. I'm doing it. It will take as long as it takes.' Rox muttered.

'Do you think we could manage a little more accurate timescale than that? I'm on a kind of schedule here!'

'It took me days to get in here... you do the math sunshine.' Rox snapped back.

Ceun ran both hands through his hair. 'Days! We haven't got days! I need that dragon back on its feet now, immediately, ten minutes ago ideally!'

'No can do John. How did I know you were going to want the bloody lizard? I'll do it as fast as I can, but molecules have a top speed, you know. Then there are all the bloody veins and stuff, and there isn't exactly a map, this is going to take some time.' The dragon was now as small as a mouse. It panted pathetically. Ceun picked it up carefully and put it into his pocket. There had to be another way.

Will was gradually coming round aided by a stinging slap across his cheek. He tried to marshal his thoughts. Opening his eyes, he wished he hadn't bothered. An out of focus, scarred face was far too close. He found himself engulfed in an overwhelming fug of garlic breath.

'This one is awake Salli.' Alfredo said.

'The girl's still out of it... hey, Alfredo don't you think she looks like Maria?' replied a voice Will assumed was Salli. The face disappeared.

'Maria? My Maria?' Alfredo walked out of sight. 'I suppose so,' he said, 'more like her sister, I think. Either way, she needs to wake up now!' There was the sound like a hand clap. Anaya had been on the end of an Alfredo wake up call. 'Nothing. You'll have to carry her.' Salvatore said.

'Why me?' his brother moaned. 'Because you were the one who gave her the stuff. Wait a minute, we're forgetting something, we have our little pack mule here.'

'Huh?' Alfredo grunted.

'We'll let him carry her. Kill two birds with one stone.' Salvatore grinned.

'What?' Alfredo asked.

His brother smacked him sharply across the back of the head.

'Think, idiot. Then he can't run away either?'

'Ahhh!' Alfredo smiled. Will was hauled unceremoniously to his feet. The bindings on his wrists loosened for a moment. The two gangsters struggled to turn Anaya and dump her heavily across the inventor's shoulders. Her head landed close to Will's ear.

'Stall!' She hissed so only he could hear. Her head then flopped over his chest, as if she had never spoken. Staggering under the extra weight, an already groggy Will sank to his knees as the morph down onto his upturned calves. A heavy boot from Alfredo in the rear completed his descent as Will collapsed on his face in the dirt.

'You're supposed to be getting them up, not putting them down.' Salvatore said crossly.

Alfredo managed to look a little sheepish. 'Force of habit.' he muttered quietly.

Ceun crept back to the edge of the clearing. Taking care that he was concealed behind the foliage, he peered out just as Will and Anaya were being untangled. The thugs were now trying to keep Will in an upright position, while at the same time trying to load Anaya. It was not going very well.

Ceun took the little dragon out of his pocket and held it in the flat of his hand. 'I have a plan?' He whispered. The Dragon lifted its head and turned a bloodshot eye towards him. 'But it does rather depend on you. I'm going over there.' He pointed to the other side of the clearing. The eye followed the line of his finger before rolling back to the bounty hunter. Ceun continued, 'once I start making a commotion I need you to fly over to Will and Anaya and burn through the rope.' The head flopped down, and the eye closed with a snap. 'I know you are not feeling exactly, yourself, but you are the only one who can do it, there's only you and me here, and I can't untie them and cause a diversion?'

There was no response. Ceun prodded it gently in the stomach with his forefinger. The creature rolled over so that it was facing the other way.

'You are charged to take care of him.' Ceun said firmly. With an overdramatic sigh, the dragon hauled itself to its four feet. Wobbling slightly, it hiccupped and nearly fell from Ceun's hand. He caught it just in time. 'Pull yourself together! You need to focus.' A waft of black soot settled on Ceun's fingers as the creature shook its head. 'Focus!' Ceun hissed through his teeth.

With an experimental flap of its wings, the dragon steeled itself. It took a deep breath and launching itself from the bounty hunter's hand fluttering drunkenly to perch on a branch.

Ceun offered up a silent prayer to whichever deity happened to be passing. Keeping half an eye on the thugs, he began to sneak silently around the clearing.

Meanwhile, Will was managing to stand under his burden, but whether he would be able to walk seemed debatable. He was putting on an Oscar-winning performance. Having already lurched into both Salvatore and Alfredo in turn, he was currently attempting a sideways kind of shuffle involving a foot forwards, two to the side and one backwards. As a result, there appeared to be a lot of movement with minimal results.

'Move!' Alfredo pushed Will sharply in the back. He tripped and staggered back, tottered forwards then dropping Anaya pirouetted gracefully and collapsed next to her.

'This is ridiculous Salli. Let's waste them now and be done with it!' Alfredo growled. Reaching into the recess of his suit, the gangster released a stiletto. It glinted evilly in the light. Grabbing Anaya by the hair, he pulled her head backwards, allowing the blade to rest just beside her jugular. Alfredo looked pleadingly to his brother. 'Let me do it now. We can tell Mama all about it. Just let me do it,' he said, his teeth grinding in anticipation.

'You see what you've done?' Salvatore said, kicking Will. 'You've made him lose his temper!'

Will's eyes opened wide. 'Ok, ok... I'll do better!'

Salli shook his head. 'I think it might be too late, my friend. You don't understand. When Alfredo loses his temper, somebody has to get hurt.'

Halfway towards his destination, Ceun stopped. He realised his mistake. He had trapped himself. There was no way he could escape from this side. The woods were thick with brambles, and, once discovered, the goons would be on him in seconds. His only hope was if the dragon could release the others. Looking back the dragon appeared to be slumped against the tree trunk, its eyes crossing as it tried to keep its attention on the bounty hunters hiding place, this was suicide.

He saw Anaya wince involuntarily as the blade pressed into her just nicking the skin. A droplet of blood began to trickle down her neck. Suicide or not he'd run out of options. Signalling the dragon, he watched as it swooped out of the tree with all the grace of a flying rock.

At the last minute, Salvatore saw the attack. His arms flapped ineffectually as he tried to bat it away, missing it completely, the creature hit him squarely between the eyes.

Alfredo gaped as his brother suddenly keeled over backwards. His wits returning too late as an enraged bounty hunter leapt out of the bushes.

CHAPTER 42

Adam shut his eyes again and tried to sleep. He'd managed to cobble together a primitive console with the parts that Murray's research and development team hadn't found which was hardly surprising given their hiding place in a plastic bag in the toilet cistern together with a backup copy of the programming and scenarios. Sometimes his partner's paranoia paid off. Adam didn't have time to be angry that the place had been cleared out, and it didn't take a genius to work out where everything had gone. That would have to wait. The only concerns now were whether this cobbled-together thing would work and if it did whether he would manage to find Will, and even if he found him would he be really Will anyway. Oh and the fact that all the concerns together were causing chronic insomnia, apart from that it was a foolproof plan. Now, if only he could drift off.

~~

Ceun rolled sideways as the stiletto whistled past his ear and embedded itself in the grass. Alfredo lifted the weapon again trying to get a fix on the wriggling bounty hunter. He lunged, allowing Ceun to use forward momentum to propel the thug over his head. In a bound, the bounty hunter was on his feet. Like a maddened bull Alfredo charged towards him, his head lowered. Dodging out of the way at the last minute, Ceun turned in time to see Salvatore lying on the ground, clawing desperately at the sick dragon clinging to his face.

Will and Anaya struggled wildly against their bonds. 'A little help here?' Anaya shouted.

'Bit busy at the moment,' Ceun called back as Alfredo made another murderous pass. One claw at a time, Salvatore began to extract the weakened dragon. Finally, it could hold on no longer. Blood dripping from his wounds the gangster regarded the virtually unconscious animal critically before tossing it idly over his shoulder into the bracken.

Ceun's full focus remained on the furious Alfredo. The Mafiosi now moved with purpose carving a figure of eight into the air with his weapon. From behind Salvatore stalked towards the unsuspecting Ceun.

'Look out!' Anaya yelled desperately, just as Salvatore launched. Ceun's attention diverted for a split second and that was all it took. The dagger held straight out like a lance Alfredo chose that moment to charge.

~~

Something green was falling on him. A vast expanse like a large tarpaulin. It must be huge because the wind was whipping his dreadlocks away from his face. He tried to raise his arms above his head in protection. Wait a minute. The green wasn't moving. He was moving. Adam's heart pounded in his ears. He was moving downwards, which equalled falling, which ultimately equalled landing, which, he tried not to think about landing. Thankfully he was distracted by what was happening to his arms. They were stretched out in front of him and Adam watching in horror as they began to shrink to wizened paws. His thumb inverted until it was no more than a node of flesh. A light down was emerging, growing thicker and darkening until it was a dense pelt of green/grey fur. Adam began to panic. Instinctively, he began to flap his arms, which is when he discovered the flaps of skin where his armpits used to be and more importantly the rate of descent was slowing considerably, in a manner of speaking he was flying. He tried a few experimental swoops. By lowering his right or left arm, he found he could bank quite successfully. Swerving back and forth, Adam was starting to enjoy himself. By pushing his left paw downwards too quickly, there was a sudden absence of current, and he began to plummet tumbling towards the earth. Struggling to right himself, he was picked up by another blast of warm air and began to bob gently, while he waited for his stomach to settle. Tentatively, he began to descend on the theory that if he did fall, the closer he was to the earth he was, the less it was going to hurt. Below the blurred landscape was becoming more pronounced. The green blanket had separated into a network of woodlands. Paths meandered between the trees emerging in clearings then rewinding their way into the safety of the wood. Just for fun, Adam tried to follow one of the trails as it played hide and seek. It was as the path crossed a clearing that Adam saw them. Standing side by side were two men. At least, he assumed they were men. Given the shapeless black robes they wore from head to toe, they could have been any sex or any species. One thing was certain, they were trying to attract his attention. Each of them held a pair of torches which they were waving frantically over their heads. Adam was put in mind of air traffic controllers. These strange-looking creatures wanted him to land.

Swooping over their heads, Adam arced around to take a second look. The monks had turned and were indeed beckoning him downwards. Descending as gently as possible, he took another fly past. He was still too high to land without crashing. He would have to take a straighter descent. Gliding over the tops of the trees, Adam swept around for the final time. With a feeling of disappointment, he began his landing. The ground whirled past as he entered the clearing. It was then he realised he was moving too fast and still too high. The comfort of gliding replaced with the sure knowledge that landing would be the hard part in all senses of the word.

The monks dived out of the way just in time. Branches were coming at him which, on the plus side at least began to slow him down, on the other, they hurt like hell. Adam closed his eyes and hoped for the best.

Ceun wrestled with Alfredo's knife hand, hampered by Salvatore's attempts to drag the bounty hunter backwards and strangle him simultaneously. Anaya yelled instructions, none of which seemed to be particularly helpful. The morph had managed to get a hand free and was desperately trying to free herself completely. Then it hit. Suddenly, a screaming grey mass rocketed out of the trees and barrelled straight into the three struggling men, bowling them over like tenpins. The new arrival rolled to a halt next to Will and Anaya and lay on the grass panting.

Anaya released herself completely and untied Will. 'Watch that!' She said to Will indicating the creature. Grabbing the rope, Anaya ran towards a dazed Salvatore. It was a matter of moments to tie his hands before dashing to Alfredo. Soon they were both immobilised to her immense satisfaction.

Ceun lay on the grass, his back to her. 'Hey,' she said as she approached, 'no time to lie around.' The bounty hunter hadn't moved. 'Hawke?' Anaya said uncertainly.

Crouching, she took hold of his shoulder. Ceun groaned. His hand pressed against his stomach and through his fingers was a gently pumping fountain of blood.

Opening his eyes, Adam couldn't believe what he was seeing. Of all the luck, Will was right there, standing in front of him. Jumping to his feet, he was shocked to see Will backing away a look of terror on his face. Adam tried to explain, but all that would come out of his mouth was a string of unintelligible grunts and growls. He took a step forward, but Will continued to back away.

'Will!' Anaya called, the panic evident in her voice. 'It's Ceun. He's hurt!' Taking care not to turn his back on the apparition Will edged to where the bounty hunter lay.

'He's bleeding! Will, he's bleeding... I don't know what to

do...' Anaya was nearly in tears. 'What do I do?' She shook the bounty hunter by the shoulder.

'Not that.' He grunted. He grabbed her hand and looked into her face. 'It will be ok. I'll be ok.' He said, holding her gaze.

'What about that?' Will whistled through his teeth.

Anaya took a deep breath. She turned and seemed to see the animal for the first time. 'You!' She instructed, 'sit down and don't move until we are ready to deal with you.'

The bear sat immediately.

Ceun carefully moved his hand and attempted to peer at the wound. 'I don't think it's that deep,' he said, 'but it's difficult to see with all the blood. We need something to stem the bleeding.'

Anaya strode to where the gangsters sat trussed together. Roughly, she pulled Alfredo's suit jacket over his head and ripped out the majority of his shirt back. His protests muffled by the jacket, she kicked him for good measure before taking the wadge of cotton back to Ceun.

His wound packed, Ceun looked around. 'I must be hallucinating,' he said woozily, 'because I can see a great big grey bear with dreadlocks.'

'Is he going to be all right?' Anaya whispered to Will, her face anxious.

'I don't know,' he whispered back, 'I'm not a doctor! We need to get him somewhere where we can look at it properly. It may need stitches.'

As if by the power of prayer, a prison cart rattled into view. The driver, a young man barely out of childhood, spotted them. He wore the uniform of an auxiliary guard, meaning that when he came of age, he would be allowed to do something more interesting than driving captives around. Of course, that would never happen if he didn't manage to find the rest of the battalion. Bad enough, the Sergeant would throw a fit when he found out about the lost cart, now he was confronted with people on the wrong side of the bars. He wasn't trained to deal with people who were free to do what they wanted. The young soldier did the only thing he could think of under the circumstances, he gaped.

Anaya marched over to the wagon. The youth sat frozen in fear as a facsimile of his fifth-grade teacher Ms Blanche reached up, grabbed him by the scruff of the neck and pulled him out of his seat.

'Hello,' she said pleasantly. The young man managed a watery, hopeful smile. 'Hello Ms Blanche,' he said in the same sing-song way he had for a whole year.

'Haven't you grown into quite the charming young man? You were always my favourite, um?' Anaya floundered. The boy was looking at her with undisguised adoration.

'Timmy,' he said dreamily. 'Of course. You were always my favourite Timmy. And what a fine cart you have Timmy, you must be very important?'

Timmy brought himself up to his full height, almost visibly glowing with pride. 'I joined the army Ms,' he said.

'That is impressive. And you get to drive this fine vehicle. I don't suppose Timmy that you would consider, no, it's too much to ask.' Anaya lowered her eyes coyly.

'What? Anything for you, Ms Blanche. You were the best teacher I ever had. You were so...' He trailed off, embarrassed.

Anaya patted him on the side of his face, the last pat perhaps little too hard. 'What I was going to ask. Timmy, my favourite pupil. I was going to ask if we may borrow your cart for a little while. These, um, robbers ambushed us, and we need to get my friend some help?'

Timmy looked at the cart with concern. If he and the cart were missing the Sergeant would be angry, if he arrived without it, the consequences didn't bear considering.

Anaya turned up the heat. 'With you being in the army and everything, you could be my hero?' She simpered.

There was nothing more to be said. Timmy found himself automatically handing over the reins. He even helped lift Ceun onto the cart. 'What about your animal?' He asked.

The bear was hopping from foot to foot.

'We'd better take it with us, find out what it wants.' Anaya said simply cradling Ceun's head in her lap.

'What if it's dangerous?' Will said quietly.

'It's one of those drop bear things from your friend's little game. Can't you see the resemblance? It's just bigger, and it's the least of our worries at the moment.'

'Wait a minute.' Will ran over to the ferns.

'Come on.' Anaya said through gritted teeth. 'What are you doing?'

Bending down Will returned carrying the mouse-sized dragon, its eyes firmly closed. 'It did try to help us?' He said by way of explanation.

Anaya rolled her eyes. 'Ok, just let's go before anyone starts to get suspicious. Oh and Timmy?'

The boy's eyes lit up.

'So you don't get into trouble, we've left you a couple of lovely gift-wrapped prisoners over there.' She indicated the clearing. 'If I were you, I'd run off and tell your superiors all about how you captured them?'

Timmy nodded.

'You don't even need to say anything about us. You can have all the glory yourself.' She said with a sweet smile. The boy scuttled off obediently as Anaya flicked the reins.

CHAPTER 43

Adam, the drop bear, climbed nimbly next to Will in the driver's seat.

'I don't want that thing up here with me!' he complained. The bear grunted something unintelligible and seemed to be trying to smile but instead only succeeded in bearing its teeth.

'Just get us the hell out of here!' Anaya said urgently, 'Ethel's cottage is the closest.'

'Are you mad? She was trying to have us mauled not so long ago!' Will replied.

Anaya fixed him with a stare that could melt diamonds. 'She must have sewing equipment,' she said as if talking to a small stupid child. 'She's always knitting this and crocheting that. If Ceun needs stitches that will be the place. Plus, we now have a bear,' she looked at the creature doubtfully, 'of sorts. Now get going!'

The bear gave Will a look that could only be described as sympathetic. He frowned. There was something so familiar about that look. The bear nodded encouragingly and lifted a dreadlock with its paw.

'It can't be.' Will said incredulously. The bear nodded again, proffering the dreadlocks.

'Adam?' Will said, amazed. 'What the hell happened to you?'

The bear clapped his hands together and attempted a double thumbs up which was hampered considerably by the total lack of the vital appendages.

'I know, let's wait until he's lost all his blood then the cart will be much lighter and easier to handle.' Anaya sniped. With a start, Will picked up the reigns.

~~

'Seems quiet.' Will said. 'Do you think they've gone?'

'Or killed each other. You go first, look for a first aid kit and a seeing basket if you can.' Anaya said, cradling Ceun's head in her lap.

'Adam, come with me,' Will pointed at Adam, who shook his head.

'Now is not the time to be shy fuzz face, you have all the hard wear. Now get in there quickly before I consider revising my views on wearing fur!' Anaya threatened.

Grumbling, Adam jumped down and followed Will towards the cottage. The inventor pushed the door cautiously and peered inside. Not a stick of furniture remained whole. Plates smashed, curtains torn, and wreckage was strewn all over the floor. On half a chair, one saved teacup teetered precariously.

'Nobody here,' he called back to the others. 'Any bodies?' Ceun coughed.

Will pushed the door all the way open. 'Doesn't seem to be.'

'Then stop messing about and help me get him inside.' Anaya shouted.

Ceun tried to get up. 'I can manage,' he grumbled.

With one finger Anaya pushed him back down. 'You are fit as a flea, it's all I can do to keep you still,' she said, 'get on with it then.'

With a filthy look in her direction, Ceun began to inch his way towards the edge of the cart wincing with every movement.

'Oh, for goodness sake!' Anaya snapped as she jumped down. 'Will you please just let me help you. it's painful just watching.'

Resigned, Ceun took her arm, and together they eased him onto the ground. With Will on one side and Anaya on the other, Ceun limped into the cottage and collapsed on the un-made bed. 'Look through the cupboards, draws, anywhere that might hold sewing stuff.' Anaya ordered. 'And you, Adam, the bear whatever you're calling yourself these days, don't just stand there, you can look too! And I'll need some boiling water to sterilise.'

~~

Anaya held the sterilised needle carefully and threaded the cotton. 'Are you ready for this, I'm sorry, it's going to hurt.' She said with a grimace.

Ceun gripped her hand. 'It's ok, don't worry about it.' He said through gritted teeth.

'What can I do?' Will asked as he peered over her shoulder.

'Try to get some sense from him.' She nodded towards Adam, who sat in the corner, inspecting his claws with amazement.

'But I don't know how to...' Will said.

'Try.' She said sharply. Anaya looked from the needle to Ceun's face, an agony of indecision.

Ceun held her hand. 'You can do this. I need you to do this, ok?'

Nodding slowly, and began to sew.

~~

'What are you doing here? You're supposed to be getting the console and returning it to my body so I can get home!' Will asked, throwing his hands in the air.

Adam shook his head. Grunting unintelligibly he tried to mime something.

'What are you trying to say? I don't understand.'

The grunts, squeals and frantic paw waving increased until Will was forced to interrupt. 'Typical about this place.

Wolves talk, pigs talk but the one creature, no offence, that you need to have a conversation with, oh no, that would be too flipping helpful,' he muttered in frustration. Adam nodded in agreement. 'Listen,' Will began, 'I know you have been having some doubts.' Adam nodded again. 'I heard you in the hospital. Long story but I kind of dropped in, I couldn't wake up, but I know you are concerned that this isn't real and that you were doing the wrong thing. How can I convince you that getting that bloody console back on me is the only way?'

Jumping to his feet, the bear began a complicated mime. After a great deal of arm-waving, face-pulling, no easy task with a bear's features, and leaping around, Adam flopped onto the floor looking at Will expectantly.

'I get the idea. Look, for reasons I don't want to go into, things are a little clearer now as far as she's concerned. Cassandra wants, well, never mind what she wants.' Will lowered his voice. 'You do what you do best and get me out of here.'

~~

'Will you keep still?' Anaya sat back irritably. Now that the stitching was almost over, she had relaxed a little.

'Stop enjoying it so much, and I will try,' Ceun replied.

'You think this is fun for me?' She exclaimed, before seeing the amused grin on his face.

She narrowed her eyes at his teasing, and silently, she continued sewing.

'I was only teasing?' Ceun said after she'd been silent for several stitches. 'Don't take everything so to heart. Anaya?'

'Keep still, shut up and let me get on with this. If you could stop bleeding, that would also be helpful.' She said huffily.

'Don't be like that. I didn't mean...' He began. Putting his hand over hers, Ceun raised himself on one elbow. 'I'm grateful for you doing this, for a lot of things you've done. You know that.'

'How do I? You think I'm some evil, selfish, vindictive bitch that would quite happily see the rest of the universe wiped out if it served her purpose!' It burst out before she could stop it.

'You forgot self-absorbed, spoiled and petulant.' Ceun said softly. Anaya raised her head and looked at him properly. He was smiling at her, still teasing. 'Anyway,' he said, looking away embarrassed. 'When did it ever matter what I thought?'

'It doesn't' Anaya said firmly, going back to her sewing, 'I'm done here.'

A crash against the front door caused everyone to start. They froze collectively as someone scrabbled for the latch. With a bang, the door was kicked open, and Ethel eased her casts through the doorway muttering to herself.

'If that wolf thinks he's coming back here after all I've done for him. Takes off after that pig without a by or leave. Will he come back when I've been all over the forest calling for him? No! Some stupid vendetta is more important than doing as he's told. Worrying me to death. If he thinks he can just stroll back here after that, he has another thing co...' She stopped as she noticed the tableau in front of her. 'Who said you could use my home!' she screamed angrily.

Wiping her hands on her skirt, Anaya stood to face the older morph, 'We had no-where else to go, and Ceun was hurt.'

'I don't care. If it's not bad enough, you wreck my beautiful things, but then you come back and, and, is that blood all over my bedclothes? How dare you!'

'Now wait a minute Grandma?' Will said suddenly. Adam nudged him. 'I know,' Will agreed, 'she isn't really Grandma Tilly, sone of those shape changer things like Anaya. Anyway' He turned back to the old morph. 'You have been chasing me, or your wolf has, and I don't think it was to ask me to tea. You threaten to kill us, and finally, *we* didn't wreck anything. So, I think the least you can do is help us!'

'You do, do you?' Ethel said menacingly. 'You think you're so clever, don't you, yet here you are, right where I wanted you.'

'And how do you think you are going to overpower all of us?' Ceun asked, struggling to his feet. 'I might not be at my best right now, but it seems your pet has abandoned you, and as you see, we have our own set of teeth and claws.' Adam waved a paw cheerfully and was shocked that he could see through to the other side. He grabbed at Will's arm, but his claws just moved through his friend like fresh air. With a look of panic on his bear face, Adam began to fade.

'What's happening to him?' Will asked.

'He's waking up.' Ceun answered.

Soon, Adam, the bear, was just a shade. 'Remember.' Will shouted. The ghost nodded and then was gone.

'That rather evens up the odds.' Ethel said, pushing the teacup from the chair where it bounced across the floor. She sat down precariously. Anaya took a step forward.

'How do you work that out? There are still two of us able-bodied, and you are in plaster.'

'Ah, ah, ah!' Ethel waggled an outstretched finger. 'Don't come to close my dear. Perhaps there is something you haven't taken into consideration, a certain item of um, neckwear that our bounty hunter friend is sporting. Anything happens to me and, oh dear, boom!'

Ceun stared at Ethel, 'You! It was you that kidnapped me and put that damned collar on me.' His hands instinctively went to his neck.

'I don't understand, why would you do that what on earth could you gain by capturing Will?' Anaya addressed her question without moving.

'Never mind that. Get this damned thing off of me!' Ceun staggered slightly before slumping back onto the bed.

Ethel laughed. 'And lose my advantage? Why on earth would I do that? I will tell you what is going to happen. The human and I will leave. When I am far enough away, I will arrange for the collar to be taken off. And I will keep my promise, Mr Hawke.'

Anaya looked confused. 'What promise?' she asked. 'Mr Hawke will tell you in due course I'm sure dearie. But right now, I need to be going. Everyone wins.'

'Except me!' Will complained. 'Oh shut up you whining creature,' Ethel spat angrily.

'It wasn't just the collar, was it?' Anaya asked Ceun pointedly. 'You're not telling me something else.'

'It doesn't matter,' he replied.

'I was just starting to trust you.' Anaya said accusingly.

Ethel laughed, 'How sweet you both are. The collar wasn't really any leverage was it, Mr Hawke? What focussed our bounty hunters attention was the threat that something could happen to you, my dear Ananya. What? Did I say something wrong?' She finished with mock innocence.

'But now I know you are nothing but an ineffectual old woman with delusions of power. No wonder you hid in the dark,' Ceun said, 'but what you haven't told us is why you want… him?'

'I don't particularly,' Ethel said with a sneer, 'but what's in his head is the means to get my revenge on the entire human race.'

'But why?' Will wanted to know, the image of his Grandma still making his brain ache.

'Have you any idea what it is like to be a perpetual grandmother for years and years putting up with snotty noses and whining and the screaming? It's all right for her,' Ethel pointed at Anaya viciously, 'she's young and lovely, she has young men falling at her feet. She even managed to touch the ice-cold heart of our own Mr Hawke. But not me. And then that… that creature, tortured me like I was nothing. Somebody has to make a stand, and I'm going to do it. I've had enough, and they have to pay!'

'What are you talking about? What creature? I haven't tortured anybody!' Will wailed.

Ethel began to advance on the inventor, her matronly face contorted with rage. 'Not you! That vile worm little Murray Leibowitz. But he's not little now, is he? He knew exactly what he was doing and, ask yourself, who was responsible for that? Hmm? Who gave him the power?'

'Um…' Will began.

'Um… UM! Is that all you can say? Thrown through the air like a cannonball I was! Look at my arms. Look at them!'

'I'm sorry.' Will said lamely.

'Bit late for sorry my lad!' Ethel said vehemently. She turned to the others. 'Now if you don't mind, we will be going. I don't want to see anyone losing their heads unnecessarily, so don't try to stop me.'

CHAPTER 44

Adam woke with a start. He raised a hand cautiously. They were all there, four pink fingers and one exceptionally welcome opposable thumb, which he kissed gratefully. Now for the big test. 'That was one weird, funky dream,' he said out loud, enjoying the sound of his voice. 'Not a moment to lose.' Ripping the makeshift console from his head, he leapt from the bed and, throwing on last nights clothes, rushed out of the door.

~~

Ringing the bell to Will and Cassandra's flat, there was no reply. 'Come on... come on...' he began thumping on the door. People were starting to peer out of windows, and it occurred to Adam that it must be very early in the morning. 'Cassandra!' he shouted, praying that someone wouldn't call the police.

The door opened suddenly. On the other side, Cassandra stood in her nightclothes glaring at him. 'Have you any idea what time it is?' she asked.

'Early,' Adam barged past her into the hallway.

'Come in why don't you,' she said to thin air as she closed the door.

Adam rushed wildly into the bedroom and began emptying the nightstand. Yielding nothing, he moved on to the chest of drawers.

Cassandra leant against the door frame calmly watching the whole pantomime. 'Coffee?' she said eventually. When she received no reply, she wandered into the kitchen. Adam was halfway through her handbag when he suddenly realised this was not a usual way for a person to react as someone ransacked her home, albeit someone she knew.

Still holding the handbag, he walked through to the kitchen where Cassandra was calmly pouring boiling water into two mugs. 'It's only instant,' she said, offering one.

He took it and guiltily returned the handbag. Not even looking at it, Cassandra threw it on the worktop and sat heavily down at the kitchen table. 'If you're here for the prototype, I'm afraid you're too late,' she said, sipping her coffee.

'What?' Adam was beginning to feel like he was still in a dream.

'Murray has screwed us both. He's got all of the research. He has a patent pending in the name of REMCORP, which is essentially him, and the only thing that could have stopped him was the daydream believer I had here. I presume that's why you're looking for it?'

Adam shook his head, trying to digest the information. 'I don't understand.'

Cassandra spoke very slowly. 'He... has... taken... it... all.'

'He can't do that!' Adam said indignantly.

'He can, and he has. We've been so distracted with Will and fighting. We didn't see it coming. He just wanted his hands on all the software and hardware. Possession is nine-tenths of the law. H has something signed that says in the event of incapacity he has Will's proxy, and you and I will keep quiet because he's going to blame us for Will's accident.'

'Cassandra, where is the console?'

'Someone came in here last night, and all they took was that silly little console. Game, set and match.'

Adam sat down opposite her. 'We can't just give up. I need that console.'

'Ha, ha... I knew it!' Cassandra exclaimed. 'I knew you weren't interested in me!'

'That's your main concern after everything that you've worked and schemed for has just been whipped out from under your nose? Really?' Adam said incredulously.

She shrugged. 'I have to feel I was right about something.' She said, taking a mouthful of coffee.

'That's bullshit. You're not telling me you're just going to roll over and say oh well!' Cassandra took another mouthful of coffee ad swallowed hard.

'You never let anyone win, or at least, not if you are going to lose.' Adam badgered.

'What do you suggest, we storm his office and demand everything back? All we'll get is thrown out with his laughter still ringing in our ears.' Cassandra slammed down her cup.

'So what about Will, you're just going to let him drift there until the doctors finally pull the plug? The only way we can get him back is to return that console, the original. And what about you? Leibowitz bested you, and now you're going to let him get away with it? That's not the Cass I know. You're the queen of schemes. We need a plan.'

~~

'Are you sure you haven't been on something... funny?' Cassandra asked incredulously as Adam explained for the second time about Morpheus. 'You are seriously trying to tell me that this dream world is real?'

'As real as this table.' Adam replied.

'You're out of your mind! The stress has finally got to you.' She snorted.

'We don't have time for you not to believe me. If Leibowitz goes into production on that thing, there will be a multi-dimensional war.' Adam insisted.

Cass looked sceptical. 'Show me. Prove to me that this place is real.'

Adam took her hands across the table. 'I have a cobbled to-gether console, but it would be too dangerous, the results are... unusual.' He shuddered at the memory. 'I need you to trust me.' He smiled. 'And isn't it enough that you will be showing that American bastard that he can't get away with treating you this way?'

'But if what you say is true, Will wants to destroy the whole project. Then no-one wins,' said Cass.

'It could be modified,' Adam lied, 'now that we know that Morpheus is real we can allow for the variables. But first, we need to get everything back.'

Cassandra regarded him critically. 'We need a weakness, some-thing that will give us back the advantage.'

'Yes?'

'Something that is going to make the Believer useless to him.' She said thoughtfully.

'Sounds like you have a plan?' Adam asked.

Cassandra smiled slowly. 'I have a plan.'

~ ~

The red-faced young man skidded to a halt in front of Lieuten-ant Fotherington-Smythe-Willowby-Smith. '

Sergeant?' The lieutenant said, looking down his nose at the panting soldier.

'Straighten up lad,' Sergeant Simpson ordered, 'deep breaths, chest out. Now tell the officer what seems to be the problem.

'Prison transport... Sir... stolen... word came on the wires.' The soldier gushed.

'Yes we heard; the Sergeant will be having a very stiff word with the man concerned.' Willoughby-Smith said dismissively.

'Not... not that sir,' the soldier gasped, 'found it. On the road close to a cottage... must be the fugitives.'

'How do we know they haven't just abandoned it and moved on?' The Lieutenant asked.

'Checked Sir. Could hear them inside. Arguing Sir.'

'Dissent amongst the rebels, eh? Well, what are we waiting for? Send a message to the committee that I will soon be apprehending the villains.'

'And get a squad together actually to apprehend them, Sir?' Simpson asked.

'Do I have to do everything man! Of course, a battalion, an army, the slippery little beggars that they are.' The lieutenant said irritably.

'Of course, Sir. But given their um... slipperiness, would it not be prudent to wait until they are actually caught before informing the committee of one's success?' Simpson added patiently.

'Sometimes Simpson I despair at your lack of faith! Look to this fine fellow here?' The lieutenant said. The soldier smiled uncertainly. 'Located the scoundrels and no doubt wanted to knock seven bells out of them, but did the prudent thing, informed his commander. He understands the nature of the beast, the machine that is the Morphean army. We don't need poopers clogging up the works! Are you a pooper Simpson?'

'No sir.' Simpson said with resignation.

With a final look of disdain, the Lieutenant strode away. 'What are you grinning at private?' Sergeant Simpson said with dangerous calm.

'Nothing Sergeant,' squeaked the young man, his face instantly devoid of a grin.

'I thought not. You've just volunteered to be first into that cottage, well done. Now get out of my sight!'

CHAPTER 45

'Murray. We need to talk.' Cass moved the phone to the other ear as Adam hovered to hear the conversation. 'On the contrary, I do think we have things to talk about. You don't believe for one moment that I didn't keep a copy of everything, somewhere you would never think to look?' She listened intently to the response. 'Uh, huh. I do understand that Murray, I could very well be bluffing, but can you afford to take the chance? The simple fact is, your boys didn't look everywhere. They didn't do the thorough job you paid them for, I'm afraid. Did you think we would be stupid enough to allow you just to sweep in and take it all?' Cass laughed at the reply. 'Not the best quality operatives it has to be said. You ask them, Murray, ask them if they looked *everywhere*. See what they have to say about that.' Moving the phone away from her ear so Adam could hear what the American had to say. 'Now, now calm down, remember your blood pressure. What I am proposing is a deal. I won't go to your competitors with, well everything to get this baby up and running, and you cut me back in, I was thinking about sixty forty.' Cassandra cooed. 'Oh, I know you won't give me sixty, but forty per cent is better than nothing. Meet me in the coffee shop on the corner. You understand I'd rather we did this somewhere nice and public.' Putting the phone down, Cassandra smiled.

'This is your plan?' Adam asked. 'Part of it. I get Murray out of the way. You have to do the rest. He always keeps his most valuable assets in a safe in his office. On the far side of his desk is a statue. Twist it to one side and enter the combination. A panel will open under the guest chair. He likes to think that anyone who visits him that their cash is going to drop into his safe.'

Adam rubbed his hands over his face. 'Apart from the obvious problem that I can't just stroll into his office and start rearranging his ornaments. How am I going to get the combination?'

'Ha! I was chatting with one of the other girls, and they let slip that it is always the last six digits of his latest victim's phone number.'

Adam opened his mouth to speak.

'If you have a better idea, then let's hear it.' Cassandra interrupted. 'Because I have to meet Murray in about fifteen minutes.'

Adam shook his head. 'Better get a move on then.'

~~

Striding purposefully into Murray's building, Adam was not entirely sure of the reception he would get. His date with the pretty young assistant had been fine, but with everything going, on he hadn't quite gotten around to contacting her again. There was a possibility she may not have taken this very well. He need not have worried. Almost from nowhere, she charged towards him, wrapped her arms around his neck and kissed him.

'Wow, Gina, that's some welcome!' He said, trying to disengage himself.

'It's a wonderful surprise that you're here! Did you come to take me to lunch?' she said hopefully, bright eyes shining.

'Not today, babe.' Adam said slowly. 'I have a bit of business, but perhaps later in the week we could have dinner?'

'Oooh goodie!' she said, clapping her hands.

'But I do have time to walk you back to your desk' he said charmingly.

'Pffft,' she said dismissively. 'That stupid job. I meant to tell you, I've been promoted. You are looking at the assistant to the head of marketing.' She beamed.

'Congratulations. So the new assistant would be?' Adam asked.

'Greta. But I'm not jealous. Greta would isn't your type. She's ancient!'

Adam laughed. 'As if she would be any comparison for you,' pushing her gently away, he added, 'I do have to go now.'

Gina kissed him gently on the cheek. 'Arrogant bastard,' she muttered as he walked away.

~~

When he got to the assistant's desk, it was completely deserted, no sign of Greta. Looking at the large clock telling the time in six different countries, he considered the possibility that even the assistants of megalomaniacs must take some time off for lunch. Slipping into the office, he carefully closed the heavy office door behind him.

Looking around, he spotted the statue. It was obvious now. Who would have thought this nubile art-deco creature would be the key to everything? He twisted the figure and revealed the keypad underneath.

'Now then, let's hope Leibowitz has not discovered the true meaning of irony.' He said quietly punching in the numbers. Silently, the panel slid back. Inside was the console together with a disk presumably containing the master blueprints.

Adam was crouched secreting the items in his shirt when from behind he heard a slow hand clap. Turning, Murray was smiling amiably at him. However, his eyes were as cold as ice. To one side, a thug had hold of Cassandra tightly by the arm. On the other stood Gina, and out of the two, she looked the most unfriendly.

'Bravo for an audacious attempt my friend. You really had me fooled oh yes, sirree!' The American said jovially.

'Leibowitz! I was looking for you.' Adam replied with false bravado.

'Under my floor? Do you think I've taken to burrowing like a goddamn gopher? Is that what you think, boy? Do you think I'm some hick from the sticks who doesn't know when he's being set up? This little darling here, she comes to me with the old, I've got what you want routine but you guys... you guys, you made mistakes.'

'Set up? Mistakes? I don't know what you're talking. You know we're not working together!' Adam bluffed.

'I know I set you on her like a dog on heat.' Leibowitz laughed. 'And she thought I was going to put up with her bullcrap and make her a partner. That kept you both busy while I cleared up a few loose ends. But you think I didn't notice sweetheart, on the phone, you said we? You've never been we in your life. It's always been you, you, you all the way.' Murray pinched Cassandra's face in his big hands. 'You think I've got where I am today by not being one step ahead of everyone?'

'He made me do it!' Cassandra said through her squashed face. 'I wanted to be reasonable, but he insisted.'

'Don't give me that doll face. I knew exactly what you were up to. When are you going to get it into that pretty little head of yours that you are playing with the big boys now?' Releasing her with a push, he turned to Adam. 'I think you have something that belongs to me,' he said. 'If you're smart you'll hand it over. If you don't want the girl to get hurt.'

'Gina?' Adam implored. 'What are you doing helping this mad man.'

'He treats me with respect. You're so dumb you don't know when you're on to a good thing. You even believed that I had a new job!' The blonde gloated.

'Shut up you empty-headed moron!' Murray snapped. 'This isn't about you and your stupid love life. Now, boy, I'm warning you.'

'Do what you want. I'm giving you nothing!' Adam replied.

Murray nodded to his guard. Cass screamed as her arm was twisted roughly behind her back. 'You think I won't do it? You're sensitive boy, you pretty ones always are, you're a lover, not a fighter. You're the one hurting her, not me, you, by being an idiot.'

'And if I give it back you're going just to let us walk out of here no questions asked?' Adam asked.

The American opened his arms. 'I'm not an unreasonable man.'

'Then let me keep the console, just this one, and you can have the blueprints and everything else. Cass and I walk out of here, and you never hear from us again?'

Leibowitz laughed. 'I said I was reasonable, not a freaking Saint! I don't think you're in a position to bargain boy. I'm holding all the aces.'

'And I'm holding your blueprints and... what's this?' Adam picked up Murray's cigar lighter from the desk. He flicked the switch experimentally. Waving the memory stick close to the sharp flame, Adam kept his eye on the American.

'Ha! Those gidgets are indestructible boy! The most it will do is burn your stupid fingers.'

Adam put down the lighter. Carefully, he held the stick in front of him, flexing it between two hands. 'Indestructible or not, it won't play very well if it's in bits.'

'That's the backup. Go ahead, break it.' Leibowitz scoffed.

Adam hesitated. There was another squeal from Cass.

'Come on, son, hand over the goodies, and it will all be over.

You have no other choice.' Murray cajoled.

'He may not, but I do!' Cassandra growled, stamping her four-inch heel hard into the instep of her captor. It was his turn to squeal in pain. Stunned, the man released his grip as Cass turned, her knee connected hard with his groin. With a stifled groan, he folded onto the floor.

In a flash, Adam was across the room barrelling hard into the American knocking him almost off his feet. Still using his forward momentum, he grabbed Cassandra by the arm and dragged her out of the door.

'Are you all right, Mr Leibowitz?' Gina asked, tentatively.

'Don't ask stupid questions, you bimbo! Make yourself useful, call the police. Tell them we have information pertaining to the attempted murder of one William Cooper.'

CHAPTER 46

'You mean you have captured him? He is in your custody?' Bango asked Captain Todd.

'We believe they have been located sir,' the captain said with a sideways glance at Winkworth.

'Located is not the same as captured. Do you think it's the same Winkworth?' The chairman banged a fist on the desk. 'No, it is very different!' he shouted before Winkworth could speak. 'The way you idiots have been running around the countryside like headless chickens, I'm surprised you can even find your own backsides without a roadmap let alone capture them!'

'Our intelligence may have been flawed sir,' Todd said woodenly.

'Flawed! , bloody non-existent!' Bango thumped the table again.

'I meant our military intelligence, sir,' the Captain continued.

The chairman gave a short laugh. 'So did I captain, so did I. I have grave doubts about your abilities captain and that of those you command.'

'Sir?'

'This is why I will be taking charge of the operation.' Bango said with a flourish.

Winkworth coughed politely, 'That is most irregular sir. You are not, in any sense, a military commander.'

'Neither are these nincompoops as far as I can tell. I am going to make sure there are no screw-ups. Captain, you will accompany me.'

Captain Todd gave Winkworth an imploring look, but the Bogeyman just shrugged in reply.

~~

'You don't have to go with her,' Ceun said, struggling onto his elbows.

Anaya gently placed a hand on his arm. 'You should be resting.' She said.

'He can't go with her. We have to give Adam time.' Ceun whispered in her ear.

'Stop stalling,' said Ethel. 'Whatever you've got planned, you've run out of time. If the two of us are not out of here and far away very soon, then you know what happens.' She made a slicing motion in the general direction of her neck, difficult with an arm in a cast.

With a resigned look towards his friends, Will opened the door then immediately closed it again.

'What's the matter now?' Ethel snapped irritably.

'I don't think we want to go out there,' Will said. Ethel shoved him with a cast.

'I told you to stop stalling. Just because I'm old doesn't mean I have to be nice. Now go'

'What does it mean when there is a man with a very nasty looking military uniform standing outside?' Will asked a slight edge of panic in his voice.

'The cart! Please tell me you hid the cart!' Ceun asked, looking from one to the other.

Anaya and Will exchanged a look. 'We wanted to get you inside...' Anaya started.

'Dangerous amateurs. I'm working with dangerous, bloody

amateurs.' Ceun exclaimed trying to get up.

'It's not like I make a habit of being on the run,' Will whined, 'There's not a course you can go on.'

'Just as well, you're not very good at it,' Ethel added.

'If it is just a wandering patrol who's found it, we might be all right as long as they haven't called for reinforcements.' Ceun said, staggering to his feet.

'I hadn't finished,' Will continued, 'what does it mean if that man in uniform has brought quite a lot of his friends along, and appears to have us surrounded?'

'What?' Ceun said, swaying slightly.

Anaya ran to the window. Keeping out of sight, she peeped out. 'He's not kidding. There must be hundreds of them out there.'

'You should have hidden the bloody cart.' Ceun said, slumping back.

'It's too late to keep going on about that now.' Anaya replied. 'What are we going to do?'

Ethel gasped. 'They're going to think I'm involved!'

'You are involved.' The others said together.

'Not how they think. You're in my cottage. I'll lose my place on the committee, and they'll believe I've been... helping you!' She said, horrified at the prospect.

Will laughed. 'Now that really is justice.'

'Ethel. Take off Ceun's collar, and we'll tell them that you had nothing to do with it. We took over your cottage, and we've been holding you as a hostage,' Anaya said.

'But...' Ceun began.

Anaya wouldn't let him finish. 'Things can't really get any worse for us, can they?' Ceun shook his head. 'Unless of course, there is another way out of here? A basement with a tunnel, anything?'

'No.' Ethel replied. 'What you see is all there is. One way in, one way out.'

'You call this a fairytale cottage!' Ceun grumbled.

'Yes.' The older morph replied. 'Very little need for secret escape hatches.'

'So do we have a deal?' Anaya persisted. 'Take off the collar.'

Ethel looked sheepish for a moment. 'What?' Anaya asked.

'Um, this is a little embarrassing.' The old woman looked at her shoes.

'Go on.' Anaya said in a voice tinged with razor blades. 'I can't actually take the collar off.'

'What!' Ceun said, his head shooting up before he collapsed coughing.

Anaya strode across to the older morph slapping her hard across the cheek. 'You had no intention of releasing him; you were just going to let him die!'

Ethel blinked back tears of pain. 'It was just lying around when I visited the police headquarters, but I didn't have time to find the key. I was going to call the authorities and tell them where you were and that the collar was on Mr Hawke. I wouldn't have let anything happen to you.'

'What if they didn't believe you?' Anaya growled. 'They might not have arrived in time… too many variables.'

'We can talk about what has been done or what could have been, but that doesn't do anything to help the situation does it?' Ceun said

'You should be resting.' Anaya said.

'Virtually impossible with all the shouting going on. If they didn't know we were here already they are certain of it now,' He replied.

'You could still let me go,' Ethel said hopefully. 'I'll put in a good word for you. I still have some standing on the committee. No reason for you to take me down with you.'

'Every reason you vicious, two-faced, hypocritical cow,' Anaya growled, grabbing the older morph by the shoulder.

'Let her go An.' Ceun said.

Will gaped. 'But...'

'No buts. There is no need for her to be involved in this. If she goes, then maybe it will buy us some time while they question her.'

'She can't be trusted,' Anaya argued. 'She will tell them everything, even things that aren't true, it couldn't be worse. She'll make sure that they know we have no way out.'

Ceun waved her into silence. 'Ethel. You owe me, and whatever happens, if you do anything to hinder us or cause us any additional problems, head or no head, I will find a way to make you pay, do I make myself clear?'

'Yes, and me too,' Anaya added.

'And me three,' Will said.

Ceun rolled his eyes. 'The point being,' he continued, 'you do not want to piss us off, we have long memories and a lot of favours that can be called in from some very unpleasant people.'

Ethel nodded quickly.

'You have been a very silly woman. You've risked losing everything, and we are giving you a chance to save yourself. If you betray us, the consequences will be severe.' Ceun held out a hand. Ethel shook it awkwardly. 'Now I think it would be best if you left.'

Will tied a piece of a white pillowcase to a wooden spoon and handed it to the old morph. 'We will be watching you,' he said with as much menace as he could muster.

Ethel nodded. Opening the door a crack, she let the white

flag wave outside for a few moments before emerging into the light.

~ ~

'You! Yes, you! Explain to me what is happening here!' Bango barked at a passing soldier.

'We're surrounding that cottage.' The youth remarked, bemused that he was being addressed at a siege by a clown.

'Do you know who you are talking to?' The Chairman exploded.

Captain Todd chose that exact moment to return with Lieutenant Willoughby-Smith and Sergeant Simpson and, like a reprieved rabbit, the soldier saw his opportunity to escape.

'I want that man court marshalled.' Bango blustered, drunk with power.

'Of course, Sir. See to it, Simpson.' The lieutenant agreed.

'Yes Sir.' Simpson replied, as he exchanged a look with the Captain. He decided to forget all about it instantly.

'Mr Chairman it is an honour and a privilege.' Willoughby-Smith gushed. 'I can't tell you how pleased I am to meet you in the flesh.

Bango found his hand being pumped up and down in a very enthusiastic manner. 'Indeed,' he said, extracting his hand. 'And are you in charge of this operation?'

'Yes, sir!' The lieutenant said with a sideways glance at the Captain. 'I have been handling the field end of things, sir. The blighters have proven jolly elusive, but we bagged them in the end. What?'

'What?' Bango replied.

Willoughby-Smith laughed, 'Very good, Sir.'

The chairman laughed uncertainly, not sure of the joke. They all stood, staring at the cottage.

'So,' The Chairman prompted, 'how are you planning on getting the um, blighters out of the cottage and safely into one of our nice cosy prisons?'

'There is no way for them to escape. We have the whole place surrounded. No-one goes in, and no one comes out. All we have to do is wait.' Captain Todd said.

'That is your great military plan? You are going just to sit here and wait for them to get bored. What about storming the cottage? You have enough men here, just get them!' Bango growled.

The Captain lowered his voice. 'There has been some talk of a Dragon sir. Caused considerable damage at the Druid camp, sir.'

'Hippies!' Bango shouted. 'These are well-trained men, not a bunch of dress-wearing, peace-loving long-haired beatniks.'

'That's what I said sir,' Willoughby-Smith interrupted. 'But the Captain felt that caution would be the better part of valour.'

Internally, Captain Todd was deciding that this particular Lieutenant's lack of caution would find him patrolling nightmares before he was very much older.

'We have to go in there after them,' Bango barked into the long-suffering Captain's face. 'We can't be seen to show weakness.' He snorted. 'I mean, it's not as if they are just going to surrender and come out of their own accord.'

'Sir?' Sergeant Simpson said, indicating the cottage. The door was opening slowly, and a white flag was tentatively being extended.

~~

With a decidedly irritated poof, the Godmother appeared and hovered a few feet above her henchmen. Taking a long draw on her cigar, she waited for them to notice her.

'This is your fault,' Alfredo griped, 'I told you we should have just done away with them and everything would have been fine. But no, you had to make an example. They had to know why they were being whacked.'

'My fault?' Salli said, outraged. 'You were the one doing the military two-step with that bounty hunter.'

'He was sneaky. Throwing dirty great hairy things at people from the sky!' Alfredo complained.

Salli looked around. 'Where did that pipsqueak go?' He muttered.

'He said something about looking for a patrol. We could be here forever.'

'You could, indeed.' The Godmother said, floating to a more visible height. The thugs visibly quivered. 'Could you,' she said, folding her arms across her chest. 'Explain to us *exactly* what you are doing?' The pair began to babble at once. Holding up the hand with the cigar, she waited for silence. 'We will tell you what you are doing. Stop us if we get anything wrong, won't you? You decided to do a little freelance work on the side, a little something to keep your hand in?'

'Our Mama was pushed into a...' Alfredo started.

The Godmother silenced him with a look. 'We understand that in the matter of family loyalty is very important,' she said before pausing to blow smoke rings. 'However, in this case, you decided to take your revenge on someone we were very interested in meeting. Someone we had put a great deal of time and effort into locating. We have no option but to question your loyalty to *our* family.'

'We didn't know Don, we swear,' Salvatore cried, throwing himself to his knees.

Alfredo, copying his brother's example, nodded wildly in

agreement. 'We could find them for you, bring them in?'

'Too late boys, we think for now the bird has flown. It seems this time we may have underestimated this human, a mistake that we will not make again. We have spent the last two hours with the Bacon Slicer. He seems to be under the very insistent impression that no-one really likes him,' she looked disgusted for a moment. 'Now we find the two of you trussed up like oven-ready turkeys waiting to be taken to the table, all down to our little human friend.'

'Revenge, Godmother. Untie us, and you will be avenged.' Salli tried.

'You have failed us...' The Godmother said thoughtfully. 'We are fair. We are benevolent...but be warned. We will not tolerate it a second time.'

~~

Timmy ran back into the clearing. He stopped dead at the sight of the fairy Godmother floating near to his prisoners. 'Careful M'am,' he said as authoritatively as he could, 'they are some dangerous men.'

'That's so kind of you to worry about us, young man.' She said sweetly, patting her curls. 'Do you really have no idea who we are?' She said, almost kindly.

'Um...' Timmy reconsidered the wings and the wand.

'We are the fairy Godmother.' Timmy's eyes lit up, what a day this was turning out to be. 'Really? He gasped. 'A real-life fairy godmother? What happens, do I get three wishes?'

The Godmother's face hardened as she flexed her wand. 'I think you had better make it just the one prayer.'

CHAPTER 47

'Wait.' Adam said as he and Cassandra crouched in her car in the hospital car park.

'What for, let's get in there, save Will and get out again before Murray comes after us.'

Adam pointed towards the building. 'Doesn't it strike you as odd that there seems to be a rather large amount of policemen milling about?'

'Perhaps something's happened?' she said. 'It's a hospital, and there will be police.'

'Or perhaps they are expecting something to happen. I don't know about you, but something doesn't smell right here. I don't think we should just go blundering in.'

'If there are looking for us, then we need some kind of disguise...' Cassandra said thoughtfully. 'Give me your shirt, pass me that scarf and get the first-aid kit out of the boot.'

It was a very odd couple that entered the hospital. In a 'borrowed' wheelchair, Adam's entire head was swathed in bandages completely, his dreadlocks now a misshapen bulge at the back of his head, across his chest and knees draped a checked car blanket. Pushing him was a strange hunchbacked figure. In an oversized shirt with a scarf wrapped around her head, Cassandra teetered after the chair in her bright-red heels. She pushed the chair past the first policeman, who barely gave her a second glance. Once in the reception hall, the presence of the law could be felt more strongly. Here and there, groups of officers milled about watching for anyone suspicious. Adam couldn't help but imagine they could not be less conspicuous, but it seemed to be working. They made it to the lifts. To their horror, the doors opened to reveal a young constable who was chatting up a pretty nurse. Too late to change plan, Cassandra wheeled Adam into the small box and prayed.

The journey to the third floor seemed to take forever. Adam and Cass stared straight ahead, both praying that the young man would remain distracted. Floor two. Floor three was fast approaching when the policeman glanced down and noticed Cassandra's footwear for the first time. He nudged the nurse and pointed, and she giggled flirtatiously. Floor three. Adam and Cass had never been so pleased to see a door open. Cassandra pushed the chair out of the lift as her heel caught in the gap. Pulling frantically, she tried to free herself.

'Let me help you,' the young constable said. Cass mumbled something and tried to push him gently away, in doing so, her scarf slipped from her head, and she was face to face with the crouching Samaritan.

He frowned before recognition appeared on his face, just as the shoe released. Shoving him backwards, Cass hurriedly pushed Adam along the corridor. Officers were coming the other way. With a mighty thrust, she launched the chair and ran in the opposite direction. Men leapt in all directions to avoid the out of control wheelchair now careering towards them. Unstopped, it careered through the double doors and out onto the stairs. Adam gripped the chair's arms as he approached the drop. As the chair wheeled left he leant right, all the years spent mastering boards of surf and snow came into their own as he and the chair bounced and lurched down the stairwell.

Finally, the insane ride came to a juddering stop on a landing. Adrenaline still coursing through his veins, Adam got up shakily and listened for anyone following. He unwound the bandages and peered both up and down the stairs. Hearing and seeing nothing, he began to creep back up the way he had

come. He opened the door a crack and could see a lone policeman standing outside Will's room listening intently to his
radio. Adam could almost make out various shouted instructions. Apparently, Cassandra was proving difficult to catch.

From above, a cough made Adam jump. 'Bloody health service
professionals my arse!' An old man was making his way down
the stairs tentatively. With one hand he hung on to the rail,
with the other he supported his weight with a stick.

'Do you need some help?' Adam asked. The man stared for a
long time. Bare-chested, bruised and with his bandages unravelled Adam looked the worse for wear.

'I think you need help more than I do, mate? Have the bastards
just left you like that? Bad enough there's coppers swarming
all over the place without leaving the likes of you and me to
fend for ourselves. What do we pay our bloody tax for that's
what I want to know?' The man said, waving his stick angrily.
When he tottered, Adam put out his arms to catch him. Fortunately, the man was still anchored by the rail.

'I can get you a wheelchair?' Adam suggested, and then considering the battered thing he'd abandoned, he thought better
of it.

The pensioner reached the bottom of the flight and waved his
stick menacingly. 'I didn't fight in a bloody war to be pushed
around in a wheelchair! They tried that caper before, and I
told 'em then, and I'm telling you now. You try putting me in a
bloody wheelchair and I'll 'ave ya.'

Adam glanced anxiously over his shoulder. 'Quite right, very
wise. Um… could you keep it down?' he whispered.

'Keep it down? Keep it down! Why should I keep it down? I
didn't work for forty years man and boy to be told to keep it
down!'

Adam could imagine the police guard moving ever closer to
investigate the noise. 'I only meant, you don't want to go

drawing attention to yourself,' he said conspiratorially.

The older man jerked his head up, birdlike. 'Why not?'

Beckoning him closer, Adam lowered his voice. 'They've decided to take the hard line. Government cuts.'

'Bloody government.' The man agreed.

'Trying to get us all in institutions. If you're not well enough to get out of here under your own steam, you're theirs,' Adam breathed.

'A home?' The OAP's eyes grew wide.

'Worse?' Adam confided. 'Human experiments?'

The old man could barely contain his awe. 'I've read about this research stuff, harvesting of bits of you when you're still using them.'

'Why do you think I ditched the wheelchair... in my condition?'

Surveying Adams bandages, the pensioner straightened up. 'They're not getting me that way. Not putting my bits and pieces in some hoodlie who's never worked a day in his life!'

'Better give me that stick,' Adam said, 'I'll get rid of it for you.' The stick was thrust towards the younger man with more force than he would have ever believed possible. He grasped it and held it aloft. 'Good luck!'

The man nodded in acknowledgement and teetering only slightly continued his way downwards. Waiting until he was out of sight, Adam tossed the stick into his other hand and muttered to himself, 'even if you manage to get away with this, at some point you are going straight to hell.'

His bandages back in place covering most of his head and face and with his body bent double over the walking stick Adam pushed open the door and began to hobble painfully slowly along the corridor.

He immediately had the attention of the guard. 'What is your business here, sir?' he barked, taking the radio from his ear.

Adam replied in a shrill quavering voice, 'Eh? What's that, sonny?'

'I said, what do you want in this corridor?' The constable said louder.

'Who's there?' Adam squawked waving the stick wildly, so the officer had to jump out of the way.

'Sir!' Almost bellowing now, the guard stood directly in front of this shambling apparition. 'WHAT...ARE...YOU...DOING... HERE?'

'XRAY!' Adam bellowed back, still using his comedy old man voice. 'SENT FOR XRAY!'

'Not on this floor.'

'WHAT?'

'I SAID,' The guard yelled, 'YOU'RE ON THE WRONG FLOOR!'

'I'M NOT ON A TOUR!' Adam said with mock horror.

'NOT A TOUR, THE WRONG FLOOR! You daft old bugger.'

Adam swung his stick in the direction of the officer's head. 'MUGGER?' he screeched.

The policeman ducked just in time, and was beginning to wonder what he'd done to deserve this.

'XRAY IS THAT WAY?' he said, pointing towards the other end of the corridor. 'TWO FLOORS DOWN.'

'DEW BORES BROWN?' Adam asked.

Turning, the policeman pointed towards the other end of the corridor. 'TWO FLOORS... wait a minute. Dew bores...?' He never finished the sentence as Adam brought the stick down sharply on to the policeman's head.

CHAPTER 48

'Prepare yourself men!' Bango shouted expansively, realising moments later that he was talking to himself.

All eyes were on the elderly polymorph walking slowly away from the cottage. The makeshift flag still clasped at the end of a plastered arm.

'Somebody get the honourable member a chair?' Bango ordered redundantly. Several guards were already rushing to help the old woman as she staggered dramatically before being caught and half carried to the chairman's carriage.

'Ethel! What happened?' The clown pushed his way through the crowd.

'Mr Chairman...' she said weakly before swooning again.

'Ethel...? Can you speak.'

'We're going to have to ask you some questions madam if you're up to it?' Sergeant Simpson said.

'Questions? Now? Look at her man. I think we should let her rest. We don't know what she's been through and to do that to an old woman. Todd! Todd? Where is that imbecile?' Bango yelled.

Captain Todd tapped the chairman on the shoulder. 'Here... Sir,' he said coolly.

'Ah, there you are. Do you see, you see what these dangerous criminals have done. Do you still think we should just wait it out?' Bango's face flushed through his make up.

'To be fair, we should really talk to the lady. We don't know what ha...' Todd began.

'Just look at her!' Bango was practically apoplectic. '

Indeed Sir, but!' Todd began.

'Oh... bugger off. Where's that lieutenant. He's the man for the job!'

The captain rolled his eyes at the Sergeant as Willoughby-Smith came running. 'Todd, I am relieving you of command.' Bango barked.

'You can't do that...' Todd protested.

'I'm the chairman, and I can do what I like. Ah, Lieutenant. You are now in charge of this operation. I want that cottage taken, do you understand?'

Beaming like an idiot, the Lieutenant saluted smartly. 'Yes, Sir!' Before rushing off to mobilise his attack force.

Rubbing his hands together, the chairman smiled humourlessly. 'Now, we shall see some action.'

~~

'Oh she is really hamming it up,' Will said peering through the window.

Anaya looked up from the drawer she was searching. 'What?'

'As long as it buys us some time,' Ceun said, shifting uncomfortably on the bed. He lay back and closed his eyes.

Anaya was now emptying the remains of the dresser.

'Just out of interest,' Will asked, 'What are you doing?'

'Looking for anything that can be used as a weapon,' she replied.

'Find anything?' Ceun said without looking.

She sat back on her haunches. 'No.'

'What are we going to do?' Will asked, glancing out of the window. 'It looks as though they are mobilising some kind of squad. We can't possibly fight them?'

'They're probably planning on storming the place.' Anaya said, joining Will.

Ceun's eyes snapped open. Wavering only slightly, he was on his feet and across to the window. 'Yep. It looks like we're going to have to defend the old homestead. Still, there are three of us and only about a hundred and fifty of them.'

~~

Adam held the console and hesitated.

'Ok, buddy. Here goes nothing!' Placing the console gently on Will's head, he pressed the button and waited.

~~

'They have a tree. What are they going to do with a tree tr... oh I see. Um, they have a battering ram,' Will said from his place at the window.

Anaya and Ceun were now frantically searching for something, anything that they could use So far their arsenal included a spatula, a saucepan and a small bundle of knitting needles.

'Pile everything that will move in front of the door,' Ceun ordered. Will and Anaya dragged the heavy bed from its place by the wall while Ceun tried to move the dresser.

'Wait. Let us help you with that!' Anaya said.

'No time,' Ceun answered through gritted teeth as he dragged the heavy dresser across the dusty floor. Soon the table and virtually every other item of furniture had been piled in front of the door and window.

Will peered through a gap. 'They're coming closer,' he said before putting a hand to his head and leaning against the barricade for support.

'You all right?' Ceun asked.

'Just felt a little woozy, that's all. Must be all the excitement.' Will rubbed his hands over his face.

'You're bleeding!' Anaya said to Ceun. 'I told you we would have moved things.'

'It's fine,' he said, brushing her hand away.

'It's not. Look how much blood there is. You've pulled some stitches. I'll have to redo them.'

'Now, woman? Are you mad? I'd say a little leakage is probably the least of our worries.'

Will was looking at his knees with great concern. They didn't seem to be quite there anymore. Also, he had the strangest feeling that all the essential parts of him were being sucked backwards, like disappearing down a plug hole. 'Guys?' he said weakly.

'We will discuss the 'woman' another time, but right now you're no good to me if you're too weak to fight!' Anaya argued wit Ceun.

'Um, something is happening?' Will said urgently.

The bounty hunter and the morph both turned quickly to look at the inventor, or what remained of him. Barely a shadow, he tried to reach out but too late. In a wink, he was gone.

~~

Outside in the corridor, Adam could hear the pounding of heavy boots. He looked at Will desperately. The console seemed to be working, but there was no sign of life. With a crash, the door burst open and a dishevelled Cassandra burst into the room. Staring wild-eyed around the room, she grabbed an armchair and dragged it across to the doorway.

'You led them here!' Adam hissed.

'I had... I had no-where left to go,' she gasped, limping across to the bed. Adam noticed she was only wearing one shoe. 'Any...

any change?' She gasped.

Someone was rattling on the door. 'Not yet. I've just plugged it in, now all we have to do is hope for the best. I see you bought company.' Adam nodded towards the door.

'You try playing tag around a hospital with the entire local police force, and then you can snipe all you want!' She said, brushing the mass of untidy hair out of her eyes.

Adam turned back to Will. 'Come on mate. We need you to come back. Will?'

Cassandra pushed him out of the way and shook her husband by the shoulders. 'Come on! Wake up!'

The door shook violently until the chair skittered across the room, followed by several red-faced police officers as they burst into the room, culminating with an officer with Sergeant stripes.

'Step away from the bed please sir... madam.' Adam found himself roughly shoved against the wall, his hands handcuffed behind his back.

Cassandra screamed and tried to fight with the two, then three police officers, who managed to push her to the ground and restrain her.

The Sergeant cleared his throat. 'I am arresting you both for the multiple attempts on the life of one William Cooper. You do not have to say anything. But it may harm your defence if you do not mention when questioned something which you later rely on in court. Anything you do say may be given in evidence. Do you understand?'

'You're the ones who don't understand. We're trying to bring him back!' Adam shouted desperately.

'Save it for the jury.' The Sergeant said with a shrug, ' And someone best get a nurse in here to check on Mr... Cooper.' He looked down at the sleeping man. 'And better get this contraption off him, can't be doing him any good.'

'Nooo!' Adam screamed, trying to wriggle out of the police officer's grip. Glancing over in disdain, the Sergeant reached out to remove the console, just as Will's hand came up to grab his wrist. The Sergeant looked down into a half-awake face.

Will yawned. 'I think I can manage, thank you.'

CHAPTER 49

Winkworth smoothed the slime on his suit. It had been a very long time, perhaps too long. But this was no time for hesitation. He grasped the handle, opened the door to the broom closet, and stepped inside.

~~

'What are we going to do now?' Anaya asked as she squinted out of the tiny gap at the window.

Ceun stroked the tiny dragon now lying on the floor. 'Rox? Rox, you useless pile of gravel. Any luck?' Ceun said to the creature's stomach.

'Which part of 'this is going to take some time' was I unclear about John?' came the echo.

'We are in kind of a tight spot here… mate. We need something, anything, there's a whole army out here about to break down the door, and at the moment the best we can do is make them some pancakes.'

'So I don't need to flush Puff here then if it's a lost cause?' There was a smile in the voice.

Ceun pointed an angry finger at the stomach, 'Yes you do! Just get on with it.'

'When I gets into a system, I does it proper. Am I right, or am I right? Undoing it ain't so simple. The more interruptions I get, the longer it'll take. You'll have to come up with something else Mr bloody smarty bloody bounty bloody hunter. Now bugger off so I can get on!'

Ceun stood up painfully and limped across to where Anaya

was sitting.

'We're stuffed, aren't we?' she said.

Slumping down next to her, he took hold of her hand. 'Here's the plan. I tie you up...'

Anaya interrupted, 'I'm sorry you what?'

Ceun continued, 'Hear me out. I go out there, um, spatulas blazing and draw them away. With a bit of luck whoever comes to check the cottage will be fooled by your feminine polymorphic charms, and when you tell them you were my prisoner, they'll let you go?'

Anaya looked incredulous. 'That,' she said eventually, 'has got to be the singularly most ridiculous plan I have ever heard.'

'No listen. It could work.'

'It really couldn't.' She began to count on her fingers. 'For one thing, you can barely walk, let alone have them chase you away from here. Secondly, the chances of them not realising what I am, that we've been working together, and that I'm an escaped convict, not great.'

'You're not giving the plan a chance,' Ceun said.

'A chance? As plans go, this one is a giant boil on the backside of one of the worst ideas that ever dared to pop into the head of someone who clearly wasn't in their right mind!' She said, throwing her arms in the air.

The cottage shook as the battering ram hit the barricaded front door.

'Ok, I get it, you're not convinced, but we're running out of options An. I think you should reconsider the plan unless you have a better one.'

Anaya looked thoughtful. 'What if we said I kidnapped you and made you help me? I wanted to sell Will for my freedom, and given the state of you they'll believe me.'

'No...' 'What's the matter, worried about your reputation, that someone finally got the better of the great Ceun Hawke?' Anaya said. The cottage shuddered again as half a chair fell from the barricade narrowly missing Anaya as Ceun pulled her forwards.

'For one thing, how did you get me to spring you out, and for another, how do you think you're going to get away, and finally, you can't go back to that place,' he said.

They were close now, noses nearly touching. 'The important thing is to get that collar off you and have those wounds properly treated.' Anaya breathed.'

'What's the point? A rogue bounty hunter? They're going to make an example of me. Get me out of this collar only to leave me in a living death? I don't think so.' He said, finally leaning back.

Anaya shook her head. She swallowed hard, 'So, we go out together then?'

Ceun nodded, smiling slightly. The dresser crashed sideways, wood splintering across the floor, they didn't notice.

'Can't take much more of this?' Anaya said quietly.

'No,' Ceun leaned in.

'Wait...' she said, starting to pull away. 'I'm not... I'm not... her.'

'Who?' Ceun said gently as he coaxed her back.

'You know what I am. I couldn't bear it if... But I'm not...Lily,' she finished lamely.

'Who said you were? You're not nearly orange enough,' he said, smiling.

'But...I'm not who you...' Gently stroking the side of her face, he stopped her, 'ah, but you are. You've never looked like anyone else to me.' He was so close now she could feel his breath on her lips.

'Eh, hem!' someone coughed. 'Sorry, am I interrupting?' Shooting apart like repelling magnets, Anaya was first on her feet, waving the spatula menacingly at the newcomer. Ceun took a little longer to stand.

'My goodness Mr Hawke, you do look in a terrible way.'

'Where did you come from and who the bloody hell are you?' Ceun demanded. Winkworth handed over a mucus-covered card.

'Winkworth, MI5, I came in through the cupboard.'

'MI5?' Ceun said wiping the card on his trousers, 'never heard of you.'

'That, my dear Mr Hawke, is entirely the point.' Winkworth tapped the side of his nose. 'Morphean intelligence.'

'And the five?' Anaya asked.

'There are five of us,' Winkworth said simply. He crossed over to the dragon and was gently stroking its head. It cooed contentedly. Anaya and Ceun exchanged glances. 'What have they done to you?' Winkworth asked the stricken creature.

'Something it ate,' Ceun said as the cottage took another hit. 'It should be fine in a week or so.'

'I wondered why I stopped getting messages. Luckily, I could still trace it.' Winkworth said, cradling the little dragon in his paw.

'You sent the homing dragon?' Anaya asked.

'Oh, yes.' The bogeyman blew his nose on an oversized handkerchief. 'Once I'd arranged to have the young lady rescued from the fortress, I had to keep track of your progress.'

'You did that? You did, you went to all that trouble. Why?' Ceun wanted to know.

'I think you know why Mr Hawke. The murder of a citizen of Realitas. He died in his sleep after inventing a dream machine?

Not exactly going to take a genius to see a link, and humans are not as stupid as we would like to believe. It was not enough to remove the inventor. We had to make sure he knew the device was dangerous and leave him in a position to go back and sort out his mess.'

'Why didn't you just tell the committee?' Ceun asked.

'Such faith in the authorities is charming, but I think our polymorphic friend knows the answer to that,' Winkworth looked questioningly to Anaya.

'Because they are self-serving, greedy idiots who would have no idea how to deal with the situation and would only consider how it could be turned to their advantage?' she responded.

'Pretty much, in a nutshell, my dear.' The Bogeyman said with a small salute.

'So you went to all that trouble, contacting me, releasing Anaya. Why us?' Ceun asked.

'Because you are the great incorruptible Ceun Hawke. Righter of wrongs, doing what is right in the face of adversity, whatever the cost.' Winkworth said expansively.

Anaya raised a hand. 'So what's your excuse for dragging me into all this?'

Winkworth positively grinned. 'Because you, my dear, know how to operate on the cold frosty side that is outside the law.'

'That's all very well,' Ceun snapped, 'but you could have asked us, helped us even.'

Winkworth stroked the dragon thoughtfully. 'Oh, I have been helping you. The guards have been running around in circles after I made sure they had some very old maps.'

'What about vengeful old women, wolves, pigs and the bloody mafia?' Ceun shouted over the smashing of wood.

'Out of my control, I'm afraid.' Winkworth said calmly brushing the dust from his shoulder. 'But it made life interesting wouldn't you say?'

'What about this bloody collar, I suppose that is outside your control too?' Ceun said.

Lifting his spectacles, Winkworth considered the collar. 'That was unfortunate, but you have to admit, it did add spurs to your endeavour,' he said. 'Allow me.'

Reaching into his pocket, Winkworth took a bundle of lock picks. Within seconds there was a click, and the collar rolled away across the floor. Ceun's hands went to his neck.

'Now,' Winkworth said pocketing the picks, 'I believe we are going to have some visitors in a moment, and there will be some explaining to do. I suggest you keep your mouths shut and let me do the talking.'

CHAPTER 50

'Mr Leibowitz, there are some policemen here to see you. A Detective inspector Todd and a Detective constable Simpson.' Gina buzzed over the intercom.

'Ah, excellent. Please send them straight in.' Murray replied.

'And err, Sir?' Gina continued.

'Just send them in Gina,' snapped the tinny voice on the intercom. With a shrug, Gina got up and opened the large office door.

'Ah officers, always a pleasure to help her majesty's constabulary.' Murray got up from behind his desk and held out his hand. 'I presume you have come to take a statement from me, nasty business.'

He stopped short as he registered Adam, Cassandra and, even more, surprisingly Will.

'A nasty business, indeed, Mr Leibowitz. These gentlemen and lady have made some very serious accusations. I am trying to clear the matter up.' Todd said calmly.

'I don't know what you're talking about. William, my friend! I'm delighted to see you up and about!' Murray gushed, rushing over to shake Will's hand.

'Delighted or extremely surprised?' Will answered coldly, ignoring the outstretched hand.

Sergeant Simpson opened his notebook. 'There is a small matter of a workshop which was emptied of all hard wear for a... um... dream machine... allegedly stolen by your employees on your instruction. Then there is the theft of all computer material ascertaining to said project. Making false accusations, wasting police time and...' Simpson looked to his superior. 'Did we decide on GBH, ABH or attempted murder Sir?'

'Attempted murder.' Will, Adam and Cassandra all said together. Simpson made a note.

'The attempted murder of one William Cooper by means of the removal of said dream device and the refusal to have it returned in the knowledge that...'

'Yes, yes, detective constable, we get the general idea,' Todd interrupted.

'Ridiculous!' Leibowitz said.

'I agree Sir; the story does seem a little out there, however, given the additional evidence. We have already obtained a search warrant for your premises and have indeed located the missing items, together with some very interesting emails. As for the other charges, we have three witnesses.'

Murray had turned a very odd shade of red. 'You can't rely on them! They took the thing off Will, not me. And her... that, that harpie, she was in on it all along!'

'Mrs Cooper and Mr Cooper have explained the situation. It now just remains for us to go down to the station and sort out the finer details. Statements are one thing Mr Leibowitz, but evidence... that doesn't lie. Constable, please handcuff the gentleman.'

Murray struggled. 'You are making a big mistake buster, a big mistake. I am a citizen of the good old US of A, the greatest superpower on the god damned planet, and when they find out how you've treated me there will be a giant can of whoop-ass emptied all over your limey asses!'

'Now that is hardly any way to talk, is it Mr Leibowitz?' The detective inspector said as the American was dragged away.

Will, Adam and Cassandra watched him go.

'You stinking bastards, you think you're going to get away with this you have another thing coming. My lawyers are going to make mincemeat of you, you hear, mince goddamned meat!'

'I'm sorry you had to hear that gentlemen and madam. With your statements and the evidence we've managed to gather, I very much doubt that Mr Leibowitz will be seeing the good old US of A for a very long time. Your property will have to be held as evidence for the time being, but in the fullness of time, it will be returned to you. I'm sure you will be anxious to pick up your project where you left off?' Todd said.

'No rush?' Will said, 'just one thing, where it will be held, it will be secure? There is some very sensitive equipment, and I wouldn't want anyone able to just walk off with it.'

'Oh, Sir. Like all of our charges, we make sure they are kept under lock and key.'

~~

'Winkworth!' Bango exclaimed as the cottage finally succumbed to the barrage, and the Bogeyman emerged through the dust cloud.

'Quite so Sir,' Winkworth said, squinting in the sunlight. 'Do you mind if we go back inside, I am afraid the sun does very little for my complexion?'

'What are you doing here?' The chairman hissed as he followed his assistant back into the gloom.

'Following your orders sir.' He replied as Captain Todd and Sergeant Simpson entered with Willoughby-Smith at the rear. Ceun lay on the floor, Anaya cradling his head and trying to stop the bleeding.

'You!!' Bango said, nearly bursting, 'Winkworth, explain yourself!'

'Indeed, Sir, if you insist.' The Bogeyman said with a small bow.

'I do insist, now what the...?'

Winkworth addressed the confused officers. 'Our Lord Elect, High...'

'Get on with it!' Bango hissed.

With a nod of acknowledgement, Winkworth continued, 'Given the seriousness of the situation, our wise chairman realised that extreme circumstances call for extreme measures. With the additional threat to the human visitor, together with the need to prevent his invention ever becoming commonplace in Realitas, something that could only be achieved if 'he' was allowed to return home, the chairman realised that any plan to eliminate the human was indeed flawed.'

'I did?' Bango said, before remembering the company he was keeping. 'I did!'

'So, under the pretext that the authorities were out looking for the human, in order to keep panic to a minimum and to show a strong presence the chairman ordered that for all outward appearances, the human should be apprehended by the army and... eliminated.' Winkworth paused for a moment to let the information sink in. 'However, besides, being the benevolent and ultimate strategician that he is, the Chairman realised that the best way to deal with the situation was to have the human shielded from those who would do him harm until he was able to return to his own dimension. Therefore, it was prudent, nay dare I say brilliant, to bring in a couple of covert operatives to undertake the task.'

'I asked you to do that?' Bango said uncertainly.

'Indeed you did, sir, although, you could not actually say so in case you were seen to be implicated. However, now that everything has worked out perfectly, we are free to revel in the glory of your wisdom... Sir.'

'Wait a minute,' Willoughby-Smith asked. 'They are on our side?'

'Indeed and I have to say, you officers put up the most splendid display of hunting them, when in fact you were giving them the 'cover',' he looked to Ceun, 'I believe that is the correct terminology?' Ceun nodded weakly.

'That's all very well, but do you think we could get him some medical help?' Anaya snapped.

'Of course, my mistake. Could you please arrange some assistance for Mr Hawke Sergeant?'

As Ceun was being stretchered away, Winkworth touched Anaya lightly on the arm.

'Remember,' he said, 'you are our operatives now. We can call on you as and when we require it.'

Eyes flashing, she responded defiantly. 'And what if we don't want to play your little game?'

'Then you and Mr Hawke will have the rest of your lives together,' he smiled, 'albeit in adjacent cells.'

'Anaya!' Ceun yelled from outside.

With a final glare at Winkworth, she walked over to the stretcher. 'You bellowed?' she said.

Ceun pointed to where the abandoned prison cart was standing by the path. 'Look where you left the cart, I mean, you might as well have put a big sign on it saying 'come and get us.'

Frowning, Anaya looked around. 'We didn't leave it there. I put it at the side of the cabin; no one would have been able to see it just walking past.' She grabbed one of the stretcher-bearers. 'Has someone moved that vehicle?'

'No ma'am. Everything just as we found it.'

'I am telling you, I did not leave it there!' Anaya said emphatically. A movement in the shrubbery caught Ceun's attention. 'An,' he said quietly, nodding towards the spot, 'please tell me it's the blood loss, and I am just hallucinating.'

Anaya stared. A slow humourless smile grew on her face. 'Sorry,' she said, 'I can see them too.'

In the bushes, a pair of cowled figures popped up and down intermittently. Realising they had been seen, one gave a thumbs-up sign before they both finally disappeared.

Ceun and Anaya exchanged a look of resignation. 'Those bloody monks!' they said together.

~~

Cassandra flopped down in the seat opposite Adam and took a large mouthful of her gin and tonic. She put the glass down and stared at him questioningly.

'How are you doing?' he asked.

'You dragged me all the way out here to this awful pub to ask me that?' She asked.

'It's out of the way for a reason. We don't want to bump into anyone do we?' He replied.

Cass gave a hollow laugh. 'God forbid that should happen!'

'So how are you?' He tried again.

'Apart from the fact that I have no money, my husband has left home to move in with another man...' She began.

'He's in the spare room, don't be so melodramatic.' Adam took a sip of his beer.

'Is he... has he mentioned me at all?' Cass asked tentatively.

Adam shook his head. 'It's not something that either of us is willing to talk about at the moment. Maybe in time.'

'But he is going to start work again, on the adjustments?' Cass asked.

'I don't know. He doesn't sleep, or at most a quick nap, it's become almost like an obsession. Understandable, I suppose.'

Cass took another drink. 'He can't go on like that. He'll make himself ill.'

'That's what I've told him, but I might as well be talking to myself. He just keeps going on about how the project needs to be destroyed. I asked him about making it safe but, I don't know he'll come around, I'm sure.'

'You think he'll come around about me?' She asked.

'We can only wait and see,' Adam replied.

'We?' Adam held her gaze. 'You know there can be no we.'

'But if Will won't forgive me. You have to talk to him, please?'

'About what exactly, the Vio, your relationship, you don't seem to understand, it's like PTSD. He won't talk about what really happened in there. I shouldn't even be here. Just there is no one else who would believe me even if I could tell them.'

'After the court case, perhaps we can all sit down together?' Cass said hopefully.

Adam finished the last of his pint. 'I don't know.' he said. 'I don't know if any of us will be the same again.'

THE END

[TT1]

[TT2]

Printed in Poland
by Amazon Fulfillment
Poland Sp. z o.o., Wrocław

50001707R00211